# Anything
## But
# *Graceful*

A second chance romance novel

# D. G. Driver

ISBN: 979-8-88653-163-3

Published by Satin Romance
An Imprint of Melange Books, LLC
White Bear Lake, MN 55110
www.satinromance.com

Published in the United States of America.

Cover Design by Caroline Andrus

*For Mom and Dad,*
*Thanks for the dance lessons, voice lessons,*
*the theatre degree*
*and a lifetime of support for all my creative dreams.*

"I was happy. I was pretty. I would love to.
    At the ballet."

Edward Kleban, A Chorus Line

"I always tell students that you've got to be practical. You do not need a dream. You need a purpose, something you can wake up to in the morning when the dream is dissipated."

Twyla Tharp, American Choreographer

"Some men have thousands of reasons why they cannot do what they want to, when all they need is one reason why they can."

Martha Graham, American Choreographer

# CHAPTER
## *One*

Here's another curious dancer who can't stop herself from staring at me. Oh, she thinks she's being discreet by watching me through the reflection in the mirrors, but I can see the angle of her eyes. The girl is pulling out all the stops. Her balance is focused, her turnout enviable, her flexibility extreme. She thinks I'm someone to impress. I could be a choreographer for a dance company or a theater. I could be scouting for new dancers. Why else would I, a woman probably a quarter-century older than her, be participating in a ballet class?

I should be used to it by now. Most of the people who take classes here are inconsistent with attendance but still regulars. This is a drop-in, pay-as-you go studio for professional dancers, so we often have new faces pop in from time to time. Kids who are on tour and want a workout. Others who need to brush up their skills before an audition. The occasional celebrity who has to dance in an upcoming movie or television shoot. We've had several of those over the years. The place has a reputation around Hollywood.

No one stared at me when I was younger. Over the past decade, that changed. At fifty, I'm the oldest dancer by a large margin. There's no hiding it. I've even started letting the gray take over my copper hair. Why not? Embrace it. Plus, I kind of like making the young girls nervous.

I *don't* like them thinking they're better than me because they're young. My plan had been to take it a little easy at class tonight. It was a long day, and I'm here more out of routine than desire. A challenge stands tip-toe before me now, and I decide to rise to it. Watching her eyebrows climb up and disappear behind those blonde bangs is worth every cube of ice I'll have to apply to my muscles later.

Spencer winks at me as we finish up with our barre exercises and spread out on the floor. He's teaching tonight. He's a bit long-in-the-tooth for a professional dancer at thirty-nine and earns most of his pay now as a teacher and choreographer. Like me, he gets lots of questioning looks from the new girls, but the motive is quite different. They're all hoping those dark brown muscled arms might belong to someone straight and single. Poor girls. They aren't going to get a date out of him or a job out of me.

The combination he teaches is graceful and elegant. It contains all the basic ballet steps anyone who has studied ballet should know. I've done this combination many times, and it's a favorite. The new girl skillfully glides through them all. Her extension exquisite. The lines of her body a bit exaggerated. She looks at me to see if I'm noticing, and she stumbles the slightest bit. It throws off her timing. Her lovely smile falters. She's a performer, though, and she quickly forces it back onto her pretty face.

After class, while I take off my toe shoes and massage my feet, I overhear her chatting with some of the other students. *Yes*, she liked the class. It was the *perfect* amount of challenge. The class was *on par* with ones she took at NYU, where she graduated with her BFA in musical theater two years ago. She *wishes* there was a class this good in New York. She'll *definitely* come again as she's in town for the next few weeks, touring with a production of *CATS*. She's making sure Spencer and I hear all of it. A couple of the regular students glance our way. They've seen this pony show before as well.

The students have mostly cleared out before the sweet young thing dares to approach us. She puts her hand out for Spencer to shake.

"Thank you so much. I enjoyed this class so much. I'm glad Delilah Yoon recommended it."

Spencer nods enthusiastically. "Oh, I love Delilah. Is she your dance captain? We were in *A Chorus Line* together a few years back. Tell her Spencer Nichols says hi and to drop by."

The girl's eyes widen. Spencer *is* somebody! "Yes, she's our captain and lead swing dancer. I play Victoria. You know, the white cat."

"So, you're not a singer then," I jab. It slips out. I'm tired and ready to go.

The joy flees from her eyes, and she juts out her chin. "All the cats sing," she reminds me. "We all have to be triple threats."

"But the white cat doesn't have any of the big solos, right?" I should let this go, but I don't. "I always wanted to be one of the cats that sings 'Macavity'."

Spencer shakes his head at me. "Grace Fuller, you know as well as I do, the only cat you can play is Grisabella, the old washed-up one."

I smack the back of his head both for the insult and for giving my name to this girl. The last thing I need is for her to look me up on the internet when she gets back to her hotel room and figure out that I'm a big fraud.

If the girl has been offended by me, it doesn't matter. She still doesn't want to hurt her chances of impressing me. "Oh no, ma'am. You're a beautiful dancer. I'm sure you could pass for... I mean... Have you ever been in *CATS*?"

"No. I've never been in *CATS*." I soften my expression to let her know I'm not bothered by her. "We'll have to get tickets and go see your show one night. Right, Spencer?"

"Oh, yes. Of course."

She looks like a toddler being handed a lollipop. "Really? Would you? I'll arrange comp tickets for both of you. Let me know what night."

She hands a headshot and resume to Spencer because it has her contact information on it. Then she asks one more question as coyly as possible. "Are you two together?"

"Us?" I point to Spencer and back to myself. We both start laughing.

"You make a cute couple," she says.

"Oh no, honey," Spencer says, laying it on thick. "Gracie doesn't date. Even if she ever did, she's not exactly my type."

The girl nods understanding, her cheeks turning bright pink. She thanks us again for the class, and then she skedaddles out of the room. Once she's gone, I take off my ballet skirt and slide into my sweatpants. I sit on the floor and tug on my sneakers while Spencer turns out the lights. Wrapping a sweater around me, I follow him out of the dance room, down the hall, and into the office where he drops the picture into the trashcan.

"What? No *CATS*?"

"Lord, no," he says. "I can happily go the rest of my life without ever seeing a production of that again. Once is exciting. Twice is interesting. After that, you begin to realize that the show is stealing away valuable hours of your life that can't be replaced. And don't even get me started on the movie."

"She'll be so disappointed."

"And yet, she'll survive somehow." He grabs his jacket. "We going out?"

"Of course."

Twenty minutes later, we are nestled in our favorite spot in our favorite place. Stomping Grounds is a coffeehouse on Melrose, a couple blocks away from the studio on Highland Avenue. It's full of mismatched cushy couches and armchairs around short coffee tables littered with *L.A. Weekly* papers, old *Backstage* or *Hollywood Reporter* magazines, and fliers for upcoming shows around town. There's a small stage in the corner that is often used for open mic nights or for local musicians or comedians trying out new material.

No one is gracing us with their talent on this early Monday evening, thank goodness. I'm enjoying the endless stream of 90s alternative rock coming through the speakers. A bar with a variety of different stools lines one wall. Along one wall is a bar with a variety of different stools. Along with coffee and tea, the place serves up whatever treats Rhonda, the owner, feels like baking that day. She has some bottled beer available in the fridge and always has some Baileys Irish Cream or Kahlua on hand for those who want to spike their lattes. Neither the treats nor alcohol are exactly legal for her to sell as she doesn't have a liquor license and her baked goods haven't been approved by the health board. In the twenty-eight years Rhonda has owned the joint, she hasn't been cited for them. The place is quiet and goes mostly unnoticed.

"It's no big deal," Spencer is saying, defending himself from my wrath about my name being given out. "She won't remember it."

"Yes, she will. She's looking me up right now," I say. "She'll show up next time with a whole different expression on her face. I've seen it before. The what-the-hell-are-you-doing-here face."

"Then you show her what the hell you're doing there." He takes his latte from Alix, Rhonda's teen son, and passes him a couple bucks as a tip.

Alix hands me my spiked iced coffee, and I put it down on one of the newspapers. He leans over and whispers in my ear, "He's right, Grace. You can dance circles around anyone." I give him a couple more dollars. He winks and walks away.

The sweet boy has actually seen me dance, so I know he's not completely bullshitting me for extra tips. Years earlier, when he was still *Sophia*, he took dance classes from Spencer at Goldie Glitz dance studio over in Santa Monica. When Sophia began his transition to Alix, the dance classes ended. Spencer offered to train Alix personally to dance as a man. Alix came to a few of our classes. He was talented and had a lot of promise. He needed more strength training to really make a go of it. In the end, it was more work than he wanted to do, so he quit. He's making his way through college now.

"I hate it when the super young girls show up," I admit. "We need to work out a system where you text me to abort my plans to come to class when one of them walks in the door."

"I won't do it."

"Why? Help protect me from the judgement of Gen Z dancers." I take a good swig of my drink. Rhonda gave it a good kick, and I appreciate it.

Spencer leans back in his cushy chair and crosses his arms. "First of all, you don't need protecting. You are a queen, and that class is your domain. Second of all, and I've said this a million times before, you can always change your status from amateur to professional. It's not as hard as you think."

"Oh, please, Spencer," I say. "That ship sailed before I even started dancing. You know that. I'm too damn old. I'm only a few years younger than Debbie, and she retired from professional dancing nearly two decades ago."

"Not a comparison. She has rheumatoid arthritis in her hands and feet. If she didn't, you bet your ass she'd be performing right now."

Debbie White owns Dancer's Room, our precious studio. She's rarely there anymore due to her condition.

"I'm one bad fall from never dancing again myself," I remind him.

"Drink your milk. Take your calcium pills." Spencer isn't putting up with my whining this evening.

"Let's drop it."

We're both quiet for a moment, drinking our coffees. Spencer's gaze drifts away from me to stare at the bulletin board on the wall. It's covered with colorful notices about band gigs, local theater productions, furniture for sale, and phone number fringe-edge fliers pleading for roommates to share apartments. After a moment, he rises from his seat and goes to the board. He pulls some tacks out and wads up out-of-date notices and rearranges the remaining ones so that everything is straight, and the most pertinent information is visible.

Alix whisks the trash away from Spencer. "Thanks. I've been meaning to get to that for a while."

Spencer squints dubiously at him. "Oh, I'm sure you were, Alix. I think there were papers up here older than you." He removes another pink flier to reveal a full-color printed image underneath. "Ooh, like this one."

His efforts have revealed a promo poster he'd made for Dancer's Room years ago. The background picture is a female dancer at the ballet barre, left leg in *front attitude*, left arm in fifth

6

position, back gracefully arched so that her arm mostly obscures her face. The copy reads: *Never Stop Learning! Drop-In Dance Classes for Advanced Dancers* with class times and the address below it. Spencer takes it off the cork board and holds it up for me to see better.

"Well, look at that. I wondered if it was hiding under there after all this time."

I roll my eyes. "Spencer—"

"Look at that gorgeous dancer with her beautiful arch, her hand so graceful, hiding under all that nonsense."

"That's not fair."

Alix takes the picture. "Wait. Is that you, Grace?"

Reluctantly, I nod. "Notice my face is indistinguishable."

"When was this taken?" Alix asks.

"Oh, about eight years ago," Spencer says. "We did some of her and some of me. Some of us together. This was our favorite because it was simple."

The memory warms a chuckle out of me. "I remember we joked about how it was an ad for a studio for advanced dancers, but the picture was of something you learn in a beginner's class."

"But you're doing it so perfectly," Spencer says with a flirty grin.

Alix hands the poster to me. "If I didn't know, I'd say that was the body of someone not much older than me."

"I've already tipped you, Alix." He shrugs sheepishly, and I shake my head. "Go get me a biscotti."

Alix wanders off. Studying the photo again, I remember how proud I'd been of that shoot. I framed some of the images we caught that day and put them up in my apartment. I was forty-two at the time, still older than most dancers when they retire.

Spencer snags the poster from me and tacks it back up on the board, right on top of other more current fliers.

"You know that the class schedule on there isn't even accurate anymore, right?"

He gives me a pointed look. "This place isn't exactly sending customers in droves over to the studio. I want people to see your sexy body."

I blush like a preteen. "Stop."

"I won't stop. Someone besides me and a handful of ballerinas need to appreciate that gorgeous figure and imagine those long, luscious legs being wrapped around him—"

"You're ridiculous." I bite into the biscotti as soon as Alix hands it to me.

Spencer sits down next to me on the couch, forcing me to make room for him. I don't have to wiggle over much. Spencer is lean. Not an ounce of body fat. I drop my head on his shoulder.

"I'm not being ridiculous. You are. All right, pushing the fact that you desperately need a lover aside," he waves his words away as if batting at a fly, "I'll get back to the main point. You are a brilliant dancer. You should do something with it. I've been telling you this forever."

I have to take a calming breath. "Look, there's no point in you telling me again. I'm too old. Get it through your head."

"You're not, though."

He sifts through the magazines on the table, checking the dates on them. Finally, he finds the issue of *Hollywood Reporter* he's been looking for. "I saw this the other day, and I wondered what you might think of it." Spencer flips to a page, points to a headline and hands the magazine to me. Before I can comprehend the words in front of me, he explains. "A film is being made based on the life of Martha Graham. The biography has been optioned, and they are going to start a search for an actress of-a-certain-age who can dance."

"Martha Graham was a famous choreographer of modern dance. Not ballet."

"You can do modern. It's like ballet with flat feet."

"Don't let Debbie ever hear you say that!"

He wriggles his nose. "Oh please. She's a purest. She hates how young people have turned contemporary dance into high school angst routines. I, on the other hand, love the shit out of it."

"Me too. So expressive."

"Annnnd, I've seen you tackle it during our Friday classes. You've got the technique."

"Yes, but—"

"But what? You can dance. You're still at the top of your skill level. Most dancers your age are not."

I shake my head and put the magazine down. "For a film? Surely, they'll be looking at famous actresses. They're not going to want a nobody to star in a film."

"Why not? It'd be a sensation! Imagine the press you'd get. *Middle-aged Ballerina Discovered to Portray World-Famous Choreographer!* The trades would eat it up."

"Mmmm, I don't know about that. Seems like people would rather pay money to see…" I fan my hand, revealing an invisible headline. *"Favorite Celebrity Trains to Master Dance Skills for Movie Role!* They'll prefer a known face dancing so-so, possibly with a body double doing the tricky stuff, rather than take a risk on someone they've never heard of."

"Let's be honest, honey," Spencer says in a low voice. "This isn't exactly the kind of movie that's going to rake in the sales. No one except us dancers know who the hell Martha Graham was."

"Good point," I agree. "So, what I'm hearing is, it's going to bomb and what's the point of this conversation?"

"The point is that you should audition for it."

"How?"

Spencer gestures wildly around him. "We are in Hollywood, Grace. Literally everyone we know is in show business. I'm sure someone can figure out a way to get to the casting agent."

"I'm not an actress," I say firmly.

He's done with my arguments. Ripping the article out of the magazine, he stuffs it in my purse. "Think about it. Opportunities like this don't come around every day. Wouldn't being in a movie be a lot more fun than selling houses? Come on. Don't lie to me about that."

I *couldn't* lie to him about that. Starring in a movie or a Broadway show was all I ever wanted to do—once upon a time.

## *1991*

"All right, everyone, say your name and tell us a little something about yourself."

It was the first day of Drama 101 at Long Beach State. Our professor, Eli Williams, had us sit in a big circle. At twenty-six students, the class was too full. Most of us were freshman. Before class, frantic whispers fluttered about that at least four people would have to be dropped. I was queasy, hoping I wouldn't be one to lose out. Planning my class schedule had taken me hours, and I wasn't ready to tackle that puzzle again. I'd mapped out exactly what courses I'd have to take and when in order to get my major in Theatre Arts and minor in Business Management, all without having to quit my part time job. There was no room to change anything without having to add summers or possibly a fifth year.

The class took place in a black box theater, the kind of performance space that was intimate and modular. The smell of layer upon layer of scenic paint did nothing to help my nausea. Currently, the four walls were solid black. White might be a blank canvas for art, but black is the blank canvas for performance spaces. All of the chairs were stacked against one wall, our backpacks tossed on the floor along another. We sat cross-legged or on our knees uncomfortably on the cement floor. I regretted not wearing my sweatshirt because the air conditioning was pumping hard against the September heat outside. It stayed uselessly wadded up on top of my backpack, and I didn't want to draw attention to myself to get it now that class had officially started.

One by one, my classmates introduced themselves. No one said anything about their favorite color or what they liked most to eat. Every single person said what high school they had attended and what show they had starred in while there. That's right. Every person in the class had either been a lead or major character in a play or musical their senior year. I'd been Charity in *Sweet Charity*. I was a big deal for a few months. Got written up in the local paper and everything. Now having been the title character of the school musical garnered nothing more than appreciative smiles and nods of "yeah, I've heard of that show" before moving on to the next person in the circle who had played Annie (either the orphan or the sharpshooter) or Dolly, or Gypsy, or Peter Pan. If I thought I'd come to a school to retain my position as *the best*, I was mistaken. We were all sizing each other up and quickly realizing that getting a leading role in a show at this school might be harder to come by than we thought. Getting a part *at all* might be rough.

My ego took a beating with each introduction, and by the time everyone had spoken, I'd nearly convinced myself that I was in the wrong major. This certainly wasn't going to get any easier when I started pursuing theatre in the real world, where there were even more people as good as, or probably better than, me.

Girls outnumbered the boys four to one in the class. Not unusual. I counted five guys, most of them 'character' types by the look of them. A little on the heavy side or too lean. Sure enough, I heard them mention their roles in shows like *Guys and Dolls* and *The Music Man*. The tall, handsome leading men types tended to get whisked away to the bigger and more expensive schools.

One guy stood out a little from the others. He had a sharper bone structure in his face. Even from across the room, I could see the brightness of his blue eyes. The green and white striped rugby shirt accented his shoulders. He pulled the sleeves up to his elbows, revealing strong forearms. His dark blond hair was long and curly on top, slicked back over his ears, and was long enough in the back to touch his collar. He introduced himself as Tyler Andrews, and his claim to fame had been playing Curly in *Oklahoma* at some high school in Northern California. Better than that, he managed to squeeze into his introduction that he did the ballet section of the musical himself—no stand-in needed. Ah, so he was a dancer. Well, that didn't necessarily mean he was gay.

Several girls in the circle were testing the water, the flirting so obvious. He seemed friendly, but I didn't get any sense he was gravitating toward anyone. I tried to be stealthy with my glances. I'd never make it as a spy. One time, I looked over at him to find him smiling right at me. Nice teeth. The corners of his lips curled up nicely so that he always looked happy, even when not smiling. I offered him a weak smile in return and quickly turned my head. My face was hot, and I prayed it didn't show.

Once the introductions were finished and Professor Williams got done telling us how important he was in the local theatre community, he had us stand up and pick a partner for some silly acting exercises. Tyler passed up three girls that were headed his way and came straight to me.

"Wanna dance?" he asked, putting out his hand.

Through a bunch of uncontrollable giggles, I said, "I think we're going to do Mirror Pantomime."

"That's fun, too." He faced me as we were given instructions everyone already knew about mimicking your partner as if looking into a mirror. "You want me to take the lead or you?"

"You first."

That's when I noticed that Tyler wasn't terribly tall. Couldn't be more than five-nine, as I was almost eye to eye with him wearing my wedges. He winked at me, and I winked right back. Slowly, he moved his right arm up and down, and I did the same with my left. He lifted a leg. So did I. Just when I thought he was going too easy on me, he snapped his head to the right. I did it, but a beat behind. He started his slow movements again. Then snap. I was closer that time, but not perfect.

"Come on," he teased through clenched teeth. "Follow me."

Slow, slow, slow, snap. I got it. There was a rhythm to it.

We switched, and I led him. I made my movements wiggly and loose. They were hard to get exact, but he matched me well. I'd frown, then smile. He did the same, but bigger, sillier. We finally ended up laughing and collapsed to the ground.

"I'm Tyler. Not sure I caught your name."

"Grace. Grace Fuller."

"Graceful? I'm not so sure about that."

I shook my head. My old elementary school nickname that the bullies favored sounded kind of cute coming out of his mouth. I allowed it.

"Nice to meet you, Grace."

"Nice to meet you, too."

Tyler tugged my arm to help me back to my feet. I popped up so fast, it felt like I could keep flying. The strength in his body was clear, and I imagined in that split second of contact that he could raise me up over his head with little effort for a beautiful lift like we were starring in a ballet. Before we could continue with the exercise, the T.A. returned from the administration office with an updated class roll. My stomach clenched. Tyler had made me forget about my nerves for a bit, but they returned with a vengeance. Six students were cut, and to my relief, I wasn't one of them. I let out a long exhale, as if I'd squeaked through a round of auditions.

"Were you worried?" Tyler asked. I nodded. "Aw, you should never worry about not making it. I can already tell you're super talented."

I rolled my eyes at him. "Really? From my mad mirror pantomime skills?"

Tyler shrugged. "You have a certain poise about you. It's different. You stand out."

I studied his face carefully. There were plenty of girls in the room better looking than me. I was thin and fairly flat-chested. Perfect body for a dancer, I'd often been told. Only, I wasn't a great dancer. I'd cut my red hair short for *Sweet Charity*, so I could look more like Shirley MacLaine from the movie. It was growing out and kind of a mess. If I stood out from the others, it wasn't for my beauty.

"Well, I'm not sure what drugs you're taking, but I appreciate the compliment."

We were told to switch partners then and started a new improv game about making sounds and movements louder and softer. Someone tapped me on the back. The girl who had been standing closest to me while I worked with Tyler tilted her head as if to ask, "How about me?" I agreed without speaking, and we faced each other. Well, sort of. She couldn't have been much more than five-feet-tall, because I looked right over the top of her head. Her frizzy brown hair was so wild her small face nearly disap-peared beneath it all, and she wore oversized denim overalls with a tight faded T-shirt underneath. I could barely make out the tips of some purple Vans on her feet. I recalled that her name was Kei. She had made a point that it was spelled with an *i* not an *ay* because everyone gets that wrong. Also, her big senior showcase had been a drama, not a musical. *The Crucible*. She played Abigail.

"Hey," I said.

"Hey," she repeated in exactly the same tone like we'd started the game.

"Oh, no. I just meant hi. I'm Grace."

"I know."

She memorized everyone's names already? I doubted that.

"Where are you from?" I continued trying to be friendly, already missing Tyler's congeniality.

I peeked over at him a few times, hoping to catch his eye again. Every time, Tyler was busy talking it up and smiling like crazy at the new girl in front of him. Ah, so it was like that.

"Fresno. Why?"

Clearly, she didn't care for that question. Or any others.

I thought about saying something about having never been to Fresno. Or asking what it was like. Kei gave me no chance. She did a big tiger growl, throwing her arms in the air like massive paws. Without skipping a beat, I copied her and did it back even louder. That finally got a tiny smirk out of her and a raised eyebrow of approval. We challenged each other back and forth until Professor Williams told us to stop.

"That was fun…" Kei had already wandered away from me. I ran a hand through my hair. "Well, all right."

Another girl in the class leaned toward me and said, "Don't worry about her. She's on my floor in the dorm, and she hasn't spoken to anyone since move-in day."

"Maybe she's shy?" I offered.

"I heard she hates people who do musical theatre."

At the end of class, I gathered up my backpack and headed out the door. On the wall right outside the building was a corkboard covered with flyers announcing show auditions both on campus and in nearby community theaters. I stopped to study them, not familiar with any of the titles of the plays being produced this semester. Someone tapped my shoulder. I looked over to find Tyler standing behind me.

"You should try for that one," he said, pointing to a flyer for *The Miss Firecracker Contest.*

"You think?" I asked. "I prefer musicals to plays and was planning on auditioning for *Pippin.*"

"Me too," he said. He pulled out a pad of paper and a pen and wrote down the audition info and handed the sheet to me. Then he copied the info again for himself. "Do you have another class now?"

"Not until ten."

"Want to get a coffee to celebrate our first day of school and you not getting dropped from acting class?"

Any final remnants of my nervous nausea vanished. I didn't even like coffee much, but at that moment it sounded delicious. "Absolutely."

We headed toward the student center while he sang "Magic to Do" from *Pippin.* He wasn't reserved about it, and he wasn't bad. He had a high tenor voice with a pleasant vibrato at the end of his long notes. Several heads turned to check him out as we made our way across campus. Looked like this guy was turning out to be a triple threat. Tyler was going somewhere at this school. I knew it. I hoped he'd take me along with him.

### Present Day

At home, I peel off my dance clothes and shower. I check my mail. I turn on the TV for a bit while I simultaneously scroll through my phone. My eyes drift to the pictures I have framed on the wall from that photoshoot with Spencer. I rarely like pictures of me, but I love these. My smiles in those shots were genuine. That's what made all the difference. It had been one of the best afternoons in recent memory. I loved being in front of the camera and showing off.

Could I realistically still have a chance at acting? At dancing professionally? There was once a time when I was certain I could do it. That confidence, that drive, it had vanished with my youth. My eyes drift to the phone in my hand. I notice how visible the veins are on the back of my hands. The skin is loose. I drop the phone into my lap and curl my fingers into a perfect ballet hand, like a princess getting ready to wave at her adoring subjects. It's pretty. I can make my hands very pretty.

Crumpling my fingers into a tight fist, forces and end to my stupid daydreaming. I've missed my turn. I'm behind the beat. With a sigh, I remind myself that I am anything but Graceful.

# CHAPTER
## *Two*

The house I'm staging smells delicious. I've done all the real estate agent tricks. I baked chocolate chip cookies and put them out on a nice platter on the kitchen island counter. I put some fresh pink carnations on the bay window shelf at the front of the house. I sprayed 'freshly mown grass' scented air freshener near the windows. Now it smells lived in, even if it is completely devoid of furniture.

I would have opened the windows, but the smoggy September heat has settled into the San Fernando Valley. The air conditioning is vital for comfort, not to mention demonstrating that there is a good, working system that can battle against the oppressive air attempting to invade this Sherman Oaks ranch style home. The AC works so well that I'm wearing a light cardigan over my pink cotton dress to stave off the chill.

Tamyra and Josh smile broadly as they arrive on time for their showing appointment. Based on the nods and murmurs to each other, their first impression is exactly what I'd hoped it would be. I lead them through the empty house, my descriptions accompanied by the rhythm of Tamyra's stiletto heels click-clacking across the hardwood floors. In twenty minutes, the sun will be at the perfect angle to turn this entire side of the house amber with light. It's gorgeous, and I need to keep them around long enough to marvel at it like I did the first time I saw it. It'll be even more marvelous today without any window dressings to get in the way.

"The family that owns this house moved to Dallas last week-end. That's why the house is empty. This property will go fast, so we haven't bothered with dressing it." Some people have a hard time envisioning how a house can look without furniture. The rooms seem smaller than they are. I've rented furniture before to stage a house more completely, and if this house doesn't sell by this weekend, I'll spend the money to make it look more lived-in and take it out of the company's profits.

"It's an open plan, as you see. No walls between the living room here in the front of the house and the dining room. You'll see there are minimal walls to separate the kitchen from the less formal eating nook and family room space in the back. Natural light is so plentiful, you'll never need lights on during the daytime. The house was built in 1975, but it's been completely renovated, as you can see." I pat the island in the kitchen as I lead them past. "This island is new, complete with a trash compactor and a spigot that has instantly hot water for tea or cocoa. We surely don't want any of that right now, do we?" They laugh. "Would you like a cold bottle of water? Or some chardonnay?"

Tamyra is a handsome woman. Her braided hair is impres-sively knotted up on the top of her head. Between that and her heels, she seems much taller than she is. She's dressed profession-ally in a button-down silk blouse tucked into a tight skirt. She wraps her perfectly manicured fingers around the plastic cup of chardonnay I pour for her. I notice that her nail polish is the same ruby red color as her lipstick as she takes a sip.

Josh opts for a water bottle but doesn't drink from it. He's a slender guy, but he likes clothes that are still a size too small on him. His pants are a touch too tight; the short sleeves of his shirt stop right above a tiger face tattoo standing out boldly against his brown skin. I'd place them both around thirty-five or maybe a little younger. They could be newlyweds, but they don't have that bubbly 'first home' energy at all. I decide they are a little further along in their relationship than that.

"All the counters are granite, and there is room here for some stools. Perfect place for the kiddos to gulp down their cereal before school. Speaking of kids, this house plan is ideal for families. Lots of room for playing. If I were growing up in this house, I would have loved having all this space to practice my dancing—"

"Oh, we don't have kids," Tamyra interrupts, making sure I get that straight. "Josh and I aren't planning to raise a family here." She defers to Josh. He nods and tosses the water bottle from one hand to the other. I notice now that neither of them wear wedding rings. I need to change my strategy.

"It's also perfect for entertaining. All this open space for mingling."

Josh strides to the far side of the kitchen to the area designed to be a bar. He opens a cabinet to reveal the wine rack inside. "This is nicely done," he says to Tamyra. He hasn't spoken directly to me yet. Tamyra is the decision-maker here. She goes to his side, her perfect fingernails tapping her chin as she studies all the built-in accessories that come with the place.

"Would you like to see the bedrooms?"

Tamyra tugs Josh's elbow, and they walk ahead of me toward the hallway leading to the three bedrooms. She'll be disappointed that there are only two bathrooms. Not enough for a party house. I'll try to downplay that and focus on other attributes, although my heart isn't into selling this place to them anymore. I almost can't bear the idea of these wide floors not being utilized by eager and creative children. It's a pure waste of space.

*1983*

Mom and Dad's bathroom counter was the perfect height to be my ballet barre. I rolled up the green shag carpet and stuck it next to the toilet. Their robes blocked the full-length mirror on the back of the door, so I tossed them as best as I could over the shower curtain rod. I'd proudly put on my new black leotard.

Now that I was starting the ten-year-old level at my dance school, I'd graduated out of the required all pink dance attire. Preteens got to wear black leotards with pink tights. The leotards could be any style, too, and Mom got me a shiny one with puffy sleeves instead of the boring cotton ones. I didn't put on my tights to practice in the bathroom. They were too hard to get on, so I danced bare-legged. A little bit of my panties stuck out, and I smushed the material back inside my leotard.

We had to wear our hair in buns for class, but I didn't know how to do that by myself. I managed to wrangle my red curls into a high ponytail. I didn't want to look at my freckled face, so I concentrated on what I looked like from the neck down in the tall mirror on the door.

My new ballet shoes were too big still, and Mom hadn't sewn on the elastic well. They slipped off my heels when I stood on my toes. It didn't matter. I was still proud of the way my feet looked in ballet slippers. I held onto the porcelain counter with my right hand and did my *plies*. *Demi demi grande*. *Demi demi grande*. I had my left hand out and then did a big circle with it when I did the *grande plie*. I always rocked a little getting back up. That's why I was practicing. Last time we had class, Allie stood behind me while we did *plies* and made fun of me for having no balance and letting my butt touch the floor.

Shoot. My butt touched the floor.

I was never going to get this right. I didn't look like a ballerina. I looked like a frog.

I started doing some kicks, but I was too close to the door. My foot connected with the mirror, and it fell off the wall, crashing to the linoleum floor.

"Grace?" Mom called out. "Are you okay? What happened?"

"I'm fine!"

I lifted up the mirror. Thankfully, it hadn't shattered, but there was a big crack going across the middle of it. I hung it back up and covered it up with the robes a moment before Mom opened the door.

"Are you dancing in here?"

"No."

She looked at me in my ballet shoes and leotard and shook her head. "There's not enough room in here for dancing. What are you thinking?"

"It has a mirror." I gestured to the big one over the sink, hoping to deflect her attention away from the one hiding under the bathrobes.

The only part of my ten-year-old body that could be seen in that mirror splattered with toothpaste spit was from my chest up. Mom could clearly see that when she looked at our reflection.

"I need you to come out of here." When I hesitated, her voice got sterner. "Now."

She took my hand and led me to the couch in the living room. She sat and patted the sofa for me to sit beside her. I didn't. I hated that ugly orange and brown plaid couch. It was scratchy and smelled like cigarettes. I stood with my arms crossed. Mom reached out and took my hands, and to my surprise she didn't force me to sit. Instead, she guided me to stand between her and the coffee table, my legs squished between her knees. Mom's hair was extra frizzy that day, like she'd been running her fingers through it a bunch. I wanted to pat it down for her, but she held my hands tightly.

"Honey, I have some bad news."

Her face was too sad. I didn't want to look at it. I squirmed to get out of her grasp. I noticed the cigarette butts in the ashtray all had Mom's lipstick on them. None were Dad's. There was a glass with melting ice making a ring on the tabletop. Why didn't I smell dinner cooking?

"Where's Dad?"

"He's not home."

"What are we having for dinner?"

"I don't know. I…" Her hands tightened their grip. Her knees clamped onto my thighs. "We'll go get some McDonald's or something."

"Really?" That didn't sound like bad news to me. We hardly ever got McDonald's. Mom always said it was out of the way. This wasn't sounding like bad news at all to me. Why did she look so upset?

"Grace. About your dancing."

She knew about the mirror. How did she know? Did she hear it?

"I'm sorry. I didn't mean to kick the mirror. I'll get you another one. You can take it out of my allowance."

For a second, Mom stared at me like I was speaking Martian or something. "The mirror? Oh. Is it...? No. Don't worry about that. I don't care about that."

Okay, that was weird. Mom would never be okay about me breaking something. "Are you all right, Mom?"

"No, Gracie baby. I'm not."

At that, I twisted my body free of her legs and climbed up on her lap. I put my arms around her and my head on her shoulder. She patted my head gently.

"Oh honey," she said, her voice the saddest I'd ever heard. Even sadder than the day Skipper, our Collie, died. "I hate to tell you this. I don't even know how to."

"What is it?"

Her hand stilled on my head, holding me in place. She sighed, much longer and deeper than those sighs of exasperation she always did with me when I messed something up. "We're going to have to cancel your dance classes."

I jolted away from her. "Why?"

"I can't afford them anymore. Not since—"

"Since when? Classes started last week. You could afford them last week. We just got new shoes and tights and leotards." I scrambled to the end of the sofa, pulling my legs into my body so they couldn't touch her.

Mom reached for her melted-ice drink and put it back down. "I know, honey. Things have changed."

"What's changed? This isn't fair!"

"No," she agreed. "It's not fair at all."

She tried to wrap me up in her arms again, but I wrenched away from her and stormed to my bedroom, slamming the door shut behind me. I tore off my leotard and kicked off my slippers. After putting on my nightgown, I crawled up on my bed and sobbed. Wet, snotty, and choking for breath, I didn't care about eating any stupid McDonald's now.

I don't know if it was minutes or hours later, but Mom came tapping at my door. The sound roused me from sleeping. When I didn't answer, she opened it gently. The room was dark except for my nightlight–a ballerina in a pink tutu. It was a Christmas gift from Grandma after she took me to see *The Nutcracker*. I remember vividly how Grandma promised me that night, "If you practice very very hard, every single day, you will get to play Clara someday." Well, I guess Grandma was wrong. I wondered what she would have to say about all of this. Maybe I should call her and have her give my mom a what-for about it.

Staying still as I could with my head sideways on my pillow, I watched Mom maneuver through the toys and clothes I'd left out on the floor before sitting down on the edge of my bed. She ran her hand down my hair so tenderly that I couldn't take it. I bunched up my knees, making room for her to scoot further back and then lie down behind me. She kept petting my head but didn't say anything right away.

I cried as quietly as I could, my hitching breath giving me away. Mom gently tugged on my shoulder, and I rolled over to find her leaning on her elbow. Her face glistened against the soft yellow light coming from the glowing ballerina.

"Are you crying too?" I asked her.

"Yep."

"Why?"

"Oh, honey. So many reasons."

I was little. I didn't fully understand what was happening. It hadn't processed yet.

"I wanted to be a ballerina," I told her.

She ran her thumb across my cheek, brushing tears away. "I know. Maybe someday…" She took a long, slow, shaky breath. "Maybe someday you can start classes again. Your dream isn't over, just maybe changed a little. We'll have to wait and see what happens. Sometimes, we have to change our dreams. Sometimes they get changed for us."

I rolled to my side again and stared at that ballerina nightlight. Behind me, Mom lowered her head to the pillow, her arm draped across the top of my head. Her breath was hot on the back of my neck. I stared and stared at the ballerina until I had bright red spots behind my eyelids when I closed them. I watched those red spots dance around until they broke apart and vanished.

In the morning, I woke up alone. I figured Mom had gotten uncomfortable on my skinny twin bed, but she wasn't in her bed when I looked for her. Her bed was still made like she'd never been in it. I found her conked out on the couch. I tapped her lightly, but she didn't rouse at all. I managed to get dressed and have a bowl of cereal on my own. Mom finally began to stir as I headed back to my room to get dressed. She mumbled apologies and said she'd pack my lunch.

Before I left to catch the bus for school, I yanked that ballerina nightlight out of the wall socket and chucked it into the bathroom trashcan.

### Present Day

Tamyra peers out the window of the first of two bedrooms that face the street. The master bedroom faces the backyard and has its own sliding glass door exit to the patio and in-ground jacuzzi. I'm eager to show her that, but she seems more interested in looking at what she apparently didn't notice during the drive to the house. "What's the neighborhood like here?"

"Mostly single families. Some retired folks who've paid off their mortgages."

"The street is narrow. Not a lot of parking."

I offer her a sympathetic nod. "It's the Valley. You'd be hard-pressed to find an older neighborhood like this one with anything different."

Josh makes a "hmmm" sound that I interpret as not being

impressed. A silent communication passes between them as she shrugs one shoulder, and he responds with an impatient eye roll.

Tamyra puts her fingertips together and points them all at me. "Here's the thing. Josh and I work for a recording company. We're looking for a place that comes across as relaxed and folksy where we can entertain our clients. Not a high-rise apartment, and certainly not an office conference room. Do you see? We've got our eyes on places in Studio City, Toluca Lake, and there's one in Glendale that's nice. This one is okay, but I don't know. What do you think, Josh?"

"Not giving me a wine and dine vibe."

"Nah, me either."

I could push them a little more, steer them toward elements of the house that might make the house more appealing. I'd like the sale. Only, I don't want them to have this house. This house is lovely and designed to have children dashing through it, unimpeded by staircases or too many walls. It has a generous, closed-in backyard, perfect for a dog and a small playset.

I nod graciously. "I'm happy to show you the rest of the house, or..." I gesture toward the master bedroom door.

"I think we're good here," Tamyra says. Josh is already heading out, checking his watch to see how much time he's wasted.

Smiling professionally, I shake their hands again at the door and thank them for coming by. I head over to the kitchen island, slip out of my heels, and eat two cookies. I pour myself a cup of wine and watch the gorgeous sunlight streak across the shiny wood floors. The light invites me to step into it and feel its golden warmth.

It's been thirty-two years since I stood basked in the glow of stage lights, and nothing has ever compared to the rush of that brightness in my eyes as I took centerstage. I turn now to face the sun and don't wince at its glow because the late afternoon has dulled its luster. I make believe that it's a special spotlight for me. It's still well above the roof of the houses across the street, forcing me to lift my chin to gaze up at it. I take a deep breath through my nose as my hands and feet find their way to first position.

Slowly, I lift my arms. My wrists lead my fingers until they form a beautiful arch above my head. I trace my right toe forward and then in a circle that pivots my body away from the sun. The house, open from living room to dining room, is now a stage. I *arabesque* and windmill my arms. Then I'm leaping and turning. I fill the space with movement.

### 1991

*Why is this so hard?* This was supposed to be a college show, not Broadway. I didn't expect the choreography for the audition to be so difficult. Kids were getting cut right and left, and I was going to be next. We were taught this faux Bob Fosse combination to the song "Magic to Do", and I couldn't get my limbs untangled enough to get it even close to correct. They were expecting a triple *pirouette*, and I kept falling out of a single. My feet clunked down after the leap like I was an elephant. No, elephants might be more graceful. I'd seen *Fantasia*.

My singing audition had gone all right. I hit all the notes and remembered all the lyrics. But the directors hadn't offered up smiles or anything encouraging. If I'd impressed them, they didn't show it. My odds of getting cast in *Pippin* were looking slim.

The choreographer and head of the dance department, Dr. Dixon, picked the next four people to step into the audition space while everyone else waited along the perimeter of the dance room. Our backs were to the mirror now, so at least I didn't have to see how bad I was. On the other hand, I couldn't cheat off the other girls who clearly had learned it better than me. We were staggered, two in the back and two in the front. I was in the front. Dr. Dixon rewound the music on the cassette in his boom box and hit play.

I smiled as wide as I could manage. My mouth twitched with nervousness. Mrs. Nell, the high school dance and aerobics teacher who choreographed our musicals used to say, "Whatever you do, make the top half of your body look good, and the audience won't care about what's happening to your feet." Now that I thought about it, this advice was only to make the non-dancers of the high school program feel better about themselves. Right at this moment, I was sure Dr. Dixon cared very much about what my feet were doing.

The combination came to an end. I wobbled on the final pose where all our balance was to be on our left foot, with the pointed right foot crossed over it, right hand flipped as if I'd tapped my invisible hat, left hand flared out behind me, and upper body bent slightly forward. Awkward. It looked cute on the good dancers. I looked like I was a breath from falling over.

We held the pose as Dr. Dixon whispered back and forth with Dr. Grisham, the director and head of the theatre department. Heads bobbed up and down. It wasn't a long discussion, but long enough for a cramp to start in my left calf. I couldn't keep my balance and gave up, lifting my leg to give it a rub.

Dr. Dixon looked up at me with a moment of bewilderment on his face. Then he said, "Oh yes, girls. Of course. Please relax." The other girls broke the pose and stood quietly as he resumed his secret conversation. Finally, he faced us again, cut three of us, and kept the cute blonde girl who had been beside me. I was confident she was a senior in the program.

"If you've been cut, stick around a moment in the hallway."

I grabbed my bag and left the room. The hallway was full with people, mostly girls, who had been cut and were waiting for whatever was going to be told to them. Only eight more people had to still do their dance call. Tyler was among them. I'd seen him learn the routine when we were all in there together. The boy could move. He'd clearly taken dance classes, and it showed not only in his ability but because he was the only guy at auditions in full dance attire—thick gray tights pulled over a burgundy tank top leotard and a dancers' cup. I'd never seen a guy up close in real ballet clothes. It was mildly startling to see the bulging, perfectly round space where his legs met. I had a hard time looking away.

Two more plays of the music, and the dance call was over. Tyler came out with a winning grin on his face and squeezed his way down the hall. Lots of people patted him on the back. He'd made it to callbacks. I shouted congratulations at him, and he paused in front of me. "Thanks, Graceful. I hope I make it." He realized I was in the cut crowd and swiftly changed his expression to sympathy. "Aw no, did you get cut? That sucks. I'm sorry."

"No big deal," I said. "I wasn't good."

The crowd pushed him to keep moving. He tossed back over his shoulder, "Hey, let's get a milkshake or something later, okay?" Then he was gone, out the door with the other good dancers. Warmth from his conciliatory sweetness helped soothe the ache of embarrassment from doing so badly in the audition. Why couldn't Dr. Dixon let us leave to sulk in privacy? Everyone around me fiddled with their fingers or chewed on their lips, wondering what he wanted with us losers.

The door to the dance room opened. Dr. Grisham and the stage manager exited, walking right past all of us without looking up or saying a word. The hallway was silent as they passed. A beat later, the door opened again, and Dr. Dixon waved us all back in. There were a couple dozen of us, and we stood in a clump while he sat on the table. He clasped his hands together and smiled kindly.

"First of all, I want to thank you all for coming today. It takes courage to audition, and you all should be proud that you have the fortitude to come out and make yourself seen. It is a first and necessary step in the life of a performer. You will hear more no's than yesses in your lives, so every attempt at getting work as a performer is important and valuable experience. At a professional level audition, when you're cut, you gather your belongings and get out of the way. I'm an educator, though, and I want this experience to be a learning opportunity for you."

He then went on to explain that most freshmen don't get cast first semester or even first year. They are competing against students with more training and experience. Dr. Dixon talked about how we'd perfect our audition technique in the musical theatre workshop class, and that we should all take that class either freshman or sophomore year. He emphasized that we should all consider private voice lessons and taking dance classes if we were serious about having careers. If anyone wanted to make an appointment with him during his office hours, he'd be happy to give some recommendations.

"Don't be discouraged," he said, his hands clasped in front of his chest and the most patronizing expression on his face. "You will improve, and you will have your chance."

Dr. Dixon dismissed us. Everyone shuffled out with heads lowered, not wanting to acknowledge each other. Most of us barely knew each other yet, having been in school only a week at this point. I know I was definitely feeling ashamed for even thinking about auditioning for the show. I got the sense everyone around me felt the same. Someone grumbled "waste of time" as he went through the doorway out of Dr. Dixon's hearing.

"I know," I agreed dully.

Then Mr. Dixon called my name. "Miss Fuller? Miss Fuller could you stay a moment?"

Did he hear me? Was he going to call me out for being rude? I tried to slip out the door, but there were too many other girls in my way.

"Miss Fuller?" he asked again with more insistence. I gritted my teeth and spun around. Dr. Dixon stood at the table, gathering up audition forms. He nodded at me. "A moment." While he wasn't smiling, he didn't seem agitated either.

As the others left the room, I walked back in. The tiniest flame of hope burned that maybe he was going to give me some kind of second chance. To do the combination again? Maybe to see if I could do any acrobatics? *Pippin* was about a circus of sorts. Maybe he needed people who could do tricks. I knew how to do a cartwheel. That was about it.

Once he had all the papers in a neat stack, he faced me. "Miss Fuller, you did a nice audition. We all thought you sang well. You had a decent handle on the choreography. I noticed that you did

*Sweet Charity* last year at school. That probably helped a lot with learning the Fosse style."

My mouth was so dry. What was he getting at? Had he changed his mind about cutting me after all? I said, "My teacher stole some of the steps from the movie."

"I'd have done the same thing," he said. "No one choreographs a Fosse musical better than Bob Fosse."

I tried to laugh at that, but it came out as a cough.

He crossed his arms and leaned against the table. "So, here's the thing, Miss Fuller. You have some talent. It's raw and untrained, but there's definitely something there. You have personality and good stage presence. Even when it was clear you had no idea what your feet were doing, your smile never faltered. I like that. However, what you don't have is a lot of skill. Not the level I need, or any professional theater will need. I highly encourage you to take ballet classes. We have courses here, and it's not too late to sign up for this semester. While you have some ability with keeping time, your balance isn't great, and you don't seem to know basic foundation steps. You will never get in a musical that requires dancing without these skills. Do you understand?"

I could only nod. The lump in my throat prevented me from speaking. At my high school, I had been one of the better dancers. I was even dance captain for *Brigadoon* my sophomore year because I remembered the routines better than everyone else.

He gave me a sympathetic smile. "Look, I'm not beating you up here. I'm trying to be helpful."

There were other dancers way worse than me in the group that left. Why weren't they all getting this pep talk?

As if he read my thoughts, he said, "I think you have promise. This is what I'm saying. Can you move your schedule around? Make room for another class? I'll make sure you get in if admin gives you any trouble about it."

I shook my head and shrugged. I didn't think so. I'd worked hard to get my schedule exactly how it was and still have time to work. I had sixteen credits already. My scholarship wouldn't let me have more than that, so I'd have to lose a different course. "I'll look," I said, "but I probably can't take ballet until next semester."

"You'll need more than one semester to get good. You understand that? Professional dancers on Broadway are continuously taking lessons."

"I took ballet when I was little."

"It's too bad you didn't stick with it."

He grabbed his boom box by the handle and picked up the stack of audition sheets. I followed him to the door where he paused to dump the sheets in the trash and turn out the light.

As I followed him into the hallway, Dr. Dixon said, "I'm serious about the ballet classes. You have to take them, or you might as well think about doing straight plays instead of musicals. There simply aren't that many musicals that require no dancing at all." He put up a finger and added, "You should take tap, too." Then he headed down the hallway and out the door to the Fine Arts quad, probably thinking he'd done me some big favor.

I was so good that I had to be singled out and told how bad I was? How was I supposed to take that? Feel inspired?

Feeling anything but inspired, I got in my car and drove home. Mom wasn't home, thankfully, so I didn't have to answer any questions yet. I went to my room and dug through my closet. Way in the back was a round, pink, shiny case. I tugged it out and sat cross-legged on the carpet with it in my lap. For the first time in eight years, I unzipped it. Carefully, I took out the tiny ballet slippers. They were still brand new, not a scuff on them. The leather still smelled spicy. Mom never did make me sell them. She could have. I'd barely used them. She'd let me keep them as some vague promise that maybe someday I'd get to use them. My feet grew. She must've forgotten about them. I pressed them to my cheek and closed my eyes.

The phone rang, bringing me out of my self-pity. I stuffed the shoes back in the case before lunging for the phone by my bed. It was Tyler.

"How about that shake? Tonight at 7:00? Hudson's Grill has great ones, if you haven't been there yet."

No. I didn't think I could hang out with Tyler that night and talk about the audition and how he'd done so well and I'd failed so badly. I'd seen Tyler dance. I saw the way the directors responded to him. He was going to be a favorite, while I got pulled aside and told how I'd never make it. How could I ever spend time with him and not despise him every moment?

"I can't tonight, Tyler. Maybe another time."

I didn't give him a chance to talk me out of it and hung up after a quick, unexplained apology.

Mom came home hours later and found me lying on my bed in my sweats with the lights out. She switched on the lamp on my bedstand and noticed the old dance bag on the floor.

"Oh, honey," was all she said. She put out her arms, and I slipped into her protective hug. She held me and patted my back a good long time with no conversation at all. She didn't ask questions. It was exactly what I needed.

### Present Day

In reality, the only sounds to be heard are my feet on the floor and the heavy breath of my exertion. In my head I hear Tchaikovsky. *The Sleeping Beauty.* The movement is exhilarating, and I love the way my skirt flows around my legs. As the music comes to a crescendo, I pull out all the stops and do a triple *pirouette* barefoot. I don't stumble out of it and stop strong. I never dance this well in class. I'm on fire.

Then I hear applause. At first it is the thunderous applause of my imagination, but I quickly come to my senses and realize it's coming from one set of hands, not thousands. I twist around so fast it tweaks my back. My right hand goes to the ache, while my left flies to my face. A man is standing in the open front doorway. He raises two fingers to his mouth and whistles before clapping a few more times.

"Bravo! I'm sold! Best open house I've ever been to, by far."

"Oh! I didn't know anyone was here."

"I didn't think so, unless this is part of your sales technique. Very original, if it is." He puts his hands up like he's reading a marquee. "The Dancing Realtor!"

It's too ridiculous not to laugh about it. My face has to be beet red, and I can't do anything about that either.

"It's so L.A.," he adds.

"I guess it is," I manage to say in response.

He steps all the way in the house and closes the door while I go slip my shoes back on my feet. He holds up a notepad. "I don't know if this is an official open house—"

"It's not. I just finished up an appointment—"

"But I was in the area looking at addresses I'd written down from a listing. This was one of them. I saw a couple leaving and another car remaining in the driveway. I was hoping I'd get lucky, and you'd show it to me while I was here."

I open a water bottle and take a sip to fix my dry mouth. I nod as I swallow and then say, "Sure. I'd be happy to show you around. I'm Grace."

"Pretty name. I knew a girl named Grace once. Forever ago. You favor her, actually." He reaches past me for a cookie and takes a bite.

"That's funny," I say. "You look a little like someone I used to know, too."

This stops him, and he stares at me for a moment with that half-eaten cookie in his hand. "Wait. You're not Grace Fuller, are you?"

My jaw loosens and I nod. "Tyler?"

"*Graceful*? Oh my God! How crazy is this?" He puts the cookie down on the counter and sweeps me into a hug like we're old friends. Maybe, technically, we are, but I'm not sure how I feel about this reunion yet. I don't hug back. Tyler steps away, and I reach for my unfinished cup of wine. Water is no longer enough.

Tyler Andrews from my freshman year of college is standing before me, running a hand through his hair, not quite as long and curly on top as it once was and definitely shorter in the back. He's unabashedly gawking at me as he matches his memory of me to the woman I am now. I'm leaner and older. I've stopped dying my hair and allowed the white roots to take over my red hair. Spencer says it looks like the smoke is putting out the fire and that I should do something about it. I'm waiting to see if I'll like it once it's finished growing all the way out. I'm patient. I've waited patiently for a lot of things that haven't come my way yet in this lifetime.

Tyler has taken care of his appearance, too. He clearly works out. The thin knit shirt he wears accents his chest and upper arms while also showing off a thin waist where the shirt is tucked into his belted slacks. His face has gotten longer since we last met, his cheekbones and chin very prominent, with some trimmed facial hair accenting his features. His eyebrows are thicker, almost wild, above his brilliant blue eyes. The man has a tan, and it looks like it's actually from being in the sun and not a tanning bed. Over all, he comes across a good five years or more younger than he is. I think he looks younger than me, that's for sure.

He's not perfect, I decide. I knock one point off because he's still barely taller than me. Who am I kidding? He's perfect kissing height.

My heart is beating too fast. I blame it on the dancing. I know that's a lie.

"It's pretty crazy," I say. "What are you…? I mean, are you looking to buy a house? For your family?"

Tyler's teeth are extra white when he smiles at me, like he's had them done recently. "Oh no, I'm not married. Not anymore. I'm looking for myself. Single occupancy. The show I'm in has been picked up for two more seasons, and I thought it was time to leave condo life behind."

He's an actor. Still. After all this time.

Of course he is.

"You're in a show? A TV show?"

He puts his hands up in mock humiliation. "It's called *Wild-cats*." At my blank expression, he continues. "It's okay if you haven't heard of it. It's science fiction about shapeshifters. Kind of crazy. See, there's this town where there are packs of people who turn into werecats. I play the football coach of the high school football team."

I'm trying hard to stifle a laugh. "Wait, don't tell me. The high school team is called the Wildcats."

"Yep. It sounds stupid when I describe it this way, but kids are eating it up. We're a hit, and they're going to put season one on Netflix this fall."

"That's amazing. I don't suppose you're singing and dancing in the show?"

He sighs dramatically. "Unfortunately, no. Unless they do a crazy musical episode like they did on *Buffy the Vampire Slayer* that one time. Although, even if they do, I probably won't be in it. I'm important to the show but not a central character."

"Well, I'll have to check it out."

"Yeah." He finally remembers his cookie and pops the remainder in his mouth. He lets his eyes roll back and he moans slightly while he chews. After he swallows, he says, "Tell me about *you*, besides the fact that you bake delicious cookies. You look great. Great's probably not a good enough adjective. You look stunning. You're a realtor?" He asks this as if he's waiting for me to explain that this is my side hustle while pursuing something more exciting. This isn't unreasonable. I know of a lot of actor/realtors. I know more of them than actor/waiters.

"I am."

An awkward silence follows. He's waiting for me to say something about myself. I don't have a big tale to tell him. Instead, I give him what he came here for.

"So, this house is three bedrooms. It's big for a single man living alone."

"I like the neighborhood."

I nod at that. "The last people here felt exactly the opposite."

"To each their own," he says.

I begin the tour of the house, reciting all the important details. The layout of the kitchen impresses him the most and he shares that he's a decent cook.

"I worked on a food truck as a day job and thought about

opening a restaurant of my own a few years back when my luck was running thin on acting gigs."

He's been acting this whole time? How did I not know? Had I seen him in stuff and didn't know it? Clearly, he isn't famous, or I would have heard or seen something. I've thought of searching his name on the internet a few times over the years, but I always stop short. I'm not sure what stifles my curiosity.

The built-in jacuzzi is a definite plus for him. The building he lives in now has one, but he's jazzed by the idea of not having to share with anyone. Privacy is invaluable, he informs me, as if he's hounded by fans. I don't know. Maybe he is. Middle-aged moms who watch the werecat show with their teen children probably salivate over him. Why wouldn't they?

We step out to the patio. The sun is setting and no longer visible. The sky is a million shades of violet orange. The colors pool into the walled-in yard, surrounding us with their vibrancy.

"I love it," he says simply. "I do. It's perfect. I'd have to make sure my contract allows me to be home by sunset every day."

Wonderful. This could be an easy sale. Do I want it? I need the money. Could I steer him away? Because being aware of where he is sleeping every night is information I'm not sure I want in my head. Does he sleep shirtless? Oh God, no. Stop.

"Is your show shooting in Burbank or Hollywood?" I ask. "Traffic getting over the hill into the city is rough sometimes."

He puts his hands on his hips as he considers this. "We do have a soundstage off Sunset Boulevard, but we do a lot of shooting out past Malibu."

"So, a house in Sherman Oaks might not be the most convenient for you."

He puts a hand to his chin, his thumb pressing his lower lip as he grins. "Are you talking me out of this house?"

"No. Of course not. I want you to be happy with your choice. No buyer's remorse, you know. It's a big decision."

I wrap my sweater tight around me. A breeze from the ocean is blowing the day's heat away.

"Are you cold?" he asks. "You want to go back inside?"

"It's colder in there."

I'm frozen with inaction. I want to stay in this moment, rediscovering this man after all this time. I don't know where to start. I don't know if I should.

"I tell you what," Tyler says. "Give me your card. I've got some other properties on my list to look at. I'll get back in touch with you to let you know if I'm set on this house or not."

I nod. That makes sense. It's practical. "I'm not sure how long this house will stay on the market. It's a good deal in a great part of town."

"You're absolutely right about that. If you get a bid from someone else, you run with it. I won't hold you up."

We head back inside. The air conditioning hits me like an arctic breeze, and I shiver. He puts an arm around my shoulders to warm me. This isn't professional, but we're more than that in some ways, aren't we? Back at the kitchen island, I hand him a business card from my stack and one of the printouts with details about the home.

"All right. I've got your number. Is this your cell, I'm assuming? Or an office?"

"It's my cell."

"And you hand this out to any stranger?"

"The ones who want to buy houses from me, yes."

He grabs another cookie. "One for the road. They're delectable, by the way. Have I mentioned that?"

"You have. Thanks."

He takes a few steps toward the front door and then spins around. Something's on his mind. "The dancing?"

I shake my head and lean against the counter, crossing one ankle over the other. "That's for another conversation," I tell him.

His grin widens. "We're going to have another conversation?"

"The house…"

"Maybe over dinner?"

Oh. Wow. My breath catches. I hope he doesn't notice, but he does. That gorgeous grin of his falters.

"I'm sorry. Should we keep this about business?"

"No, I…" I gather myself. This has been the strangest afternoon. "I would love to have dinner with you. To... you know... catch up."

He is visibly relieved. "I'm free tomorrow night."

"I have class on Tuesdays," I say. I can almost hear Spencer yelling at me to blow off class. I could *not* tell him. Oh, please, I will *have* to tell him about this. He'll pull it right out of me. Spencer has a knack for noticing everything, and he'd know if I were keeping a secret. "You know what? I can skip it. Tomorrow sounds great."

After Tyler tells me he'll call with details, he leaves. I watch him drive his BMW away. The man has done well for himself. My nine-year-old Camry waits patiently for me in the driveway. I've not done as well, but I'm doing okay.

I pour myself another cup of chardonnay, a little higher up to the brim this time. I sip at it as I put the remaining cookies in a container and clean up after myself. I make sure the doors are all locked and the lights out. Streetlamps have turned on outside. The glow from them infiltrates the front window, dim and haunting like a ghost light in a dark theater. The show is over. The players have gone home.

# CHAPTER
## *Three*

It's been difficult not telling Spencer about my impending date with Tyler. I've picked up my phone to call or text him at least twenty times. I know he'll be encouraging. Probably too much so, considering I haven't been on a date in a while. Okay, a couple years. All right, *several* years. He'll be sure to remind me of that fact and how I *need* this in my life.

I'm not convinced this date with Tyler is going to lead to anything, so why get Spencer's hopes up?

I've been able to avoid seeing Spencer face to face easily enough. That's helpful. Dancer's Room is rented out on Monday nights for small troupes or individuals needing rehearsal space. Sometimes the movie studios use it to rehearse dance numbers for upcoming features. Spencer assists or choreographs for an extra fee. We've had a number of local high school dance teams or show choirs come for pointers before a competition. I've been pulled in once in a while to help, but I always feel like a fraud. Spencer tried to get me to come lend a hand tonight with some *pas de deux* routine he was hired to choreograph for a high school couple who are planning to audition for *So You Think You Can Dance*. I begged out.

I wish I hadn't. Sitting at home, I feel antsy. I don't have enough to do to keep my mind off of meeting Tyler again. I've thought of nothing else since he left the house I was showing.

Now, I've got my second glass of merlot, a heated up Healthy Choice meal, and am scrolling through the internet with his name in the search engine.

It turns out he's done all right as a performer. IMDB has him listed as having been a guest star on twenty-two TV shows or films since the nineties. Some of them are shows I know and have watched. From what I'm seeing, he never had recurring parts on these primetime shows, just a guest spot here and there. The burn victim on *Chicago Hope* or a gruffy homeless witness on *Law and Order*. I guarantee I saw him at some point and didn't recognize him. Now I kind of understand why people don't connect Clark Kent to Superman when he puts on the glasses—they simply aren't paying attention.

Tyler spent a year or so on a daytime soap opera, and he was in a short-lived kids' show. I assume he's done some commercials, too. The only video clips I find of him are from *Wildcats*. I find a whole episode on YouTube and hit play. Fifteen minutes in, I've completely tuned out. The show is moronic, and he's barely in it.

I search to see if he has any Broadway credits but don't find any. It's a shame. A guy who could dance as well as he should have been on Broadway. I hope that he's been doing some kind of stage work throughout the years. Tyler was built for musical theatre.

A feeling niggles at me, and it's something unfamiliar when it comes to how I recall handling Tyler's success. I'm disappointed. Not jealous or envious, the way I always used to feel with regard to Tyler Andrews. No. I'm sincerely bummed out that he's not famous. He's simply a working actor. One who had to also have a day job on a food truck. I wonder what other day jobs he's had over the years.

I close my laptop. I need to stop this searching. Who am I to judge the status of his career? He's a *working actor*. He's still at it after all these years and making money from his craft. Who am I? Nothing. I never even gave it a chance. I just... I want to live vicariously through him. I want to feel like saying *I knew that guy when we were kids* should give me some validity. It's stupid. It's all I have.

## 1991

Within a few weeks of school starting, I realized that the commuting time between school and home, plus homework, made it impossible for me to keep my job at Clothestime at the mall where I'd been working since turning sixteen. I'd chosen my classes specifically so that I could keep the same work schedule I'd had in high school, but it wasn't working out at all. I wound up quitting and taking a job in the student center on campus, working at a hot dog and concessions stand.

The job was awful, but I got more hours, and the hourly pay was better. A lot of the professors tipped, which was nice. The students absolutely did not. I missed my friends at the store. We used to laugh and joke all the time. At Eats and Treats, I mostly worked with Fresno Kei. In fact, I spent a lot of my time at college with Fresno Kei. We were in two other classes together besides Acting 101.

It was now too late to add a class or change my schedule. No ballet. No fun job. No musical. Lots of this sour-faced girl who seemed to hate me for existing. First semester of college was not turning out the way movies depicted it. So far, I hated every second of it.

Fellow students from the theatre department came by now and again, trying to convince me to give them free drinks or food —'cause we were good friends, of course. The first time it happened, Kei tugged me back to the meat slicer. "Look," she said. "They don't know you for shit. Got it? You don't owe them anything. Is one of them going to get you a part in a play? Is one of them going to help you out later on? No. Theatre is a dog-eat-dog world, and they don't care about you. All they care about is using you for free stuff. Notice how they didn't ask me? They know they can't play me."

I thought they didn't ask Kei because she was mean. I wasn't mean. I wanted to be liked and included. I wanted to make friends. Surely, a free Coke now and again... Although, I didn't want to lose my job. I couldn't afford it.

"I don't need the lecture, Kei. I wasn't going to give them anything."

Kei raised an eyebrow. "You sure looked like you were. No is a fast and easy word to say, and you haven't said it yet."

I spun around and smiled at the faces I barely knew from the arts department hallways and said, "I'm sorry. I can't. Policy. You understand."

"A cup of ice?" one of them asked. I remembered her from auditions. Cute. Perky.

"Ummm."

"No." Kei stepped up to the counter beside me. "If you're not going to order anything, there are people waiting behind you."

The girl, whose name I think I remembered to be Tiffany, or I might have thought it was Tiffany because she looked like the singer, and her two friends said a collective "aww" and then walked away without ordering a thing.

"Moochers," Kei muttered as she tugged the scrunchie off her ponytail and proceeded to try to tame that thick, frizzy mess into a newer, neater pony.

I smiled at the next customer, a tall student in a hoodie, holding a backpack in place over one shoulder and digging in his pocket to get out some cash. He ordered quickly, his eyes darting up from his hands at Kei a couple times as if waiting for her to attack him. I understood his concern and wondered about my own safety sometimes.

Kei lived in the dorms, as did Tyler. They had become friends when they did a scene together in acting class. Living so close, they were able to practice a lot. Their performance was impressive. So much so that Dr. Williams gave them an entirely different set of constructive criticism suggestions. For the rest of us, it was generic stuff like: "You could turn to the audience more on that line" or "Use your upstage hand when you gesture so you don't block your face." Basic stuff that didn't help improve our acting much at all. With Kei and Tyler, he did the kind of directing I'd always imagined should happen at college level. "I hear your longing in that line, but why? What are you trying to get from him?" or "Brilliant gesture to show your anger, but don't waste your energy. How can you show the same thing without moving at all?" On and on. He took an entire class period perfecting their scene and then suggested they rehearse it some more because he might use it in the one-act showcase at the end of the semester.

My scene was fine, I guess. The biggest thing Dr. Williams said to me was that Angela and I had miscast ourselves. Pretty, petite Angela should have played the ingenue role, and I should have played the comic relief. We'd done that casting on purpose to challenge ourselves, but it didn't fly. He said, "Practice it again the other way around, and if we have time next week, I'll look at it again."

We never had time. There were too many people in the class who still had to do scenes, and all the attention on Kei and Tyler ate up what could have gone to Angela and me.

I hated the fact that Tyler was the only person who could make Kei smile. And she smiled all the damn time when he was around. Oh, and go figure, if Tyler showed up at Eats and Treats, you bet he got a free drink and chips.

Tyler remained consistently friendly to me, but there was always some shared joke or comment between the two of them. All the dorm kids had the kind of friendship of a secret club, and us commuter students were most definitely not in on it.

Kei got cast in some play being directed by a grad student that I'd never heard of before. Nor had I even known about the auditions for it. I was grateful in a way because this kept her away from work a lot. Between her rehearsals and Tyler's rehearsals for *Pippin*, I rarely saw either of them except for class. I was beginning to feel a bit like a ghost around the theatre department halls. I knew I was there, but no one saw me, especially if Tyler or Kei were around. They were the freshmen superstars. I was the girl that didn't give anyone free food.

The choosing of scene partners in Acting 101 was a little like picking teams in P.E. back in elementary school. The best kids got paired up first. Dr. Williams announced the scene choices and flung the stapled copies to the floor at the front of the room. We frantically went through the crowd shouting stuff like "I want the Mamet one!" or "Who wants to do *Streetcar* with me?" You had to be fast and determined. The first two times this happened, I was way too slow and timid.

This time I was going to jump in there and be at the head of the pack. I clenched my fists and leaned forward like I was at a racecourse. Dr. Williams raised that stack of paper ceremoniously before scattering the pages. As the papers smacked the ground, hungry actors leapt forward. My way was blocked. I felt like a starving beggar pushing through for a scrap of bread. Everyone had learned how this worked, and no one was going to be polite and let me walk through. I glanced over at Dr. Williams standing beside Jeff Holland, his grad student assistant. The smug smiles on their faces as they watched the frenzy let me know that this was how they got their kicks, watching desperate theatre students duke it out for choice scenes. Why not put two in a cage and let it be a real fight? I could picture Tina Turner shouting, "Two actors enter! One actor leaves!"

I quit. I didn't feel like being part of their entertainment. Instead, I backed away and leaned against the brick wall under the window for the lighting booth. I crossed my arms, put one foot against the wall, balancing on the other, and waited. Whatever scene and classmate were left at the end, I'd go with. What did it matter, anyway? I shut my eyes to the chaos and worked at tuning it all out.

"Grace! Grace!" I opened my eyes to find Tyler standing in front of me waving two stapled scenes. "I got it. *Barefoot in the Park*. It's the best scene up there. I knew the second Dr. Williams described it that I had to do this scene with you."

What was happening? Tyler, Mr. Hotshot, had emerged from the battle with spoils for me?

"With me?" I clarified. I knew he couldn't do another scene with Kei. No repeat partners allowed. There were plenty of other talented girls in this class. Cuter girls.

"Yes, you," he said sweetly. He handed me a script. "I decided on the first day of this class I had to do at least one scene with you this semester, and I've been waiting for the perfect one."

I met his eager blue eyes. "I'd love to do a scene with you. If you think I'd be good enough."

He wriggled his nose like he tasted something sour. "Come on, Graceful. You're one of the best in this class, and you know it."

"I don't know that."

"Well, I do."

I accepted his vote of confidence.

"Besides," he said. "I've been wanting to get to know you better, but we're both so busy. This'll force us to spend at least a little time together over the next week or so."

How could I resist? I caught the glares of six different girls as Tyler and I sat down together and did a quick read-through. I was proud as hell.

Even though Tyler told me not to, I rented the movie from Blockbuster and watched it at home with my mom before the next time he and I got together to rehearse. It was cute and helpful. Tyler totally noticed that I had adapted my acting style to match what Jane Fonda did and scolded me gently for it.

"Knock that off and get back to acting," he said. "You won't impress anybody by being a copycat."

Only, this is what I'd always done before. I mimicked the actors in the movies. I figured they had mastered the roles and why not borrow their style? In high school, I was praised for my impersonation ability. Tyler said he never watched the movie versions of plays or musicals he was in. He wanted to have his own unique stamp on it. He wanted his opinions to be fresh. He told me that some actors don't even read the novels that a movie is based on because they don't want to be biased by anything.

We got together to rehearse in the commons area at his dorm. The room was designed to have a home family room appeal to it for the kids who wanted to gather and watch a movie together or hang out. It wasn't as inviting as it might have been a decade or two earlier when the sofa had been less ratty, the end tables less wobbly, the coffee table absent of stains and scratches, and the armchairs less worn. The boxy TV in the corner had broken antennas, and I suspected it didn't have a cable connection. I did see a VCR on the shelf below it, so that was something.

Tyler and I rearranged the furniture to be set like it would be in an apartment. When it came time to perform the scene in class, all we'd have at our disposal would be folding chairs, but we both liked the idea of doing the scene in a realistic setting to see how it felt. Tyler said it would give us "affective memory" that we could call on when we performed the scene in class. When I asked where he learned that, he told me about *Method Acting* and Stanislovsky. He was excited to share this knowledge with me and didn't patronize me for not knowing it. Still, I felt dumb being a theatre major in college never having heard of this style of acting or this great theatre guru. My high school drama teacher didn't have us learn stuff like that. We just had fun. Before I started college, I thought doing theatre was supposed to be fun.

The only thing we couldn't avoid or incorporate into our acting were the constant intrusions. This was the main pass-through for everyone living in this dorm building. Girls entered and headed to the halls on the right, boys to the left. It was four in the afternoon, so lots of kids were coming in from finishing their classes. A couple of students had the decency to hush up as they passed. Most didn't even notice us and kept chatting nonstop.

We'd been assigned the biggest scene in the play between the two main characters, newlyweds who had moved into a problematic apartment. It was a big fight between them when they realized they didn't have as much in common as they had once thought. Every time Tyler and I got deep into our acting, someone would walk through and check to see if we were okay. The fifth time broke Tyler. It was the campus security guard. The man strolled into the room, his thumbs in his pockets, and said, "Is this boy bothering you, miss?"

"Yeah," I answered. "He won't stop picking on the way I deliver my lines."

Tyler collapsed on the sofa and started laughing. It was infectious, and giggles bubbled up in me, too. Confusion washed over the security guard's features, which only made us both laugh harder. Finally, he figured out that everything was on the up and up, even if it didn't make sense to him, and he exited the building.

I plopped down next to Tyler. The uneven cushions forced me to roll slightly into him so that our shoulders and legs touched. "I guess we're getting it right," I said, as I struggled in vain to get more centered on the cushion. "People think we're really fighting."

Tyler ran a hand over his face in a poor attempt to calm himself. "Well, I guess that's something. This is a terrible place to practice."

"It is," I agreed. We both turned our heads to face each other, our noses practically touching, and we burst out laughing again. His laugh was high and light, matching his tenor voice. If it was possible, the blue of his eyes brightened when he laughed, like his laughter blew away the clouds in the sky. Our shoulders bobbed up and down against each other, and it was everything I could do to not lean forward a bit more and press my lips to his.

"Can we rehearse in your room?"

Tyler shook his head, sighing. "It's too small, and Terrance is probably studying in there right now. Could we go to your place?"

"I don't live on campus. It's a good thirty minutes from here."

He groaned. "I've got rehearsal in an hour, so that won't work."

"Yeah, I have to work later, too."

I picked up my script from the coffee table and fiddled with it in my lap. Tyler had stopped laughing. I'm sure his thoughts were consumed with finding a quieter place to go. On the contrary, I wasn't much interested in moving at all. Our upper arms were still touching. He made no effort to get away from me, and I certainly wasn't going to make an attempt to get away from him.

After a long minute, he put a hand on my leg. The warmth of it went right through my jeans. Why hadn't I worn a skirt or shorts? Tyler squeezed my leg softly, conciliatory, then gave it a quick pat before standing up. "I guess we'll have to practice quietly. We'll definitely have to get together again at least once more before we have to present this so we can practice full out."

"Sure." I folded the script long-ways along the same leg he'd touched as if protecting the spot from any other sensation. "It's a good thing we didn't do the first scene in the show. We'd really get a reaction around here."

"What do you mean?"

I tapped the script to my chin, barely touching my lower lip as I debated whether or not to continue with my thought. "Have you seen the movie? Ever, I mean?"

"I don't think so. My mom likes it. She got jazzed when I called and told her I was doing a scene from it. She's a big Jane Fonda fan. Does her workout video every day."

I nodded, tilting my head a little and offering my best flirty smile. "Well, I don't know if it's in the play, but in the movie there's this scene right at the beginning, right after their first night as newlyweds, when she won't let her husband leave for work without giving her a big, juicy kiss right there in the hallway. It's romantic."

"Oh yeah?"

"Yeah. And she's only wearing a robe."

Tyler sat on the coffee table in front of me, his knees on both sides of mine, his elbows resting on his knees. "That sounds like a way more fun scene than this one."

I leaned forward so that our faces were only an inch apart. "I think so, too."

He'd been looking me in the eyes, but his gaze drifted to my lips. "Wanna switch and try that scene instead?"

"We probably shouldn't."

"No, not for class, anyway. But maybe... Just for fun, you know."

"Yeah. For fun."

Tyler closed the gap between us, pressing his lips to mine. His arms reached for me, wrapping around my back and pulling me even closer. I opened my legs so that one of his knees slipped between mine, and I scooted to the edge of the couch. The script fluttered to the floor as I snuck my arms up his chest, over his shoulders, and then intertwined my fingers behind his neck. The kiss intensified. Our mouths opened and our tongues met. A soft moan escaped me as his hands ran up my back, pressing my chest against his.

The coffee table creaked dangerously. Tyler's eyes widened in alarm. He put his hands on my shoulders to steady me so I didn't fall into him as he abruptly stopped kissing me. "This could be dangerous."

"I know," I said with a giggle. We were both talking about the rickety table—and maybe a little bit more than that. "You sure you don't want to come over to my house? My mom won't be home."

Tyler got off the table and sat beside me on the couch again. He reclined into the cushions and draped an arm over the back. I took that as an invitation and leaned into him, putting my head on his shoulder. "You live with your mom?" I nodded. "Just the two of you?" I nodded again. "Cool."

I wasn't sure what he meant by that. It didn't feel judgmental, but, honestly, he was a good actor. Maybe he liked the idea of having somewhere to go off campus.

"I can't go now," Tyler said. He put a finger to my chin and turned my face to his. His blue eyes twinkled. Those natural upward curls of his lips were pronounced. "But I really want to."

He kissed me again, his fingers brushing my cheek and finding their way to my hair. We heard some whistles from people walking through the common room. He didn't pause to look up or respond. I put a leg across his. He lowered his hand to my hip and hooked one finger through the belt loop of my jeans and tickled my exposed skin above it with another. A tingle ran through my body, and I gasped from the sensation.

The kisses stopped, and Tyler's expression grew serious. "I didn't expect this to happen, Grace. Is this okay?"

I nodded eagerly. "Yes. It's okay. It's awesome."

Tyler smiled. He didn't take his hand away from my hip. I didn't move my legs. We were practically nose to nose. "We can't do this here," he said. "I want to so much. Wow. You have no idea. But not right here. You know what I mean?"

I gave him my best pout.

"God, you're so cute."

I put a finger to my dimple and said in my best Betty Boop voice, "Thank you."

He gave me one more light kiss and then got up, scooping up my script from the floor and grabbing his from the table. As if nothing had happened, we were right back to rehearsing.

Oh, but something had happened. Our chemistry was lightning now. The scene was brilliant. It was the best acting I'd ever felt come out of me. I decided I might be good at this after all.

We got together to practice twice more, both times at my house. Both times ending in passionate make-out sessions in my bedroom. Acting turned him on. While I thought of little else but wanting to kiss him while we practiced, he was all business and didn't get frisky until we'd hit the desired level of passion within the confines of the scene. It was as if our kissing each other was our reward for great work.

I tried not to wonder if he had done the same thing with Kei when they rehearsed. I tried not to worry that he'd do the same thing with the next girl he partnered with, or the girl who acted opposite him in *Pippin*. What would happen to us after we presented our scene in class and didn't have to rehearse anymore? We wouldn't have to even see each other anymore. I hoped Tyler was as crazy about me as I was about him. It seemed like it. But Tyler was a great actor.

Our scene was well under control, but then in the class before the one where we were slated to perform, Dr. Williams told everyone to add an element to our scenes. He had us read a chapter from Uta Hagen's book *Respect for Acting*. She had a whole exercise for learning how to make the fourth wall real. The fourth wall is the imaginary wall of the set where the audience sits. Our job as actors was not to see the audience but to instead see the rest of the room where our scenes took place. We were told to find three specific things on that imaginary wall to focus on during our scene and incorporate it into the blocking.

Tyler and I didn't have time to rehearse again, but we got together in the quad for a few minutes and discussed what that extra wall of the apartment our characters lived in looked like. He was going to focus on a crack in the wall, a window that needed cleaning, and the noisy radiator. I was going to focus on where I could put a flowerpot on the windowsill, a painting that could be moved to cover the crack, and a small bookshelf that still needed books. Specific thoughts that fit our characters. Tyler didn't want to plan specific lines for us to look at these imaginary things, but to let them come naturally as the scene progressed. Without telling him, I totally planned when to look at everything so I wouldn't forget.

When we performed the scene, Dr. Williams was complimentary—toward Tyler. He commended Tyler for his pacing and character choices. He asked what Tyler was looking at for his three objects, and when Tyler answered, Dr. Williams nodded appreciatively. "Yes. See, everyone? This is how it should be done. He not only noticed things, but he noticed them with objective and as his character." The class mumbled their understanding, and I saw a few people nibble on lips or scratch heads as they realized they hadn't thought of the exercise this way.

Dr. Williams asked me what I was looking at, and I told him what I'd chosen and why, sure that I'd get the same praise. He frowned. "Okay. Okay. I noticed you look out three specific times. It was fast, more of a glance, like you were remembering that you had to do it rather than because something caught your eye and forced you to focus on it. See the difference? If something is real, you really look at it."

That was all I got. Nothing about my actual acting. I learned more about acting from Tyler in our practices than I was getting from this stupid class. Why was I even bothering?

Dr. Williams congratulated us again, patting Tyler on the shoulder, before sending us back to our folding chairs to watch the next couple of suckers. As I sat down, Kei, who was sitting in front of me, leaned back on the back two legs of her chair. With all that bushy hair practically in my lap, she looked at Tyler beside me and said, "You were great." Then she sat up straight again.

Tyler linked his pinky with mine and whispered in my ear. "Want to skip your next class and hang out for a bit?" A thrill spiked through me. My frustration immediately dampened it. Tyler might want to celebrate his awesome acting, but I hardly felt the same. Yes, I wanted to ditch my next class. Not to go make-out with Tyler, but to drive miles and miles away from this place. Maybe go to the beach and walk around, allow the salty air to clear my head. Every thought in there was a jumble of negativity.

I unhooked my finger from his, clasping my hands together in my lap. "Not today," I whispered.

Tyler said nothing. He accepted my no, which was good, but I can't say I wouldn't have preferred him to try a little harder to convince me. A couple extra tantalizing words might have gone a long way toward convincing me that he cared about me and not that he wanted to be with me because he was on some acting high. I don't know.

When class ended, other students surrounded Tyler, wanting to congratulate him on the scene. I snuck out without saying goodbye. I went to my next class like a good little girl and doodled pictures of monsters in the margins of my notebook while my psychology professor droned on about Freudian theories.

Fortunately for me, the next set of scenes in the class were all same sex. Basically, Dr. Williams wanted to see some scenes with the guys acting with each other. Our final for the semester was a monologue. All of this meant, at the very least, I didn't need to have any jealousy about Tyler kissing his rehearsal partners. He and I found time here and there to go out for a burger and steal some time to kiss in my car in the parking lot of a neighborhood playground after dark. He was too busy to ever make it all the way over to my house between *Pippin* rehearsals and homework.

The show opened in November, and it was amazing. The best show I'd ever seen. Way better than a high school production, that was for sure. Tyler was even better than I imagined he would be. He became an instant star on campus. Getting close to him was nearly impossible, alone time out of the question. Finals arrived before we knew it, and then he was packing up to head home to Palmdale for winter break. I noted that while Palmdale was a good two or more hours from my house in Los Alamitos, it was not far at all from Fresno.

Tyler and I stayed in touch by phone over the break when we could catch each other at home. Our conversations were always awkward. He talked incessantly about his friends from college and what everyone was up to and the fun things he'd been invited to do with them. I knew the names and faces, but these weren't people who had befriended me. If he hadn't told me about the parties, the ski trip, and a gathering at Universal Studios, I would never have known about them. I wouldn't have been jealous. I wouldn't have wondered why I wasn't invited. I was a heck of a lot closer to Universal Studios than he was.

Tyler never offered to come down or have me come up there the whole time. He did tell me at the end of every phone call that he missed me and then would say something flirtatious, like, "I hope you're saving up your kisses for me. I want to collect soon."

So, were we boyfriend and girlfriend or not? I'd had a couple of boyfriends in high school. Nothing serious. If a date ended with kissing, it usually went unsaid that we had become a couple. We'd date until it didn't work anymore and one of us broke it off. With Tyler, everything was ambiguous. He never directly said he liked me. He didn't stick to my side when we were in the same vicinity as each other. Sometimes he was so busy being popular, he never noticed me at all. I'd left the cast party for *Pippin* after only forty-five minutes, and he never said anything about it. I'm not sure he ever knew.

Second semester was even worse. Thanks to his work in *Pippin*, Dr. Grisham bumped Tyler out of Beginning Musical Theatre and put him in Advanced. I still couldn't figure out how to put Ballet in my schedule, but it wouldn't have mattered because Tyler was in Ballet III. We had no classes together. The school didn't do a spring musical. Instead, a grad student directed a review of current Broadway songs for her Masters Thesis project that went up in February. I had no idea when auditions had been for that or if there had even been auditions at all. Tyler, of course, got cast in it. He got some juicy solos like Jack from *Into the Woods* and Marius from *Les Miserables*.

No sooner did that show end, but members of Advanced Musical Theatre and Advanced Acting were invited to audition for a study abroad program in New York. We were told that freshmen were never picked. Tyler was, though.

Right after spring break, Tyler took off to spend the second half of the semester studying in NYC with the best of the best kids in the school's theatre department. Our musical theatre professor went with them, so the second half of the semester was taught by a first-year MFA student who either didn't get chosen or couldn't afford to go to New York with the rest of them. I took extra shifts at work to keep myself busy. I ate most of my lunches and dinners at Eats and Treats, which wasn't doing much for my figure.

Tyler stayed in a sublet apartment with three other students. They didn't have a phone, so he couldn't ever call me. He sent me postcards of the awesome Broadway shows he got to see with notes about how hard the classes were and how it was so stressful. Imagining the golden boy disheartened and overwhelmed gave me guilty delight, fueled by my incessant jealousy. I imagined him coming back in May feeling defeated at the reality of professional theatre, ready to slink back into the trenches with me where we could daydream about the life of being actors "someday" and know how much work we still had ahead of us. We'd be back on the same plane again.

Except, a few days before his flight back to California, Tyler sent me a letter in a large manila envelope. It contained a black and white photo of him. His note said the picture was a headshot taken of him in New York and that he had gotten some printed out in 8x10 so he could do a few auditions. They were all required to do at least two professional auditions to see what they were like.

*I can't believe I'm writing this, but I got cast in summer stock in Phoenix, AZ, for the whole summer. I'll be in three shows!* The Wizard of Oz, A Chorus Line, *and the play* Our Town. *It pays a stipend, plus room and board. I'll be acting professionally!*

*I'll be coming back to pack up everything at the dorm and take it home before I leave for Arizona, so I'll be able to see you for a little bit.*

*There are tech positions available in the costume shop and lighting booth and stuff. Why don't you come with me and work? I can talk to someone and get you in if you want. Wouldn't that be a blast?*

*I miss your pretty face and that gorgeous red hair. I hear it's hot there in the desert. It would be even hotter if you were there with me.*

I kissed his picture. I absolutely wanted to go work at that theater all summer if I could.

Mom put her foot down. It was too far away, and she didn't want me chasing Tyler out to the desert to feel as left out there as I'd been feeling all second semester.

"You need to stay here and work. Earn some money. Meet a boy that gives you the time of day. Not one that only wants to see you when it's convenient for him."

She had a good point, and I listened to her.

The New York group returned, and there was a huge party for the theatre department celebrating them. I wore a sleek black dress that used to be loose on me but now hugged my curves. I'd always been fairly flat-chested in the past, but the extra weight I'd been putting on gave me a little something to show. I bought a new underwire bra to help out the situation. I used a banana clip to pull back my hair that I'd been growing out all year and teased my bangs to be as big as possible. My plan was to tell Tyler that night that I wouldn't be joining him for the summer, but I wanted him to hurt a bit over it.

The party had been on the empty stage of the school's theater, and it concluded with a slideshow of all the awesome activities the students had done while there and announcements of who had gotten what great summer gig. This time I didn't leave early. I sat in a chair in the theater lobby for an hour and a half waiting for Tyler to be done mingling. Nearly everyone had left, and the lights shut off except for a few near the exits. Tyler came out of the auditorium with two other New York students. He saw me, stopped, and said goodbye to his friends. They left the building, and he came over to me.

"You're still here."

"I wanted to see you."

"It was nice of you to wait."

"I guess so," I said with a shrug. "I'm not sure I ever have a choice about that."

He frowned. "Are you okay?"

I nodded, paused, then shook my head. "No, Tyler. Not really."

Tyler sat on the padded bench next to me, sideways with an arm around my shoulders. "What's the matter?" He placed a hand on my knee below the hem of my dress.

Tentatively, I put my hand on top of his, fighting the urge to flick it away. "I don't fit in. Not with this school or with you."

"Come on, Graceful. You're so talented. No one's seen it yet, but they will. I knew the first day I met you."

"You're sweet, Tyler, but you know that's not true."

He turned my face toward his. Half of his face was in shadow, making him look exactly like a comedy / tragedy theater mask. A chuckle burst through the knot in my throat in a strangled sound. I looked away again.

"I can't compete with you."

"Who's asking you to? Why do we need to compete?"

"I don't know," I answered. "I guess I got used to being one of the best people. At my high school, you know? Even as a freshman, I got noticed in high school. Here, I'm nobody."

"Every single freshman in this theatre department feels like you," he told me.

"Are you sure about that?" I challenged, looking him in the eyes.

"I had a lucky year," he said. "They picked a show that had a young character as one of the principles. I'm short. I fit that part better than all those six-foot-tall upper classmen. Luck is half of what this business is about. They talked about that a lot when we were in New York. Don't doubt yourself."

"It's hard not to," I replied. "It's all I feel right now. Doubt. I even doubt that you care about me at all."

"Care about you?" He acted like this was the most incredulous thing I could have said. "I think about you all the time. I missed you so much in New York. It's why I want you to come to Phoenix with me."

My face grew hot, and as much as I tried to fight it, a tear managed to sneak out. I was hoping the darkness hid it, but it must've glistened against the light from the exit sign. Tyler wiped it away with his thumb. "I can't go to Arizona. Mom won't even discuss it. My car would never make it, anyway. She said maybe I could fly out there to catch one of your performances. So, make sure I have the dates and pick the one you most want me to see."

"I won't know which roles I'll have until I get there. The way it works is that they hired all the actors they needed for the company, but when we arrive, we audition again for specific roles. I'm going to be one of the youngest people there. I'll probably be a person who lives in the Emerald City and the newspaper kid in *Our Town*."

"I'll come see *A Chorus Line* then. You'll have to have a speaking part in that, right?"

"Well, there are some people who get cut in the opening scene—"

I put a finger to his lips to stop him. "Tyler. You and I both know you are not going to play ensemble roles in all three shows."

He grinned and nibbled gently on my finger. I pulled my finger away, and he leaned toward me. He cupped my head with both of his hands and drew me toward him. He kissed me so tenderly. Over the past year, we'd shared a lot of passionate kisses, but this was the first one that I felt had substance. It felt like something true. My heart hammered in my chest as if it were trying to warn me to protect it. I couldn't. My armor failed, and my heart exploded. Emotion coursed through my veins like I'd been poisoned.

When he stopped kissing me, Tyler continued holding my head and stared into my eyes. "You're so beautiful, Graceful. Please. Please come with me to Phoenix. I want you with me."

## *Present Day*

I have that headshot of Tyler somewhere. It's in a box underneath a bunch of other boxes. A moment passes where I think about digging through all my stuff to find it. That's more effort than I want to make at the moment.

Why did I even save it? Probably because I have so few tangible remembrances from my college days. I'm thinking the photo is tucked inside the program from *Pippin*. I remember it was a horizontal image. Headshots are always vertical. How unprofessional Tyler must have looked showing up with a horizontal headshot printed at some corner photo shop. I've had too many glasses of wine, and the thought of this makes me chortle.

I should go find it and bring it on the date tomorrow night. It'll give us both a good laugh. It'll be a conversation starter. But what conversation will it start, I wonder? The one about how far his career has come since then? Or the one about what happened to us?

I'm not sure I want to talk about that yet. I leave the picture where it is. Hidden. Hard to retrieve. Like the memory had been until today.

Tyler Andrews has reappeared in my life, and I'm not sure I want him here. I decide that when he calls to affirm where we're meeting, I'll beg out. He can buy the house or not. Either way is fine. I'm not interested in going on a date with the guy who broke my heart when I was nineteen.

The phone rings as I'm washing dishes. I take my time drying my hands, hoping I'll be too slow and the voicemail will pick up before I can. No luck. Tyler is on the other end after I swipe to answer.

"I thought you were going to ghost me for a minute."

"Sorry. I was just—"

"I'm joking," he says, laughing. "Sorry it's so late. Is it too late?"

"It's only ten or so," I say. I'm used to talking to Spencer past midnight sometimes if he's having a crisis or there's some juicy gossip to share.

"Great. So, here's the thing…"

Oh. He's going to cancel on me. Of course. I should have expected this.

"I have a shoot tomorrow, and they're saying it's going to go through sunset. I won't be done until after eight o'clock."

Same old Tyler. The way I remember him. Busy acting. Too busy for me.

"This is what I'm thinking," he goes on. "We're shooting at Zuma beach. We could either reschedule, or, if you're up to it, we could meet for drinks in Santa Monica at nine. What do you think?"

"I'm up for drinks," I hear myself say. No! That was the out. I could have easily said no. I could have told him it was inconvenient. I don't live near Santa Monica. I'd rather not…

"Orrrrr," he says, drawing it out like a game show host, "you could meet me at the lot. You could watch some of the filming. I could give you a tour. What do you think?"

What did I think? It would be fun to see a TV show being shot. It's something I could check off my bucket list. What would it be like to watch Tyler in that environment? Would it be thrilling, or would it bring back all those old feelings of inferiority?

*Stop it*, I think. I'm not pursuing acting anymore. I don't need to compare my life with his. It's incredible that he's still making it in that crazy career. I should celebrate that. I need to get over myself.

"I would love to watch you work," I tell him. "That would be thrilling."

He shouts a "whoo-hoo!" and it makes me laugh. I think I like this new Tyler. He seems like a fun guy. I jot down the address and the instructions for getting access to the site. I'll get there at five and hang out until he's done. Then we'll have a nice dinner.

It sounds magical.

# CHAPTER
## *Four*

Aware of how long it takes to get from my apartment in Hollywood to Pacific Coast Highway on a Tuesday afternoon, I canceled everything I had on my side of town and scheduled some meetings with prospective clients in West Los Angeles and Santa Monica for the day. I wear my best sundress, turquoise blue cotton with spaghetti straps and a skirt that flares out at the waist. All of my best dresses have full skirts. I have another back-up outfit in the car in case something happens, but based on the response I've gotten all day from my male clients, I know the dress I have on has the desired effect. I signed to represent all three houses that I visited, and I got one solicitation to marry the owner of one and move with him to Vegas.

I get to the filming location a bit early. The security guard at the parking lot entrance has my name on his roster and lets me in. He has a twinkle in his eye, and I guess that he gets a little glee out of welcoming non-movie people to the lot for the first time. A sweet intern named Alina finds me wandering around the service trucks and leads me to a couple of gazebo tents where guests are allowed to sit and watch the filming. She tells me to make myself comfortable, enjoy the food and drinks available, and that Tyler will be finished soon.

"He's such a sweet guy," this college-age girl says to me. "Everyone loves him."

I smile back at this pretty young thing as politely as I can. "That's always been the case."

"He's like everyone's dad."

I can't help but laugh. Alina looks confused for a second but shrugs it off. Tyler's like everyone's *dad*. Of course. He's fifty-years-old. Attractive to me, but probably not so much to the kids working on this show.

"How do you know him?" Alina asks.

"We went to school together," I say simply.

"Wow. So, you're like old friends."

I nod, trying not to laugh again. "Old being the correct description."

Alina puts a hand to her mouth as her eyes grow huge. "Oh no. That's not what I meant. I'm sorry. I didn't—"

"It's fine. No harm done."

Alina grabs a water bottle from the cooler and hands it to me. "Please don't tell Tyler I said he was old."

"You didn't," I tell her. "And I wouldn't."

After the most grateful look I've ever seen, Alina takes off to go do whatever her job is. I'm sure she has more to do than find lost souls wandering around on the beach and make them feel ancient.

I settle into the cushy beach chair and focus on the activity down by the lifeguard station. The camera operators and tech people block my view of the actors. At one point, I see Alina approach the action. She taps someone on the shoulder and talks to them while pointing back at me. A few moments later, Tyler pops around the whole group, his feet almost in the surf, and waves at me. He's wearing belted khaki slacks rolled up to his shins, no shoes, and a light blue button-down work shirt with the top couple of buttons undone. I wonder what could possibly be happening in the scene.

Someone shouts, "Andrews!" and Tyler looks over at the fray and jumps back into it.

The weather has cooperated nicely for them. The clouds are airy and light, reflecting all the hues of the sunset. They film different shots around the beach for the next two hours, making that setting sun earn its pay. A breeze and the shade of the gazebo keep the late afternoon cool enough that I reluctantly have to slip on my sweater. I also request a hot green tea from Alina when she comes by again. Watching the filming gets dull after a while, due to not being able to see or hear much of what they're doing. Gradually, I shift my attention to enjoy watching the waves change from green to purple as the day turns to evening. It's mesmerizing, and I find myself wondering why I don't go to the beach more often. It's so close, and I don't take advantage of it nearly enough.

### 1992

I lived ten minutes from the beach and didn't go there one single time all summer. I'd been working hard to save up my earnings, and my mom pitched in a little so I could get tickets to fly from LAX to Phoenix in late August. Using the help of her travel agent friend Marilyn, I booked a room at the Red Roof Inn. I was too young to rent a car, but I learned the bus routes and figured out how I'd get around. I was only going to be there for one night, long enough to see Tyler perform in *Our Town* and maybe have breakfast with him if he had time before I had to fly back out again. I wanted to get out there in time to see *A Chorus Line* because I prefer musicals and wanted to see him sing and dance again. That was the first show of the summer, though, and I couldn't get my funds together in time.

Tyler had been great about writing to me all summer, at least once a week, to fill me in on all the activity happening in his life. It sounded exhausting. They rehearsed non-stop. He wrote that between all the heat and dancing, he'd gotten heatstroke twice. The college dorm rooms they'd been sharing had terrible air conditioning units that barely puffed out enough air to bring the temperature down to eighty-five degrees. He complained a lot in his letters. I decided he was trying to downplay everything so I wouldn't feel bad about skipping on my chance to be a part of it all. It worked. I was awfully glad not to be serving popcorn at an amphitheater in the desert.

We didn't get to talk on the phone much. I was working two jobs and running kind of crazy myself. Clothestime took me back for the summer, and I was allowed to keep my job on campus even though the traffic wasn't as busy. The transmission on my car went out. Instead of getting it fixed, I bought another car. A 1982 Ford Escort. This time I didn't buy it from a neighbor. My dad helped me get it from a car dealership. It was a much better, slightly newer car, but now I had a monthly payment I couldn't afford. Dad didn't offer to help pay for any of it at all.

Similar to when Tyler was in New York, he didn't have a phone in his room. His access to the pay phone was limited. It didn't matter. I was barely home enough to answer a call if he made one. Missing him had become such a normal feeling for me over the past half year that I wasn't sure how I was going to handle it when he came back to school and was around all the time.

I did tell him I was coming. For a while I thought about surprising him. I'd never been great at keeping big secrets, though. I hoped he'd turn around and surprise me by being at the airport when I got off the plane. He wasn't. I stood at the arrival gate for a good fifteen minutes in case he was running late. When he didn't show, I went ahead and got my luggage and headed for the shuttles. Standing in the oppressive Arizona heat, I let two of them pass by while I double-checked that he wasn't driving one of the many cars going through the arrival pick-up lanes.

Maybe he'd be waiting for me at the hotel. I'd told him where I was staying, and he'd asked why I didn't stay at the Sheraton, as it was walking distance from the amphitheater. That's apparently where everyone's guests got rooms. Marilyn mentioned it to me, but when she informed me of the room prices, we looked elsewhere. Tyler wasn't at the hotel when I got there, either. Nor was there a note waiting for me when I checked in.

My suitcase felt like it weighed a thousand pounds, and my

purse strap dug into my shoulder as I strode through the lobby and waited for the elevator to take me to the third floor. The busy red, black, and gold pattern of the corridor carpet looked like a long series of stop signs and warning signals to me. I had to tear my eyes away from their hypnotic repetition of images to locate my room number.

The strange disinfectant smell of the room and the hum of the wall conditioning unit immediately pushed away my self-pity. I was in a hotel room all by myself! I'd never traveled alone before. It made me feel so grown up. I tossed my bags onto the dresser top and flung myself down on the queen bed. A bad painting of desert cactus flowers hung on the wall over the headboard. I kind of loved it. It was impersonal, so visitors wouldn't want to keep it. I wanted to take it home and hang it in my bedroom to help me make believe I was always on vacation.

With a couple hours to spare before showtime, I roamed the halls of the hotel. I got ice just because I could. I went outside and put my feet in the pool. Why didn't I remember to bring a swimsuit? Finally, I grabbed some snacks from the hotel's convenience store and went back to the room where I watched reruns of *Cheers* while I snacked on Oreos and Ruffles chips. I figured that would be cheaper than any of the concessions at the show. My hope was that Tyler would take me out for a late dinner after the play so we could spend some time together.

I got dressed in a cute sundress I'd picked up at work. It showed off my new curves. I had a little cleavage now, and I made sure it was visible. Due to the heat, I wore my hair up in a ponytail on the top of my head, teasing it a bit so it puffed around my ears and the back of my head. Normally I would wear some foundation, but I didn't want to sweat it all off. I kept my makeup natural, wishing I'd taken some time to get a tan. What kind of Southern California girl was I?

This was as good as my face was going to get. I winked at my reflection in the bathroom mirror, grabbed my clutch bag, and headed out the door. The bus took me right to the amphitheater. I got there thirty minutes early, plenty of time to get a cold soda and find my seat. The main seating area consisted of folding chairs placed on the cement risers, but there were grassy areas up top for people to sit on blankets, picnic style. The stage was completely bare. I didn't know much about *Our Town*, but I remember Tyler writing something about the play being famous for not having any set.

*It's challenging me to be the best actor I can be in order to help the audience see what isn't there.*

Humble brag. Very like him.

The sun was declining, but it was still light out when the show began. A woman who was part of the producer's team that ran the summer stock program made a few announcements about exits, future shows, and fundraising efforts. Then the show began. It was kind of boring at first as a man called "The Stage Manager", who was really a narrator, rambled on and on about the town and introduced characters. At long last, Tyler's character "George" was announced. He ran in alongside the actress playing his younger sister. They were sibling-fighting and full of energy. As short as Tyler was, she was much shorter. Her hair was wound into two fuzzy braids.

Wait. I knew that face. That voice. Fresno Kei. How on earth had Fresno Kei wound up in the show? I clenched my jaw, seething as I wondered further why I hadn't known about this until now. Seemed like the kind of tidbit Tyler might pop into a letter or phone call. "Hey, wouldn't you know it that a friend of ours is out here doing this show with me?"

Even though Kei wasn't exactly a friend of mine. She hadn't been working at Eats and Treats all summer, but I figured that was because she was in Fresno. Not because she had also gotten cast in a professional summer theatre company. When did she even audition for this show? Tyler auditioned while in New York. Had the company held auditions in California? Was this yet another audition that only certain members of the theatre department got to know about?

Or had Tyler set this up specifically for her? He never asked me to audition for a show. All he wanted was for me to sell popcorn or help people backstage with fast costume changes.

I was glad her part was tiny. I counted her lines. I think it was five.

As expected, Tyler was awesome. He was absolutely yummy in the role of this sweet baseball player in love with the prettiest girl in town. Their malt shop scene where he asked the girl, "Emily", to be his girlfriend was the best scene in the show. So good, it made me uncomfortable. He broke down crying in the final scene when she died. I believed it. The boy was talented.

After the show, I lingered in the aisles as the audience exited, dodging purses and small, sleepy children on hips. The actors came out in front of the stage to meet their friends, still in their 1900 era costumes, Tyler in a dark brown suit with a bowtie. When I got closer, I saw that he had some stage makeup accenting his cheekbones, with some eyeliner and mascara intensifying the look of his usual blond eyelashes and bright blue eyes. People surrounded him and showered him with congratulations. I waited, straight in front of him, hoping he'd look up from shaking hands, hugging people, and posing for pictures. I'd take a hesitant step toward him as it looked like some people were about to clear away, and then another person or three would butt in front of me.

The throng took a while to move on its way before he finally saw me standing there by myself, my hands clasped behind my back while I chewed on my lower lip.

"There you are!" He beckoned me toward him. I dashed forward and went right into his waiting arms, not caring that he was sweaty. "It's good to see you," he said as he held me tightly. "I was looking for you but didn't see you anywhere." His cologne and deodorant couldn't quite conquer the musky body odor coming from his warm body.

"I've been right here."

"Well, you put up your hair. I was looking for that wild mane of red hair. It distinguishes you from everyone else."

My hair was still red and rather wild, I thought. It wasn't like I put it in a tight bun or under a hat. I smiled and wiggled my head, so my high ponytail bopped around a bit.

"Did you like the show?"

"I did. I really did. It was so good. You were the best." I knew that was what he wanted. It didn't bother me to say it because it was true.

He pulled back but kept his hands on my arms. "I'm so glad you came to this one. *A Chorus Line* was fun, but I put my heart into this one. Alicia, our director, was so great to work with, and Jillian, that plays Emily, is a genius. Would you believe she's thirty-two and has two kids already? Doesn't she look young?"

Well, I liked hearing that news at least. Despite how much they looked like they were in love, Tyler didn't seem like the type to go after a woman thirteen years older than him with kids.

"She's very talented," I agreed. "Does she live here?"

"Yeah. She's an acting professor at Arizona State. She played Dorothy in *Wizard of Oz*. Us short folks, we pull off the kid roles. I bet I'll also still be playing teenagers into my thirties."

I laughed and nodded because that was also true. I was show-girl height, but I couldn't dance like a showgirl. What was in store for me, I wondered?

"Jillian also played Connie in *A Chorus Line*. Rumor has it they picked the whole season around her. She was the only person to have a major role in all three shows."

Speaking of short people. "So... Kei? Tell me about that."

Tyler's grin got even broader, if possible. "She's in the show! Isn't that great? Totally happened by chance. I invited her to come out and work, like I did with you, and she wound up getting cast in the play. With Jillian and I playing George and Emily, we still needed one more young-looking cast member. They had some kids come in to be munchkins, and we pulled Tommy from that group to play Jillian's brother, but they wanted another adult actor to play my sister. I told them about Kei—"

"I thought you invited me to work out here because you wanted us to be together this summer." I couldn't help it. It blurted out.

He continued to hold my arms, and he squeezed them gently. Confusion washed over his face. It seemed genuine. "Well, yeah. I wanted you here with me. It would've been fun."

"Then why did you invite Kei? Because I said no? Was she your backup?"

Tyler shook his head. "No. No, you've got it all wrong. I invited her because she told me how much she didn't want to go home for the summer. I thought it would be an excuse for her to stay away. I was trying to do her a favor."

I didn't know if I bought it, but I accepted it. Kei made no secret about how much she hated her hometown. After all, it was the first thing she expressed to me. I still couldn't quite let it go. "But. I mean. If I had been here, do you think I would have gotten cast in a show? Would you have recommended me?"

His hands dropped to his sides. "Look, Grace. I recommended Kei because she's petite and I knew she could pull off the role. You could hardly pull off being my twelve-year-old sister. We're practically the same height, and you're a gorgeous redhead."

I cocked my head and pursed my lips. "Gorgeous, huh?"

"Ravishing!" He wrapped his arms around me and pulled me close. "I want to kiss you all over, but I'm sweaty and have stage makeup running down my face. Give me a few minutes to change and clean up, and I'll come back out. You can come with me to the cast party tonight." My reaction to that invitation must've been all over my face because he immediately asked, "What? Aren't you sticking around?"

Maybe it was selfish of me. I knew his time with this group was limited and coming to an end. Still, I hadn't seen him in months. It was my turn. "I was kind of hoping we'd have some time alone together. My mom is at home wringing her hands worried about you coming over to my hotel room. We might as well make her worries valid."

"Oh, Graceful," he moaned. "I want to. You know I do, but I've got to go to this party. At least put in an appearance. I'm one of the leads of the show. It would look bad." He took my hand and caressed the back of it with his thumb. "I can introduce you to everyone. I'll tell them how awesome you are and that they should remember you for next year."

I swallowed back my disappointment. Introductions were good and all, but what I wanted were his arms and lips. All I wanted was to know was that I was still his and he was still mine. That is, if we ever belonged to each other to begin with. It never seemed crystal clear. "That's fine," I relented. "Sounds fun."

"We can cut out early," he said. "I promise."

Kei rushed over to us. My presence didn't surprise her one bit. She must've known I was going to be there. That was something, at least. Tyler had told at least one person I was coming to see him. "Hey, Grace," she said off-handedly. To Tyler she said, "Mabel wants all the costumes on the rack pronto so she can get them washed. I told her I'd drag you back to the dressing room."

"You *wish* you could drag me."

They pretended to spar like real siblings for a moment. He wrapped an arm around her neck and dug his knuckles into the top of her head. Clearly, he hadn't hurt her, because she backed away from him, giggling. My brain had a hard time accepting that serious, sarcastic Kei was capable of giggling. "Come on! You can talk to her later." She looked at me one more time and said, "He'll smell better next time you see him. I'm doing you a favor." Then she ran off.

"I've got to go," Tyler said apologetically. "Wait for me?"

I did. I waited almost forty minutes as the sky turned black and all the lights went out. I sat in the dark amphitheater as cast and crew members strolled past me, full of conversation and jokes I knew nothing about. It seemed like every member of the company had left before Tyler finally emerged. He did look much better. Clean and free of makeup, in a peach polo, white jeans, and loafers. Kei was right about him smelling better. When I hugged him, I got a fresh whiff of soap, hair gel, and a fair dousing of Nautica cologne. He guided me out to the parking lot where his car waited and drove me to the party at one of the producer's houses.

It was a nice, sprawling terra cotta home with a red-tiled roof. The front yard was designed to survive the hot, dry weather. Lots of cacti and succulents. There was a saltwater pool in the backyard surrounded by a beautiful, stained deck. Nearly everyone gathered out there. The night had finally cooled off a bit, and a good breeze was going, aided by a couple of ceiling fans attached to the lovely pergola that stretched out over half the deck.

I got myself a soda and a plate of appetizers while Tyler circulated amongst his new friends. Kei sidled up next to me as I leaned against a railing and stared out at the manmade lake and walking path centered in the circle of homes.

"It's a nice neighborhood, isn't it? Nothing like this in Fresno."

"Nothing like it where I live either," I said. "Unless you know someone who lives in the uber rich communities closer to the beach, which I don't."

"Well, at least you have a beach to go to, so that's something. And you can still walk around campus whenever you want. It's pretty. I wish I lived closer to school."

I turned and leaned sideways against the railing. Kei had her elbows up on it, nursing a beer in a plastic cup. No one was concerned about underage drinking at this shindig. She continued taking in the view and didn't look at me.

"Do you like it here?" I asked her.

She offered no expression one way or the other and said simply, "It's better than almost any other thing I could think of to do this summer, although I could have probably gotten a much bigger part in a show if I'd gone back home. There's a dinner theater in Bakersville, and I've worked there a couple times. It's a commute, but it pays enough to cover my gas and usually gives me free dinner. They've got the best barbecue sauce, and I love to get a plate of fries and dip them. Makes my mouth water thinking of it."

"You don't like doing *Our Town*? You were good. You had some of my favorite lines in the play."

"I have six lines in the play, Grace. I sit backstage and read the rest of the time. I've been on a Stephen King kick. I've read both *It* and *The Stand*. Those books are massive, so that shows you how much time I have doing nothing. Also, you know the worst thing about playing a fourteen-year-old and looking like a fourteen-year-old?"

"What?"

"Everyone thinks you're a fourteen-year-old."

"Someone gave you a beer." I pointed at the cup.

She tapped my can of soda with her cup. "Yeah, well, no one is manning the keg, so I took it. Not the first one either." She raised the cup like she was making a toast and sighed. "Honestly, I think I had more fun selling the snacks and handing out programs. You should be glad you didn't come out here."

"If I had come out here it would've only been for one reason," I confessed.

She put her drink on the railing and pulled herself up to sit beside it, facing into the party. Kei was wearing her trademark denim overalls, but these were cut off mid-thigh. Her legs dangled, her sneakers rhythmically thumping against the slats on the railing. "I know. I came out here for Tyler, too. That was a mistake. He barely notices me. He's too busy being 'that guy' like at school. I thought here I'd have a chance…" She snuck a look at me and then took a swallow of her beer. "I'm sorry. I know you two had a thing."

"Have," I corrected. "We have a thing."

She raised an eyebrow. "If you say so."

"It's why I'm here."

Okay, so Kei had her eye on Tyler. It was a bit of a gut punch to hear it said out loud, but I wasn't surprised by this news. Who didn't have a crush on him? Kei chased him all the way out to the desert, and he still wasn't interested. Too bad for her. Good news for me. I thought I was jealous of her being here with him, but clearly she wasn't Tyler's type. That's because *I* was. I was a good five inches taller than her and, in my opinion, better looking. Shoot, even with her sitting on the railing, I was still looking at the top of her head. The weight I'd gained gave me more of a figure, and I thought he might like that compared to the flat-chested stick I was at the beginning of the school year. He wasn't into Kei because of me. I ate a brie-topped cracker as I chewed on that thought and allowed my confidence to bolster.

Kei pointed into the crowd. Over by the bar, Tyler sat on a stool, smiling and laughing, surrounded by a group of people. "It's not that he doesn't care about you, Grace. He probably does. You're really pretty. If I looked like you, I'd skip school and go straight to Hollywood, get an agent, and get this acting career started, you know." I bit the inside of my cheek to keep from smiling at the compliment. "But the thing is, Tyler mostly cares about himself and what's going to make his acting career take off. You and I, my friend, aren't able to help him, so we end up sitting at the fringe of a party we probably shouldn't even be at." She took a final gulp of her drink and then crumpled the cup in her hand. In a swift movement, she hopped over the fence to the grass below. "I'm leaving. You want a ride someplace? I've got my car." She dangled the keys she dug out of her pocket.

I shook my head. "I'll stick around. It'll look weird if I take off without saying anything."

"Suit yourself. Don't say I didn't warn you." She walked away, disappearing into the deep night shadows between the houses.

I took a fortifying breath before plunging into the crowd to get to Tyler's circle. Grateful wasn't a good enough word to go with the feeling when he noticed me right away, gestured for me to come to his side, and then promptly introduced me to everyone. Tyler put his arm around my waist and handed me a clear plastic cup with some kind of cold white wine in it. I sipped at it while the group chattered about mishaps that had been happening backstage all season.

Midnight came and went. Around one-thirty, I finally pulled Tyler aside and told him I needed to get back to the hotel and get some sleep. I had a flight the next day. Politely, he excused himself from his friends and led me into the house. I dashed to the guest bedroom where I had tossed my purse on the bed with everyone else's. When I came back, Tyler was finishing up a phone call with a taxi service.

I sat on the sofa beside him, my arms crossed over my purse in my lap. Another couple moseyed past us and went out the front door. The man's arm was around the woman's shoulders. That's how Tyler and I were supposed to look, and I despised those people for sharing something I couldn't have.

As soon as Tyler hung up the phone, I asked, "Is the cab for me? You can't drive me yourself?"

"I'm gonna crash here. I've had too much to drink to drive. I don't know this area well enough to risk it. I'd probably get us both lost or in an accident."

He didn't seem all that drunk to me. His conversation was still lucid. I didn't hear him slurring, and he didn't seem off balance. Was he blowing me off or that clueless about why I came all the way to Arizona?

"I could drive your car," I offered tentatively, tasting my words like I would a soup to see if it was too hot and might burn my tongue. "You could stay with me and head back to your place in the morning. I want to spend some time with you, just the two of us. Catching up and, you know, other stuff."

His eyes widened. Clearly, he hadn't considered that option, which was crazy to me because it had been the only thing I'd thought about since I bought the plane tickets. A full night alone with him in my hotel room. Why didn't he want this? Why weren't we there already?

"Oh man. Oh, Graceful. I'm so sorry. I didn't realize you wanted me to… Aw, honey. I wish you'd said something earlier."

"I kind of did, I thought."

He stared at me like I'd spoken in a foreign language for a moment. "You know what? Let's do it. I like your plan." He called up the taxi service and cancelled the cab. As soon as he hung up the phone, he handed me his keys. On the way out, he grabbed a can of Coke from the cooler in the kitchen and popped it open. "I'm not that drunk. I only had a couple beers, but I don't trust myself, you know. Some caffeine'll straighten me right up."

After I adjusted the driver's seat in his two-door silver Cutlass, Tyler handed me a city map he kept in the glovebox. I figured out my route and told him to hang on to it just in case. We sang musical theatre duets at the top of our lungs and laughed hysterically every time I pulled over to check the map again. We had to stop four times. We were in the middle of a rousing chorus of "Suddenly Seymour" when a policeman approached us the last time we stopped and let us know that it was awfully late for us to still be out. "Nothing good happens after midnight, kids."

I agreed. "We wouldn't still be out, but I keep getting turned around."

The policeman gave us directions and thankfully sent us on our way without a ticket. Once we were away from him, we burst out laughing all over again. The cop was right about it being super late, though. It was well after two before we stumbled into my room. We collapsed onto the bed, both of us exhausted. I'd turned on the light in the entryway when we entered the room but not the ones beside the bed. The thick blackout curtains on the window were still partially open, so a hint of moonlight snuck through the cream-colored window liners. We were both on our stomachs, perpendicular to the bed. Tyler turned his face to me and kissed me above my right eyebrow, his mouth slightly open so that his tongue licked my temple ever so softly.

"Thanks for coming to see me out here. It means so much to me."

"Does it?" I asked. I didn't want to start anything, but I craved some kind of real acknowledgment that I mattered to him. I wanted Kei to be wrong.

"Oh yeah," he said. "I missed you so much."

He pulled the band out of my hair, and my locks tumbled around my face and neck. Switching to lie on his side facing me, he ran his hand over my hair to where it stopped below my shoulders. His hand paused for a moment at the small of my back and then traveled on to my rear where he explored my soft curves. I adjusted to my side as his fingers tugged my skirt up and found their way under it to my panties. Electric shocks ran through me as he slipped a finger under that material, too.

"You sure you want this?" he asked. "It's so late. We could cuddle and sleep. I'd be okay with that."

"No," I said too quickly. My body was on fire, and my voice was the last thing I thought I needed to control. "I want this. I do. If you do."

"Of course I do," he murmured. His free arm slid under my body and tugged me tighter to him. "I've wanted this since the first day I met you." He kissed me then. Full, deep, and passionate. If he was tired, he didn't show it. My body forgot all about being tired and arched into him. In a blink, our clothes were off, and we were fully naked together for the first time. It had been all hands under clothes before. I was grateful for the lights being off so he couldn't see the imperfections of my body with its extra twenty pounds, but I was also disappointed that I couldn't see every distinct line of his body molded by years of dance training. I felt it, though, as my hands ran up and down his chest and then his back.

When it was time, Tyler felt me stiffen up from fear. "I can stop," he said.

"No," I whispered. "I'm… I don't know what it will feel like. If it'll hurt."

Tyler kissed me as gently as possible, a totally different kind of affection than what he'd been showing me so far. He stroked my face lightly with his left hand and looked right into my eyes. He stayed like that until he entered me, easing my fear and helping me to relax. It did hurt a little at first, but then I gasped as my body took him in and it was incredible.

I didn't know what I was doing, and I'd never asked Tyler about his experience. From the way he moved, I gathered that this was not his first time. A tiny piece of me was sad that I wasn't his first lover, but the rest of me that was enjoying the benefits of his knowledge quickly got over it. The way he made my whole body tingle had to be better than it ever would be as some awkward stumble-through with a guy who'd never done this before.

Afterward, Tyler rolled to his back, one arm over his head, keeping the other hand on my bare belly. I stared at the ceiling, tears rolling down the sides of my face. I wasn't sad or ashamed. It was so much emotion.

"Was that okay?" he asked.

"I was going to ask you the same thing."

"It was incredible. I kind of can't believe it. You sure you have to leave tomorrow?"

"Today, actually."

"That's right. Today."

I nodded sadly, then pepped up quickly as I had a thought.

"But summer's almost over. Classes start back up in a couple weeks."

"That's right," Tyler said, his voice quiet and slow. "Not long at all now."

"I wasn't looking forward to school at all, but now I can't wait."

I couldn't wait to rub Kei's nose in the fact that Tyler and I were going to be a real couple. She had been so wrong about him.

Tyler didn't say anything else. I glanced over to see that he had fallen asleep. My heart and mind were racing, so I stayed awake a while longer watching him breathe deep and evenly in the soft glow from the window. All of the negative thoughts I'd had the past year vanished. Everything was going to be great from this point forward. I could see it all. My perfect, handsome, talented boyfriend and I would finish college, get married, and head off to our amazing Broadway careers together in New York. Hope filled every cell of my body, and I reveled in the joy it brought me.

### Present Day

Someone shouts it's a wrap for the day. Interns and crew buzz all around me, cleaning up equipment and clearing everything away. I feel my phone vibrate through my purse on my lap. Tyler lets me know that he is up at the beach house the show has rented for the actors to use for dressing rooms. I can meet him there. Alina magically appears before me when I look up from the phone, ready to guide me.

I wait on a wooden swing on the porch of the beach house. It's a little nippy out, but I take off my sweater so Tyler can get the full effect of my dress when he steps outside. He's been surrounded by beautiful people all day. I need to do what I can to impress him.

Thanks to my years of dancing, I'm quite lithe. I'm proud of my thin, tight arms. My collar bones are sharp and prominent. The cut of this dress accents them well. I can't do much about my bust, though. Losing weight meant losing what few curves I ever had. My body is that of an aging ballerina. I have cultivated it over years of hard work and love every bit of it. I hope he will, too.

Tyler finally steps outside. He's now wearing blue slacks and a short-sleeve button-down open over a white T-shirt. A jacket is hooked on a finger over his shoulder. I rise as he spots me, and his grin is magnificent. Goose pimples rise up and down my arms, and they aren't from the chilly ocean breeze.

"Thanks for waiting for me. I tried to hurry, but Brett wouldn't stop talking. Man, you look amazing."

"Thanks."

"You've got to be freezing, though. You want my jacket?" He opens it for me, but I shake my head and grab my cardigan from the swing. I slip my arms into it. "I know you're probably hungry, but do you want to walk on the beach for a minute? It's so lovely here."

"I'd love that."

He takes my hand and leads me down the steps to the sand. He kicks off his loafers, and I notice then that he isn't wearing socks. I'm amused that he's stuck to this style all these years. I hesitate kicking off my pumps and take a step into the sand wearing them.

"Oh, come on," Tyler says. "Kick them off. You'll ruin your shoes if they get wet and sandy."

I grimace at him. "I have ugly toes."

"What?"

"Don't look."

"Are you serious?"

I nod weakly. "I'm a dedicated dancer."

Tyler seems to not comprehend anything I'm saying. "Wait. So, the dancing at the house? That wasn't goofing around? You're a professional dancer?"

I put up my hands as if to stop him from saying more. "I *was* goofing around. I'm not a professional dancer, but I do dance. All the time. Ballet. It's my hobby, you could say."

"Take your shoes off," Tyler says.

I slip my foot out of one and immediately dig my toes into the sand.

"That's cheating."

I bend my knee and take the left shoe off with my hand. Pointing my toe expertly, I swing it forward for him to get a quick glimpse before leaping into the sand away from him. I toss my shoe back to land beside the other. Tyler dashes two steps to catch up with me.

"I don't remember you being a dancer way back when," he says as we walk toward the water. The sand is quickly losing the heat from the day and is cool against my feet. The bumps and divots in the sand fit inside my arches.

"That's right. I wasn't."

"You weren't bad though," he amends. "I only saw you dance the one time, at auditions for *Pippin*, but I remember you were pretty good. You stood out."

"I stood out enough for the choreographer to pull me aside and tell me personally how bad I was." I say this with a self-deprecating laugh like it was a funny memory.

Tyler shakes his head as if it doesn't compute. "You're kidding. Dixon said that? It doesn't sound like him. He was always so nice to me while I was there. How come you never told me?"

I wave the comment away, wishing like hell I'd never brought it up. "It was nothing. Really." I bite back the urge to say something snide about how of course Dr. Dixon treated him well. Tyler was the theatre department's pet. Instead of talking about my failure, I switch topics to his success. That should lead to a much easier conversation. "What were you filming today?"

Tyler allows the change of subject and tells me about the plot of the episode. Something about one of the main high school characters being upset that a friend has gone missing. He thinks it might have been his fault. Tyler's character finds him at the beach and tries to calm him down. Then the other kids show up and tell them the body of the friend has been found. Exciting stuff.

I can't help it, I start snickering.

"Don't laugh," he says playfully. "It's serious. He thinks he ate his friend."

I laugh harder and wipe away a tear. "I'm sorry. I'm sure it's very touching."

"When it airs, there will be girls crying all over America."

"I'm sure." I pull myself together and ask, "Why is the scene at the beach?" I ask. "Isn't the show about werecats? That doesn't seem like it goes with a beach setting."

"Ha! I know, right? I said the same thing to my agent when he first called me about this gig. A werecat show set near Malibu. It's ridiculous. But the idea is that the kids turn into mountain lions like the ones all over the hills in this area. They said in season two the writers might introduce some were-coyotes as a rival gang."

"Oh my!"

"Exactly."

It's gotten darker. Tyler gets a text that they are shutting down the beach house for the night and he should get his stuff. We hustle back to the house. I dust sand off my feet and slip my shoes back on. Tyler watches carefully.

"You weren't kidding about those toes. Those are some gnarly calluses."

"Is it a turn-off?" I ask.

"Not at all. They're kind of sexy." I roll my eyes at him. "I'm not kidding. It makes me imagine you in your leotard and tights, legs taut while you balance on your toe shoes. I'd like to see that in person sometime." He slips an arm around my waist and uses his other arm to twirl me in a circle like a partner dance. I wind up at his side, looking up at his handsomely aged face. "What do you think?"

"Let's see how tonight goes."

I follow him back down the coast to Santa Monica, where we stop for a late dinner. He tells me about living in New York up until getting the gig on *Wildcats*. It has been an adjustment after all this time, but he's liking it so far. Enough to buy a house and make a go of it. He's got an ex-wife but no kids and is surprised to find that I've never been married or had children.

"You don't look like you've ever had kids," he admits, "but it's rare to find someone our age who hasn't."

"Not in showbiz," I say. "A lot of my friends out here have kids late. One woman I know had a baby at forty-nine. I can't even imagine it."

He asks me. "Do you miss it? Having a family?"

"No." It's an honest answer. "From time to time I've wondered about it, but I never felt I was ready. Now it's too late."

"But your friend…"

"Was an anomaly. Let's be serious here." His face is blank for a moment until he understands what I'm saying. His cheeks pinken a little.

Tyler takes my hand across the table and caresses my knuckles with his thumb. "You're stunning, Graceful. Simply stunning."

"You turned out all right yourself," I respond.

The small talk stays sweet and flirty. After dinner, he walks me to my car. His condo isn't far, he tells me. I remind him how late it is.

"It's a school night," I tease.

"Oh yeah," he says, raising my hand to his lips. "I remember that old excuse. I also remember some foggy car windows." I open my fingers and lightly push his face away. "I didn't realize until today how much I've missed you."

The old line. He misses me combined with something flirty. He did it backwards this time, but it's still the same. And it still gets me.

"I've missed you too."

He opens my car door for me. I sit down sideways in the driver's seat, holding my purse awkwardly in my lap. Tyler leans in, and I tilt my head back to allow his kiss. His lips are warm and soft, his breath smelling of the wine we drank. I open my lips a little, inviting him to do more. He moves his mouth so that his lower lip fits neatly between mine. As he pulls away from me, he allows me to hold onto that lip a moment longer, a promise of more to come. "Can we do this again? Soon?" he asks, his face still so close to mine.

"I'd like that."

He knew that would be my answer, but he still smiles as though he's won a challenge. A tingle runs through me at the thought of pleasing him.

He stands there as I close the door and back out of my spot. He waves at me one more time before I drive away. As soon as he is out of sight, I run a hand down my face and rest it over my thrumming heart. Oh my. Is this happening? Am I really going to start seeing Tyler Andrews again after all this time?

# CHAPTER
## *Five*

Class is exactly what I need tonight. I had a hard time getting any sleep last night after the date. Work was mostly paperwork and phone calls at the office. I crave movement. I need to get some of this electricity coursing through me out of my body.

The class size tonight is low. Not great for the studio, but perfect for me. It gives me more room, and I take advantage of it, especially during the floor work and combination. Spencer is teaching, and he comments a few times about me being off count because I'm overdoing it. I don't care. It feels good to fly.

I'm in the middle of an across-the-floor combination of *piqué* turns, *échappé*, and *grand jeté* when I see Debbie's reflection in the mirror. She's snuck in and is leaning against the doorway, her wooden cane gripped in both of her gnarled hands. As usual, she watches me without a hint of amusement. I've known her twenty years now, and I've yet to glean a single outward expression of joy from her while watching me dance. She's told me a number of times that I have talent and ability, but her body language and facial expressions share a different opinion.

Class comes to an end, and Debbie calls Spencer over to her. I change out of my toe shoes and slip into my sweats while they talk. I'm curious what has brought Debbie here tonight. She owns the studio but rarely comes by anymore. I know it's hard for her to drive now, especially when her rheumatoid arthritis is having a bad flare. I act like I'm minding my own business, but I'm trying my best to filter out the chatter of the other dancers so I can hear the two of them.

Spencer guides Debbie across the room and pulls out the piano bench from the old upright that is rarely ever used anymore. The top of the piano is covered with an equally old boom box and a much newer Bluetooth speaker and iPod port. Debbie uses her cane to balance as she lowers herself onto the bench. I see the relief in her eyes immediately. Even standing still is hard for her these days. I know she'd never want me to say it, but I can't help feeling sorry for her. She's only seven years older than me. You wouldn't know it to look at her. Granted, I look a little young for my age. Debbie looks a good ten or more years older than hers.

"Grace," Spencer calls. I dart over to them, trying not to look too eager to be included in their business.

"What's up?" I ask as I gather near them.

"You look good tonight," Debbie says to me. "Lots of extra energy. A little spunk. I like that. It makes the younger dancers work harder to keep up."

"Thanks," I say, meaning it. Compliments from Debbie are few and far between.

Debbie watches the rest of the dancers exit, and once they're gone, she says to both of us, "Look, I came by to pick up some files from the office for my attorney. We're working up a will."

"A will?" Spencer drops to a crouch and puts a hand on her knees. She's wearing loose cotton pants with an elastic waistband. Her tunic blouse hides some of the weight she's put on since she stopped dancing. It's hot outside, but her sleeves are long. Too long for her arms, covering her knuckles. I haven't seen her in short sleeves for a few years now.

She pats his hand softly. "Don't get all excited, Spencer. Nothing to worry about. I'm getting to that age." Debbie looks at me and raises an eyebrow. "It wouldn't be a bad idea for you to write one up, too, kiddo. I can give you Arnie's number."

"If I had anything to give to anyone, I'd take you up on that."

"Well, it's not like I'm loaded, either. This studio takes more than it gives."

She's downplaying, of course. Debbie was a professional ballet dancer with New York Ballet for five years, straight out of high school. For a few years after that, she joined the Rockettes. Then she married a film director and moved to Hollywood. With his help, she landed small parts in *Center Stage*, *The Company*, *Showgirls* and a few other movies and music videos that featured dancing in the nineties. His career flourished, too, and they bought a lovely home in Hollywood Hills. When she retired from dancing, he helped her put together this studio. The mortgage is paid, so her only expenses are the upkeep, taxes, and paying Spencer and other guest teachers. She stopped advertising a long time ago.

"Enrollment is down," she notes.

"Just tonight," Spencer says. "It was packed in here last Thursday."

Debbie nods that this is acceptable information. "Jamie drove me here, so I shouldn't keep him too long." Her son, Jamie, is an aspiring writer who moved back in with his mom after his dad died a couple years ago. I've watched him grow up over the years. He's a good kid, if not a terribly good writer. He's still working on the novel he started when he was at UCLA. He's twenty-six now and says he hasn't got it right yet. Debbie has muttered her frustration over the whole situation more times than I can count.

Both Spencer and I offer to help as she rises from the bench. Debbie accepts Spencer's hand and bats mine away. I take a step back, pushing the familiar rejection I feel aside.

As she shuffles toward the door, Debbie looks back at Spencer. "Hey kid, you make Grace take over some of these classes. There's no reason for you to run yourself ragged teaching all of them yourself."

"I do," he reminds her. "Grace teaches every other Wednesday. Tonight was her off night."

"Have her take over the lyrical class on Fridays."

I interrupt. "I'd rather stick to ballet. I'm not the best at—"

"If I think you're good enough, you are." Debbie isn't in the mood for my modesty. I appreciate her confidence and whisper my thanks. This way she hears it but doesn't have to acknowledge that it happened.

Ultimately, it'll be up to Spencer if he wants me to teach more classes. He's the one who's running everything at Dancer's Room these days.

Spencer leads her to the office, and I go back to gathering my things. I check my phone messages and find two sweet texts from Tyler thanking me for a lovely night and asking when we can see each other again. My heart beats wildly. All my old schoolgirl feelings for him bubble up to the surface. I'm in the middle of texting a response when Spencer comes back in the room.

"Must be something good," he says.

"What?"

"You're smiling while you text. Not normal. You usually look like an old blind lady poking out messages with your one finger. Thumbs, girl. Use them. They're what separate us from the animals." He reaches for the phone, but I drop it quickly into my purse. He puckers his lips with intensified interest. "Ooh, what's going on?"

"Nothing."

Having no shame at all, Spencer reaches into my purse and pulls my phone back out again. Without hesitation, he types in my code to unlock my phone and see the messages. He gasps and covers his mouth with his hand. "What am I seeing? Is this a man? Texting you? Writing about... a date last night? Oh, this can't be real. You skipped class for a date? I cannot believe it."

I try to get the phone back, but he holds it out of reach. I jump, but Spencer's arms are long, strong, and un-budging. He flings himself away from me and dashes across the room. He scrolls through the messages. "Wait a second. I know this name. Tyler Andrews. Oh my God! Is this the same Tyler Andrews from *Classroom Chaos* back in the nineties?"

I have no idea what he's talking about. "Um, I'm going to go with a no on that."

"Is he an actor?"

"Yes, actually."

"It has to be him. Oh wow." He opens the internet on my phone and quickly punches something in. A second later, Spencer is back by my side showing me a picture of a young Tyler Andrews in the wildest of early nineties outfits and a head of teased out hair posing against a locker in the hallway of some colorful high school set. "I watched this show every afternoon when I got home from school. I had the biggest crush on him. You have no idea." Disappointment crosses his face. "So, he's not gay, huh? I would've sworn he was gay. He danced on the show a lot, and he was good."

I'm still staring at the picture. It's the Tyler I remember, except for the over-the-top clothing. He's probably in his young twenties, but he's made to look as though he's seventeen tops. I didn't have cable back then, and I surely wasn't a kid, so I never knew this show existed. He's adorable.

Spencer is still going on about it. "I liked it way better than *Saved by the Bell*, but it couldn't compete. I think it only had two seasons. Maybe only one." He makes an 'eek' face and hands me back my phone. "Is this the same guy?"

I nod, still staring at the picture. "Yeah. Yeah, it is. I knew him in college, and we ran into each other the other day." I click off the phone and drop it back in my purse. Spencer presses me for details, and I tell him the whole story of him showing up at the open house and how the date went.

Spencer's eyes are twinkling by the end of my story. "Nice first date, hon. Very promising. A successful, hot actor? I approve."

"Well, I don't know what I would do without your approval."

From the doorway to the classroom, Debbie chimes in. "Don't rush into anything."

"I didn't know you were still here," I say, heading over to her.

"I'm leaving," she says, waving a thick file with her free hand. "I overheard a little bit. You say you knew this guy when you were in school?"

"College, yes," I answer, offering to take the file from her. She allows it. I can tell her hands are struggling to hold it. "Freshman year. We kind of dated then. Nothing big."

Spencer flicks off the lights to the room, and we walk with her to the stairwell that leads down to the front door. Jamie is waiting down there for her. He comes up a couple steps to help her navigate the stairs.

"So, this is some kind of serendipity? You think you're getting a second chance encounter with this fella?"

"Maybe," I say.

Spencer squeals a bit. "It's romantic. I love it. Besides, it's been forever since you dated anyone."

"It was one date, Spencer."

"One awesome date. What will you do next?"

"I don't know yet."

The steps are slow-going, and we finally make it to the small front lobby. Debbie puts a hand on my shoulder and looks me in the eye. "Be careful. Sometimes we want to make things seem more important than they are. Just because you had something with him a million years ago doesn't mean that it's meant to be because you ran into him again. Be smart, kiddo."

Debbie knows I hate her calling me kiddo. I also hate the way she always dumps on everything that's good in my life.

"I'll keep that in mind, Debbie."

Jamie helps his mom outside and into the Cadillac he's parked in the handicap spot. She waves at us as he backs out and then drives away.

I face Spencer. "Well, since you're meddling, anyway. What do you think Tyler and I should do for a second date?"

"I'm curious if he can still dance," Spencer says. He gasps as an idea comes to him. "You should go dancing."

"For a second date? I was thinking coffee—"

Spencer looks at me seriously, both hands on my shoulders. "Honey, you got to snag this boy. Use all your skills." He winks at me, and I laugh.

"You're ridiculous."

"You're always saying that. But you have to love me." We go

outside, and he locks up the building. "Let me know if you go, and I'll happen to show up. Please. You owe me this."

"I don't, actually."

"I won't make you teach lyrical classes and won't tell Debbie."

I cross my arms and stroke my chin with my fingers as if mulling it over. "Okay. It's a deal."

Spencer doesn't believe me. "You're going to chicken out. I can see it all over your face. Come on, get out your phone. I want to witness you inviting him."

Groaning at him, I fish out my phone again and text Tyler. I name a place and time, late enough for Spencer to be able to come by after class tomorrow night. Tyler doesn't answer immediately, which clearly disappoints Spencer.

"He's in the middle of filming a TV show, you know. I'll let you know what he says," I promise.

"You better."

The thought of going dancing with Tyler was lovely and fun for a moment. Once I'm alone in my car driving away down Highland Avenue, the worries settle in. Dancing might lead to questions I'm not sure I want to answer. I'm not sure I'm ready to tell him my story because I'm not sure I'm ready for his reaction to it. It's one thing to have to explain my hobby to new people I meet. Telling Tyler feels different. He was always a person who had big goals, and it looks like he's met a lot of them. How exactly do I explain that any and all big goals for my life vanished a long time ago?

### 1992

The trip to Arizona took up a fair bit of the money I'd earned all summer, plus my mom made me get and pay for my own birth control pills. The week before classes were set to resume, I used my employee discount to buy necessary new clothes. I'd outgrown everything by two sizes. I was laying out my new outfits on my bed at home, deciding which one I'd wear first, when the phone rang.

"Hey, Graceful." Tyler's voice seemed less enthusiastic than I expected. We'd only talked a couple times since I left Phoenix, and he'd been full of energy and lots of over-the-top romantic thoughts both times.

"Are you okay?" I asked. "Are you here?"

"Oh, no. I'm not down there. Yet. I mean…" His words trailed off.

"I know move-in day isn't until this weekend," I said, helping him out. "I wondered if you came in early or something. You sound tired."

"I am. I actually just finished a long drive."

"Where to?"

He hesitated. The silence from his end unnerved me. "So, here's the thing, Grace."

Grace. He called me by my actual name. Something was up.

"Is everything okay?"

"Yeah. It is. It's what I'm calling about. I wanted you to know that… well…" I heard him take a deep breath, probably through his nose. "I'm not coming back to Long Beach."

The handset dropped out of my clutches as if it had shocked me. I watched it fall and dangle by its cord from the base on the night table. I heard his voice calling me, muted by the carpet. I sank to the floor, leaning back against my bed, and picked up the phone. With a shaky hand, I put the handset back to my ear.

"Are you there?" Tyler asked.

I nodded and gave a weak "Mmm-hmmm" because I knew he couldn't see me. I was glad he couldn't see me. Tears were already running down my face, and he hadn't even started explaining himself yet.

"I kind of knew when you were here, but it wasn't for sure yet. So, I didn't tell you." He went on, "The thing is, the woman who played Emily in *Our Town*. Well, she's a professor at University of Phoenix. I told you that, right? Several professors from the school were involved with summer stock out there, and they were all impressed with me. They had a meeting and decided to offer me a scholarship to their BFA in Musical Theatre program. It's a big scholarship and an amazing program. Our school doesn't have anything like it. I can't turn it down, Grace. You understand, don't you?"

Did I understand? "No, not really, Tyler."

"Graceful," he said softly, as if begging me to feel something different from what I was capable of.

"We have a good school. You're a star there already. Plus, you and I. We're... I thought we were... You're just leaving me?"

"I know how it looks. Especially after that night in Phoenix. I'd say we could stay together and make a long-distance thing work, but you know it won't. We've kind of proven that between me being in New York and then all summer in Arizona." He paused, and when I didn't say anything, he added. "You know I care about you, Graceful."

"Not enough, apparently."

Not more than his career. Kei had been right after all.

"I'm sorry," he said. "I really am."

"No, you're not."

It was the last thing I ever said to him. I slammed the handset down on the receiver. I stood up and flung all my new clothes off the bed. Then I crawled onto my bed and rolled up in my comforter. I was still crying in the dark when my mom got home from work. She came in and held me the same way she used to when I was a little girl, and I wondered when the world would stop being full of disappointment and she wouldn't have to do this for me anymore.

*Present Day*

Crosby, Stills, and Nash singing "Our House" breaks me out of my memories, thank goodness. Any more thoughts about Tyler and our long-lost love might take away any ounce of courage I have left to see him again. It took many years to forget about him, my first, and open my heart up to the possibility of dating again. There had been boyfriends and lovers over the years. None of them ever won me over completely. I'd run if things got too serious. I never did and still don't blame Tyler Andrews for screwing up my life. That was all my fault. I was a weak kid who was easily broken. I never learned to toughen up.

The song is the ringtone for my father. It's about to stop, and I consider letting the call go to voicemail. I can call him back later, after I'm home, showered, and have had some dinner. Dad doesn't like to talk on the phone when his favorite TV shows are on, so that will help keep anything he has to say brief. It's going to be about business. He never calls me about anything else. Since he retired from actively working in the real estate firm he owned, he bothers me all the time for updates.

I hit answer on my earpiece a heartbeat before the ringing stops. "Hey Dad."

"Hey girl," he says. He's chipper. Must be on his second gin and tonic. "Haven't talked to you this week yet. Wondered how that showing went the other day."

"Good. No sale. There's one person expressing some interest, but he's not committing to it yet." I hear what I'm saying about Tyler and cover my mouth and nose to stop myself from snorting out a sardonic laugh. Ah, Tyler, not committing to something. That didn't sound like him at all, did it?

*Stop it*, I think. I don't know him anymore. I'm not even sure I knew him all that well back then. He's obviously committed to acting. He's still doing it. He's not married. Doesn't have kids. But he's still acting. Bet his ex-wife could tell me a story or two about his priorities.

"It'll sell, Dad. It's a great house. Wish I could buy it myself, honestly."

"I wish you could too, sweetheart. I'd love to get you out of that apartment."

Dad hates that I live in an apartment in Hollywood. It especially irks him that I moved away from being near them in

Alhambra to be closer to the ballet studio. The horrible traffic made me so tense by the time I got to my classes. I left my dad's office and joined a realty company in the area. A couple years later, my dad bought out that company and made me the manager. I still tease him that he could have left my job alone and spent the money on a house for me instead. Dad knows as well as I do that he made the right investment. He's retiring in style with two offices making money for him.

He worries for no reason. My building is a concrete fortress at nine stories high on the corner of Wilcox and Franklin. It's withstood some powerful earthquakes without any substantial damage. Every couple of years, my income allows me to move up a floor or two. I'm on eight now, as high as I can get without being in a penthouse. I've got two bedrooms and a balcony overlooking the city. One of the bedrooms has a desk for my computer but is otherwise empty. It's where I practice my dancing and work on choreography. The apartment is old and could use some new carpeting and fixtures, but I like it well enough. I've decorated it with framed posters of my favorite dancers. I've got an autographed 8x10 of Baryshnikov, a still from the movie *White Nights* that I loved so much when I was in middle school. It's my prized possession. People give me ballerina figurines as birthday and Christmas presents. Every tabletop and counter are covered with them. Sometimes I tease Spencer that I'm going to tell everyone I'm super into penguins so I can get something different.

But secretly, I adore all the ballerinas.

"I'm fine where I'm at," I tell him for the millionth time. "I've got access to a pool which is always super warm, and my newest place has its own washer and dryer, so I don't have to use the laundry room downstairs anymore."

I can almost hear him rolling his eyes. "What a luxury."

"You don't do laundry, so you wouldn't know."

"You got me," he says.

I turn into the parking garage under my building as he asks who this interested buyer is. I'm kind of hoping the signal will cut out like it sometimes does. Then he'll have to wait until I park, go up the elevator, and get settled in my apartment before I call him back. Maybe he'll have started his third drink and won't care anymore.

The signal stays strong. "You still there, Grace?"

"Yeah. Yeah, I'm still here. The interested buyer is an actor from New York. He's in a show that films here and is doing well, so he's interested in getting a permanent place." I know he'll ask, so I go ahead and tell him, "His name is Tyler Andrews."

"Tyler Andrews." He says it one syllable at a time like he's puzzling it out. "No, I don't think I know who that is."

"He's not famous. Just an actor that's making good."

"The name is familiar, though. Hang on." I hear him calling out, "Do you know an actor named Tyler Andrews? No? Tyler. Tyler Andrews." I'm sitting in my car in the dark parking lot under my building because I know the phone call will for sure cut off the second I get in that elevator. Dad speaks into the phone again. "Hold on. The name has triggered something, and she's marching over here to take the phone—"

"Grace?" It's my mom. "Does your dad have that name right? Is it Tyler Andrews? Like the Tyler Andrews you dated in college?"

Why is her memory so damn good? I grit my teeth and answer. "Yeah. One and the same."

"He's still acting?" The wonderment of it sets me on edge. "At his age?"

"Mom, you know not all actors are young people. Watch a movie or TV show once in a while. Nearly all of the actors are over thirty-five. Especially the men."

"Oh, I know, honey. I know. But they've all been acting their whole lives."

"So has Tyler," I say. "That's how I met him, remember?"

Mom clicks her tongue, a sound that is sharp and grating in my ear. "Well, it's amazing. And you met him? Was your dad saying you're selling a house to him?"

"Yes, I met him. I don't know if he'll buy the house or not." Should I go on? Should I let her in on my business? I feel like I need to sit on the news of me dating Tyler until I see if it's going anywhere. I have my doubts that it will no matter how much he complimented me last night.

"Oh, wouldn't that be exciting if he did?" she says. "After all this time, the boy that broke your heart is now a big Hollywood actor and comes back to win you over again? It's fate. It *is*. Were you dressed nice when you met? Not in one of those sundresses with the full skirts that practically look like ballerina tutus. They don't do anything for your figure."

My figure is flat and straight. Full skirts give the illusion of hips. As usual, my mom doesn't know what she's talking about. Then again, she's never been particularly thin, and she rarely wears anything besides jeans and oversized button-down shirts.

"Mom, I'm in a parking lot. It's not the safest place to be, so I'm going to get off the phone—"

"Okay, honey. You get inside. But hey, if he calls, even if he says no to the house, consider asking him out for coffee or something. Maybe there will be a spark after all this time. You were brought together again for a reason. I'm sure of it. Things have their right time and place."

Mom is a big believer in second chances. She's got a good reason.

Dad gets back on the phone and gives me a couple of messages to take to the office tomorrow. He tells me he loves me. Mom shouts it from her end of the sofa. I hang up and sit in my car in the dark a little while longer.

*1992*

Sophomore year started up without any fanfare. My schedule was heavy on general education classes, so I wasn't in the performing arts department much. I had Theatre Lit and Beginning Set Design, that was it. I still hadn't managed to figure out how to get a ballet class onto my schedule. To be fair, I hadn't tried that hard to figure it out. I didn't see how starting ballet at nineteen-years-old was going to help me be any good at this point. People who did ballet well started as children. All I was going to learn were the basics, certain steps that everyone should know, so I didn't look dumb at an audition when a choreographer said "*chassé glissade pas-de-bourree.*" I was taking French, did that count?

Eats and Treats went back to being my main source of income. I limited hours at Clothestime to the weekends. Kei came back to work as well. When I saw her name on the shift the first time, anxiety wracked my nerves so hard that my neck stiffened and gave me the worst headache. I almost called out. I almost quit. But as soon as she showed up, she looked up at me with doe eyes, opened her arms wide, and drew me in for a big hug.

"Are you okay?" she asked.

I nodded, struggling to hold back the tears I hadn't expected.

She let go of me and grabbed an apron from the hook on the wall. "I know, Grace. It sucks. Tyler's such a jerk. In all honesty, you should be glad he's gone. He'd have broken your heart more if he stayed. My opinion." She put up a hand like she was taking an oath.

The weakest of smiles crept across my lips. "You're probably right."

"Probably?" Kei tied her apron behind her back. "I'm absolutely right. That guy doesn't think about anyone but himself."

I figured Kei knew as well as I did that was true. She'd followed him out to the desert, too. At least she hadn't slept with him. Only I had to carry that regret.

We got to chatting about our class schedules and the year's season of shows. The shift flew by, and we were both a little sad to clock out and head home. Kei invited me back to hang out with her in the dorm for a bit, but I begged off. I wasn't ready to go back there yet. I headed home, my head buzzing because I'd finally made a friend at this stupid school.

Auditions were posted on the bulletin board for the fall musical. *Hello Dolly.* That seemed fun. The leading roles of Dolly and Horace Vandergelder were not available. Two members of the faculty were pre-cast, which was a big deal to everyone. Seeing our professors strut their stuff was exciting—and a learning opportunity. However, it also wiped out the two biggest parts. It didn't matter much to me. Getting a major role was off the table for me, even as a sophomore. This was a fact, not an opinion. I considered auditioning for the ensemble and picked out a song to sing from the ones I'd worked on in Musical Theatre class last semester.

On the day of the auditions, I walked into the theater and saw all the students lining up to sign up for a slot. Too many. There were too many people. How could there possibly be so many people in this theatre department? Were there people who weren't from the department auditioning, too? How was that even fair? I stepped into the line and moved steadily forward for ten minutes. With each second, my will evaporated. My skin got clammy and my head light. Breathing seemed to be a real chore, and I hoped I wasn't wheezing loud enough for anyone to hear. Oh God. I was going to pass out right there on the steps in front of everyone.

I stepped out of line, muttering some excuse about needing to use the restroom like the people around me needed an explanation. As calm and collected as I could manage, I walked back up to the top of the auditorium and out to the foyer. A moment later I breathed in that familiar Long Beach air that smelled of equal parts ocean and sulfur. I went straight to the restroom across the way and threw up my breakfast. After splashing water on my face in the sink and destroying my makeup, I stared at my reflection. My throat was now raw from the retching. I couldn't possibly sing, even if I could drum up the nerve to go back in there. I grabbed a handful of scratchy brown paper towels and wiped the combination of water and tears off my face, rubbing way harder than necessary until my face was ruddy. I left the bathroom and went the opposite way of the theater, around the fine arts building to get to the parking lot. I tossed my songbook in the trunk and slammed it shut.

I was about to get in my car and drive away when I heard someone shouting my name. Kei waved at me from the grassy hill between the parking lot and the path to the dorms. I liked her, but I wasn't in the mood to chat or be cheered up. She wouldn't understand. She didn't do musical theatre, and odds were that she'd be cast in one of the dramatic plays being done this semester. I had serious doubts I could beat out my fellow acting students for any of those roles. Nothing so far had given me an indication that I had real acting chops.

With large windmill arm motions, Kei beckoned me to come join her. "Come on! Let's go get a coffee!"

Politely, I waved and then opened the door. Kei put her hands on her hips and cocked her head, overacting her disappointment. She looked a little like Punky Brewster in her oversized denim overalls and bright colored T-shirt. I shrugged like I couldn't help it and got into my car. I drove away from the only person trying to be my friend.

The next time we worked together, the conversation was back to being stiff. I'd blown it. Kei had offered me an opening, and I turned it down. Even though I apologized profusely, and she said she understood, it didn't look like she was going to throw open that door to her friendship again anytime soon. Then, as expected, she got cast in a play. Not at school. A community theatre production of George Bernard Shaw's *Caesar and Cleopatra*, where she was going to play Cleopatra. She quit Eats and Treats.

Not only did I miss her company at that stupid job, but I missed the way she could always deflect the theatre arts kids who came to get hot dogs and gossip about Tyler. Kei and I were apparently the authorities on what happened to the school's vanishing star. One afternoon shortly after Kei quit, a group of them showed up with a bunch of new questions.

"Is it true that one of the professors was having an affair with Tyler? Is that why he got accepted into the school without an audition?" This was from Tiffany, now a senior and playing one of the only four available female speaking roles in *Hello Dolly*.

Kei would have said something smart and sarcastic. She always had a quick tongue. I didn't. I stumbled through explaining how he'd done three productions out there that summer and that showed his abilities well enough.

One of Tiffany's friends, a girl named Heather, followed up with, "Well, you were kind of his girlfriend, right? You wouldn't know if he'd been sleeping with the professor. It's not like he'd tell you. Where's Kei? She'd know."

I didn't answer.

"Are you still so sad he's gone?" Tiffany asked, her lips in a pout. "Do you know that he shared a room with Caroline Janowitz the whole time in New York? I heard they shared the same bed. From the first day they got there."

I put too much mustard on her hot dog. I hoped she choked on it. "We were never officially a couple, so…"

"Oh," Heather said. "I thought you thought you were. Everyone knows you chased him all the way out to Arizona this summer."

How did everyone know that? Did Kei tell them? That seemed unlikely since she did the same damn thing. Oh, but she could play it off like it was work, and they'd probably believe her because she'd proven herself as an actress in this stupid program.

"I didn't *chase* him. He invited me."

"Not how I heard it," Tiffany replied. She handed me money for her food but refused to take the hot dog when I handed it to her. She sneered and ordered me to make her a new hot dog because the one I'd assembled for her was gross. While she wasn't looking, I put a layer of onions on the bun and hid them with the dog. She'd find out soon enough.

At home that evening, I looked through my registration packet for the semester. The final date to drop classes without penalty was in five days. I circled that date on the hanging calendar my dad's real estate office always handed out to customers for free. The picture for October was a couple of jack-o-lanterns on the front steps leading up to the doorway of a house. It was inviting, and I wanted to be ten-years-old so I could go trick-or-treat there.

I wanted to be ten so I could have a do-over on choosing my goals and dreams. Maybe I could choose something that wasn't so romantic as wanting to perform for a living. What was that, anyway? A dream to play and pretend for the rest of my life. Time to be a grown-up and put silly, childish dreams aside.

Well, what was stopping me? I was only nineteen. Hardly old. Hardly too late. What else interested me? What else could I do? I stared at that decorated house with my dad's name, business, and phone number printed on the lower left corner. Without really thinking about it, I picked up the phone and called him. He lived in Alhambra on the other side of town, so we met up for a late lunch of pizza and chicken wings and had a good talk.

Dad followed me home so we could discuss with my mom as well. I did the right thing and called ahead to let her know this was happening. She had the house tidied up nicely when we arrived, and she put on some makeup. I hardly ever saw her do that anymore.

"You look happy," she said to my father when we entered. It was true. His face beamed with joy and pride. I honestly couldn't remember him ever looking like that toward me. Not even at my high school graduation. Certainly not after seeing me in *Sweet Charity*. He never bothered to attend a single performance.

"Well, our daughter has finally gotten some sense in that head of hers."

I wished my joy matched his. Maybe he was right, and I was finally being sensible. That was indeed how it all felt. Sensible. Smart. Practical. And yet, as I watched my parents smile at each other about their clever child, my mind drifted backwards. Suddenly, I was a little girl again carefully placing my brand-new ballet slippers in my pink dance bag and burying it in the back of my closet.

From this day forward, I would never be extraordinary. Childhood fantasies were gone.

We sat at the dinner table, Mom and Dad allowing me to share some wine with them. It was bitter and dry. We discussed how I was going to drop out of my current classes and transfer to community college in January to get my real estate license. It would be cheaper and faster. Then I'd go work for my dad's office out in Los Angeles. Oh, and the icing on the cake? Dad was going to pay for all of it. Mom and I didn't have to worry about college tuition anymore. It benefited him in many ways, including a write off on his taxes.

"Are you sure?" Mom asked me several times, the lines deep between her eyebrows. I assured her this was what I wanted. It was a better plan for me. She reminded me that community theatre could always be a hobby. Yes, I supposed it could. Maybe someday.

Dad patted me on the shoulder. "Selling a house is like acting. You gotta set the stage. You gotta perform. You'll be a natural at this."

Sure. Yeah. It was exactly the same.

I left them to finish the rest of the wine. From my room, I heard them laughing as they caught up with each other. They hadn't spent any significant time together in nearly a decade. So, this is what it took for them to get along? The destruction of my ego? The crumbling of my confidence?

Sitting on my bed, I thumbed through the phone numbers in my address book from back to front. I considered calling some old friends from high school that were still around, but I didn't want to answer questions about how college was going. I found Kei's number. Would she try to talk me out of this decision? Did I want her to? Ah, she was probably busy anyway.

My finger stopped on Tyler's name. He was the only person since high school that encouraged me. He said I had talent that was worth something. I don't know if he meant it, but he seemed sincere when he said it. Was it something he said to all the girls? Was he just being nice? If I called him now, would he convince me that I was giving up too easily? I knew deep down that was true, but I also suspected I didn't have the fortitude someone needed to be in show business. Maybe a guy like Tyler who cared for little but making his dreams come true would have some advice for me about how to toughen up.

I had several numbers for him—home in Palmdale, the Long Beach dorm, and how to reach him at summer stock in Arizona. None of those numbers would work. I didn't have a phone number for his new school. He hadn't given it to me when he broke things off with me. The realization that I had no way of ever talking to him hit hard. I threw the address book across the room where it plopped onto my worn yellow beanbag.

That beanbag had to go. I'd had it since I turned twelve. A birthday present. Looking around the room, I noticed how childish my room was. Posters of Michael Jackson, Prince, George Michael, and *The Breakfast Club* left over from high school. Knick-knacks of unicorns and fairies on the shelves beside the window. Pink curtains and matching bedcovers. A mirror over my dresser with wallet-sized school pictures of friends I hadn't spoken to in a year and a half tucked into the wooden frame. I couldn't afford to move out, but I could at least do a makeover. If I was going to start acting like a grownup and make grownup goals, then my room needed to reflect it, too.

As soon as Dad left, I came out to the kitchen where Mom had started making some grilled cheese sandwiches and tomato soup for us. She hummed as she smiled pleasantly. I wanted to remind her that the person who had made her feel this way was the same person that walked out on us nine years ago, but I held my tongue. Instead, I grabbed some black trash bags and headed back to my room.

Mom called after me, "What are you up to, honey?"

I shouted back, "Nothing."

# CHAPTER
## Six

I gave Tyler an address and told him to meet me. I also directed him to wear loose-fitting pants and a comfortable shirt. I am not surprised to find him waiting for me outside Rusty's Rhythm Club in a pair of pleated khaki slacks and a tight black T-shirt with an unbuttoned bowling shirt over it. He hands me a pink rose as I approach.

"You look perfect," I tell him. "Did you look up the venue?"

"I did. Had to know what we were getting into."

"Have you ever done swing dancing before?"

He tilts his head both directions. "Kind of. I was in a production of *Swing!* at a dinner theater in Florida one time."

"Not the same," I tell him. "Real swing dancing isn't choreographed. There are several basic moves, and then you get in the groove."

"Sounds good to me."

He opens the door, and I lead him inside where our IDs are checked and we're given stamps on the backs of our hands. I pay for our dance lessons, ten dollars each.

"I'll get our drinks later," he says. I agree to the deal with a wink and pull him toward a table where we can put my purse and sweater. I'm wearing a 1950s vintage dress with a skirt that is going to twirl like crazy when I spin. It cost me a pretty penny, but it's so worth it. I change into my saddle shoes. I never wear them outside where they can get scuffed. They cost me even prettier pennies.

The club is a renovated warehouse in Playa Del Rey, not too far from the beach. It's a ritzier stretch of coastline south of the more popular Venice Beach. A bar stretches along one side, and the round tables are set all along the perimeter of the room. A platform stage is at the far end from the entrance, with a drum set and microphones waiting for people to use them. For now, we'll be dancing to recorded music. The live musicians come in later. The large, square, hardwood dance floor is slightly raised. Everywhere else is cement.

All over the red-painted walls are giant posters of jazz musicians and movie posters from the 1940s and 1950s. It's not fancy, but it gets you in the spirit.

It's almost seven o'clock and the place isn't too busy. Our class will have about eight couples. Not too bad. Tyler watches me get ready and looks around at the other people gathering for the level one swing dancing class. "You're serious about this, aren't you? Shoes and costume."

"It's fun. I don't swing dance much anymore, but I do love it. You will, too." I grab his hand and lead him out to the floor. "You should stretch your calve muscles," I suggest. "It'll get you two days from now if you don't."

He does a couple lunges like he's getting ready to go jogging while I do a few quick *plies* and *releves*. Judging from his physique, Tyler works out regularly, so he'll probably be fine. I'm not worried about my calves. I dance on a regular basis.

Our instructor for the evening is Tim. He's been with Rusty's for a couple years, and he gives me a big smile when he recognizes me. "Good to see you, Grace. Got a rookie with you?"

"Oh, he's a dancer," I tell Tim.

"Not a swing dancer," Tyler amends.

Tim laughs. "You will be after tonight, especially if Grace is your date."

We get started learning the side, side, back-step combination that is the base for everything else that happens in this form of dancing. He gets it in a wink. While the other couples are still stepping on each other's toes, Tyler and I are already in each other's arms, going around in circles. I lead until he's comfortable, and then I let him take over.

Tim comes over and teaches Tyler how to let go of me and bring me back in, then how to let me turn under his arm. By the end of class, we've got enough moves to fill up a full version of "Jump Jive and Wail" without being super repetitive. The other class members applaud us and then Tim to thank him for the lesson.

We head over to our table and drain some big glasses of water. Tyler is dripping sweat and uses a napkin to pat himself down. "That's exhausting."

"Yeah, but fun, right?"

"You're not sweating at all," he says. I'm not. I am breathing hard, and my heart rate is up. "Was that too easy for you?"

"I don't sweat that much," I tell him. "I tend to get red in the face when I overdo it instead of sweating. I can tell when it's bad because people give me worried looks and ask if I'm all right."

He shakes his head. "You look amazing right now. Simply glowing."

I smile and raise my glass to my mouth.

The beginning dancers leave the floor, and the next class gathers. "These are the more advanced level dancers," I tell him. "They're here to learn different styles and all the tricks. The lifts and spins."

"Are we allowed to stay and watch?"

I nod. "They have some food here. After this class, the place opens up as a club for the evening. We can dance again then with the live band. Want to stay?"

"Absolutely."

We order some beers, wings, and fries. I'll regret the meal later, but it tastes delicious. Tyler talks about dances he's done in different shows over the years and points out when the couples learn something he's had to do once. During the time after the class and before the band gets set up, he finally asks me, "How did you ever find out about this place or get into swing dancing?

It's another mystery about you I can't put together. The Grace I knew in college wasn't a dancer."

"I'm different from that girl."

"That's clear." He gestures to the room. "So?"

I put my elbows on the table and prop my chin on one hand. "Okay, I'll tell you, but you have to promise not to laugh. It's silly."

He makes the most serious face he can muster. "Promise."

"So, I put on some weight in my twenties. A fair bit, actually. At the end of 1999, I made a New Year's resolution—a millennium resolution—for the year 2000 to do something to lose weight. I tried different exercises, like jogging. Ugh." I stick out my tongue, and he laughs. I give him a sharp look.

"Come on," he jokes. "I hate running, too. A necessary evil for me."

"I got some old Jazzercise videos to do at home, and they were kind of fun. I wasn't consistent with doing it, and my downstairs neighbors complained a few times about my jumping on the floor. I joined a gym, but I always found excuses not to go. Nothing worked." I stick my finger in the splat of ranch dressing on my plate and draw circles in it. "Then one day a friend of mine from work invited me to go to The Derby to see a friend of hers sing in the forties cover band there."

"The Derby?"

I grin sheepishly. "Remember that movie *Swingers* in the nineties with Vince Vaughn? Did you ever see it? Well, it made swing dancing huge, and this club called The Derby was *the* place to go because they shot some of the movie there. Getting in was a big deal."

"I remember that movie."

Licking the ranch off my finger, I say, "Yeah, well, I was excited to go but scared about being at a swing dancing club because I didn't know how to do it. Turned out they offered classes on weeknights, so I went to one. I caught on fast, and the instructor moved me up to the intermediate level after only one class."

Tyler points at me. "I always told you that you had talent. You never believed me."

"*You* were just flirting with me," I remind him.

"Graceful, I never flirted with anyone who didn't impress me."

I take that in for a moment, trying to figure out which wound to bandage with it. "Anyway, I turned out to be adept at swing dancing and started going there regularly. My body trimmed up a bit. One night, a woman approached me and pulled me aside. She said she was with some professional dance troupe that did a touring show of swing dancing. She wanted to know if I had any formal dance training. I had to confess that I didn't." I take a long drink from my beer and put it down.

"Did she want you for the troupe or to audition or something?" Tyler asks. "Don't leave me hanging."

"Oh, no. She gave me her card and said I had some raw talent. If I took some classes and strengthened my core skills, and lost a little more weight, I might have something."

Tyler's jaw dropped. "That's amazing! She was basically telling you to call her after you took a few basic classes in what? Ballet? Jazz?"

"I guess. Yeah."

"So? What happened?"

What happened? I quit. I hit a wall. I was told once again that I could never be good enough to make it. I stopped going to the club.

I don't answer right away. I wish I had a good ending for him.

"Is this when you started doing ballet? I saw you dancing ballet at the house, and you were astonishing."

"Yes," I answer as though it were that simple. "Yep. That's when I started doing ballet classes. At thirty-years-old."

"I mean, it's unusual, but better late than never, right? Did you ever call the lady back?"

I shake my head. "Oh no. I didn't get to a level she would need fast enough. I let that go."

"Aw, you shouldn't have. She gave you an opening, and you should've taken it." He means it. This is a man who pursues his dreams. He would've called whether he thought he was ready or not, I bet. He'd have faked it and used that charisma of his to win a spot in the troupe.

Most of the tables at Rusty's are full now. The room is full of conversation, and we are leaning over the table to be able to hear each other. The members of the band are tuning their instruments and doing mic checks. It'll be hard to keep talking. I'm glad of this. I'm ready to get on my feet again.

"How come you didn't want to meet at The Derby tonight?" he asks. "Isn't it closer to where you live? You live in Hollywood, right?"

"It's closed. It closed a few years ago. It's a shame, really."

He nods right as the lead singer of the band says hello to the crowd, shouts the name of the band, The Retro Gang, and launches into a cover of "Zoot Suit Riot". Dancers in colorful vintage outfits rush to the floor. I grab Tyler's hand and pull him out of his seat. We dance, and I let all my thoughts about failure fall away as I enjoy the way my limbs move so easily to the music and the easy grin on his face as he watches me come alive.

### 2003

"Are these for your daughter?"

The woman behind the counter at the dance supply store looked at me expectantly. Everything about me shouted newbie. I was a good twenty pounds overweight and stood frozen at the entrance of the store with one hand clutching the leather strap of my purse and the other one pressed to my face as I stared at the round racks of brightly-colored leotards The lady came around the corner of the counter to escort me further inside. Her graying hair was in a loose bun held up with a pencil. Reading glasses hung from a chain around her neck.

I'd told her I was looking to get some dance shoes. This apparently meant she had to wrap her arm around my shoulders and guide me through the obstacle course of clothing racks to the back of the store where there were a couple of wicker chairs to sit in while trying on shoes and some curtained-off dressing room stalls.

The answer to her question caught in my throat, and I shook my head until I could wrangle up some sound. "Uh… no. They're for me. The shoes are for me."

As if I'd given her an electric shock, her arm jerked off of my shoulders. Her open expression transformed into something more judgmental. "Oh. Well, of course we have shoes for adults. Many members of the studio's dance team go on to study dance in college and we've even had a couple join professional companies. I'm Nora."

The studio she referred to was Razzle Dazzle Dance Company, and it used the space next door to this shop in the strip mall. From outward appearance, the space used to hold a grocery store. Now it contained two dance rooms, an office, and a large front lobby for parents to wait while their darlings took class. I'd been in there already to register for the adult ballet class they offered that had been advertised in a free community newspaper. When I registered, I was informed that the adult class did ballet, jazz and tap alternately. It wasn't exactly what I wanted, but I didn't know where else to go that was close to my apartment in Alhambra and cheap. Everything I found was only for kids. This was the first place that had classes for grownups.

The same people owned this dance supply store. A clever move. I was told I didn't *have* to purchase from them, but I might as well because they had exactly what was needed. After writing my check for the first month of classes, I immediately went next door.

A mom was in the store with a cute, bubbly thing that was probably no older than five. All curls and sticky fingers. They were being helped by a slim teenager that was most likely Nora's daughter. Some black patent-leather tap shoes were slipped onto the child's feet and the ribbons tied to hold them in place. In a flash, she jumped up and tick-tick-ticked all over the tile floor.

She wiggled her tiny tush and put her hands up to the sides of her face in a Shirley Temple pose. The girl's glee was precious and infectious. I felt my nerves melt away and absorbed the joy of this adorable girl. I remembered being her once upon a time.

"I absolutely love starting little girls out with their first pair of dance shoes," Nora said, her face beaming. "It's truly my favorite part of the job. Is your daughter a new student here? I don't remember you coming here before."

"Oh, I don't have a daughter."

Confusion swept over her features. "I thought you were signing up for the Mommies class."

"The Mommies class?"

The teenager spoke up then. "A lot of the dancers' moms thought it would be fun to have their own class. So, they started one up a year or two ago. My mom doesn't do it even though she'd be better than all the rest of them."

Nora's face flushed a bit as the little girl's mother and I both looked at her. "Are you a dancer?" I asked.

"Was," she clarified. "A long, long time ago."

Nora didn't seem all that old to me, so I wondered at what age she gave it up.

The teenager leaned over and said to the tiny dancer, "She can still do the splits."

"Ooh!" baby Shirley Temple said, slapping a hand to the side of her face. "I can't even do that."

"You will one day," the teenager said. Then she got back to making sure the shoes fit and asking the mom if they wanted to try another pair.

Nora returned her attention to my needs. "So, you'll need ballet slippers, tap shoes, and jazz shoes, right?"

"That's right. And some tights and a leotard or two."

"We'll get you all set up. It'll be fun. Especially if you've never danced before."

Driving home an hour later, after dropping another hundred and fifty dollars, I found myself wondering why the class would be fun *especially* if I'd never danced before. What could she have meant by that? Icky doubts that I had wasted a ton of money for nothing took over my brain. I nearly turned around and returned everything, and if it weren't for the fact that I couldn't get back there before the store closed, I probably would have.

While shopping, Nora had told me that the children had specific colors they had to wear. All pink for the little ones. Older girls wore black leotards with pink tights. High school students and adults could wear any color they wanted with nude or pink tights. Sometimes the mommies wore leggings instead of tights, and that was fine. Parachute pants were only okay for the jazz portion of the class.

For my first class, I wore black stirrup leggings and hot pink leg warmers. The leotard had a pattern of pink, turquoise, and purple shapes, and fit high on the hip bones and straight across my collar bones from one shoulder strap to the other. I put my hair up in a tight ponytail to keep it out of my face. I appreciated that the leggings hid the dimples of my thighs, but nothing could hide the bulges from the lines of my underwear and bra underneath the skintight clothing. I hated the way my bare arms sagged when I held them out to my sides. I covered everything up with a track suit, having no idea how I'd get the courage to take it back off in front of other people.

I drove to the studio, so nervous that I drank nearly all the water from my water bottle before I even got there. I parked and watched all the teen dancers get out of their parents' cars and stride into the building like they owned the place. The mom dancers parked and met their friends in the lot before walking in. The clock in my dashboard clicked away. If I didn't get going, I'd be late.

I took a deep breath and let it out again. "This is better than a treadmill or spin class," I reminded myself. "This'll be fun." The whole reason I'd signed up for the class was to find a fun way to get in shape. I wouldn't look flabby in my dance clothes for long, right?

Grabbing my duffel bag and my nearly empty water bottle, I got out of the car and headed inside. I followed the adult women into dance room A. The teens headed to the bigger studio, B. Inside the classroom, women stepped out of their sweats or track suits and lined their bags up along the back wall. The amount of color splashed about on these women's clothing made the room look a bit like a Jackson Pollock painting come to life. I was the only person in the room wearing a leotard by itself. Everyone covered their bottom half with either a ballet skirt, bicycle shorts, or nylon running shorts.

From the subtle nods and fingers up to mouths, I could tell a number of women seemed to be commenting to each other about my choice of dance attire or mere existence in their world, but no one bothered to come over and say hi or introduce themself.

The only person in the room younger than me was the instructor, Sally, a freckled girl probably fresh out of college that stood no more than five-foot-two with hair knotted up in a loose bun. She wore a too-big T-shirt over a pair of leggings. Her black ballet slippers were scuffed so much the toes were nearly white. A CD player and speaker were on a rolling stand in the front corner of the room. Sally busied herself with choosing music to play while the ladies got ready. She looked up long enough to notice me and beckon me over to her.

"Hey, you're Grace, right?"

I nodded.

"Cool. Well, on Tuesdays we start with ballet exercises for forty-five minutes, take a quick break, and then we work on our dance routine for thirty minutes. We do jazz and tap on Wednesdays."

"Right," I said. They'd told me as much when I signed up.

"Find a spot. You'll catch on quickly. Have you danced before?"

I confessed, "Not in a long time."

"That's okay," Sally said. "No one else in this class has either."

She snapped the CD player shut and hit play. A Sarah MacLachlan ballad played, hardly what I expected for a dance class. Sally shooed me away and then called lazily to the class, "Let's do this, ladies."

She centered herself in front of the mirror, sat down and spread her legs open wide, ready to start stretches. The students made their way to their spots, creaking and groaning as they lowered themselves to the floor as well. I finally found a place on the floor toward the back after two ladies informed me that I was in their spot. We started with floor stretches, where I quickly learned that although I could touch my toes, that was the extent of my flexibility. I didn't get embarrassed, though, because no one else in the room could do much either. It didn't take long to realize that none of these ladies, all thirty-five or older, were real dancers. This was the mom class. Each one of them had a young dancer in the program, and they were doing this for kicks.

Sally sent us to the barre next, where she had us work on positions, *plies* and *tendus*. It was easy, and despite twenty years passing since my parents made me quit dance, I remembered all of these basic movements. I was a bit surprised that the class wasn't doing anything more advanced at this point. From what Nora had told me, some of them had been taking the class for a couple of years. Not to mention the fact that it was January, and the year's classes had begun back in September. I had expected to struggle to catch up. My legs were already stinging a bit from the stretches and *plies*, but I wasn't feeling at all tired.

Sally never smiled once at our class. Occasionally, she would look at the ladies over her shoulder and ask them to hold their conversations for after class. She taught like it was an obligation and not a passion.

"We aren't going to do across-the-floor today," Sally told us. "Everyone, make two lines. Windows please. We're going to start choreography for recital."

What were windows? Recital?

"Um. Sally?"

I raised my hand, but one of the moms grabbed my wrist and tugged me into the back line with her. "Stand here so you can see yourself in the mirror between Cathy and Denise." Cathy and Denise weren't exactly thin, so I saw a sliver of myself through them. "You started on a good day. If you'd come a week or two later, you'd be so behind. I'm Jan. My daughter is a senior on the team. Is your daughter starting, too?"

The faint lines around Jan's eyes and mouth indicated that she was a good decade older than me, but her body was in good shape. Her legs were muscular, and she wore bicycle shorts over her leotard to accent them. I suspected she did more exercise than this dance class offered.

"Oh, I don't have a… I'm Grace."

"Nice to meet you."

"We're doing a recital? Like a performance of some kind?"

"They didn't tell you that when you signed up?" I shook my head. Jan's eyes sparkled at getting to be the person to tell me the awesome news. "Yeah, there's a giant recital every spring. The studio does it up right and uses the high school auditorium. Costumes. Lights. It's a blast. Every class does a performance. We'll do three numbers. One jazz, one tap, and the ballet one we're about to start learning."

"We perform with the kids?"

"Not *with* the kids," Jan said, punctuating that statement with a high-pitched laugh that caught Sally's attention. She whispered the rest. "We have our own numbers in between theirs. It's a real hoot."

"Ladies," Sally called out, specifically looking at Jan and me. "Let's get started. This is a harder dance than last year's."

A lady at the end of the back row moaned slightly. I shared her sentiments, and then I wondered what last year's routine was like.

Questions rang out from the group. "Do you have costumes picked out? What are we dancing to? What's our tap number? What's the jazz song? Can we do more hip-hop this year?" And so on.

Sally took a deep breath. "I'll show you the costumes I've picked out at the end of class. This number will be to 'My Heart Will Go On' from *Titanic*." Lots of oohs and other happy comments. I fought rolling my eyes. That song was so over-played. Did I have to listen to it every time I came to class? "You'll all be wearing white for this. Pretty dance skirts that are blue at the bottom. You'll look nice."

*We'll all look like icebergs*, I thought.

The class finally settled down, and Sally taught us the first four counts-of-eight and then went over them repeatedly until everyone got the steps right. By then, the class was coming to an end, so she led us in a cooldown. Women gathered their bags and wiped down their necks with little towels even though no one was sweaty.

Jan stepped up behind me as I put my tracksuit back on. "You did remarkably well for a first day. Better than some of the women in this class who've been here the whole time. Some people have natural talent. You should see my daughter, Allie. She's amazing. That's not just a mom talking. She has real talent."

"She does," Sally said, approaching us. "Jan isn't exaggerating. Allie is a talented girl." She put her hand on my elbow and guided me away from Jan. "What did you think of your first class? The number is going to be pretty, I think."

I kept my voice low so Jan couldn't overhear. "Class was fine, but… Well, what I'm looking for is a class that will teach me the basics of ballet. I want to know the names of the steps and how to do them correctly. Kind of like going to a guitar teacher to learn all the chords and some strumming styles."

Sally nodded her head at me like she was listening, but her answer wasn't exactly what I wanted. "All the basic steps will be in the choreography for your recital number, so you'll learn them as we go."

"But a recital? I'm not interested in that. Will I have to pay extra for these costumes?"

At that, Sally tugged me even further from the other ladies. "Look, Grace. I hear you. Recital is kind of a big pain in the ass, but it's what the parents want. They need an end of the year parade of their children in shiny costumes to invite all the relatives to see. It validates how much money they spend on this activity each year. The moms want their own numbers to steal back a little of the attention lavished on the kids. It's a good time. I know you don't have a kid here and could care less about this, but you will learn how to dance. From what I see, you move well. Plus, you're the youngest person in this class. Maybe it'll motivate some younger people to join or some of our graduates to come back. I'd love a class of people in our age group. We could turn things up a notch."

"How old are you?" I dared to ask.

"I'm twenty-eight," she told me with a wink. "I'm just short."

The moms filed out of the classroom. Jan paused at the door. "Sally? Grace? Want to join us at Starbucks?"

Sally waved at her. "Not tonight."

I shook my head. Jan shrugged and joined the noisy ladies in the waiting room.

"The dance team rehearses for another hour, so a lot of the moms hang out together while they wait. Usually, it's coffee. During competition season when rehearsals run longer, they go grab adult drinks."

It felt nice to have been invited. Maybe one night I'd go with them. I doubted it, though. I didn't have much in common with a bunch of suburban moms—unless I could talk one of them into buying or selling a house.

I walked over to get my bag. Sally put the CDs we'd used in a box and moved toward the light switch. As I passed her at the door, she said, "Hey Grace. Don't quit the class. Give it a chance. I kind of like the idea of having a student in this class who is actually interested in learning technique." She put her lips together and let her eyes drift to the corner of the ceiling like she was thinking about something. "Yeah. It gives me some ideas of things to do with you." She leaned toward me and whispered. "To be honest, I'm usually about as motivated to teach this class as the three-year-olds. No. Less motivated. You, my friend, are giving me a challenge."

I liked her. Even if the class was dumb, and I had to flit around dressed as an iceberg, I would keep going simply because I thought Sally was a kick in the pants.

On Wednesday, I returned for jazz and tap. I came to every class after that. I never once went out with Jan and the moms. Occasionally, Sally would help me after class with some small things like the positioning of my feet and my *port-de-bras*, and then we'd go for a drink together afterward and gossip about the moms. We made plans for our younger adult class for the following season and got excited about it. I didn't love dancing at Razzle Dazzle, but I was certain I'd like it a lot more once we got past this dumb recital and I could move on to this better class.

*Present Day*

A man asks me to dance as soon as Tyler and I sit back at our table. I check with Tyler, and he nods that it's no problem. "I'd love to watch you show off."

I recognize the man who leads me to the floor as someone who's been to the club before. "Is your name Ralph?" I ask.

"Yeah. It's Grace, right? You're friends with Spencer?"

"Yes."

"Sweet. You okay with lifts?"

"Bring it on."

We do a full Lindy Hop routine. He leads well, the right pressure on the small of my back and hand to let me know where we are going. Ralph is much taller than Tyler, so the lifts have me flying. It's exhilarating. When that number comes to an end, another guy cuts in for a turn. And then another. My heart rate is through the roof. I'm having a blast.

Tyler has been asked to dance a couple times. He's a handsome man and looks the part, but I notice he's at the table more than on the floor. The girls here want an experienced dance partner, not a beginner. After my fifth dance, I glance over at him and see him swirling the remnants of his beer at the bottom of the glass. It's time to rejoin him.

"Bored?"

He acts affronted. "Are you kidding me? It's like a show. I'm enjoying the hell out of watching you dance like that. Don't stop on my account."

"You look lonely."

"Not lonely, Graceful. Envious. I want you in my arms, not

theirs." He puts a hand to his face. "I'm so sorry. I didn't mean that to come out that way. You know I mean dancing, right?"

The band gives him a break by easing into a slow dance. Some of the crowd groans, but the lead singer of the band tells them he has to play a slow one once in a while to make sure people are stopping to buy drinks. "It's how we all get paid, folks." Then he launches into "Blue Moon".

I put out my hand. "One more dance. No fancy steps required."

"Absolutely."

He takes my hand and we head out to a dance floor that is much emptier than it was a minute ago. I put my arms around his neck, and he wraps his around my waist. "You weren't kidding. You don't sweat."

"Nope. If it were brighter in here, you'd see how red my face is." I touch my forehead to his. "See? Hot."

As I pull away, he leans in and presses his cheek to mine, murmuring in my ear. "Very hot." A shiver runs through me as if to argue. "Don't look embarrassed. You're amazing. Not a lot of women at our age can say that they are better looking now than at nineteen, but you can. You absolutely can. Don't get me wrong. You were pretty then, but damn. You're fire now."

I look in his beautiful bright eyes that haven't dimmed one bit since our teen years. "Thank you."

"I'm thanking whatever divine providence has put me back in your presence after all this time."

"Yes, me too."

We dance silently to the remainder of the song. No twirls. Simply holding each other close, allowing the moment to exist. The final chords play, and I know that I don't want to dance with anyone else that night.

"Wanna leave?" I ask.

"Only if you're done dancing. Don't let me stop you."

*Oh, Tyler. You're starting me. I've been stopped for too long.*

"Let's go."

We grab our things and head out. Spencer is coming up the walk as we exit, dressed in cream linen pants and a violet rayon shirt with the top three buttons undone. He puts both of his hands up to stop me.

"No. No, Grace. I came all the way here to dance with you. Do not tell me you're leaving already."

I shake my head. "Sorry, pal." I introduce Spencer to Tyler. They shake hands, and Spencer definitely gives Tyler a good once over. Before Tyler can get uncomfortable or Spencer blurts out anything embarrassing, I interject. "Spencer is one of the instructors where I take ballet." I shake my head. "I don't know why I said *one of* the instructors. He basically runs the studio and teaches all the classes."

Spencer puts a finger to my lips to hush me and speaks directly to Tyler. "Don't let her downplay herself. Grace here is also an instructor. It's mostly the two of us, but we have some guests come in once in a while."

"You should have her teach swing," Tyler said. "She's amazing. I would pay money to see her dance a whole show."

"I know," Spencer agrees. "I keep telling her, but she's all, *I'm so olllllld*, all the time."

The two of them laugh while my face gets hot. I drift out of the lights at the front opening into the darkness of the parking lot so they won't notice.

Tyler puts a friendly hand out to Spencer. "Hey man, I don't mind waiting around a bit longer if you two want to dance together—"

"No, no. I'm giving her a hard time. You two go have fun. I have a room to conquer."

He winks at me and then turns with a flourish and heads into the club. Tyler joins me on the asphalt and takes my hand.

"I like him."

"Best person I know."

Tyler walks me to my car. Before I can dig my keys out of my purse, he gently twists me and presses my body against my car door. His hands slip into his pockets, as though he's keeping them locked up. Even though he's not touching me, every inch of him is so close I can feel the heat radiating off of him. Those blue eyes are focused on my lips.

"My ears are buzzing," I say.

"Mine too."

"Did you have fun?"

"Are you kidding?" His hands escape his pockets and tentatively settle on my waist. While we danced, his touches were firm. Necessary. This touch is intentional. Inviting. "It's still kind of early."

"Yes," I say, answering all the questions he's actually asking.

Quickly, I unlock my car and toss the rose and my saddle shoes inside. Without another word, Tyler leads me to his car and opens the door for me. I slip inside, enjoying the smell and feel of the soft leather seats. He gets in and starts the engine.

"I have a lot of great memories of being in a car with you." Tyler grins and checks his mirror before backing out of the space. I have no idea where he's planning to take me. "We're not far from Long Beach, are we? Do you ever go back there?" After putting the car in drive, his right hand stays on the shift in a position that allows his pinky finger to faintly touch my thigh.

"No, I don't." And I don't want to, if that's what he's getting at. Even though it scares me, I'd rather go to his condo than go back to Long Beach. This new Tyler is intriguing. Going there will bring up all my feelings about old Tyler. Nothing good will come of that. I think of an alternate. "I know a cozy bluff near here that overlooks the ocean. It's a nice night for that."

"Cozy? Sounds perfect. Guide me."

I direct him to Pacific Coast Highway and then tell him where to turn off so that we wind up at an empty neighborhood park. We pull into a spot in the parking lot, and he looks around. "I like the privacy, but I don't see any ocean."

"There's a little path between the shrubs over there that leads down to a cliff edge. Want to see?"

He's game, so we get out of the car. I take his hand and lead him. I'm crossing my fingers no one is using the spot. It isn't exactly a secret in this neighborhood anymore. The path that used to be hidden is now fairly wide. The break between the bushes is obvious where it used to be subtle, and the twigs don't catch on our clothes. I don't hear anyone, so I'm hopeful. Being fairly late on a weeknight is helpful for keeping the teenagers away.

We come out the other side, and I let go of his hands and do a small spin in triumph. Tyler chuckles, watching me instead of taking in the lovely expanse of ocean that has been revealed to us.

The spot is a small ledge with a giant boulder on it that has been tagged many times by visitors. It's terribly unsafe and should have been blocked off years ago by a fence to protect children playing in the park from plummeting over the edge. When I first found out about it while roaming about after helping a client in the neighborhood put his house up for sale, I thought the lack of safety was because no one knew about the ledge. Looking at it now, it's clear the place is no secret. Trash collects in the scrub— fast food remnants and cigarette butts mostly. A few beer bottles. I wish it were prettier, but the view can't be matched. The ocean waves roar below us and as far as we can see. Dots of light on the horizon mark ships and oil tankers. Rather regularly, a jet flies over, having departed from LAX.

"It's not the most romantic spot—" I start to say.

Tyler stops me with his lips. He pulls me into him and kisses me deeply. My body goes so limp in his arms, he could easily toss me over the cliff like a bundle of rags. He holds me tight, clearly having no intention of doing anything to get rid of me. His fingers circle into my hair, and when I pull back to breathe, his mouth moves to my chin and throat. His tongue finds my sharp collarbones and tickles them. I giggle out a "stop that".

"Grace," he murmurs as he kisses his way back up to my face. "Oh, Grace. I've been wanting to do this since the moment I saw you dancing in that empty living room."

His eyes meet mine, and I nod. So have I. Still, we have to slow down. Don't we? I shift my body around, so that he's holding me from behind, and I lean my head back on his shoulder. With his face pressed into the side of my head and his arms around my middle, I sigh. It's perfect. This moment is perfect.

"This is one of my spots where I go to think sometimes. I used to believe it was my secret, but as you see, it's been discovered by more than a few people."

"I like it. The view is breathtaking." I glance up at him, but he's not looking at the ocean.

I lead him to sit beside me on the boulder. He keeps an arm wrapped around my shoulder, toying with the strap of my dress, while we watch the surf below.

"So, that Spencer thinks you're something," he says.

"He's my best friend."

"How did you meet?"

"At the studio," I say simply.

Tyler leans over and nibbles on my shoulder as he says, "That's right. The dance studio. You still haven't told me exactly how all that came to pass. Last thing you told me was that you turned down a chance to become a professional swing dancer."

And I want to leave it at that. Still, I feel obliged to tell him something. "It took me a while to find ballet classes for adults. Everything was for kids or classes through a community college. I asked around a lot and was finally told about Dancer's Room. It was hard at first, but once I caught on, I got kind of addicted. I've been faithfully attending for twenty years. The only person who's been there longer than me is Debbie, the owner."

"You must be good friends with her."

"Oh, yeah," I say, hoping he doesn't catch the hesitancy in my response. "Yeah. We are."

The strap finally relents and dangles off my shoulder. Tyler runs his hand over my shoulder and up my neck until my face is nestled in his palm. Tenderly, he turns my face and leans in to kiss me again. I stop thinking about Debbie or the studio, or ballet, or just about anything.

*2003*

The night of the recital had arrived. We were using a local high school auditorium. Their dressing room area was miniscule, so

the Razzle Dazzle students were broken up into age groups and placed in classrooms down the hallway. Being that the mom class only had three dances, the least of any group besides the preschoolers, we were furthest down the hall. I thought it was humorous that we were in a French classroom. None of the other moms laughed when I pointed out the irony.

In their defense, they were busy. Not only did they have to take care of putting on their overdone makeup and organizing their costumes for the quick changes, but they had children to manage. The moms of the super young dancers were practically frantic, running back and forth down the hallway to fix their kids' hair and pin sequins in place. The moms of the teenagers were more relaxed, but their phones buzzed like crazy with things the teens needed. Kids everywhere forgot bobby pins, lipstick, mascara, hair nets, tights, and one kid forgot her tap shoes. That eleven-year-old borrowed mine. I've always had small feet despite my height. They were the wrong kind of tap shoes. Mine had heels, and she was used to flats. Intense whining and foot stamping occurred. I honestly thought that mom was going to slap her kid right there in front of everyone. We all kind of wanted her to. But she took a deep breath and won the Mother of the Night Award by talking her kid down and explaining how grown up she'd feel wearing adult tap shoes compared to everyone else. Ooh. The girl sauntered off like she'd been told she could drive a car and stay out late on a date. I was impressed.

I also barely got my shoes in time for our number because the girl forgot to bring them back for me. The mom and I had to go scrounging through her stuff for them.

On top of all that, the moms struggled to get out to the audience or to the wings backstage in time to watch their little monsters do their dances, where they'd clap madly and cry, "Go Baby!"

Panic. That was the word for the whole night. The recital ran on panic and adrenaline with a tiny bit of "thank God that number is over" relief.

I didn't put on enough makeup at home and didn't bring any with me. Jan pulled me aside and slapped a ton of rouge on my cheeks and blue eyeshadow on my eyelids. "You should have bought eyelashes for this," she complained at me, while digging through her makeup kit to find a bright red lipstick. "Wipe it with a tissue and toss it back in here when you're done."

Ew. How many people had used this thing?

When I finished making myself look like a tramp, I put on the fishnet tights and hot pink satin costume to complete the look for our jazz number "Steam Heat" from *The Pajama Game*. I headed out to the hall to wait for my turn and watch the crazy pageant of over-sexualized children go back and forth in organized chaos. Unexpected feelings of jealousy rose in me as I watched the young people walk around so comfortable in their skintight clothing. Not every girl in the studio was slender, but some had amazingly trim bodies. This was especially so for the thirteen and older dancers. I tried reasoning with myself, reminding myself that they were children who not only hadn't finished growing but had been dancing their whole lives. Their heartaches, weight gain, and metabolism slowdown were far ahead of them.

There wasn't a lot of time to sit. The show was made of a long string of three-minute routines, and the music never stopped. Time clipped by at a fast and even pace. Sally and the other instructors dashed back and forth, shouting out who needed to be "on deck" and who needed to line up in the hall. The fact that it all came together was a minor miracle.

At last, it was time for us to make our way to the stage for our final number—the ballet. We moved down the hallway in a titter. These white costumes were ice-skating costumes, in my opinion, and they did not look good on any of us. We all wore new, white ballet slippers. We'd only rehearsed in them once because we were told not to scuff them up. Mine were stiff, and I was angry that I couldn't get a good arch when I pointed my toes. Sally had worked hard with me on that skill. That and keeping my foot turned-out and not sickled inward.

We passed children who grew in age with each step. When I peeked into classrooms, I saw that some of the tiniest kiddos were asleep. The teenagers were closest to the stage, with some of the competition team changing backstage because they were on so often. Sally had us wait in the wings while the class before us finished their piece. It was a pretty lyrical number being done by the junior team, mostly middle school girls. That envy stirred again. Those flexible bodies. They all could kick so high and spin with such ease. What must that feel like?

Then I heard someone behind us trying to shush a group of girls from laughing.

"Stop it!" someone said, but that person was laughing, too.

"I can't. I mean, don't they look like a herd of polar bears? Stomp. Stomp. Stomp."

Someone else said, "No, wait. This is better." Then she changed to a ridiculous English accent and said "Iceberg, straight ahead!" in a pure imitation of a line from the movie *Titanic*. This girl knew which dance we were doing. Her friends giggled maniacally.

The music of the lyrical dance came to an end. By the time I craned my head around, the teens had covered their mouths and were trying to look innocent. Except their shoulders still bobbing gave them away. Beside me, Jan let out a slow, even breath. She bit her lip, probably getting lipstick all over her teeth. No time to fix it. Our pack was moving onstage. I looked back one more time and recognized one of the girls in that group to be Allie, Jan's daughter. I'd put money on it, she was the one who'd said the dig about us.

There was no time to confront Allie about how rude and ungrateful she was. We walked out and stood on our spots. A heartbeat later, the lights and music came on. Sally had told me not to worry about seeing the audience, and she was right. The lights were blinding. If there were people out there, I couldn't tell. I didn't remember lights being this bright when I'd done shows in high school. This was a little overboard. The intensity helped me remember to do my head positions correctly, because it kept my eyes away from the light grid.

At one point, we all faced each other in a circle of arabesques. Jan's cheeks sparkled. For a moment, I thought she had covered her face in glitter. Glitter had been everywhere on the younger girls. When we turned closer to each other, I saw that what I thought was makeup was tears. My face must've betrayed me, and she gave me a brave smile. The choreography forced me to move away from her before I could express anything else. Anger roiled up in me. I wanted to march offstage and punch that girl in the face. I wanted to tell all these spoiled girls what I thought of them and the way they took advantage of their mothers. I wanted to grab the microphone offstage and let this audience of indulging parents and grandparents know what ungrateful little bitches they were molding with these lessons and overblown recitals.

How many of them were going to go on to be professional dancers, anyway?

I didn't, obviously. That would ruin everything for everyone. All I could do was steam. I was so hot I was surprised my white outfit didn't catch fire. It felt like I could shoot flames out of my fingertips or propel off the floor like a rocket. If I'd ever felt angry like this before, I couldn't remember it.

The number came to an end, and we did this flitty ballet run we'd learned to exit stage right. This kept stage left open for the next group to come on. Allie's quartet. We moved as a group toward the stage door, but one woman lingered. Standing alone in the wings, Jan held her hands together, fingers to her nose and mouth, and watched her daughter dance. I went to her and tugged on her elbow.

"Come on," I said quietly. "Walk away. Don't honor her by watching her."

"She's a senior," Jan said. "This is it. This is the last time I'll get to see her do this."

I watched Allie and her friends for a moment. They were lithe and light on their toes. They moved in ways I couldn't imagine. So flexible. So clean. Slightly mesmerizing.

"Is she going to dance in college?"

"No. She wants to be a lawyer." Fresh tears rolled down Jan's face. "Can you believe it? I raised her right."

Had she?

"Are you going to keep dancing? Next year? In the mom's class?"

"Oh no. This was it for me. The mom's class is for, well, moms. You know?"

Jan never tore her eyes away from her child. She couldn't miss a moment. The seconds of her daughter's dancing life were ticking away.

"Right," I said, understanding. "Only for moms." It was okay. I'd never made an effort to be her friend. Why should I care about her feelings now? She clearly didn't care about mine.

I left her there to watch her perfect offspring and went to join the other moms in the hallway. We were supposed to stay in costume for the big finale and bows at the end. I stood there, waiting until Jan came out from the stage door to join us. Then I decided I was done. I turned heel and headed toward the classroom. I was zipping up my jeans when Sally rushed into the room.

"What are you doing? They told me you came in here. You have the finale to do."

"I'm skipping it. I think they can bow without me. I don't have anyone here watching me, anyway."

Sally paused in the doorway. "You didn't invite anyone?"

"Who was I going to invite?"

"I don't know. Your parents or something."

"No thank you," I sang. I tugged on my ankle-high boots.

"Well, you should have. You did a great job."

"Please."

"No, seriously, Grace," Sally said. "Your dancing in the ballet was the best I've seen you do. You were into it. I saw real promise. I'm excited about you coming back in the fall."

I shook my head. "I'm not coming back, Sally."

"Look, don't make that decision right now. Let's talk about it, okay? Next week? Call me?" She glanced down the hall and then back at me. "It's too late to get you changed again. I gotta run. Call me. I'm serious." With that, she ran off.

In the parking lot, I passed some grandparents hobbling out to their car muttering, "Why does it always have to be so damn loud?"

I snorted and got in my car, driving home to the noise of ringing in my ears.

A few days later, Sally called me. She tried hard to convince me to start this younger adult class with her, but when I wouldn't relent, she let it go. She told me if I was really interested in taking ballet to learn skill and technique but not have recitals, then I should go where the dance teachers go. It was a place in Hollywood, and it wouldn't be easy.

### *Present Day*

"Do you want to come over?" Tyler's hands are spread around my ribcage so that his thumbs gently caress the outer curves of my breasts.

"I shouldn't leave my car where it is. It'll get broken into or stolen or—"

"We can go get it, and you can follow me." I hesitate, and he kisses me again. "I don't want this night to end yet."

I don't want it to end either. But I know that as soon as I get in my car I will come to my senses. I'll do the responsible thing. I'll head home. I think he senses this.

"Graceful. I'll do whatever you want. If you need things to go slower, I'll do that. I'm afraid to let you go again."

Let me go again? He never let me go. He left.

Reality rushes back at me like a tidal wave. "I should head home. I do have to work tomorrow. I imagine you have filming in the morning."

"I do, but—"

I give him a quick kiss. A friendly one. "We'll see each other again. Soon."

He nods reluctantly. His hands drift around to my back until I'm being held in his comforting embrace. He presses his lips and nose to my forehead and holds me like this for a long tender moment. "I care about you, Graceful. I've thought about you over the years. The one that got away, you know? Seeing you again now? It's crazy. You're astonishing."

*The one that got away.* Real or bullshit?

I need to go home.

Without responding, I take his hand and lead him back up through the bushes and across the playground. We settle in his car, and he leans across to kiss me again. It stirs me, and everything in me wants to give in and go with it. I don't. I slowly pull away and sit back in my seat. Tyler starts the car. Aside from directions, we don't talk. Small talk seems awkward now.

Rusty's is closed and dark when we get back. My car is the only one in the lot. When Tyler stops the car, he moves as if to jump out, full of chivalry.

"It's okay. I got it," I say, unlatching the door.

Tyler reaches out and grabs my hand before I exit. "Grace. Is everything okay? Did I say something wrong?"

I smile, hoping the tear that's forming in the corner of my eye won't fall and reveal itself. "Tonight was wonderful, Tyler. Thank you."

"Don't say it like it's a goodbye."

"It's not. I promise it's not." He tightens his grip on my hand, and a genuine smile crosses my lips. "I promise."

"Okay." He lets go. "Call me."

I get out of the car, but I hesitate before closing the door and walking away. I need to know something. I duck back into the car, one knee on the seat for balance. "Tyler, I was wondering…"

"What is it?"

"Did you really like watching me dance tonight?"

He drops his jaw incredulously and puts his hands up to emphasize him saying, "Are you kidding me? You were amazing to watch. I've already said it, but I'll say it twenty more times if you need a confidence boost."

"I don't need a…" I run my hand through my hair. This position of my body is awkward. Should I sit back down? "I'm not asking how well I did. I guess what I'm asking is how it made you feel. Watching me dance while you stood aside."

"Like, was I jealous of the other guys? Sure, a little. I hated that I didn't know enough yet to be on your level. Then I could dance with you myself. We'd dazzle the hell out of everyone, wouldn't we? Look at those old folks go!" He laughed. I only smiled, and only a little. His laughter halted.

"So, you weren't jealous that I was getting the attention. You were jealous that you weren't the one dancing and also getting attention. Sounds about right." I bow my head to get all the way out of his car. I'm about to close the door when he shouts.

"Graceful, wait!"

I shut the door anyway.

He launches out of his side of the car and bounds toward me before I can finish the two steps to mine. "Grace. Wait. What do you mean? I thought we were having a good time. What happened? What did I say?"

Sighing, I face him. "It's nothing, Tyler. Old wounds."

"That I caused?"

He seems so innocent about it all. Does he not realize how much he hurt me?

I roll a pebble back and forth with the toe of my shoe.

"I used to watch you perform with this crazy combination of pride and jealousy. It tore me up inside, and I didn't know what to do with the feelings. I thought you were my boyfriend, or at least someone I was dating." I stop for a second to check his expression. He's showing nothing but concern. No validation. I look back at the ground. "I was proud of it. That's *my* guy wowing everyone, I used to think. But then you'd get swept away by the crowd, whether it was the kids at school or the people out there in Arizona. They all claimed you, and you seemed to prefer their attention to mine. Always. Every time. It was always about you."

Sounds of the city fill the silence between us. Cars drive by. A horn honks. A plane flies overhead. I'm about to apologize and leave, when he clears his throat.

"I'm sorry. I… I didn't know you felt like that. I always liked you, Grace. I thought you were special, but I didn't think we were officially a couple. It never seemed to work out."

"Because you were too busy and not around."

Tyler nods reluctantly. "I feel like a jerk."

"Not now," I clarify. "You were a jerk in 1992. In fairness, you couldn't help it. You were a star."

Tyler steps closer and lifts my chin with his fingers. "And tonight was supposed to be your turn."

I nod, then immediately shake my head. "No. I wanted to have fun. Not show off."

"You *totally* wanted to show off." He grins at me.

I can't help it. I grin, too. "Yes. A little bit."

"You shined, Grace. You did. I can't express how impressed I am with your dancing. It astounds me that you're not a professional dancer." He's kept his fingers on my chin this whole time. He leans toward me. "Let me be clear about this, okay? I did not want to dance better to draw attention from anyone but you. The room could have been empty for all I cared. I want to be what you need. That's all. I swear." He puts a hand over his heart.

"Okay, okay. I believe you."

He pulls me into his arms for a warm, genuine hug. After a moment, he says, "You're still a puzzle to me, Graceful. I can't get my head around why you take dance classes but never plan to perform. What's that about? Pardon me for saying this, but it seems like such a waste of time."

I shimmy out of his arms. It's not the first time I've been asked this, and it won't be the last. I've got this answer memorized. "Not everyone who goes to the gym is planning to become a professional weightlifter. Not everyone who jogs is planning to win a marathon. Not everyone who plays tennis is going to Wimbledon. I could go on." I have before.

"Got it. Do you even do community theatre or anything like that?"

"Nope." The expression he's making is both insulting and hilarious. He's so baffled by all of this, and I try hard to dismiss the waves of judgement coming from him. "You should see your face right now."

Like we're back in Acting 101, he physically wipes his face back to neutral. "I'm sorry. I don't mean anything by it. I've never met anyone like you. Everyone I know is dead-set on making a buck with their talent. I've lived my whole life this way."

"I don't know what to tell you. I like dancing. That's all there is to it." He opens his mouth like he's about to give me another argument, but I don't allow it. "Think of it this way. I'm like the end of the movie."

"The end of what movie?"

"You know how in the movies there's always this person who wishes they were super successful, and then they get everything they thought they ever wanted. The fame, the money. All of it. Time passes, and they realize it's not enough and long for the simple life when they did art for art's sake. When there were no pressures or fake people. They give it all up and go back to being ordinary." I flash him my coyest smile. "I just skipped all the fame, fortune, and chaos part and went straight to the ending where I dance for the fun of it."

Tyler runs his hands over my hair and then cradles the back of my head. "The end of the movie, huh? There's one thing missing from your plotline, you know that?"

"What?"

"A romantic interest." He kisses me. My fingers tremble as they find his waist and pull him closer. We stay like this, enjoying each other's warmth, hands, and lips until someone shouts at us. We break apart to see a man shaking his head as he rolls up the window of a car that has pulled out from behind Rusty's. Probably the owner, maybe Rusty himself, finished with counting his receipts for the night. We pull apart, smiling goofily at each other.

"I guess we should go before we get in trouble for loitering," I whisper.

"I'm willing to risk jail-time."

With promises to see each other again soon, we finally say goodnight. Tyler holds my hand until I'm sitting in my driver's seat. I close the door, and he waits until I've started the engine and backed out of my spot before getting into his own car. This is not the same Tyler I used to know. I want desperately to believe that he won't break my heart again.

# CHAPTER
## Seven

It takes me a while to understand what I'm feeling, and I come to the conclusion it's anger. I didn't feel it right away. I buzzed all the way home from Tyler's kisses and charming demeanor. He'd managed to erase thirty years of my life and turn me back into a lovesick schoolgirl. By the time I got home, he'd already texted three times to thank me for a wonderful evening with lots of red hearts after each note. When I got up to my apartment, I texted back some cute, pithy responses of my own and a selfie that he requested. As much as I wanted a picture of him in return, I was kind of glad he didn't send one. If we'd had cell phones back in the day, we'd both have been stupid with selfies.

By the time I got my makeup off and my nightshirt on, the bubbly feelings began to pop. Doubt, my old grumpy friend, slides into bed with me and keeps me from sleeping. Tyler is a rare catch. He's handsome and fit for his age. He's a television star. He could have girls much younger than me, if he wanted, and probably has.

I should have gone home with him. We're adults. We don't have to wait. It's not like we're teenagers reserving our virginity for that special moment. What was I holding out for? Some kind of validation that I wouldn't get used and tossed aside? That's such old-fashioned thinking.

If I'd gone over there, we'd have made love, and maybe we'd

have declared that we were officially a couple. Now, I'm in that same in-between as we used to be back in school. I know he likes me, but...

Toss. Turn. Don't think about the way it was when we were kids. It doesn't matter. We're different now. He's different now. Making him wait is good. It'll make him try harder to impress me. At least I hope so.

Unless my lack of drive turns him off. He's impressed by my dancing ability, but he's disappointed in my life choices. I don't want to be thought of as unmotivated. It took a lot of drive to keep going to those classes all this time. They're damn hard. I bet he couldn't do them. I'd like to see him try.

Stop. Settle. He hasn't said anything discouraging to me. I've gotten that same reaction from people for years, since the day I started taking classes. I'm used to it. It doesn't hurt. Well, maybe it still stings a little bit.

I rise for work in the morning, shower off my frustration, and let my first cup of coffee soothe my nerves. Tyler texts me a good morning with a photo of the beach. He's on set already. It's a pretty day outside, and I respond that I'd rather be where he is. I head out to my ordinary car, and drive to my office to do an ordinary day's work while my potential boyfriend films a TV show.

Doubt sits in the passenger seat, grumbling in my ear about the traffic and other things that hold up my life.

### 2003

In all the time I'd lived in Los Angeles County, I never had much reason to go to Hollywood. Most of my dad's real estate properties were in our area and further east like Rosemead, Arcadia, and even Pasadena. I felt like a tourist, using my Thomas Guide map book to help me find my way to Highland and Melrose. I missed the address several times because it wasn't posted prominently anywhere. Turning around wasn't the easiest thing. My nerves had my bladder about to burst, and I was terrified I was going to be late. At five minutes to the hour, I nearly gave up. I was going to stop at the nearest Burger King, relieve myself, get a shake and some fries and head home. This was a stupid idea anyway.

Then I saw it. Sally described it well. A two-story commercial property that had been painted a drab olive green back in the 1970s and was never updated. It had its own parking lot but not many spaces. A lawyer, a place that printed headshots for actors in town, and an optometrist with one usable door and one that was blocked made up the ground floor. In the middle was a navy-blue awning over a glass door. That was the entrance to the dance studio which was on the second floor. I parked, gathered my dance bag and what remained of my courage, and headed through that door.

Immediately inside to the right were a row of brass mailboxes on the wall for each business and a unisex bathroom I was more than grateful to find and utilize. I was also pleased that someone kept it stocked with lavender-scented soap. Strains of "At the Ballet" from *A Chorus Line* flitted through my head as I climbed *up the steep and narrow stairway* that filled the left side of the foyer. Up top, the only choices were to go right, down a hallway where I'd find a closed office door and a dead-end wall, or to go immediately left through the open door to the brightly lit dance studio.

Or to go back down the stairs to the safety of my car.

"Are you here for class?" a voice asked. "We're about to start, so come in if you're joining us. Debbie doesn't like people coming in late."

The woman asking me was so thin she seemed like she could simply fade away at any moment. Past her shoulder, I saw that the entire class was made up of stick-like women. There were nine of them, and not one of them had an extra ounce of fat. Everything was so different than what I was used to. The dancers stretched, doing splits or putting their upper bodies flat to the floor between wide open legs. I didn't have time to join in the stretching. My flexibility had been better than all the moms in my other class, but I'd look like a humpback here. The half year of dancing at Razzle Dazzle hadn't done much to help me lose any weight, and I felt like a blob.

"This is Ballet 1, right?" I checked.

"That's right. You can put your stuff over there." She backed up a few paces to give me a wider entrance to the room. Dance bags and outerwear lined the floor against the side wall. Floor to ceiling mirrors covered both the front and back walls, with barres attached. An upright piano was in the front corner, a man seated at it and tinkling with a tune. Next to him stood a woman in a black elbow-length leotard cut so low on her back I wasn't sure how it didn't fall right off her shoulders. Each vertebra of her spine was visible. Long legs in light pink tights poked out beneath a sheer black dance skirt. She flipped through pages of a music book until she found a piece she wanted and handed it to him. Sharply, she turned to face the class, and all the students dashed to the barres, placing themselves at equal distances from each other.

"There's a spot here," the girl who'd spoken to me at the door said. She was at the barre at the back of the room and indicated that I could fit between her and the wall. I kicked off my sneakers and slipped my ballet shoes on. I wore my pink ones, not those awful white ones we got for the recital. They were more worn in but didn't look nearly as used and abused as the ballet slippers of the other dancers. Some of theirs had holes in them.

When I got to my spot, the girl whispered to me. "Your ties are out."

"What?"

"Your ties," she repeated. "Tuck them in."

I ran my fingers over my shoulders to see if my bra straps were sticking out of my leotard.

"No," she said. "Your shoes. Hurry. Before she's sees."

I looked down at my ballet shoes. They looked the way they usually did with the bow that tightens them right in the front. Was this wrong? Quickly, I glanced back at her scuffed slippers. No bow. The strings were tucked inside. Behind her, the other two girls also had their laces tucked. Was this a thing? None of the dancers in the mom's class tucked their ties. Some of them even put beads on them to give them a little bling.

The pianist started playing a soft classical piece of music. I didn't know what famous composer had written it. I knew nothing about classical music. As fast as I could, I took my shoes off and put them back on with the ties nestled up against my toes.

"You might want to either pull those leg warmers up or chuck them," my helpful dancing friend suggested. "Debbie doesn't allow any loose-fit clothing in her classes."

Once more I looked around to see what everyone else was doing or wearing. None wore bright colored leotards. No bike shorts or parachute pants. No skirts, except for Debbie, who was older than everyone else. At least, she looked older than everyone else, including me. The dancers mostly wore black, but I saw some brown and maroon leotards, too. Tights were black, white, nude or pink, but every pair of legs sported runs and several dancers had cut their tights off at the ankles and wore their ballet slippers over bare feet. One girl wore her black tights over her leotard. Two girls wore leg warmers stretched from ankle to thigh. I saw that one girl wore a tight cotton camisole with dance trunks and no tights at all. She could get away with it, though, because her legs were nothing but muscle. I'd never seen such toned legs in my whole life.

I tossed my floppy leg warmers toward my bag. They were loose and would never stay up. I only wore them for looks anyway, never knowing their purpose exactly. They were also aqua-blue, matching the swirls on my hot pink leotard, so they stood out. It had been one of my most complimented outfits at Razzle Dazzle. Now I felt like a clown.

Debbie had been fixing her bun with a few extra pins, so she hadn't noticed all my fumbling about, thank goodness. She put a hand out to the piano player, making him stop. She twirled a finger, and he started over.

"First position!"

All the dancers snapped into place. No introduction or "welcome to the class." Debbie was about as warm as a popsicle. I hated being at the end of the line with all the dancers behind me.

I couldn't see what anyone was doing without moving my head. Directions were shouted, and when I tried to look around, Debbie snapped, "Heads forward." Thankfully, I knew how to do *plies*, *tendus*, *dégagé*s, and *battements*. Sally had taught me the positions for feet and hands and helped me make them look good in our after-class sessions. I thought I was following along pretty well until we turned in the opposite direction. That's when I saw how deep the dancers could go in a *grande plie* without falling and how high they could kick on a *battement*. My legs weren't that flexible or strong.

Debbie had us face the other way again and directed us to do *ron de jammes*. I had no idea was that was, and she wasn't demonstrating up front. She wasn't dancing at all. Debbie paced back and forth in the center of the room.

I craned my neck around to look at my helpful friend. Her eyes went wide, and she nodded for me to face front. I did before Debbie barked at me again. I tried watching the dancers on the far side of the room through the corner of my eye. It was some kind of kick with a twirl of the leg and then another kick. I couldn't figure it out. We turned around, and my left leg wasn't cooperating with the step at all. I looked like a clod.

Our barre exercises hadn't used up much of Sally's class time. She liked to get through that quickly and get on with her choreography for the recital. That's what the moms enjoyed the most. In this class, the barre exercises went on for what seemed like forever. Each round of steps harder than before, topped by a pattern of arm movements called a *port de bras*. It felt pretty to do. I didn't dare look at myself to see that I was not doing it prettily at all compared to the others.

I thought it would never end, but the pianist played a flourish bringing that repetitive piece to an end. My muscles throbbed already. I had no idea how far we were into the class because there wasn't a clock anywhere.

We were directed to find a place on the floor. Debbie never seemed to smile. Sally wasn't a big smiler during our classes because she didn't like the moms. Debbie seemed liked she didn't like ballet; she was that sour-faced about it. She rarely corrected anyone's form. She might tell someone to lift higher or straighten out, but she wasn't mean to anyone. Just firm. Just precise.

All of the dancers skipped over to their dance bags and swiftly tied on their toe shoes.

"I'm waiting," Debbie said.

My grip on the ballet barre was so tight, I wondered if I took a step forward if I'd take the whole mirror with me. Toe shoes?

I leaned toward the dancer who had been kind to me so far. "I thought this was Ballet 1. Beginning."

The girl looked up at me, eyes full of pity. "Oh honey, Dancer's Room doesn't have a beginner class. I thought that might be the problem. Ballet 1 is the class that people take when they're a little rusty and want to tighten up some skills. Ballet 2 is for ballet dancers who are regularly working and are looking to be challenged." She grimaced. "This might not be a great fit for you."

"Let's go, ladies," Debbie shouted, her gazed fixed on us.

The dancer stood and dug her toes into a box of rosin and then found a spot on the floor. I stood as far back as I possibly could, hoping to be mostly hidden by the others. I still stood out like a plump flamingo in the middle of a flock of swans. I hadn't even thought to put my hair up in a bun. It was in a ponytail dangling down my back.

Debbie again directed us into a combination of movements by using dance terms and not showing us a single step. The dancers around me knew exactly what to do and floated about beautifully. Next, they worked on their *pirouettes*. Everyone easily landed triples. I kept falling out of a single. When they moved on to working on *tours jetes*, a lump formed in my throat. It was everything I could do not to start crying in front of everyone. I'd seen some of the girls on dance team at Razzle Dazzle do these, but they certainly hadn't taught them in the mom's class. I tried, but eventually I was so turned around and frustrated, I couldn't take it any longer. I dashed over to grab my stuff and ran out of the room. As I stumbled down the stairs, I heard the music stop and the dancers all murmuring to each other.

I was almost out the door when Debbie appeared at the top step. "Where are you going?"

"I'm sorry," I said, wiping my face with the back of my hand. "This was a mistake. I'm sorry I bothered you."

She shook her head like she had not been bothered at all. "I would like you to stay and finish."

"I can't. I don't know what I'm doing."

"I'm aware of that, but there's only one way to learn." She beckoned me with her hand, and that's when I noticed the knobbiness of her fingers. Her knuckles were swollen, and her fingers didn't line up straight. Something was wrong with her hands. "Come along. You're holding up my class."

I shook my head. "It's embarrassing."

"If you don't finish this class today, you will never dance again."

I don't know how she knew that, but she was right. I felt it in the depth of my soul. I refused to go back to stupid Razzle Dazzle. I didn't know if there was an in-between option between there and here, but I was so mortified at my lack of skill that I doubted I would ever get brave enough to try another class elsewhere.

Why did it matter, though? I was thirty years old. I didn't need to take dance classes. I was fine being a normal person who could exercise at a gym. It's not like I was planning to be a professional dancer. Most dancers start planning what they're going to do after their dance career at my age. That was evident by the median age of those girls upstairs in the classroom. If any of them were over twenty-six, I'd be surprised.

Debbie called into the room, "Ellie, lead the class in some across-the-floor movements. The usual stuff, but make sure everyone is staying light on their feet. I do not want to hear a herd of elephants stomping around in there. Jake, do the Rossini piece I pulled." She looked at me again. "Come with me."

I climbed back up the stairs, each step feeling impossibly tall to my sore legs, and followed her to her office. She flicked the overhead light on as we entered, but the room stayed a soft amber. Pretty orange and red shawls covered the florescent lights in the ceiling. Wood paneling, probably left over from the seventies, covered the walls. Two tall, mismatched metal filing cabinets were in the far corner, a dark wooden bookshelf opposite them. Linoleum checker squares made up the floor with a light blue shag carpet covering most of it. Debbie sat behind a desk that I noted didn't have a computer on it and leaned back in her faux leather office chair. I sat stiffly in one of the two hard, black plastic chairs on the far side of her. Behind her, a large window with open blue shades faced the alley at the back of the building. The sun had set since I had arrived, and the only light coming through the window was from distant streetlamps. Still, it was enough to highlight the loose strands of her blonde hair and make her glow.

"I'm Debbie White." She didn't offer to shake my hand. Instead, she put her hands in her lap where I couldn't see them. "You called last week about classes? Grace, right?"

"Yes, Grace Fuller."

There was a briefest of sparks in one of her green eyes and a twitch in the corner of her lip, and then it faded. Not everyone heard the joke that was my name, but she did. "Why are you here?"

"I was taking a class at more of a family-oriented studio, and my teacher told me—"

"Yes, yes. You explained that on the phone. I'll speak to Sally another time to remind her of qualifications." She took a breath and let that thought go. "What I want to know is why you're here."

"To learn ballet."

As with everyone who'd asked me this over the past half year, that answer didn't satisfy.

"Do you have a show coming up? An audition?"

"No. All I want is to learn how to do ballet. I've always wanted to but have never done it. Maybe it's a bucket list thing, I don't know. I wanted to give it a try before I get too old."

This time, the corner of her mouth slid all the way up. "Oh, you're already too old. I don't want you to be disillusioned."

"I'm not under any illusion. I promise you, I'm not. That's why I was leaving. I don't belong here. I realize that."

Debbie didn't respond. She didn't try to make me feel any better. I couldn't tell if she was nice, but she definitely wasn't fake. After staring at me for a moment and then making some silent decision, Debbie pulled a notepad toward her and grabbed a pen from a mug with a Degas painting on it. In beautiful handwriting, she jotted out a name and a phone number on the pad. She tore the page off and handed it to me with an explanation.

"First, we need to get you outfitted correctly. Call Angelica at this number, she's got a dance supply shop here in Hollywood. She only works by appointment. Your slippers are fine, but you'll need everything else and a pair of pointe shoes."

"pointe shoes?" I balked. "I'm not ready for that."

"No, you're not, but you will be sooner than you think. If you practice, that is." She winked at me. "There's no reason to pursue this dream of yours if you're not going to do it full out."

Was she making fun of me? It was hard to tell if she was pulling my leg or not. I folded up the paper and put it in the side pocket of my dance bag.

Debbie strode over to a bookshelf. She pulled out a VHS tape and then knelt down to thumb through some record albums on the bottom shelf. She glanced over at me. "Do you have a record player?" I shook my head. "Who does anymore?" she said, pushing the records back in place.

She came back to me and placed the VHS on the desk in front of me and tapped it. Her nails were manicured with a pretty shade of lavender. I wondered why someone with such gnarled fingers took the time to get manicures. Did it somehow help her pretend her hands weren't so ugly?

"Practice with this at home. It's not ideal, but it has a lot of basic instruction to give you better foundation." The title on the cardboard case read *Learn Ballet at Home* and had a picture of a beautiful woman around our age in a shiny yellow spaghetti-strapped leotard and attached skirt, holding on to the back of a kitchen chair with one hand, while she held a tight *sous sous* up on her toes with her other hand in fifth position over her head.

Her chestnut hair was full around her face and shoulders. She wore white ballet slippers, not toe shoes, with yellow leg warmers around her ankles that matched her costume. A counter and sink were slightly out-of-focus behind her.

I turned the case over and read the quick description that it was a tape for ballet enthusiasts who would like to learn how to do the elegant form of dance themselves. *Tone your muscles through beautiful movement* the ad copy declared.

Debbie leaned back on the desk in front of me and nodded like she knew how silly it seemed. "That's Stephanie. She's a friend of mine from our Rockettes days. She was trying to get in on the crazy video fitness craze. I'm in the video. A little younger then. We did this back in '89." She laughed at the memory while I wrapped my mind around the fact that this woman used to be a Rockette. "When you get past the outfits and music choices, it's a pretty good tape. It'll help you learn the names of steps and the correct way to do them—if you have any room in your home to do it. Do you?"

"I can move some stuff around."

"Oh, and you'll need this." She practically did a *grande jete* leap back to the shelf to grab a spiral-bound book and brought it back to me.

"A cookbook?" I asked.

Debbie shrugged. "I know you don't want to do this professionally, but if you don't want the other dancers to keep giving you the side-eye, you'll want to lose a couple pounds. Your weight is a bigger tip-off than your attire that you're a novice." She put the VHS and the book together in my lap. "It has a perfect diet plan and recipes."

I didn't think the other dancers were giving me the side-eye. Were they? The one dancer near me had been quite nice and helpful. Was she protecting me as much as possible from the scorn of the others?

"This is very nice of you, Debbie," I said, scooting my chair back so I could stand up. "I'm not sure why you're offering to help me when you know I'll never be able to dance at the level of your other students. I don't want to embarrass myself."

She crossed her arms, still leaning back on the edge of her desk. "I run a business here. I don't have one without students. You want to dance? You want to pay for classes? This is some kind of personal goal for you? Fine. Use these tools I'm giving you and get yourself on a level that I can work with. Ballet isn't fun. It's not like taking an aerobics class where you show up and jump around in your fashionable dancewear. We won't be outfitting you in sparkly costumes and doing a recital like your last studio. Ballet is an artform. It's a discipline. If you want to get even close to what my weakest student can do here, then you need to practice diligently, and you need to come to class regularly. Tough out the stares and questioning eyes and focus on what it is that you want to do. Children take ballet to be pretty. Adults take ballet class to be indomitable."

Laughter and chatter filled the corridor and stairwell. Class had come to an end, and the students were heading out. I turned my head toward the sound.

"Can I count on you to be back?" Debbie asked.

I nodded weakly. I had my doubts I'd ever see this place again.

Debbie put out her hand. "It'll be fifteen dollars for today's class. If you pay fifty up front it guarantees you four classes, saving two-fifty a class. I recommend doing that because when people pay ahead, they're less likely to skip." She raised her eyebrows at me.

I got out my checkbook and began filling it out. Before I wrote the amount, Debbie pointed at the price line and said, "That'll be fifty plus ten for rental of the materials." I wrote the check for sixty. She traded me the book and VHS for the check. "I'll see you next week. Be early. Students are required to stretch before class starts, and I don't let anyone in past two minutes late."

"Gotcha. Thank you."

I couldn't stand another moment with her. I might have been intimidated out of sixty bucks for classes I'd never take, but with a polite smile and nod, I left the room. As I passed the studio, I saw Jake the pianist gathering up his music books in a pile while talking to the nice dancer. She turned in time to catch sight of me before I walked past.

"Hey!" she shouted.

I paused in the doorway. "Hi. Um. Thanks for helping me earlier."

"Not a problem." She made her way across the room to me, still in her toe shoes that gave her a bit of a duck walk. "I'm Ellie. Are you going to come back?" She held on to that last word as she fished for my name.

"Grace. I'm Grace." I showed her the stuff Debbie gave me. "And yeah, I guess so."

"I hope so," she said. "You did well for a beginner. Don't give up too easy, okay?"

Her voice was as light as her step, like she was used to talking to young people. "Are you a teacher here?" I asked her.

"No, I help out sometimes. I teach dance at a school in Santa Monica. Kids."

That explained it. She was another Sally.

"I also dance with a troupe in West L.A., mostly modern but some classical. We have a show coming up if you want to see it." She went over to her bag and dug out a green flier. "We're good, I promise."

"They are excellent," Debbie said over my shoulder. "I recommend them. You'd learn a lot by watching some professional dancers."

"I'll be there," I said, smiling at both of them before heading down the stairs.

Debbie went into the studio. Neither of them followed me or pursued any further conversation, thank goodness. By the time I made it outside, there were only two dancers left, and they were smoking and talking next to a car on the far side of the lot. Easy to avoid. I flung my stuff into the passenger seat, started the engine, and turned up the radio to some loud alternative rock. I got in line for the drive-through at In and Out. As I waited for my turn, my eyes drifted to the seat beside me. *Learn Ballet at Home* was right on top, spiting me. Daring me.

144

Was I going to be a quitter again? Was I going to be like that my whole life?

The car in front of me moved, and it was my turn to pull up and order a burger, fries and shake. I froze. The person behind me honked. No. I wasn't going to do this. I wasn't going to let Debbie steal my money.

I pulled out of the line and drove home. After some quick rearranging of the furniture in my apartment, I stuck that tape in my VCR and hit play.

"Are you ready to dance?" Stephanie asked with a voice bright enough to match her yellow leotard and attached nylon skirt. The camera pulled back to reveal what was clearly a ballet studio decorated to look like an over-large kitchen. Sure enough, a much younger Debbie and another dancer, both in neon colors and big eighties hairdos, stood at angles to Stephanie. "Great! Let's start with first position."

**Present Day**

I beg out of teaching the Friday lyrical class. Spencer isn't too surprised and says he'd been planning to teach it himself anyway. When I don't show for our Saturday morning core strengthening class or our Sunday evening jazz workshop with a special choreographer visiting from San Francisco, I finally tip Spencer's curiosity into high gear. I'm sitting on my sofa with two pieces of pizza growing cold on a paper plate next to an empty bottle of merlot on the coffee table, staring at the fifth episode in a row that I've binged of NCIS, when I hear a knock at my door.

I've turned off my phone to avoid Spencer and Tyler, so it shouldn't surprise me that someone's come looking for me. Still, at my Hollywood fortress, any visitor has to go through Ralph the doorman to get buzzed into the building. That is not supposed to happen without me leaving notice or Ralph calling up to get my approval. I wonder if it's a neighbor needing milk or sugar or something.

"Just a second," I say, wrapping my throw blanket around my shoulders to cover my thin pajamas.

"Oh, don't get all dressed up for me, honey," rings Spencer's voice from the hallway. "I know you probably look like death."

My shoulders drop. Of course, Ralph would let Spencer up. He's seen Spencer hundreds of times. Why wouldn't he be welcome? I'll have to have a chat with Ralph about assumptions.

I open the door and Spencer immediately touches my forehead with the back of his hand. "Are you sick? Is it the flu? I don't want to catch anything."

"Then you shouldn't have come," I say. "Hello, by the way."

"You're not hot." He gives me a once over and sneers. "And I mean that more ways than one. Let me in." He says this as he pushes past me. I close the door and turn around to find him putting a couple of bags of take-out from Sweetgreen on my counter. He pushes the pizza box to the side. "Pizza? I'm disappointed."

"I need comfort food."

He notes the uneaten slices on the table and the empty wine bottle. "You're getting comfort from something, anyway. Here, have a salad." He squeezes some dressing into a plastic container of salad, shakes it and hands it to me.

I take it and sit down at the kitchen table. He joins me with his own salad and two water bottles. He passes one to me and says, "Hydrate. Water fixes all things. Now, are you actually sick?"

I shake my head. He sits back in his chair and frowns as he looks me over. "I apologize for not calling you Thursday night to see how things went with Mr. Hotshot, but you two looked eager to leave Rusty's, and I figured you'd be having a late night together. I also figured you'd call me back by now. So, what happened? Was it a bust?"

"It went great. We had a wonderful time."

"This is not how people look when they've had a wonderful time with a new lover." He puts a forkful of salad in his mouth.

"I like him, I do," I tell Spencer. "I'm not sure I'm ready for someone like him. He's so driven. It's a lot."

"You're driven," Spencer says. "It's why I'm here. You missed three classes. In a row. Normal for everyone else at our drop-in studio, not normal for our superstar. I think even the building misses you when you don't show up. Everything creaks and groans more."

I'm instantly sad that I've been ignoring my best friend and enormously grateful he's clever enough to know that I need him, anyway. I pick at the salad with my plastic fork. It'd probably taste delicious after nothing but Lean Cuisines for the past several days, but all that dark green spinach looks like poison to me.

"Maybe it's a good thing, me not going to the studio all the time. It's too much. The young girls, they probably laugh about me behind my back because I'm relentlessly there. Or that I dance at all. I'm too old. Everyone knows I'm too old for all this."

"Oh, is this happening now?" Spencer gets up and grabs the remote to turn off the TV. "Is today the day you finally quit? Twenty-odd years of dancing and today is the day you finally prove Debbie right, that you're not good enough."

I push the salad away and plop my arms on the table in front of me. "This isn't much of a pep talk, Spence."

He sits on the arm of my gray sofa. "Who says I'm giving you one? You *are* too old. That's a fact. You were too old when you started. How many times have we both heard Debbie rant about that at you? So, what changed all of a sudden? Some new aches and pains? I've got some Tiger Balm in the car."

"Why are you being such a shit?"

He shrugs. "Why are you being a wimp?"

I've changed my mind about being glad he showed up. I stand up and open the door for him, gesturing for him to leave. He doesn't budge. All he does is smirk at me until I close the door again. Without a word, I walk around the far end of the sofa and then plop onto the cushions and pull a loose pillow over me. Spencer shifts around to face me. He's wearing his favorite kelly green skinny jeans with a tight black, short-sleeve button-down shirt that shows off the muscles in his chest and upper arms. He kicks off his Toms and puts his bare feet on the sofa.

"Are you done?" he asks.

"Why are you here?"

"To make sure you're not sick or dead. It's not like you'd call anyone for help."

"I'm fine."

He raises an eyebrow. "I'm sure you are. Now tell me all about why you're not dancing anymore. Was swing dancing at Rusty's your last hurrah? Did you embarrass yourself in front of the new beau?" He leans over his knees. "Did he get jealous of you dancing with other guys? Is he like that? Are you giving up the thing you love to keep your man? So last century of you."

"You're annoying."

He fans his face dramatically. "I take that as a compliment. Now spill."

With a huff, I tell him how great the night went and how it ended.

"Sounds promising, but I don't get how it leads to this." He gestures at me. "Have you even showered?"

"Stop it, Spencer. I'm serious."

"Fine." He slides down to the couch and wraps me under his arm. "Tell me."

"There's no reason for me to keep dancing. I'm tired of answering all the questions. I'm tired of the looks I get. I'm tired of defending myself. I can get the same exercise from yoga or Pilates. I was thinking of a Tai Chi class—"

Spencer puts a hand to my mouth to stop the noise. "That's enough now. Breathe and let it go." He takes a deep breath and lets it out. When I don't copy him, he gestures dramatically for me to do it with him. It does help, damnit. "Now, let's think about this. You can do yoga or Pilates if you want to. You might enjoy them. But you won't enjoy them as much. You love dancing, and you should do it until your body tells you that you can't. Then you can go do Tai Chi in the park with the grannies."

"You don't understand."

"Don't I?"

He pulls his phone out of his pocket and quickly finds a video for me to watch. It's a girl we know named Alyssa doing rehearsal for her debut in the ensemble of *The Lion King* national tour. I remember how she came to every class we offered for three weeks to get ready for that audition. After Spencer thinks I've seen enough, he types in a different search and pulls up a performance dance piece featuring Janyce and Shannon who took classes with us for a couple years. It's a gorgeous duet that combines ballet and contemporary in a way that shows off both of their strengths. Spencer pulls the phone away before it's over and searches something else, mumbling "not that one. Ah, there it is." He shows me a video of Christina, a girl who took classes with us for a while to rehabilitate after breaking her shoulder and clavicle in a car accident, now dancing like a dream in a Chicago production of *Swan Lake*.

"I can find more of these," he says. "You've danced with dozens of professional dancers over the years."

"I'm not sure what point you're making. Showing me that I'm surrounded constantly by young, amazing dancers doing well with their art isn't exactly changing my mind."

"It should, though." He shakes his head at me. "Don't you get it? You dance with these people. On an equal level, if not better. You've taught most of them. That leap Shannon did? I remember someone teaching her how to do that. Oh yeah, it was you! You think these students look down on you? They look up to you. I promise, the only chatter going on behind your back is marveling over your dedication and skill level and a little bit of wonder about why you're not famous."

He starts laughing, and when I glare at him to let me in on the joke, he says, "I've heard some pretty funny fairy tales they've made up about you to explain it all. My favorite is the one where you were once a member of the American Ballet Company, and you broke your ankle falling out of a lift during rehearsal right in front of Baryshnikov himself. It was so demoralizing and devastating you left New York and quit dancing. Then you suddenly re-emerged like some Greta Garbo of classic ballet, dancing anonymously at our little school."

"That is a detailed story. I like it."

"Thanks. I'm proud of it."

I swipe at him. "Dork."

He snatches up my hands and holds them tightly. "The point I'm making, hon', is that you're talented. Everyone knows it. No one is making fun of you or looking down on you. Those girls that come and go wish they'll still be able to dance when they're fifty. And, by the way, most of them think you're in your thirties. They have no idea you're not all that much younger than Debbie."

I let this sink in. Debbie is only seven years older than me, but the chronic pain, meds, and chain smoking have weathered her. When I look at my face in the mirror, I see the lines around my eyes and mouth. Secretly, I enjoy the ones in my cheeks that increase the size of my dimples when I smile. Despite having a long, thin neck, I still have a crisscross pattern of age creases forming that lotion isn't halting. Back that camera up a few feet, though, and you can't see all that, especially if I put on some make-up. Debbie's wrinkles are deeper, especially around her lips. They bring down the corners of her mouth to make her look like she's constantly frowning. She never comes to the studio without a scarf tied around her throat and wears loose-fitting clothing to hide her extra weight. Put side-by-side it wouldn't be obvious to someone who didn't know us that we were born within ten years of each other.

"How's she doing?" I ask.

He sighs. "She's struggling. I met with her the other day, and she officially asked me to take over managing the studio. I'm getting a salary and benefits."

I nod. "Good. I think that's overdue. You've been pretty much running everything for a while now. Does this mean she won't be coming to the studio anymore?"

"She wants to stay home. It's hard for her to get around."

"I need to go visit her."

"That would be nice."

We sit silently for a while thinking about the friend that

brought us together. I let the warmth of his body infect me, and I snuggle into him. "Thank you for coming."

"Feeling any better?"

"I guess so."

"Good, because now that I'm in charge of Dancer's Room, my first action is to hire you. I'm too busy to run the studio by myself. I still have shows I'm contracted to choreograph this season, and I have to judge that show choir competition in November and the dance competition in March. I need you to take over some classes."

I get up and take my empty wine bottle and plate of pizza to the kitchen counter. "So, your whole pep talk was a ruse?" I grab the salad and fork and come back to the couch.

"I meant every word of it, but I'm a selfish person. You already know this about me." He plucks a tomato off my salad and pops it in his mouth. "I can count on you, right?" I hesitate to answer. He practically swallows the cherry tomato whole. "Grace? I can count on you, right? Don't tell me this whole dog-and-pony show was for nothing."

"I guess if I'm officially a teacher then there's value to my dancing," I say at last.

He spreads his fingers over his chest and drops his jaw with a fair amount of over-dramatic offense. "Um, hello? Becoming a dance teacher is the end result for *most* little girls and boys who start ballet classes as snotty-faced five-year-olds. Some of us are damn proud of this career choice and exceptional at it."

Horrified that I came across as insulting my best friend's chosen career, I kiss his cheek. "I didn't say that to demean dance teachers. I'm thanking you. You making me officially a member of staff of Dancer's Room gives me something I can say to people. 'I'm not just a student. I'm a teacher'." I flip my hair for effect.

"So, you're looking for validity? Why now?" When I don't answer, he gasps. "I was right. Tyler said something to you. What? Do I need to go kick his ass?"

"It's not just him. It's everyone all the time. He's… It's different, is all." Spencer waits for me to go on. "When other people wonder about my dancing hobby, it makes me defensive, but not to the point of doubting myself. Tyler makes me wonder why I dance if I'm not planning to do something with it. Like, what's the point of doing anything if there isn't an end goal? If there isn't a way to monetize it."

"I know lots of people like that. I once dated this guy who was pretty decent at costume making, but he wouldn't make us costumes for fun. You know, for Halloween, or whatever. If he wasn't getting paid to make them, he simply wouldn't do it. Some people don't get doing something because it's fun."

"Which way is normal?" I ask.

"All of it." Spencer wraps his arm around me again. I rest my head on his shoulder while we look up more videos of our dancing friends on his phone. Before he leaves, we divvy up the class load at the studio with plans to update the website before October. I've led classes there before, but I'm excited to be able to say that I'm officially a teacher at Dancer's Room.

Feeling heady, I call Tyler to tell him the news. He cheers so loudly I have to hold the phone away from my ear. I've impressed him.

"Let's have lunch tomorrow to celebrate," he says. "I'm off for the day. Can you meet me?"

I'm so grateful he hasn't commented on how long it's been since we've talked or asked why I haven't responded to his texts. I don't want to answer those questions. They may come out over our lunch date, but I'll be more prepared then. "Lunch sounds wonderful." We make a plan before hanging up.

Even though it's bedtime, I slip out of my pajamas for the first time that whole weekend and tug on a leotard and my ballet slippers. I'm not a bit sleepy, and my body feels twitchy. In a moment I've got Gershwin's "Rhapsody in Blue" playing through my speakers and I'm doing my best Leslie Caron impression, imagining that Tyler is my Gene Kelly whirling me around Paris.

# CHAPTER
## *Eight*

I arrive at the restaurant early. I know how hard it is to find parking in this part of town. After driving up and down the nearest streets, I finally give up and pull up to the valet in front. Beverly Hills seemed like a good halfway compromise for both of us, with his condominium being in Santa Monica. I have to get back to work after this for an appointment in Glendale at three. It's noon now, and everyone is rushing out of their offices to grab a bite to eat on this bright Monday.

Tyler is waiting for me. A hostess leads us to a table in the front patio as soon as I join him. He must've arrived early, too, and got his name on the waiting list. If he was trying to make a good impression on me, it worked. Adoration bubbles inside me.

"It's such a nice day," he says, holding my chair for me to sit down. "I hope you don't mind being outside."

"I love it."

He sits down, taps the menu, and whispers conspiratorially. "So, I know the place is called Pink Taco, but do I have to get the tacos? It sounds kind of gross."

"You do! This place has great fish tacos. It's their specialty. I recommend the salmon ones. They're not gross, I promise."

He grimaces. "I'm not a fish guy."

"Fish is the key to staying slim," I tease him, like this is a problem for him.

He pats what there is of his belly. "I stay slim based on a diet of too much coffee, enough water to stay hydrated, and basically only eating lunch." He winks. "I make it a good lunch, though."

"You agreed to this place."

"I did. I did." He opens the menu, gives it a quick glance and closes it. "I saw something with chicken. I'm safe."

Pink umbrellas at each table provide shade, but the way Tyler kicks back in his seat puts his face in the sunshine like it's his personal spotlight. His blue eyes absorb the glow, and the effect makes me gasp. Age has improved everything about his face, and his eyes are more stunning than ever. I suddenly seem unable to think of anything to say to him beyond small talk. If he notices, he doesn't let on. He discusses the weather and traffic with me until the waitress arrives.

As predicted, she teases him mercilessly about not ordering fish, and he shrugs pitifully. "I'm sorry, I'm that same person who chooses pizza at a Chinese buffet. Shameful, I know." She brings us our tortilla chips, salsa, and mango tea promptly, knowing full well that this guy has all the markers of being a good tipper.

Before she walks away, she asks if we are done with the menus. Tyler puts them on the place setting to his left. "We'll hang on to them for now."

I assume he's keeping them to order desserts afterward. It's a thoughtful gesture, albeit unnecessary. I don't want to spoil anything by telling him that I never eat desserts, so I decide to deal with it when it comes up.

Tyler asks me to tell him more about being asked to teach at Dancer's Room and how that all came about.

"Well, I've led classes there many times over the years when Debbie, Spencer, or one of our other teachers were unavailable. Debbie has given me cash for it a few times, but usually she lets me take a few classes for free as our trade."

"Oh wow. I didn't realize you still pay for classes."

"It's like taking classes at a gym." I take a sip of tea.

"No special privileges for being a member for so long?"

"I'm grandfathered in at the old prices. Debbie has raised

prices twice since I've been there, and Spencer and I are thinking about raising them again."

Tyler sits forward and wraps both hands around his tea glass. "That's cool. That's something. Now that you're going to be staff, will they still make you pay for classes that other people teach?"

"I'll have to bring that up with Spencer when we start negotiating all the details."

"Drive a hard bargain, Graceful." He looks over my shoulder and his grin explodes. "Speaking of someone who can work a deal." Tyler stands up.

I twist around in my seat and see a man walking toward us with the hostess. He points at Tyler, and the hostess nods before returning to her stand in the lobby. This man is probably in his early sixties, bald on top but peppered hair over his ears and wrapping around back. He wears a fitted slate gray dress shirt with black pressed pants. My guess is that his suit jacket and tie are in his car, and he's glad he didn't wear them. Tyler is in jeans and a vintage Rolling Stones T-shirt. I'm in a blouse and skirt, business attire, hardly anything I'd consider dressy. It took me a while to figure out what was casual enough for a Monday lunch date. My other five outfit choices are strewn about my bedroom.

The men shake hands and slap each other on the shoulder. Tyler gestures to the spot with the menus, and the man pulls out the seat. Before sitting down, he reaches a hand across the table to me. I take it. His grip is firm.

"Grace, this is Alan Bergman, my agent."

"Oh! Hi!" I rise out of my seat and shake his hand with a little more vigor.

"Nice to meet you, Grace," Alan says. He sits down, and I see Tyler has already taken his seat as well. I lower my body back into my seat cautiously, almost as if I'm expecting a whoopy cushion to be there or something. "I hope you don't mind me joining you two for lunch. Tyler has told me a lot about you."

A parade of feelings rushes through me, and I'm the sad kid in the crowd too short to see any of it clearly. "I, uh… It's nice to meet you, too."

"I hope you don't mind," Tyler says. "I was talking to Alan

this morning and mentioned I was meeting you for lunch. He wanted to know a bit about you, and I told him what an amazing dancer you are."

"And I asked if I could crash your date."

"Oh, how nice. That's nice." I don't have words. I'm not sure what's happening.

The waitress comes by. Alan orders a gin and tonic and some guacamole to go with the chips. Both men are so at ease. This all seems normal to them. I'm fighting the urge to bolt from the restaurant to avoid saying or doing something embarrassing in front of this person who finds movies and TV shows for Tyler to star in.

They talk about how filming is going for the show, leading me to wonder what their phone conversation earlier had been about, if not that very subject. I find out as soon as Alan gets his drink and has a chance to take a swallow from it.

"Now, Grace," he says, focusing his energy on me. His eyes have a permanent squint to them, like he spends a lot of time in the sun without his sunglasses. That or the majority of his time is spent like this, peering into the souls of wannabe actors and deciding if they have value. "Tyler bragged a lot about you to me, and I have to say that everything he said about you is true. You are absolutely stunning. Just beautiful. And so thin!"

The compliments are coming so rapidly, I don't have an opportunity to fit in a humble thank you.

"He says you're his age, but I don't believe it. Show me your driver's license and prove it." His teeth are exceptionally white.

I must look like a squirrel staring down a Mercedes in the middle of Mulholland Drive, because they both start chortling.

"You are precious. Precious!" He finishes off his drink and signals for another one by raising the glass and tinkling the ice. He puts an elbow on the table and points at me. A shiny silver Montblanc watch pokes out from the cuff of his shirt. "I'm going to be frank with you. When the young actresses come to my office fresh out of drama school, I tell them that if they don't make it by thirty, to forget it. Go get married and have babies. Unless they're character types. I can always do something with them, if they have talent. The pretty girls, though, don't have a long time. There are plenty of aging actresses of note, and they are all fighting for those coveted leading lady roles. Do you hear what I'm saying?"

I feel myself twitch instead of fully shaking my head. "I think you're telling me that I'm too old to start acting?"

He nods. "Yes. Yes, that is what I would normally say."

I can't imagine why Tyler's face is so full of glee at this moment. I hardly need another person to tell me I'm too old to do something in entertainment. I wasn't asking for this verification. All I wanted was to have a date with my handsome boyfriend and celebrate a little success that I'd had. That I earned. Now it all seems stupid. Big deal. The fifty-year-old dancer has graduated to teaching classes at the same place where she'd been a student. Nineteen-year-olds do this at other studios. Of course Tyler would think it was lame and need to show off his bigger, fancier life. He has an agent! Wow! Same old Tyler.

All I can think to say to them is, "Not sure what point you're making."

Tyler must see the sour expression that I know is all over my face and bursts in, "But Grace, wait. Listen to him."

"Okay. All ears." I'm grateful my food has arrived, but now I'm wondering how to eat these messy tacos in front of this opinionated man. I drink more tea.

Alan dips a chip into the guacamole but doesn't eat it. He waves it around while he talks. "Aging dancers are a dime a dozen in New York, but you're unusual for Los Angeles. You're an unknown face, which is good for commercials. I don't think I can get you a lot in the way of dramatic roles with your lack of resume. No, I absolutely won't be able to do that. But I think I *can* get you some work. Enough to pay a bill or two."

"Work? Like acting?"

Tyler clinks Alan's glass with the bottom of his tea glass. "She's stunned. You've stunned her." He reaches toward me and rubs my shoulder. "I told you it wasn't too late. Isn't this amazing?"

This is the craziest moment of my life. This kind of thing

doesn't happen, and I'm not prepared for it. "I don't know what to say right now."

"You don't need to say anything. I know this is a bit of a surprise. Tyler said you did some acting when you were young and had some talent. I'm willing to take a chance on that. What I need is for you to get me some headshots. Do you have one? Probably not. Selfies aren't good enough. And I'll have one of my interns work with you on a resume."

"I have my realtor picture."

I'm about to reach into my purse for one of my cards when Tyler pulls out his phone and lifts it up to show the screen to Alan. "Will this work?" I lean forward to see what he's showing his agent. It's one of my pictures from the photoshoot I did with Spencer for the studio.

"Where did you get that?" I ask.

He shows two other shots of me that he's saved on his phone. "I looked you up on the internet and read up about Dancer's Room. I found these promo shots. They're gorgeous." He swipes back to the first one, cropped to reveal only my shoulders and head.

"That one is great," Alan says, nodding. "It'll do for now. I'd like something updated, but you still look enough like that for it to work. We'll need to discuss what to do with your hair. Go all the way with the white or go back to red. I'm not sure which is going to sell better." To Tyler he asks, "Can you send me that?"

My head is buzzing as if I had been the one to drink those two gin and tonics on an empty stomach. I feel like I might faint right out of my seat. "I... um..." I look at my watch and fake alarm. "Oh, my goodness! It's so much later than I thought. I have to run. I've got an appointment—"

"I thought you said it was at three," Tyler said. "You haven't eaten anything."

"I know. This was all so... unexpected. And exciting... that I forgot. Can you box it up for me? I'll get it from you later?"

"I'll keep it for twenty-four hours max," he says. When I stare at him blankly, he explains, "It *is* fish after all."

I laugh. There's too much air in it. I think I'm going to faint. "That's right. I'll have to see you within a day then."

"I'll count on it."

Carefully, I stand up and put my purse over my shoulder. I notice that Alan is looking me over from toes up, making sure the package he bought is good. The glint in his eyes suggests he's pleased. He puts out his hand for me to shake one more time.

"It was a pleasure, Grace. I'll be in touch if it's okay for Tyler to give me all your contact information."

"Sure. Yes. Yes, it's okay." I shake his hand. "This was nice. Thank you."

I walk away, hearing Tyler call out my name. Too rattled, I forgot to say goodbye to him. I'll deal with that later. For now, I must escape and get back to reality.

Tyler politely stays quiet for the next couple hours. I assume he believes that I'm working and hasn't put together that I ran out of that ambush of a meeting on purpose. I'm sure that it would never occur to him that someone might not welcome a sit down with a Hollywood agent. Everyone wants to be famous, right?

But do I? I have some regrets about not pushing harder against my doubts when I was young, but do I honestly feel like I ever had a shot at it? I might have been cute in *Sweet Charity* when I was eighteen—I've never watched the old VHS recording to find out. I know for a fact I was nothing special, though. One of a million girls who experienced the rush of popularity that comes with starring in a high school musical. It all went to my head, and I needed to be humbled a bit to get back to reality. Reality was becoming a realtor, not a movie star. I made the right move. Not exciting but correct.

Plus, I didn't care for the way Alan Bergman spoke to me. Maybe from his perspective it was flattering, but not from mine. All I got from it was that I looked good for an old gal. Like this was some huge feat. Not everyone lets herself go after forty. I know lots of women my age that are attractive and fit. I'm in Los Angeles. People exercise here and eat right. For that matter, I bet there are hot moms in Arkansas and Wyoming, too. He didn't need to be so amazed by this concept of a healthy middle-aged woman.

Or maybe it was all fake. An agent of any note has a strong client list already of good-looking actresses and models. He gets submissions from more who dream of their shot in front of the camera every day. He doesn't need me in his life. He does need Tyler. Tyler is making him money, and dropping in on our lunch like that was probably some clever manipulation to keep his client happy and satisfied that he's being represented by the right guy.

I decide to put it all out of my mind. I'm not going to get a call from Mr. Bergman or his office. Tyler and I will laugh about it when I go retrieve my fishy leftovers. We'll have a drink and that'll be that.

At the office, I go through some listings and answer some emails. I gather up what I need for the showing at three o'clock and start out the door. Then my phone rings. I don't recognize the number, but that's not unusual in my profession. I answer.

"Is this Grace Fuller?" a woman's voice asks.

I've been told never to answer "yes" on the phone to strangers. There was some scam going around where they recorded people saying "yes" and then used it to steal identities. I don't know if that was a true story or not, but now I always fumble a bit when someone starts a phone call this way.

"Uh-huh."

"Hello?"

I try again. "May I ask who's calling?"

"This is Carla Steyer from Screen Talent Agency. I work for Alan Bergman. Is this Grace Fuller? Do I have the right number?"

"Yes. Yes, this is she."

My heart. It's pounding so hard it hurts. I don't want anyone in the office to see me pass out, so I make my way to my car and get inside. I leave the door open for some air. It seems particularly hot for late September.

"Great. So, good news. Amazing news. This rarely happens.

We haven't even got your photo loaded onto the website yet. Anyway, you have an audition."

I'm so happy this pleasant-voiced lady can't see my face right now. I glance at my reflection in the rearview mirror and mouth to myself, *Oh my God!* before saying out loud, "Really? Wow. How does that work? For what, exactly? I'm new to this whole thing."

Carla has a soft sweet chuckle at my expense, like she thinks I'm adorable. The jury is out with regard to how I feel about her. I wonder how old she is. I wonder if she even knows what I look like yet. I picture her to be some hot brunette model with huge boobs. That seems like Alan's type.

"No worries, sweetie."

I do not want this girl calling me sweetie.

She goes on because I'm too startled to correct her. "It's for a commercial. They're looking for active middle-aged and senior adults. Mr. Bergman thinks you should go in workout clothes. Something that shows off how fit you are. He says you're a dancer, is that right?"

"Yes. But he doesn't want me in dancewear?"

"No. More like a workout. Think something you'd wear to jog in or take a class at a gym. Okay?"

"Sure."

"The audition is tomorrow morning at 10:45 sharp. I'll text you the address. Bring a printout of the headshot you showed him at your meeting. You don't need a resume for this."

I nod and then speak a moment later. "Yes. Yes, I can do that."

"I can count on you for this, then?"

"Mmm-hmmm." My breathing is shallow. I need some water.

She sounds doubtful. "Okay. Let us know if you aren't going to make it for some reason. It reflects poorly on our office to promise to send someone and then they don't show up. We have a policy that if you miss three auditions, we cut you. That's agency-wide."

"Wow, just three. What about people who work?" I dare to ask.

"This takes priority over work," she says simply. Then there's a sharp breath on her end as she remembers something. "Oh, and Mr. Bergman said there's something about your hair. It's got some gray or something? If you have time to fix your hair before this audition, that would be great." Then she whispers into the phone like she doesn't want anyone to hear her, "I know getting a last-minute appointment will be hard but do what you can."

Impossible, actually.

"Did he decide it should be bleached white or dyed? He wasn't sure earlier."

"I don't know," she says, stretching each word out musically. Okay, that was cute. I'm starting to like her. "I'll have to get back to you on that." Then she says, "You know what, Grace? Don't worry about it. Let the commercial casting director decide how old he wants you to look."

"Is there anything else I need to know or do?"

Carla holds out a long "Hmmmm" while she thinks about it. "Nope. Just relax and be the beautiful, charming lady Alan met at the restaurant. And hey, I know it's your first time. Feel free to call me for a little pep talk right before, I'll text you my personal number."

I get off the phone with her and within seconds, I have her number and the address for the audition. I text back my thanks and look at the time. If I don't leave right now, I'll be late for my appointment. My mind whirls. Can I handle trying to sell a house right now? I have an audition to think about.

No. Stop it. Selling houses is my job. It pays my bills. One little commercial is not as important. Besides, selling and auditioning aren't that different. I decide to use this as practice. I'm going to impress these people with my poise and upbeat energy and get them to buy what I'm selling.

# CHAPTER
## *Nine*

I have to dance. My energy after that audition has been through the roof all day. Sitting for more than a minute at a time is difficult, and I do most of my work that afternoon on my feet. The only way I survive driving through L.A. traffic is playing the stereo as loud as I can and singing at the top of my lungs.

It was so much fun. I was terrified before arriving, and I almost turned around and drove right back home. I didn't, though. Both Tyler and Spencer gave me motivational speeches over the phone. Carla called me fifteen minutes before the audition to make sure I was on my way. I assured her that I was already in the parking lot.

"Get on up there, sweetie," she said to me. "Dazzle them."

I fluffed up my hair and touched up my lipstick before heading into the building. The assistant in the waiting room didn't ask for my headshot, choosing to take a picture of me on her iPad. A half dozen people sat in the room with me, men and women all on the downhill side of forty. All of them were in peak health, from what I could tell. One silver-haired man that I guessed to be around my father's age range was dressed like he was going straight to the golf course after this pesky audition. He was aging much better than my dad. He could rival Pierce Brosnan. I'd buy any pills that guy was selling.

When it was my turn, I went into a conference room and

shook hands with three friendly men and a woman who sat behind a table. Their professional attire was starkly different from the workout clothes I wore. They introduced themselves. I'm not one for catching names quickly, so none of them stuck. Plus, my heart pounded so hard in my ears, I could barely hear them speaking. One of the men was the director of the commercial, but I wasn't clear on which one. Perhaps the one not wearing a tie? I answered some questions about what I do to exercise and stay healthy. I told them about studying ballet, and that triggered some excitement in all of them. Lots of nods and grins at each other. For the first time in my life, my confession about being a dancer didn't prompt judgement or confusion. None of them asked how long I'd been dancing or why I started. Their interest was more in regards to what I liked about it and if I'd recommend it to other women my age to stay fit. I'd been preparing to lie and say I'd been dancing since I was in school. I didn't figure they'd factcheck. It turned out the only thing they needed to prove I wasn't lying was a demonstration of my ability.

I took off my sneakers and backed up further into the open space where tables had been pushed against the walls to make room. I hadn't been sure what to wear to this audition, and I was glad that I'd chosen my black leggings with the sheer nylon stripes running from ankle to mid-thigh. They showed off the muscles in my legs when I danced. I wore a thin, pink V-neck shirt that hung loose over my shoulder, revealing the strap of my black cotton camisole and the sharpness of my collar bones. My thought was to look more like a yoga mom than a dancer, but it was a good outfit for showing off some movement.

After a quick assessment of the limited space, I decided on a combination I've done many times in class before while humming some of "The Nutcracker Suite" quietly to keep my tempo even. It didn't occur to me until much later in the day that I could've pulled up some music on my phone. There wasn't any room for leaps, and doing any kind of turn on the carpet in my socked feet would be a mistake. So, I focused on movements that showed my balance, flexibility, and strength. Like a drug, the dancing soothed me as I concentrated on pushing through my extension and tightening my core. They murmured "oohs" and "aahhs" throughout like I was doing some kind of magic show. It brought a smile to my lips. I finished with an elegant *arabesque* and then a modest curtsy.

All four of them stood and clapped. Compliments flew my way, including when the woman said, "And you sing, too!"

I felt my face heat up, not realizing they'd heard humming.

They asked me to sit down for a moment, and as I tied my shoelaces, I answered some questions about my availability over the next couple of days. When they had all the information they needed, we all stood and shook hands again. One of the men said, "Lovely. Just lovely. Thank you so much for coming today."

I was over the moon.

Carla called three hours later to let me know I'd booked the job. I nailed my first audition. I was going to be a working actress.

I called Tyler right away. Then I called Spencer.

Working wasn't really a thing for the rest of the day because I couldn't concentrate. All I wanted to do all day was keep dancing.

I arrive at Dancer's Room forty-five minutes before class and let myself in. I've had a key for a while. For now, I leave the lights off and let what's left of daylight infiltrate the room from the windows high up on the wall. I enjoy the dusky shadows as I stretch and do some barre work. Now that I have the space and my toe shoes, I do all the leaps and turns I know, giving my energy and taking energy from the room. It's exhilarating and exhausting. I'll have little left for our actual class.

The overhead lights flick on, and Spencer enters. "Well, hello, superstar!"

I stop dancing, putting my hands on my hips while I catch my breath. "Hey." I know my grin is wild.

"Anything interesting happen today?" he teases.

"Oh, not much."

I dash over to him, and he gives me a tight hug.

"Thought you'd be with Handsome tonight."

"We're meeting up after class," I say. "I told him I had to dance tonight to get my nerves out. He's filming today, anyway."

"Good. I get to celebrate with you first—by making you sweat and get all gross before your hot date."

"You know it takes a lot to make me sweat."

"Oh, I know, honey," Spencer says, "but I'm up to the task. My goal is to get you some shower sex with that man of yours tonight. He deserves a treat."

I smack him playfully. "*He* deserves a treat?"

"Yes! He's the one that made this happen. It's not like you would've gotten that Viagra commercial without his interference." He puts the back of his hand to his forehead dramatically, "*Oh, Spencer! Tyler's so mean to me. He thinks I'm beautiful and talented and wants his agent to put me in the movies, and I hate him so much.*"

"Stop it."

"Well?"

"You're right. He was right. I'm glad he did it."

Spencer grabs his dance bag from the doorway and heads to the old piano and Bluetooth speaker on top of it. I miss old Jake, our piano player. Debbie let him go about twelve years ago when she had to tighten the budget. I wonder what he's up to these days.

I get my water bottle and take a swig. "It's not Viagra, by the way. The commercial."

"What's it for?"

"I don't remember the name, but it's for Rheumatoid Arthritis."

Spencer's brow creases, and he doesn't respond right away. He turns on the speaker and fiddles with getting his phone synched up to it. A blast of violins sound, and he quickly stops it. Without looking at me, he says, "Maybe we shouldn't share that fact with Debbie."

"Maybe not," I agree. I feel bad that this is the first time I've thought about the possibility that this commercial might upset her. I brush my concerns away. She'll probably never see it, anyway.

The students arrive, catching up with each other. In walks that cute, perky dancer that I still think of as Victoria because she's in *CATS*. I learned her name at one point, but I've put a block on remembering it. This is the third time she's returned. She tosses me a snide glance, and for the first time since I've met her, I don't care. I booked a commercial today. Because of my dancing. So there!

Spencer leads a great class, and by the end, I'm officially tired. The endorphins released in my bloodstream from that audition are finally subsiding. He leads us through a cool-down with long muscle stretches and movements designed to make us take deep breaths. It feels good, and I close my eyes. I've done this combination of steps many times before, so I don't need to see him or look at myself in the mirror.

A burst of giggles from the girls brings me out of my meditation. Tyler is in the doorway with a bouquet of pink carnations and a bottle of champagne.

"Oh my God. Is that Tyler Andrews?" Victoria squeaks behind me. "He's in *Wildcats*. I love that show!"

Two of the other girls join in with their appreciation of the show and 'Coach Sanders'.

Spencer waves his hands at the girls. "I guess class is over. Good night." He makes a face at me, and I stick out my tongue. Tyler walks toward me and hands me the flowers. I can feel Victoria's envy burning behind me.

"I enjoy watching you dance," he says. "I can tell it's your happy place."

"It is."

"Carnations are the right flowers for ballerinas, right? I looked it up."

That's right. I bring them to my nose to take in the sweet scent and feel the fluffy petals against my hot face. Tyler presses them down and leans in to kiss me.

Several girls squeak like they are still in school.

Victoria steps up beside me. "You're dating Tyler Andrews?"

I'm somebody again.

Tyler signs a couple autographs and takes selfies with the

dancers while I get dressed and pack up. Spencer chases them out and asks if I want to lock up.

"We're not staying," Tyler tells him. "We've got plans."

"We do?" I ask.

"We have to celebrate."

Whistling softly, Spencer turns the light out on us and drifts down the hall to the office.

In the yellow glow coming up from the lamps on the stairwell, I lick my lips and wrap my arms around Tyler's waist, pulling him close. "Do you mind if I get a shower first?"

# CHAPTER
## *Ten*

We shot the commercial the following week, starting early in the morning. I don't know what the original concept for the commercial had been, but they went full in on basing it around me being an aging ballet dancer. They asked me to bring the most traditional ballet dancewear I had, and they chose all the pinks and a sheer ballet skirt when I insisted no one wears a tutu for a ballet class. They set up in a lovely dance studio that had lots of natural sunlight. Mostly they had me doing poses at the barre, so they could get angles with my reflection in the mirror. I was asked to keep my expression light and joyful, like I loved what I was doing, but not too exuberant. To my surprise, they did not ask me to dye my hair, saying they preferred the natural white coming out.

"It's like we see that age is starting to take over, but you're winning the battle against it. Perfect for our theme," said my makeup technician, a sweet young woman named Kashvi who had a head of gorgeous magenta colored hair. "Also, if your hair was completely auburn, you'd look too young." Kashvi was instantly my favorite. She was skilled at her craft, too. With a mysterious use of shading, she made my hands look a little swollen and definitely more fragile. She also somehow managed to make my face look fresh and bright continuously throughout the day. I gravitated toward her to hang out whenever we had a break.

The last shot of the day was outside at a grassy park. They put me in an orange sundress that was the same color as the drug's logo. They tried putting me in open-toe sandals, but after seeing my ugly toes they let me wear my white pumps instead. I had to walk along like it was an ordinary day and then suddenly spin and throw my arms up like the world is full of wonderful things and I can do and see them all because I have no pain. It was silly and fun. Expressing the needed jubilance with my body wasn't hard at all because it had been a great day. Everyone on the crew was nice as could be, so easy-going, and treated me like I was a star. For that day, I was everyone's focus. The time flew by.

When the shoot came to an end, a melancholy took over that I hadn't expected. The only times I'd ever felt show let-down was after closing night of shows back in high school. I chalked all that emotion up to hormones. Now I realized there was something to it. It's very different from the rejection of not getting cast at all. Returning from being treated as a special member of a group hyper-focused on a creative goal, back to normal life was a little like driving through the scenic mountains and right off a cliff. I knew it was just a dumb commercial and didn't matter that much in the grand scheme of things. We weren't filming an Oscar-worthy movie or anything. Maybe there would be other days like it in the future if my agent got me more work. Fingers crossed. Hope was my only weapon against the sadness, which only grew worse as the days rolled by.

Carla only called me once over the month that passed with an audition notice. Another commercial, this one for a hotel chain. I didn't get that job. At least that's what I guessed when I didn't hear anything for a week. I called to check, and Carla told me that casting directors only call when they're hiring. No call means a no. I wasn't a big fan of that open-ended form of rejection. "Don't worry. It'll pick up, sweetie," Carla said, trying to reassure me. "You're new to this. Most people don't get bookings their first week out like you did."

I convinced myself it was fine. It's not like I was expecting to be at auditions every day. As each day went by, I kind of wished that the commercial hadn't happened at all, because it had given me a false sense of success. I knew better.

Tyler also let me know the slowness was typical, especially for someone starting out. We spent most nights together now, and his presence in my life kept me from wallowing about silly things like why the phone wasn't ringing nonstop with job offers.

I found out the commercial had started airing when a customer recognized me during a house showing. "I thought I recognized her," she said to her husband. "She's the ballerina in that commercial. Oh, my goodness, what a funny town Holly-wood is. I've got a TV celebrity selling me a house." She had her husband take a picture of us, which she immediately texted to her sister Caroline back in Bowling Green who would never believe it.

I sold the house.

The commercial aired regularly once an hour during the after-noon talk shows on CBS. I set my DVR and caught it. Then I invited Tyler, Spencer, and my folks over for a viewing party. It was a fun way for them all to officially get to know each other, and to demonstrate to my parents that all my years of dancing weren't a complete waste. Dad was in a great mood as he enjoyed thinking about the fact that I would get a royalty each time the commercial aired. Spencer was his usual delightful self, and Tyler managed to make my mother forgive him for breaking my heart by being completely charming.

Everything is on an upswing for me, yet I remain uneasy. My usual pessimism has worked its way into the cracks of my armor. As great as my friends and family are at making me feel like a winner right now, a part of me craves criticism. Someone who can speak right to my weaknesses and put me in my place. It's what I'm used to feeling, and I know exactly who can oblige me.

## 2015

The new teacher was a tall, handsome black man. We didn't get many male students at Dancer's Room, so I was blown away a few weeks back when Debbie brought him in and introduced him as her new assistant. Assistant wasn't exactly the word I'd use for a person who taught the entire class while she watched. I felt he needed a better title. After the first class went according to her expectations, she didn't stay in the room at all, letting him run the class while she remained in her office. His name was Spencer Nichols.

I liked his energy a lot compared to the heavy-handed way that Debbie taught. He also actually danced and demonstrated steps. Due to her chronic pain, Debbie rarely did more than stand and call out directions. About a month before Spencer started teaching, she got a cane, and she loved pounding it on the hard floor to help us keep time. Spencer's demeanor was cheery. He smiled constantly, and his smile was terrific. I know that's not a descriptive word. It's the word I thought every time those lips widened. *Terrific!* It was as if he enthusiastically whispered it into my ear like the Master of Ceremonies from *Chicago*. "Hotcha!"

When I learned Spencer had done a lot of professional dancing, it didn't surprise me. Debbie had originally introduced him as a teacher she was borrowing from a children's dance studio in Santa Monica. She super downplayed his actual credits. He eventually told us about the many other gigs he got around Los Angeles and Orange County as a choreographer and professional dancer. The man worked all the time.

I'll admit I hovered around him with the rest of the girls after classes to get all his information. I was curious about him and his experience. He was also amazing looking and didn't seem too terribly young. At forty-two, being single was getting annoying. If it meant being a bit of a cougar to get a guy, I'd do that. It was a cliché to assume that because he was a male dancer that made him gay.

Except he was, and proud of it.

We were in the middle of his fifth time teaching Ballet 2, when Debbie showed up at the doorway to watch, leaning heavily on that new cane. I felt myself instantly stiffen. We'd been laughing over a story Spencer had been telling us about a time in high school when he busted his ankle coming down from a leap while dancing in a Disneyland parade. He'd been wearing the Goofy costume at the time, and the sweatband he wore under the big head slipped over his eyes. He was completely blind and limping, and they were only halfway through the parade route. He hilariously acted out how he wandered about trying to find someone to help him. The laughter must've caught Debbie's attention.

I explained to her, "He was talking about when he worked at Disneyland. I bet it was a blast to work there."

"You should try out sometime," Lettie said, one of our younger dancers. "I have a friend older than you who works there. She plays Mary Poppins sometimes. She's like thirty-five or something."

Debbie snorted. "Grace doesn't try out for things." That comment seemed unnecessary, but I was grateful that at least she didn't correct Lettie about my age.

"Sorry, Ms. White," Spencer said. "Just telling them about my stupidness." He looked at all of us. "Anyway, the quick end of the tale is that a parade assistant held my hand while I hopped my way through the rest of the parade route, waving constantly at people I couldn't see. Show must go on, right?"

"Class must go on, at any rate," Debbie said. It was light in tone, but no-nonsense. Spencer got the drift and told us to find our spots on the floor.

I had become accustomed to Debbie's combinations over the past twelve years. She had several that she rotated through. I'd been coming regularly a couple times a week since I started. I knew them all by heart. Spencer still hadn't repeated anything yet, so I had to pay attention. The combination today required a lot of balance. We had to hold an *arabesque en l'air*, *plié*, straighten, then slowly *promenade* in a circle on the supporting leg before lowering that pointed back toe to the ground. It concluded with a *pas-de-burree* into a *pirouette*, then the back foot came to the front in fifth position to start the whole thing again on the other side.

Five students took class today. No one new, but no one who'd been dancing there more than a year or two. People used Dancer's Room for specific reasons. Nobody ever stayed permanently. Rarely did we have students much older than thirty. So many teary-eyed girls stopped in over the years to tell us they were quitting dance to be mommies. This was the usual reason we lost students, but I also noticed that as dancers got older, they simply got tired of training. They figured they knew enough. Plus, they weren't getting as many jobs anymore. These particular five girls were strong dancers, especially Mariah. That woman had to be pushing six feet, and her legs were pillars of strength. They were all in their twenties, and I thought I was good enough to be in their company. Over the years, I'd become an acceptable ballet dancer. I stopped getting questioning looks long ago.

It had taken a long time to feel this confident. Between class, practicing religiously, some weightlifting, lots of sit-ups and running laps on the weekends at the local high school, I'd thinned considerably and exchanged my fat for lean muscle. Debbie wasn't nearly as tough on me as she used to be.

Until this day.

I felt her staring me down, and it finally got to me. I wobbled.

"Tighten your abs, Grace," she snapped, banging her cane on the ground to the tempo of the music. "Get that leg up."

I zipped up my core the way she had taught me and concentrated.

"Watch your turnout." She walked through the other dancers to stand beside me. Then she grabbed my elevated leg and pushed it up higher and yanked my toe outward. I struggled to keep my balance. "Why are your fingers twitching like that?"

My fingers were twitching? That was new.

I lowered my hands into first position and then prepped for my *pirouette*. I fell out of a double.

Naturally, Debbie had to comment. "If you can't do a double, do a single. Better to land clean than show off and fall out."

Doing a double wasn't showing off. It was an expected minimum at the level of this class. Debbie had me rattled. I continued to bob and flail, and she continued to point out every bit of it. Finally, I couldn't stand it anymore. I stopped and put my hands on my hips.

"What's the problem?" I demanded to know. "Why are you after me like this?"

"You're being lazy."

All the other dancers stopped as well. Spencer went over and hit pause on the CD player.

"You're making it hard to concentrate," I told her. "Why are you being so critical?"

"If you can't take it, then you should leave. This is what taking dance class is about. Not hanging out with your friends for social hour."

A circle of slender arms and legs formed around us, but I only looked at one face. "I know what class is about. In case you haven't noticed, you aren't teaching this class. Spencer is."

"He's being too easy on you."

From the front of the room, Spencer put his palms toward us. "Hey now. I'm still new and trying to get everyone feeling good about the change…"

"You're fine, Spencer," Debbie said, not looking at him, keeping her eyes only on me.

"Then what is it?" I challenged. "I'm here all the time, working hard to be a dancer."

This was the wrong thing to say, apparently. Her face reddened. Through clenched teeth, she seethed, "You are not a dancer. Until you do eight shows a week, full out, for months on end, you're not a real dancer. Until you dance on broken toes and twisted ankles, with your back screaming in pain with every movement because it's your job and you have to go on, you're not a dancer."

I glanced around at the other girls in the room. Their faces were full of shock. None of them knew what was going on.

I wanted to scream at her to mind her own damn business and get out of my hair, but I didn't. I knew her better than anyone else there. I fought back the frustrated tears and forced myself to stay calm. Leaning close to her ear, I asked quietly, "Are you okay?"

The wildness in her eyes wilted. It was as if whatever had been haunting her had fled at being discovered. "I'm fine. I'm heading home. I left a key on my desk. Lock the place up." I nodded at her that I would. She waved her hands at us. "Get back to dancing."

Without a word, the dancers took their spots again, and Spencer pushed play on the music. I watched Debbie walk with careful steps toward the exit. I noticed then that she was wearing her soft-soled suede clogs. She favored those on days when her feet were extra swollen. At the doorway, Debbie looked back over her shoulder before Spencer counted us off and said, "Spencer. Don't ever call me Ms. White again. It's Debbie. Just Debbie."

He gave her a thumbs-up and then said to all of us, "Arms up. And five, six, seven, eight…"

I watched Debbie leave, catching sight of her grabbing the rail on the stairs with all her might as she slowly took a step down and out of sight. Part of me wanted to rush and help her, but I knew the woman's pride would never allow it. Also, frankly, I was kind of pissed off and wanted her to suffer a little for taking her pain out on me.

"What was that all about?" Mariah asked when class ended and everyone knew for sure that Debbie was gone. She wiped her gorgeous long neck with a soft towel. Spencer collected money from the students as they gathered around me.

"It's nothing," I said, not wanting to share Debbie's personal information. "She's having a bad day."

Lettie said, "I thought you two were best friends."

"Oh, I wouldn't say that exactly."

Another student, Rochelle, said, "But you've known each other forever, right? I heard you two were in the Rockettes."

"Debbie was a Rockette," I correct. "I met her here."

The girls came at me with a hundred questions, and I did not want to get into all the details of my relationship with Debbie and lack of professional experience.

"Was it my question about you trying out for Disney?" Lettie asked, her precious face all scrunched up. "Is it because you still dance, and she doesn't? I'm sorry if it was my fault."

"It's fine, Lettie," I said, but I knew she'd hit the hammer on the head.

Spencer put his duffel bag over his shoulder and said loudly, "Class is over, ladies. I have a date with a tasty morsel I met the other day at the gym, and I do not want to be late. Out, out, out." To me, he asked, "Do you want to lock up or me?"

"I got it." I headed to the office to retrieve the key.

About the time the noise of the girls clunking their way down the stairs and out the door faded, I got back to the studio to find Rochelle in conversation with Spencer. They both looked up at me and smiled.

"What's up?" I asked suspiciously.

Rochelle waved a hand that it was nothing. "I was telling Spencer that I've been focusing on my photography a lot lately. I'm thinking of doing it professionally. You know, something I can do to supplement my earnings as a dancer. Plus, I'll be able to keep doing it after I'm retired."

"That'll be a long time," Spencer assured her.

She didn't look so sure about that. "We'll see. My knees are telling me otherwise. Anyway, what I wanted to say was that I know you two are kind of the faces of the studio here, and I was wondering if I could do a photoshoot with you both. It would be for my portfolio, but I'd be happy to give you the images to use for your own purposes—or maybe for advertising the studio. Would you be interested?"

I was absolutely interested even though I had no need for professional photos. It sounded like a great time. Something I'd never done before. Still, I found myself wondering aloud, "Don't you want to use the younger dancers?"

She grinned sheepishly. "Honestly, the reason I want both of you is because you are a little older. I think you make much more interesting subjects for photography. Please don't be offended."

"I'm not," I said.

"I am," Spencer said, nudging me in the side with an elbow. "I am not nearly as ancient as this old thing." Rochelle's eyes grew so big. Before she broke out in a stream of apologies, Spencer laughed. "I'm kidding. Take all the pictures you want, honey."

We made plans for the day and time of the photoshoot, and I told them I'd run the whole thing by Debbie to get permission to use the studio. I doubted she'd want the photos for advertising, but at least it would be a fun day.

As Rochelle headed down the stairs, Spencer put a hand on my arm to stop me from following her.

"Hey, are you really okay?" he asked. "I know I haven't been here long, but I've never seen Debbie tear into anyone like that. Is that normal for her?"

I shake my head. "It's not. She and I have some history."

"Yeah, she said you'd been taking classes here a long time and that if I needed any help with anything to ask you. I assumed that was because you were friends. Didn't seem like it today. She kind of had it out for you."

"You know, you'd think Debbie and I would be tight after twelve years and being fairly close in age. *She's* older," I pointed out quickly, and that made him smile. I liked relieving the worry in his face. There were no lines in his face yet, not that I could see. I didn't want to be the one to put them there. "We've never gone out for drinks or met for lunch. We've never even gossiped about the other students in her office after hours. She's never warmed up to me, and she's certainly never stopped letting me know that I'm beneath her. Today was one of those days."

My throat tightened unexpectedly. I hadn't spoken about my relationship with Debbie to anyone before. Saying it out loud made it real. Debbie and I weren't friends, and I doubted we ever would be. It hurt more than it should to say it out loud.

"Why would you be beneath her? She should be proud of what an incredible dancer you are."

"You'd think," I said. "She's the one who taught me. I didn't know diddly-squat about ballet before I walked into this place."

"You're kidding."

I put my hands up innocently. "Not."

"Well, honey, you completely snowed me, and I have seen thousands of dancers in my *short* lifetime." He nudged me with his shoulder. "Just pointing out that I am the youngest of this trio."

"Noted."

"Well, the way I see it, Debbie is missing out. I, however, am not making the same mistake. I'm cancelling my date, and you and I are going for coffee together. Right now. I know a great place."

I bit my lip. "You don't have to cancel a date for me. I'd feel terrible about it."

"Don't. He's a bore." Spencer wriggled his nose. "He's also kind of a whore, so he'll come over later if I ask him to."

I giggled. I couldn't help it.

"Let's go," he said.

We locked up the studio, and he took me around the corner to introduce me to Stomping Grounds.

**Present Day**

I arrive at Debbie's house in Hollywood Hills on a Saturday afternoon. October has brought some windy days, but the sun has kept the temperature in the seventies. Debbie's property isn't too high up in the hills and not terribly large. No front yard to speak of, just some overgrown shrubs around the short path to her front steps. The driveway is barely long enough for me to park my car without the tail sticking out in the road. Jamie, her shaggy-headed son, greets me at the door and leads me through the house. "Mom's out back." I know my way, having been here many times before, but it's sweet that he's guiding me.

"How's she doing?" I ask.

"Same stubborn self." He reaches for the sliding glass door

but pauses before opening it. "It's getting worse. She's not getting enough sleep because she can't get comfortable at night. Sometimes she cries out. I'll go to her, but then she yells at me that there's nothing I can do for her and to go back to bed. It's hard, Grace. I want you to know that before you go out there. She's very bitter."

I put a hand on his shoulder. "I would expect nothing less from her than a sharp tongue. It's how she's always been with me."

"What do you mean? You've always been her favorite."

I let out one loud sarcastic laugh. "Ha! That's hilarious."

Jamie opens the door for me. "Calling it like I see it."

"You're pretty blind then. Go have your eyes checked."

The backyard is shallow. It's fenced in on two sides with arborvitae trees lined up in front of them taking up another several feet. A brick retaining wall along the back keeps the cliff from avalanching down on her. The remaining yard is mostly pool and attached jacuzzi with only enough cement between where I stand at the sliding glass door and the water to allow for a couple of lounges and an outdoor table and chair set. Debbie's love for the color aqua-blue is evident in the furniture, the cushions, and the knitted cover-up abandoned on one of the lounges.

"Where is she?"

"Swimming. She spends most of her time in the pool now. She feels weightless in there and says it's the only place she can go where nothing hurts."

I step outside, and Jamie slides the door closed behind me, leaving me to deal with his mom on my own. I walk around the table set with its wide-open umbrella covering and find her floating on her back with her eyes closed. The pool is clean and inviting. The jets are on in the hot tub, which I imagine is boiling hot. I didn't bring my swimsuit because Debbie has never, not once, in all the time I've known her asked if I'd like to come over for a swim or soak.

She looks so peaceful as she floats. I'm sure the water is warm, and it soothes her tender body. In this moment, she's not angry or bitter. I've never seen her face so relaxed. All the lines on her face borne from aggravation are magically gone. For the first time, that seven-year age gap between us doesn't seem so obvious. I hate to be the one to disturb her. I consider sneaking back out without her noticing. As I turn, my purse bumps one of the chairs. This rouses her from her meditative state. She groans when she sees me, and she aims for the steps at the far end of the pool.

"You can stay in the pool if you want," I tell her.

Debbie doesn't respond to that, but she does beckon for me to bring her towel. She's left it near the edge of the pool. I hold it open and wrap it around her shoulders. As she dabs herself dry, she shuffles over to her lounge chair and sits down, tossing her cover-up over the back of the chair. Carefully, she slips her feet into a pair of soft flip-flop shoes before reclining into the chair. The flip-flops show her swollen and crooked toes. Her long middle toe has crept over the top of the one next to it. I pull my gaze away from them and back to her face. She's not overjoyed to see me.

"I did call," I say.

"Jamie told me."

I pull the other lounge chair closer and sit on it sideways. I want to take off my shoes, but after seeing the condition of Debbie's feet, I decide to keep them on. I'm in a yellow jumpsuit. It feels like it's catching the sun and burning me alive.

"You want something to drink?" she asks.

I see the pitcher of what looks like lemonade on the table but is probably margaritas. I shake my head. "I'll get you more if you want."

She sips from what is left of her watered-down drink and then puts the glass back in the cup holder attached to her seat. "I'm good." Debbie lays her head back on the cushion, her sunglasses get darker as she looks straight up at the sky. I can't see if her eyes are open or not.

I guess I should say something. "How are you doing? It's been a while since you stopped coming to the studio, so I thought I'd check on you."

"How nice of you to think of me. It's been what, five weeks?"

"Y-yes. A month or so sounds about right."

"Glad you found the time."

Whew, Jamie wasn't kidding. I go over to fill up a glass of mid-day pick-me-up after all.

"Have you gotten out of the house at all?"

She waves a hand like the question is pesky. "Not much. Therapy. Doctor. Hair appointment."

"Your hair looks nice," I say quickly.

"No, it doesn't. She botched the whole thing."

Her hair is wet, so I can't tell what it looks like. It appears to be freshly dyed back to its lustrous blonde shade and is shorter, curling naturally as the sun dries it.

"Well, it looks nice to me."

"Are you ever going to do anything with yours?" she asks. The white continues to take over my hair. I've had it trimmed recently, and now all that remains of the red are the tips. I kind of think it looks cool. Several of the students at Dancer's Room have complimented it, and every time, Spencer rolls his eyes and tells them they're not helping. "It ages you. Or is that what you want? To look like an old lady?"

"I thought I'd look my age for a change. It was a challenge I gave myself on my birthday, to see how long I could grow it out before it drove me crazy. All the young girls are rocking the fake silver hair, so I thought why not give natural a shot?"

She blows a raspberry. "You have another forty, fifty years to look old. Look young while you can."

It's a good point. "I'll think about it," I tell her.

"Are you still hooking up with that high school flame you were talking about?"

"College."

"What?"

"He was my college flame." She shrugs like she doesn't see the difference. "And yes. It's going pretty well. He's an actor, did you know? Did Spencer tell you? In a popular TV show. And he got his agent to sign me on."

"To do what exactly?" she asks.

"Acting."

"Is that what you call it?"

That makes me pause. She taps out a cigarette and grabs a box of wooden matches that were on the ground beside her. I assume they are easier to light than regular matches or using a lighter. She still struggles enough that I rise out of my seat to help. Before I take a step, she gets the end burning and puffs smoke my direction.

She says what I've been waiting for. "I saw your commercial." She pushes her sunglasses on top of her head and meets my eyes with hers. Her eyeliner is smudged.

"You did?"

"Yeah. I did. The one no one told me about." She gives me a tremendously fake smile and cocks her head. "I called Spencer and got the lowdown on your famous boyfriend and his attempts to make you someone he can brag about."

I take a breath to keep from saying anything I'll regret. I'm convincing myself that this is Debbie's take on the conversation and not Spencer's opinion. If it *is* Spencer's opinion, he sure has been hiding it. He'll be hearing from me soon.

"What was the point of that ad, do you think?" I hear the challenge in her tone. "If you take their magic potion your arthritis will vanish, and you can be a ballerina? Wow! Will little fairies appear and help you fly, too?"

My body stiffens. "I didn't write the commercial. I don't even think it was supposed to be about ballet originally. There were people at the audition who looked like golfers or tennis players. The director thought my sport was unique, is all."

"Yeah, it is," she agrees, sitting upright. "It's so unique that it kind of looks a little like you were mimicking the only person you know that is older than you and can dance ballet. Oh, and who happens to have rheumatoid arthritis. Funny. Isn't it?"

"I wasn't mimicking you—"

"No," she says sharply. "You weren't doing it well, anyway. Because RA is fucking painful. And it's ugly. Your hands. Your feet. Your posture. Nothing about that commercial looked like you had any-damn-thing wrong with you."

I speak slowly, choosing my words carefully. "Like I said, I didn't write the commercial, Debbie. I did what they told me to do."

Debbie reaches for her glass in the holder behind her. "That was clear. The moves you were doing. Did they tell you to do that shit? Basic ballet skills an eight-year-old can do. At least they could have had you do something impressive. Represent our age group." She brings the drink to her mouth, but her grip isn't tight. The glass slips from her fingers and smashes on the cement between us. The toes of my yellow wedges are soaked. Fragments of glass scatter everywhere. A spot of red catches my eye. A shard has embedded itself in the top of Debbie's swollen left foot.

I rush toward the table and grab up all the napkins. I open the back door and call out for Jamie to come and bring some bandages. Quickly, I return to Debbie and squat beside her, hearing glass crunch under my shoes. As carefully as I can, I pluck the glass out of her foot and put it aside. The cut is deeper than I thought it would be. I press the napkins on the wound to stop the bleeding.

Debbie hasn't said a word or made a sound. I know this has to hurt. Her feet are so messed up already. I look at her face. She's pinching her lips bravely as the tears running down her face betray her true feelings.

"I've got it," I tell her. "I'll get it all cleaned up for you."

She puts her hands on both sides of my face and lowers her forehead until it touches mine. "I'm sorry," she whispers.

"It's okay. The glass was sweaty. It could've happened to anyone."

Debbie tilts my head back, so we are looking in each other's eyes. I've never been this close to her face before. I've never noticed that her irises have flecks of lavender. The corners of her mouth tug downward, and I see her struggling against the emotion sweeping through her. "No, Grace. I'm sorry about the way I've been. The way I'm being. I don't mean it. I don't. It just hurts. You know. To see you. It always hurts to see you dance, but this was like a slam. Like you were mocking me. Do you understand?"

I nod. Tears run down my face, too. "I didn't think about how it would come across to you. I was caught up in the excitement of it."

"And you should have been. It was exciting for you. Your first professional gig as a dancer. At fifty, no less. When does that happen?"

I shrug weakly.

"It doesn't," she answers. "There *are* dancers our age, but they've been dancing professionally all along. No one starts a career at our age."

I sniff. "I'm not trying to be a professional dancer. It's a commercial. If I get another one at all, it'll probably be as some-one's mom, selling peanut butter or something. It was all a timing thing."

She swipes at her face, and I check to see if the bleeding has stopped on her foot. It hasn't, so I apply more pressure. Debbie winces. I lighten up. Jamie either didn't hear me or has no idea where the bandages are kept.

Debbie says, "You have the weirdest timing of anyone I've ever met."

"I'm a bit of a misfit," I confess.

"When you first showed up at Dancer's Room, I never thought you'd stick with it. No one stays for long. Just you. Then Spencer, and that was more because of you than me."

"And because you pay him."

She rolls her eyes. "Not enough. Not compared to his other jobs."

I tip the margarita pitcher to strain the drink through my fingers and keep a handful of ice. I press it on her foot. She twitches at the cold and then relaxes. I have her replace my hands on the ice and then work on cleaning up the broken glass on the ground, carefully sweeping it with one hand into the other. I'm not sure what to say to her.

"I'll need a broom for this."

"Grace." She says my name like it's weighing her down. I don't look at her. There are lots of small pieces of glass that need my attention. "I've always been too hard on you."

"You're a ballet teacher," I say. "It's expected. Stereotypical even." Although I know as well as she does that she has never been remotely as hard on any of the other dancers. They all come to the studio with years' worth of previous training, simply wanting a workout. She helps them without discouraging them. She provides them a safe place to hone their skills. Debbie has always treated me as lesser than, even when I started showing some real ability.

"Stereotypical?" she smiles painfully. "I didn't have a cane until recently." I shake my head but still won't look at her. "I was hard on you at first to test you, to see if you had the mettle for this. Part of me wanted to chase you away. I didn't want my other students thinking my studio wasn't quality. You didn't flake out. You worked hard and improved. Then I saw it as my duty to train you. I don't know why. But ask any of the girls who dance, and they'll all tell you their best teachers were bitches."

"I don't think that's true."

"The bitch part? Please." She laughs.

"Oh, yes, the bitch part is true. I don't think you were interested in me being a great dancer, though. Why would you be? No one starts dancing in their thirties. You told me over and over again I was wasting my time and yours." With a handful of glass that I'm mindfully not clenching into a fist, I raise my face to meet hers. "You were hard on me because you were pissed that I kept showing up."

"Of course I was pissed. Your ability to dance was growing, as mine was declining. It wasn't fair. What were you going to do with it? I'd have sold my soul to go back to dancing in New York. I still would. And you? You just want to take classes forever. That's all. A pretty workout."

There. It was out now.

I take the broken glass over to the trashcan and wipe my hands free of it. A sliver catches in the pad of my thumb. I get it out and then suck on the sore spot.

"Come back," Debbie says. "Come here."

I open the sliding glass door and call out to Jamie again. This time he shouts that he's coming and asks how bad it is. "She'll live," I respond. I glance back at Debbie. The ice has melted, and the top of her foot is bloody.

"I need to get something for your foot."

She wraps her foot with the bottom half of her beach towel. "Please, come here," she insists.

Reluctantly, I walk back over to her and sit back down on the other lounge chair. "I shouldn't have come today."

"I'm glad you did. I needed to get this off my chest. Your commercial got me all wound up. But..." She takes one of my hands with her cold ones. "This is a talk we've needed to have. You know I gave control of the studio to Spencer. He told me he's hired you to teach officially, and that's good. I want you to do more than that. I want you to run it with him. He's too busy to do it by himself, and he knows it. Both of you need to make the studio what you two want it to be. I know you have ideas. I won't argue. I won't fight you. It's yours."

"Me? Are you sure?"

"Damnit, Grace. I want twenty years of dancing to be worth something more than one commercial where you didn't even dance that much. If you're not going to be brave enough to try out for a show, then at least pass on what I've taught you. Give me a legacy."

We're both crying again. "I will. Thank you. Of course I will. I'm happy to do it."

Jamie comes outside with a roll of paper towels, a bag of cotton balls, a box of bandages, and some hydrogen peroxide. "Did you both get hurt?"

"Just your mom," I tell him. "But I think we're fine now."

He sits on the end of her lounge chair and cleans her foot. "You ruined this towel, you know."

I rise, needing desperately to clean my hands and face. "I'll come visit again soon. Before another five weeks pass. I promise."

"Ouch. Jamie! Gentle. What are you, a baboon?" Debbie smacks her son on the head. He looks up at me helplessly. To me she waves. "Fine. Fine. But pour me a fresh glass before you leave."

After putting her new margarita in the cup holder for her, I kiss her on the top of the head. "Goodbye, my queen."

"Ah, get out of here already."

I rinse my hands and face off in her downstairs bathroom and then head out to my car. It was a wasted effort. As soon as I sit down in the hot car, my body shudders with all the feelings I've been keeping trapped inside. I can't drive the skinny winding roads of Hollywood Hills crying like this, so I sit in my car with the air conditioner on high and the radio blasting.

I'm not even sure what it is that has me so worked up. I'm grateful to Debbie, but I'm so angry, too. All this time I was certain how she felt about me. Hatred. Pure hatred. I was always a dagger in her side, and she was always a sword at my back. And that was the thing, wasn't it? No matter how hard she was on me, she never discouraged me. She never told me I couldn't dance. She never told me not to. She pushed and pushed. If her intention was to make me quit, she failed. Debbie made me stronger than I used to be. She made me the dancer I am. I owe her so much.

Now I hate myself for doing that stupid commercial. That was a mistake. I should have been more respectful.

I pull tissues out of my glove box and wipe my face dry. My makeup is destroyed. I'm going to go home and clean up and then head to the studio. Spencer and I need to talk and plan. We're going to make Debbie's Dance Room—yes, we're going to rename it—the best studio in town.

# CHAPTER
## *Eleven*

Sunlight sneaks in through the cracks of my vertical blinds. I've hit snooze on my alarm twice. After my third time reaching over to give myself eight more minutes, Tyler hooks me under the arm and pulls me back into him. During the night I had slipped on a long-sleeve shirt to ward off the air conditioning, but I have nothing on waist down. He's completely naked beneath me, our bodies warm against each other. Tyler nuzzles against my ear and cheek. His trim beard is scratchy, and my skin is tender from the intense kissing last night.

"I need to get up," I say. "It's a workday for me."

His breath is hot against my neck. "I thought you made your own hours."

"Kind of. I don't own the company. My dad does."

"He's retired."

"His idea of retirement is different from what most people think. He checks in."

I scooch away from him. Tyler grabs my waist and pulls me back again.

"Come on," he says. "I don't have a shoot today. Sleep in with me."

"I don't think sleeping is what you want."

I roll my body so that I'm facing him. He grins. "You're too clever."

He slips his hands under my nightshirt and pulls me to straddle him. In a flash, my nightshirt is flung to the floor. Tyler runs his hands down my body, then pulls my hips as he slides further down the mattress. I gasp as he pushes his tongue into me. I hold tight to the headboard as the sensation sends me wild. It's impossible to suppress my moans of pleasure. When I can't stand it a moment longer, Tyler rolls me over and opens my legs. I'm more than ready to take him inside me.

Our love making is morning-clumsy but satisfying. We're both much more awake by the time we separate and lie back on our pillows. I don't want to, but I sneak a peek at the time.

"I really have to get up now," I groan. I kiss him and scoot out of the bed before he can grab me again. I watch his hand swipe across the empty bed sheet. As I head for the bathroom, I tell him, "You can stay as long as you want. Don't feel like you have to rush."

Tyler has spent the night before, but he's always had to leave before sun-up to get to the lot. Due to my schedule at the dance studio, we tend to get together on my side of town and wind up here. He hasn't seemed to mind, although he's mentioned more than once that he'd like a leisurely Sunday morning with me at his place, drinking mimosas and enjoying each other's bodies in the sunlight that streams in through his balcony windows. I'd like that. His condo is much nicer than mine. Not one porcelain ballerina anywhere.

I smile as I remember the first night he came over. While I was pouring us drinks, he stealthily moved all the fragile dancers off the tables around the couch and put them on the kitchen counter. "Keeping them safe," he'd told me. "You never know what might happen in here." The wine glasses got left on the kitchen counter, too.

The hesitation we'd had as kids was long forgotten. His touch was sure and confident, and I gave myself to him without reservation. We moved from the couch, to the floor, and, yes, eventually to the shower before finally collapsing onto my bed, fully spent but never more alive. It was an incredible night, and every night with him continued to blaze with passion.

Before I step into the shower, I think I hear my phone ringing. It's in the bedroom, so I'll let whoever's calling leave a message. The water feels wonderful on my skin. The lather soothes the skin left sensitive from Tyler's attention. I don't have time to linger and enjoy it. Despite what Tyler thinks, I do have things to do this morning for both of my jobs. I've got a house to stage in Glendale for an open house tomorrow. Spencer is going to meet me there to discuss plans for giving Debbie's office a makeover. My thoughts wander to paint color choices for the walls that are hiding under those wooden panels. Or should we do wallpaper? The desk has to go. I can find us another one.

A few minutes later, I emerge from the bathroom wrapped in a towel, my hair still damp. Tyler isn't in my room anymore. I hear him talking in my living room.

"Yes, I'll tell her. Like I said, I don't know what's going on... Okay. I think I hear her. Do you want me to...? I will... See ya."

I push my bedroom door all the way open, and he turns to face me. Normally he would give me a lascivious look, seeing me in only a towel. He'd suggest that I take it off and we hop back in bed once more. Not this time. His face is stunned, but not from anything I'm doing. My phone is in his hand.

"You're answering my phone calls?" He glances at the phone like he's surprised to find it still there. "Who was it?"

Tyler puts the phone on the arm of the sofa beside him, face down, so my black cover with the hot pink etching of ballet toe shoes stands out against my gray upholstery. The phone case had been a forty-ninth birthday gift from Spencer last year. Super cheesy and perfect.

"Sorry. I recognized the name and number."

I wait for more of a reason.

"It was Alan's office. I thought they might have an audition for you, and I didn't want you to miss getting the information."

That made a certain amount of sense but still bothered me. Carla could easily have left a message. She'd done it before. In fact, she's left three messages over the past week, and I haven't called her back. I'm sure she and Alan Bergman are fairly annoyed with me right about now.

"What did she want?" I ask. Might as well skip the argument about his right to answer my phone and get to the meat of this conversation. The lack of happiness on his face suggests that I didn't have an audition to go to.

He runs a hand through his thick hair. All he has on are his navy-blue boxer briefs. His chest is bare, and as if he suddenly seems to notice that fact, he crosses his arms. "Carla said you're not returning her calls. She's lined up two auditions for you this past week, and you've ignored her."

"I was busy."

"Then you call her back and tell her," Tyler says. "She's not asking you out to lunch. She's trying to get you a job. Not calling back is unprofessional. You know that, right?"

I nod weakly. "I know. I just—"

"It's embarrassing for me, Grace. I stuck my neck out for you."

This hits me all wrong. "You stuck your neck out? Really? Is your agency going to drop you or something if I don't work out?"

"No."

"Then you're fine. I'm sorry if I'm not the perfect client for them. I have two jobs that I'm juggling right now. The timing is bad."

Tyler runs a hand over his face and then abruptly walks into the bedroom. I find him picking his clothes up from the floor. As he tugs on his jeans, he says, "You live in Hollywood. It's not like auditions are out of your way or take a long time to do."

I lean against the doorframe. The smell of coffee wafting in from the kitchen makes my stomach grumble. I wish we could have this talk after I've had a cup. "If I book a commercial, it'll eat up a day or more."

"But you said you had fun filming. Don't you want to do it again? How are you not hooked?"

I don't know what to say to him, so he'll understand. "It was fun. It was in my wheelhouse because I was doing ballet. Some of these other jobs are not me. One of them I was supposed to be a business executive or something. I don't have a suit or anything to wear for that."

"It doesn't matter if you have the exact costume." He's got his shirt on now and sits on the foot of the bed to put on his shoes. I come closer and prop one knee up on the bed, putting pillows in place. "It matters if you show up, look good, and read the sides well. That's all. You can do that."

"Okay," I say. I don't feel like fighting. "I'll call her back."

He twists around and takes my hand. "Alan got on the phone and talked with me for a minute, too."

"You know I wasn't in the shower that long, right?" I quip.

Tyler continues. "He says you still haven't sent him any printed headshots or a resume to use. Some of the casting directors still like to work old school and not solely through the internet. He needs those. What's the hold up? Do you need help paying for it? I can pay for it. I can find you a photographer for new pictures. What do you want me to do?"

His face is so sincere. This matters so much to him. He can't comprehend that it doesn't matter as much to me. I see that so clearly at this moment.

"I'll get to it."

"When, honey?"

Honey. I'm honey now. Interesting. I get the loving nickname when he's frustrated with me. I guess it's better than the way he said my name a minute ago.

"Alan says they'll stop calling you if you turn down any more auditions. They have a strict policy unless you have a valid reason. Like if you're vegetarian and they're sending you for a hamburger commercial. Even then, it's a push to say no. There are ways to fake eating."

I pull my hand away and tighten my towel, which has been slipping. I feel vulnerable enough without being flat out naked. "He can go ahead and drop me. It's okay."

His posture droops. "Grace. This is a big deal. Alan is one of the best agents in town. He can help you be somebody."

"I am somebody."

I grab some underwear from my dresser. I pull a dress from my closet without looking to see which one it is and disappear into the bathroom, slamming the door shut behind me.

193

"Ah, come on. That's not what I meant. Grace!" He's right behind the door.

The dress is not one of my favorites, but it's stretchy and easy to pull on over my head. It's royal blue with a pattern of small black flowers. I don't answer him while I dress. The steam from my shower has mostly cleared from the mirror. My face is in desperate need of some makeup. My freckles are shouting. Let them be seen, I decide.

"I know you wanted to be an actress once. I don't want you to have any regrets. That's all. I thought you'd be into this, a second chance to have your dream."

I open the door and walk past him, heading for the kitchen. I grab a couple of mugs out of the cupboard and pour us both some coffee.

"Graceful? Talk to me."

I hand him a cup. It's olive green with the letters D-A-N-C-E engraved in the ceramic. I don't have anything not like that to give him. "I've decided that's not the dream I want. I don't regret not being an actress. I'm fine."

"You're lying," he says, putting the cup down on the counter without taking a sip. "I knew a girl once who did a scene with me in my first college acting class, and she was and remains one of the best acting partners I've ever had."

"Nice try."

"I'm serious."

I know he's blowing smoke. It still feels nice to hear it. "I liked acting back then, but I didn't have the stomach for competition. I still don't. What I like now is dancing. Running the studio with Spencer is what's important to me at this moment. I'm not saying I wouldn't go to an audition if it was the right one and suited me. If Alan isn't interested in me picking and choosing, then he can let me go. I'm fine with that."

"You won't get a chance like this again."

"I might not."

We stare at each other, neither of us knowing exactly how to end this conversation. Tyler finally shakes his head and says, "Fine. I'll talk with Alan and see what we can do."

"I'll talk to him myself," I say. "You don't need to do that for me."

"What are you going to say?"

"I'll think of something."

"I know how this works better than you do."

"Why are you being like this? It's my problem. It's my life. Why does it matter to you so much?"

"I care about you and want you to be happy. I want to help you be successful." And yet his face doesn't match the words he's saying. There's a sneer on his lips and the creases between his brows are deep with resentment.

"Why do you think I'm not?" I challenge. "Maybe we measure success differently. You ever think about that?"

"You don't get what I'm trying to do for you."

"You're trying to turn me into you, is what you're doing. It's always been about how *your* talent and *your* work are more valuable than mine."

"I've never said that."

"No? Are you sure about that?"

This shuts him up. I've definitely struck a nerve. He walks across my living room to the back window and looks out on the sunny morning. As he watches the traffic down below, he says, "I don't do anything valuable. I'm an actor. It's a selfish job, and I know that. Yes, I want to entertain people, but I'd be lying if I said it wasn't also about pride and accomplishment. I like acting. Always have. It's who I am, and I'm good at it."

He pauses. I'm not feeling in the mood to pet his ego for him, so I stay quiet.

"I lost my wife over my ambition." He speaks quietly, and I have to step closer to hear him over the TV playing in the other room. We haven't talked much about his marriage yet. I'd been wondering what happened but haven't braved the subject. "She wanted me to settle into a regular life with her out of New York. She was tired of auditions and living gig to gig. Ready to give up that life for the suburbs. Raise a couple kids and join the PTA. Maybe do community theatre once in a while for kicks. I wasn't there yet. I don't know if I'll ever be that guy.

"I'm having a good run right now. I don't know how long it'll last. My hope has been that the success of *Wildcats* will give me a boost into better guest starring roles on major networks or maybe a movie." He looks at me. "Then I meet this gorgeous woman who is passionate, if not slightly obsessed, about her talent, and I think, 'This is her. This is the person who will get me. She couldn't be more perfect, and we can live out our crazy dreams together. No compromising'."

"Tyler, I—"

"So, I give her performing career a nudge to help us get on some even footing. Something I regret not having done when we were teens. I always thought she was amazing, but I was, as noted, a little self-absorbed. I thought I was doing it right this time." He laughs painfully. "I guess I'm still wrong. There's no winning with Grace Fuller."

How is it possible for a wound three decades old to still be so fresh? My chest aches as I remember how discarded he made me feel back then. I hear him telling me his feelings, but I can only remember the way he treated me. I don't know if I have the ability to let him all the way into my heart again.

"Tyler, it isn't that I don't appreciate what you've done for me."

He puts up a hand to stop me from talking. "You don't, though. That's the thing." He grabs his wallet, keys, and phone. "I'm gonna head out." At the door, he stops and faces me. "You know your whole thing about being the end of a movie?" He makes finger quotes to emphasize what he's saying.

I nod slowly, not sure where this is headed.

"You can't be the end of the movie if you didn't have a middle to your story. A character needs an arc. You're a flat line. You're still that scared teenager no one noticed because you were hiding in the corner."

"That's not fair," I say, but my throat is so tight it barely comes out.

"Plus, endings are supposed to be happy. A single fifty-year-old woman living alone in an apartment in Hollywood? You don't even have a cat. What kind of ending is this? And if that's the ending you want, there's no place for me in it."

He doesn't give me time to answer.

I press my ear to the door after it closes behind him. I can hear the bell of the elevator stopping at my floor to take him away from me.

I'll call Carla and fix everything. I'll go to all the auditions. I'll make him proud of me.

Familiar music plays on the television in my bedroom.

"Eases joint pain and helps reduce swelling..." a pleasant woman's voice narrates.

That damn commercial. I wander into my bedroom and sink onto my bed in time to see me joyously spinning through a park on a sunny day. Where is that woman now?

# CHAPTER
*Twelve*

"The studio sits empty all day long," I tell Spencer. "I don't see why we can't make more use of it during daylight hours."

We sit in our newly renovated office on a Sunday afternoon. It's my favorite place to be now that it's been finished. We both agreed to lighten the whole room up by painting the walls a pale pink, replacing the chunky, mismatched furniture with white shelves, cabinets for files and books, and a small desk that is hardly ever used. We have two cushy chairs and ottomans, and we tend to do most of our office work sitting in those with laptops balanced on our knees. Spencer always has some essential oils burning to ease our souls and to eliminate the hint of Debbie's endless cigarette smoking that we are sure will never completely fade. That old ratty carpet went in the dumpster, and we brought in a cute rug with a rose pattern Spencer found at a garage sale in West L.A.

Spencer wraps a soft blanket around his shoulders and tucks his feet under him. "Well, I don't wake up until noon, for one thing, and we both have other jobs." It's chilly in here since November blew away the last gasp of summer. The heat in this old building doesn't come upstairs as strong as it does for the businesses on the ground floor. Jeremy, one of the stylists in the hair salon that took over the old optometrist office, complained to Spencer and me the other day about how sweaty he gets while working. Spencer's reaction was to tell him to come upstairs some night and see how sweaty he can get. They've been practically inseparable since that moment.

"My job is flexible, and I'm also talking about more guest teachers."

"We can't pay them."

"Their pay would be dependent on how many students they get. It'll force them to hustle. Like this lady, for example." I turn my laptop to show him a picture of a woman in layers of full-length, colorful, cotton skirts and a jeweled bra top. A belt of bangles wraps around her hips, and she poses with her arms above her head, palms out. "Her name is Lana, and she teaches belly dancing. She wants to know if we'd be interested in having her teach once or twice a week."

"We don't have room in the schedule," Spencer says, shaking his head.

"We do if she teaches during the day, or at least a little earlier. Like four o'clock."

He shakes his head. "People work at four o'clock."

"Not everyone. Think about it, will you? It seems like a waste of space to not use it. If we could bring in more revenue, we could purchase the space over George's office, break through the wall and have a whole second dance room. It's a big space, too. We could offer ballroom or swing classes. We could rent it out for show rehearsals. From what I saw in the files, Mondays are our best money-making nights because we rent the space to companies that pay. It's more lucrative than students popping in and out. When do we ever have a class with more than six students?"

"How many lattes have you had today, Gracie?" Spencer asks.

"I know. I know it's a lot, but I want this place to last. Right now, it feels like we're some secret society, with only a tiny handful of people who know about it. We need a better website. A better schedule. Something to draw in new bodies."

Spencer rolls his head around, and I hear his neck crackle. "You're stressing me out. Debbie hasn't asked us to save the studio from ruin or anything. All she wants is for us to run it as it has always been run. It has a reputation for integrity, for legit dancers. She won't like it being turned into some community center."

"Then you probably won't like my idea of a free class for low-income kids on Friday afternoons. I was also thinking about creating a small troupe to tour schools, to teach stories through ballet. We'd pay them. There's this grant we could apply for—"

Spencer throws off the blanket and stands up. "Stop. Take a breath, Grace." He takes a deep breath himself as he walks around the room. I don't. "We don't need to do so much."

"I want to refinish the hardwood floors."

He puts up a finger, and I close my mouth tight. Spencer leans over the back of my chair and puts his arms around my shoulders, his face next to mine. "You still haven't heard from him?"

I press my face against his. "No. I'd say it's official that I've been dumped."

It's been nearly three weeks since our fight, and Tyler hasn't called or texted. I reached out twice, but he never responded. I'm still not clear on who needs to do the apologizing. He somehow managed to compliment and insult me all at once, leaving me to wonder what's true and what's not.

The day after he walked out, I had my hair dyed back to its full flame and had Spencer take some pictures of me that didn't completely suck. I sent them to Alan's office. Carla never acknowledged the email and has not yet called me for another audition. So, that part of my life appears to be over, too.

"Well, I'd say his loss is my gain, but you're kind of driving me crazy." Spencer kisses my cheek. "Can't you go sell a house or something?"

"You know that would be nice," I say. "I've had this one precious house up in Sherman Oaks, and no one will bite. I think I've shown it a dozen times now."

"Did you bake the cookies?"

"Of course. Always. I love the house, and I can't figure out why no one wants it."

"Probably too expensive."

I nod. "Yeah, that could be it. I'd buy it in a heartbeat, but I certainly can't afford it."

Spencer grabs a Powerade out of the refrigerator in the corner. "I don't know what you need a house for. You live here, don't you? That is your egg salad in there?" He points over his shoulder.

"Leave me alone."

He rifles through mail and papers on the desk. "Jamie called me this morning. Said he was taking Debbie to church."

"That's... that's weird. Right?"

"Yeah, that's what I said. Didn't know she had a church. Turns out it's a Methodist one up in Burbank."

"What's that about?"

He shakes his head and shrugs. "Jamie said the family used to go there when his dad was still around. He's hoping it'll help her. She's been in a real funk, he says."

"Yeah, she wasn't great when I saw her. I should get back over there soon."

"Me too."

Spencer lifts up a flier advertising our guest teacher workshop. We have them posted on the windows downstairs and handed them out to our students over the past week. There's one pinned to the board at Stomping Grounds. "I hope the word got spread. Only an hour away."

The flier, printed on light blue paper, is a picture of a handsome male dancer in a Fosse-style pose, the buttons of his short-sleeved, fitted shirt mostly undone, his legs crossed while his body looks about to lose balance. You trust he won't, though, because his arms are stretched toward the opposite direction, fingers splayed. The copy boasts that film and stage choreographer Arthur Montoya will be teaching a contemporary class for advanced level dancers. It's forty-five dollars to attend. He's the highest profile teacher we've ever had come teach for us. As such, he's asking a lot for his fee. We're desperately hoping we get enough students to cover it.

Debbie knows him and set this up before she retired. Spencer talked to his rep on the phone, so neither of us have dealt with him personally. We're both pretending we're not nervous. If this program is popular, I'd like to start doing something like this at least once a month. It could bring in a lot of new dancers.

Contemporary isn't my strongest style. Debbie ordered me to stay away from her modern and contemporary classes for the first few years I studied with her. With me being so behind, I needed all my focus to be on learning the specific litany of ballet steps correctly. She was determined to get me on pointe, and with a lot of work and even more pain, I succeeded. I continued to stay away from the other forms of dance she offered at the studio. I didn't know if I could handle the differences, and I didn't want to go back to that feeling of being a beginner again.

It was Spencer that finally pushed me out of my comfort zone. He said he was offended that I never came to his contemporary class on Friday nights. "I always knew you were a fake friend," he teased. Under extreme pressure from him, Rochelle, and Mariah, I gave in and took the class.

I caught on better than I thought I would. It was nothing like the flailing about that I did at my first few months of ballet class. Thankfully, I had enough musicality in me now to be able to make my movements flow. The styles are different in the way the body expresses movement. Contemporary is much looser, using the back muscles more expressively. Lots of contractions and releases. Feet are sometimes flexed; angles of legs and arms aren't always pretty. I can hold my own in a contemporary or lyrical dance now. I've even led class a few times. Ballet still holds top spot in my heart.

Spencer and I end our planning discussion to grab a quick, light meal before coming back to change and get ready for the class. My favorite part about contemporary is the break from the toe shoes and that we can wear looser attire. I wear a workout bra instead of a leotard under a loose T-shirt with a pair of black yoga pants. Spencer wears a black tank that shows off the glorious muscles in his arms and shoulders and some cut-off sweatpants that are tight around the butt.

"You trying to get some attention?" I tease. "You'll make Jeremy jealous."

"It's not every day a male dancer shows up around here, let alone one that has finished puberty."

We tap water bottles.

The door downstairs opens, and we hear a man's voice call up, "I'm looking for Spencer Nichols?"

"Hello!" Spencer dashes out of the office to the stairs. "You must be Mr. Montoya. Our studio is up here."

"Everyone calls me Art," he says, making sure to look my way and include me.

I linger up top as Spencer leads Art into the building. I notice his hair first, as I'm looking down on him. It's the darkest shade of brown and thick with waves. When he raises his face to look where he's going, I see that his eyebrows are equally dark. A bit of gray streaks through his sideburns, belying his age. His skin is a warm brown that makes me think of whiskey and hot summer days. He's wearing a wool jacket over his dance clothes and a scarf around his neck, giving away that he is a New Yorker. I don't know anyone who owns a scarf.

I put my hand out to shake his when he reaches the top of the stairs. "I'm Grace."

The corner of his mouth lifts as he appraises me. There is a hint of a goatee, like he hasn't decided whether or not to shave it off. By the glint in his eye as he takes my hand into his warm one, I know that Jeremy has nothing to worry about. Spencer will still be his when this class is over.

"Pleasure to meet you," Art says. "Debbie told me you two run this place now?"

"Mostly Spencer. I help."

"Great. You can help me get set up."

Spencer gestures toward the office. "You can stow your personal belongings in the office over here."

Art heads toward the dance room instead. I follow and click on the lights for him. "We've got the music you sent us ready to play through the Bluetooth speaker. If you want to check that…"

He waves that away. "I trust you've checked already."

I have. A couple times. I want this to run smoothly.

He takes off his coat and scarf and puts them carefully on the piano bench. "I didn't know you had a piano. I like dancing to live music."

"It's badly out of tune."

He pops open the lid and plays a quick allegro with his right hand, grimaces and makes a show of closing the lid carefully as if to trap the evil inside. "We'll leave that alone then."

I laugh. He smiles broadly, revealing deep dimples in each cheek and gorgeous crow's feet to the side of each brown eye. He's wearing loose white linen pants with a beige V-neck short sleeve shirt. His muscles aren't as large as Spencer's, but his pecs and arms are defined. The girls coming to class are going to have a hard time concentrating. He steps out of his loafers and bends over to put them neatly in place under the bench. Yep, no one will be concentrating.

"Do you need anything?" I ask. "Water? I think I'm going to get a bottle." I need one. My throat is crazy dry right now.

"Sure. I'll take one," he says.

I dash down the hall and bump into Spencer. He gives me a look to say, "Oh my God", and I mouth, "I know."

Turnout for the class is better than expected. We squeeze twelve dancers plus Spencer and I into the space. None of us are used to being so tightly packed. There's a lot of bumping elbows until we get it all figured out. Another male dancer shows up that I haven't met before, so Spencer isn't the only one. They don't dance near each other, and I know Spencer well enough to see that he's competing.

Art is an exceptional teacher, pushing all of us to a higher level without making any of us feel inadequate. He's a hands-on teacher, too, and has no problem grabbing an ankle or wrist of a dancer to put a leg or arm in the right place. None of the girls seem to mind. Gauging by all the blushing faces, I think they'd be okay with him touching them anywhere.

The dance routine, which is the main portion of the two-hour class, is a complicated piece of choreography, and he teaches fast. We're still struggling with some of the hardest parts when time comes to an end. I have to remind myself that this was one class not a rehearsal for a performance, and I can see some of the other dancers are a bit frustrated, too. Maybe next Friday we can work on it without Art in our regular class. I'll mention it later and see if anyone is interested. I'd love a reason for more of these dancers to return.

By the time class is finished, the room is steamy with sweaty bodies. Even I have passed my point of red-faced-ness and have sweat beading up around my hairline. I've had to put my cold water bottle to my face and neck multiple times, so I don't look like I'm about to have a heart attack and die.

Art invites us to sit on the floor while he pulls the piano bench over and parks on it. Spencer offers a softer chair from the office, but Art waves that away politely. Spencer leans against the wall, and I scooch over to sit by his feet. For the next half hour, Art talks about casting for Broadway shows and what he looks for in dancers at auditions. He answers questions from all the eager young dancers in the room and is forthcoming with information. These people paid for a master class, and they're getting their money's worth.

When it's over, all of the dancers thank us as they leave.

"This was so good," Elise, one of our Friday night lyrical students says. She's a nursing student at L.A. Valley College who has told us many times her real dream is to dance in Vegas. There's no reason in my mind why she wouldn't make it, but she's scared to go. "Please, please, please do more of these."

"We will," I promise her.

"Can't guarantee they'll all be like this guy," Spencer says.

Elise says in a low voice, "No one is like this guy."

At last, the place has emptied out. Spencer goes to the office to write Art a check. I hang out in the dance room while Art puts his shoes back on and stretches his back.

"Thank you," I tell him. "It was a great class."

"I enjoyed it. And you were terrific. You keep up with the tykes."

"Tykes!" I burst out laughing.

He grins wickedly. "Can't help it. Anyone under thirty seems so young to me now."

"It's very disrespectful," I kid.

"I suppose. I'm serious though, you're a great dancer. Where did you train?"

"Here."

That catches him off guard. "Here? I thought this was a school for professional dancers, not a training school."

"It's a long story," I say with enough weight to let him know I'm not in the mood to tell it.

"Well, I'd like to hear it sometime." He puts his coat and scarf over his arm. It'll be cool outside, but it's still hot as blazes in this room and smells of perspiration. "What are you doing tomorrow night?"

Now I'm the one that's thrown. "Oh... I'll be *here*. We have a dance team coming in for some critique and fine tuning from Spencer before they head off for competition season."

"What time will that be over?"

I'm short of breath, much worse than when we were in the middle of the dance. I have to lean against the wall for a second. This handsome man, made extraordinarily so now that his skin has a sheen of drying sweat on it, steps closer to me. It hasn't been long since Tyler and I stopped seeing each other. I'm still reeling from that ending so abruptly. Is it wrong to be this attracted to a man already? Why do I feel guilty at the prospect that this man might be about to ask me out on a date?

"We should be done by eight o'clock."

What do I say when he asks? Should I make an excuse? All those gorgeous dancers that just left, and I'm the one that caught his eye? To say I'm flattered is an understatement.

"Will anyone be using the studio after that?"

Not the question I was expecting at all.

"No. No, they're a high school group and for sure will be done by eight."

"Great." He drops his jacket and scarf on the ground, and backs into the center of the room. He does a couple dance steps, watching himself in the mirror. The movements are broad and masculine, quite different from what he had taught our class earlier. My opinion of his talent goes up another notch. While still dancing, he says, "I'd like to rent the room out for the remainder of the evening. Can you set that up or do I need to check with Spencer? Or do I need to ask Debbie?"

From the doorway, Spencer says, "I can take care of it." I wonder how long he's been standing there. Had he seen me squirming while I thought Art was about to ask me out? Did either of them notice that? I pray they did not.

Art stops dancing and addresses Spencer. "Let me know how much that'll be. I'll probably want a few hours. Is that okay?"

"One of us will have to be here," Spencer says.

Art gestures to me. "Do you mind, Grace? I could use your help. I'm working on choreography for a duet. I can pay for your time."

"You don't have to pay me for that," I say. "It'd be like another master class for me. I'd be honored."

"That's kind and generous of you. However, your talent and time have value, and I insist on honoring that with proper compensation."

Spencer and Art go down the hall to work out the details. I pick up Art's coat and scarf and can't stop myself from doing a fist pump when neither of them can see me.


I'm late to the studio because I changed my dance clothes too many times and put on more makeup than usual. I was torn between wanting to look the same as last night. Not trying too hard, right? Or looking more desirable. I know now that Art's interest in me is purely professional. Still, it couldn't hurt to look nice for him. First, I put too much makeup on and had to wipe it off and start over. I wanted to wear enough to hide my face when it got hot and red from dancing, but not so much that I looked like I was purposely vamping up. Did I want to wear loose-fit dancewear or tight? I ultimately chose an elbow length wine colored leotard and nude, footless tights. He had us all dance barefoot yesterday. For the workshop with the teenagers, I wear a matching wrap-around skirt over the leotard.

When I arrive at the studio, Spencer immediately starts

singing, "Music and the Mirror" and tells me I look like Cassie from *A Chorus Line*.

"You know what? I feel a little bit like Cassie tonight." I strike a pose and sing a line. "God, I'm a dancer. A dancer dances!"

"I always forget how well you sing," Spencer says.

The girls on the dance team laugh at us. One of them shouts, "You're hot, Ms. Grace!"

I curtsy.

Spencer has been judging dance competitions for about fifteen years now, so he knows what is required of a number to win. He does his magic with this team, and I mostly watch. I help demonstrate a step or two when people get confused, but that's about it. At the end of the session, the team is in top form. Their dance teacher starts crying, and then all the girls get teary, too. Spencer and I get pulled into this giant, smothering group hug.

When I finally escape, I see Art crouching in the front corner of the room. He's charmed by the kids and how grateful they are to us as they pack up and leave. The teacher thanks Spencer again, saying this was worth all the car washes the girls had to do to pay for it. He walks her out, leaving Art and I alone.

"Are you warmed up?" he asks, as he moves across the floor to put his things down by the piano. I see that he's in tighter dancewear tonight. Black jazz pants and a light blue compression shirt that leaves little to the imagination. His body is firm. He has a duffel bag with him. A change of clothes for later? I wish I'd thought to bring regular clothes to wear. Maybe we could go for a drink afterward? "This number is challenging, so make sure you've stretched."

I untie my skirt, feeling awkward about taking it off in front of him. This is a normal thing to do in a dance room, and yet I feel like I'm baring myself. I crouch to put it down instead of dropping it. I don't know why.

"Thank you again for doing this," he says. I put a leg up on the barre to stretch. "You look great, by the way."

I accept the compliment as politeness, nothing more, and continue with my stretching. He is now doing warm-ups of his own on the floor. We're quiet while we concentrate. Spencer comes back upstairs.

"Whew, you're here. I thought maybe you two had snuck out a window or something." He winks at me to let me know what he thought "or something" really meant. "Do you need me to stay?"

I never intended for Spencer to waste his night by sticking around. If he leaves, I'll be alone all evening with this man I barely know. I've made sketchier decisions in my life. Besides, I'm ninety-nine percent positive that this professional choreographer is interested only in working on his dance.

"I'll be fine. I'll lock everything up."

"Thanks, man," Art says to Spencer. "I appreciate the use of your space. I'm meeting with some producers of a film project this week and want to show them an idea of mine."

"What's the project?" Spencer asks. I want to know, too.

Art puts out his hands helplessly. "Sorry. Not allowed to say at this point. It's still in the planning stages. A lot of debate over whether they want it to be a movie or do a TV limited series kind of like what they did with that Bob Fosse biography."

Spencer's eyebrows shoot up, and I know he's wondering, like I am, if Art is talking about the movie being planned about the life of Martha Graham. It seems like forever ago when he showed me that article in the *Hollywood Reporter*. "Sounds like it'll be awesome whatever it turns out to be. You'll be the choreographer on it, then?"

"I'm auditioning for that, yes. It's not cemented."

"Well, break a leg." Spencer starts out and then stops to say to me. "I'm going to grab my things and get out of here. Jeremy wants sushi tonight."

"Have fun."

"You too." He blows me a kiss and mouths "hot!" behind a hand so Art can't see him. I have to stifle a laugh.

Art takes a long, soothing breath and spins in a circle with his arms wide open. "There is honestly nothing I love more than a wide-open dance floor." He faces me, arms still open. His fingers beckon me toward him. "You ready?"

I am.

I haven't had much opportunity to dance with a partner. Most of our students are women, and we normally stick to perfecting the craft of dancing rather than working on creative stuff. Every opportunity I've had to work on lifts and partnering has been with Spencer, and usually during the Monday evening specialty sessions. I feel terrible about not disclosing that information ahead of time, because quickly into the choreography Art is trying to get me to do a complicated lift I've never done before. He explains it first, but doing it is another thing.

"You need to tighten your core, Grace. Don't be afraid. I won't drop you."

I squeeze everything in me, and he lifts me easily above his head and then rolls my body until I'm in a low dip. When we succeed, I start breathing again.

"Oh, my gosh! I've felt less of a thrill on a roller coaster."

"Let's try it again."

"Hang on," I say, holding my chest to still my heart. "I need a moment."

He peels my hand off of my body and gets me back into position. "The more you do it, the more natural it will feel."

The second time isn't as frightening. I'm able to smile.

"Wonderful," he says, holding me in the dip longer than necessary. "Let's put everything together up to this point."

We move apart and he starts to count us off. I interrupt. "Why did you choose me for this, Art? I'm hardly the best dancer that was in your class last night. I know I'm the least experienced."

"Best is subjective," he says. "I wasn't judging to see who was best or not. I like the way you move, and, if you must know, I'm intrigued by your age. If I get chosen to choreograph this project, I'll be working with a more mature dancer."

That makes sense to me. "Did Debbie tell you how old I am?"

"She told me nothing about you. I hope you won't be offended if I guess?" I gesture for him to try. He peers at me like he hasn't already thought about it. "I'm guessing late thirties. Forty-two tops."

"I'm flattered," I tell him.

"What? Don't tell me you're older than that? I'm forty-six."

"Well then, you're a baby."

I would never have put him at forty-six, so we're both guessing young.

"No. No! You can't be older than me. I refuse to believe it."

"Fifty."

"No shit." I nod my head, and we both laugh. He takes my hand and kisses it. "You move well for an old lady."

"Thank you kindly, young man."

We dance through what he's taught me already and nail the lift. Immediately, he teaches me the next sixteen counts. He's choreographed this dance so that once we get through that first lift, we are constantly touching each other with some part of our bodies. We remain extremely close to each other, at one point touching foreheads as we promenade in a circle. Then we roll out of it in a way that our heads never stop connecting until we are almost face to face again. At that point, his hand juts out and takes mine to lead me into another preparation for a lift, this one more complicated than the one before.

Despite the difficult work and his dedication to staying on task and getting the work completed, his banter stays light and flirtatious. If there is a world outside of the room, I've forgotten about it. All of my body and mind are controlled by this dance and the impossible energy of this man. The time flies by, and before I know it, it's already eleven o'clock. My body will scream at me tomorrow for what I'm putting it through.

We take a break, and I go to grab cold waters from the office. When I return, he's setting up a tripod and a video camera. I put his water bottle on the piano bench.

"We're recording this?" I confirm.

He nods. "This is what I'm bringing to my meeting. Do you want to sign a release or anything?"

"No, it's fine. I hope I don't mess up. Cameras make me nervous."

He comes toward me and brushes a couple stray hairs away from my eyes. "You should never be nervous around a camera." I shiver slightly despite being hot from all the dancing. He heads back to the camera and clicks open the lens. "Besides, you've done this perfectly several times now, so I'm not worried."

Art indicates that I get into position. He clicks record on the camera and play on the music and dashes toward me. We do the number flawlessly, but he wants another take to be safe. In the final moment of the dance, I have my leg wrapped high around his hip, my body close to his, and then he swings me out to a high kick where I completely separate from him and fold into a full body contraction. The final pose has him crouched over me in an identical contraction, neither of us touching.

Only, this second time through, when we get to the leg wrap, he doesn't spin me out. He keeps an arm tight around my back and slips a hand onto my thigh that clasps his hip. I make as if to move away, but he firms his hold to keep me in place. We breathe heavily, our chests connecting with each inhale, air hot in each other's faces.

There is no holding my core tightly now. Everything inside me is jello.

I whisper so I can't be heard by the microphone. "The video."

"The first one was fine." His hand runs up my spine and cradles the back of my head. Sweat glistens on his face. The heat of his body has only intensified the musky smell of his cologne. Those gorgeous brown eyes gaze into mine. "This has been a pleasure," he says in a voice of silk.

"I'm so glad—"

He stops me with a kiss. For a split second, I think of pulling away. His tongue moves between my lips, and I let it in. The kisses are deep and urgent. I grip my arms around his torso and squeeze his butt with my leg. We should lose our balance, but Art is a dancer. He picks me up in this position and carefully lowers me to the ground. His hands roam from my head, around my face, over my shoulders, and find my breasts.

My glance flickers to the camera. He chews his lower lip for a second, as if debating my unspoken request, and then gets up. He saunters over to the camera, and a second later the red light goes out. This makes me feel much more at ease. Still, I sit up and pull my knees to my chest. I'm not sure what's happening and if I should allow it. For all I know, he's a predator and does this with all the girls.

And yet. He didn't choose a young, naïve girl. He chose wizened, old me. We worked hard and professionally all night. The dance was intense and put our bodies in close proximity. I'd be lying to say I haven't felt the pull of desire all evening. I fight the part of my brain telling me that it hasn't been long enough since Tyler left. That it's not appropriate. That I might never see this man again. What is the point of resisting? There are no rules for a woman my age. If this man wants me, why shouldn't I give myself?

Besides, in the twenty years I've danced in this room, I can't count how many fantasies I've had about having sex on this damn floor.

Art takes two steps and then slides the rest of the way across the wooden floor toward me. It makes me laugh, and I trace the dimples in his cheeks with my fingers. He trails the neckline of my leotard with his finger, hooks the material and pulls it off my shoulder. His tender lips kiss my bared skin. I open my legs and trap his body within them. He grins as I push my leotard off the other shoulder.

He takes his time exploring my body and finding ways to make me shudder. When he is ready to take me, it's as intense and passionate as his dancing. The reflections of his incredible body twined with mine in the mirrors on both sides of the room heightens the thrill. The hard wood beneath me that has bruised my body so many times when I've fallen over the years seems as if it is yielding to us both. It could be made of feathers.

We lay together on the dusty floor when we are both spent. Our dance clothes are scattered around the room. I only now notice that music is still playing from the speaker, obviously long past the song we danced to on the playlist. The song playing now is soft and quiet, perfectly accenting our repose. It's almost as if the choreographer had planned it. There's a part of me that wants to ask, but I also want to bask in this delicious moment and not care about his conquests or how he achieves them.

"Remember to edit your video," I say.

Art wriggles his nose. "I don't know. The second one might be better." I'm about to give my opinion when he pulls me into his body and tells me not to worry. His kisses begin again with fresh energy. This time, to save our knees and backbones, I guide him to the office, and we enjoy each other on my soft chair.

We both doze off for a bit. I open my eyes to find him dressed and sitting in Spencer's chair. He's watching me, his chin on one hand. "No, no," he says. "Keep sleeping. You look so beautiful and peaceful." He's found Spencer's blanket and put it over me. The sky is still dark outside, so I assume it's sometime after midnight. I haven't slept until dawn, thank goodness. My muscles are stiffening and cry a little when I stretch.

"I should clean up and get going," I say. He nods toward the pile of my dance clothes folded on the desk. Very considerate.

"Do you live far?" he asks.

"No. Not far at all."

"Good. I'll be here through Thursday, staying at the Hollywood Roosevelt. Any chance I could see you again? I'd love to tell you how the meeting goes. Drinks? Dinner?"

I'm naked under a fleece blanket, and that doesn't make me feel nearly as vulnerable as this man's offer to take me out to dinner. We've danced. We've had sex. We have not had to talk.

"I could, after class on Wednesday. Do you want to meet here?"

He stands and crosses the floor to me. Full of chivalry, he lifts the blanket and holds it open. I stand, and he wraps it around me like a ballgown. "We'll pick a place, and you meet me there. I want to see you without dance clothes."

"I think you already have."

He spins me under his hand and the blanket drops to the floor. "Yes, I have, and you are exquisite." Art appraises my body once more, moans, and then hands me my clothes as if to stop himself from ravaging me again. "Wednesday," he says, walking out of the room.

After I'm dressed, I lock the office and find him waiting for me on the stairs with his duffel bag over his shoulder. I lock up the dance studio and then follow him downstairs where he waits once more as I lock up the building. Our two cars are alone in the small parking lot. The traffic is light but steady. The bars are still open.

"Thank you, Grace," Art says, wrapping his arms around me once more. It's much chillier out than I anticipated. I regret not bringing a coat. I shiver slightly, so he rubs my arms and kisses my cheek. "Okay, I'll let you go."

It's only after I've driven away that I realize I haven't given him my number. I guess that'll be the real test. If he wants to see me again, he can reach me through the studio. I'll leave it up to him to make that move. No expectations. Besides, I can hardly get in a relationship with a man that lives across the country, can I?

My windows fog as I drive. I'm not sure if it's the heat from the vents or me as memories of the night flash through my mind.

# CHAPTER
## Thirteen

Spencer about loses his mind when I tell him.

"Right here. You did it with that gorgeous mass of muscle right here?" He points to the floor of the dance studio. He puts his hands on his hips and shakes his head. "You have finally officially surprised me, Ms. Fuller. I wondered why the floor was so clean." He gasps. "This hard floor. That had to have hurt."

"It didn't seem like it at the time, but..." I turn and let him peek down the back of my leotard at the purple circles on my spine and he clucks at me. "It was worth it."

It's Wednesday evening. It hadn't been my intention to tell Spencer all the details, but I haven't heard from Art yet and I had to know if he'd called the studio. This conversation started with Spencer telling me no.

"Well, honey, you have gone years thirsty in the desert and now two delicious drinks back-to-back. This is something. *I'll* take you out tonight to celebrate your new slutty side."

I know he's joking, but some old-fashioned notions about shame hang on like prickly burrs. I'd never had a one-night stand before or even slept with a man on the first date. The more I think about it, the more my mind tarnishes my shiny reminiscence of the spontaneous passion.

I've barely slept the past two nights, guilt and regret nagging at me. My moment with Art was wonderful. I have no reason to feel bad about it. Tyler has made it clear through his silence that we're over, so it wasn't cheating. If I never hear from Art again, it shouldn't matter. I hardly need another relationship right now. There is nothing wrong with a woman sharing a consensual night of passion with someone alluring.

All the same, I was hoping he'd call. A chance to talk and get to know each other, even if it went nowhere, would make me feel more comfortable with what happened between us.

"Thanks, Spence, but I'm going home after class. I'm tired."

"Tired of strutting your sexy ass around?"

"You're ridiculous."

"Always."

At ten to seven, dancers begin showing up for class. Elise comes in, which is a surprise. She rarely comes out for Ballet 2. It's not her strongest form. I'm about to approach her when she turns to a group of girls and shows them something on her phone. I walk away, not terribly interested in whatever funny gif or meme she's sharing. After beginning my stretches on the floor, I realize they are still watching whatever video Elise is showing them and beckoning other dancers that arrive to come watch, too. They're murmuring to each other, their eyes wide with astonishment.

"What's going on?" I whisper to Spencer. He shrugs and heads over to the group.

"Have you seen this?" Elise asks him when he pushes into the group.

Now I'm curious. I get up and start toward them as well. As soon as she sees me, Elise turns the phone to her chest, and the rest of the dancers scatter. I feel like I'm in high school—if there had been cell phones when I went to high school.

"What is it?"

"I don't know," Spencer says. "But I really want to."

From behind me, one of the newer dancers says, "It's so good, Ms. Grace."

I don't like them calling me Ms. Grace. I'll fix that later. "Let me see," I say to Elise.

She turns the phone over and taps it to bring the video back.

"You haven't seen this yet?"

"I don't know," I say. "Depends what it is." Honestly, I'm not that big into social media, so I probably haven't seen it unless it's been shared two million times.

She hits play and holds it up for us. It takes a second for me to register what I'm watching. It's the video of Art and me dancing. I grab the phone from her and pull it closer to my face to see it better. Spencer leans in, his chin over my shoulder. The dance is more impressive than I realized. Other than in a mirror, the only time I've seen myself dance was that stupid commercial. That was hardly anything. Watching this is like watching someone else. A twin. One who can bend at impossible angles and soar to unimaginable heights.

"You're amazing in this," Elise says timidly. "You should be proud."

"This is on the internet?" I ask. How? Did Art post it? Why? He didn't tell me he was going to do that. I didn't give permission... I didn't sign anything saying he couldn't.

Beside me, Spencer gives a low whistle. "This is incredible... *ly sexy*! Grace! Look at your hotness! I am literally losing my shit!"

It's the second take, the one ending with us kissing passionately. My face is on fire, and I feel the stares of all of our students. Elise in front of me has pinned her gaze firmly on the floor. I want to look away from the video, but I can't. I have to see it all. The video comes to a stop before his hands explore my body. It's been edited and has at least spared me that extra embarrassment.

"It's got so many likes so far," Elise says. "It's fire."

I'm so confused by all of this. "What do you mean? How did you even find this?"

"Oh, it's on Arthur Montoya's channel. I subscribed to him before the master class so I could learn more about him. He posts a lot of his choreography on there. He's got a lot of followers. This went live this morning."

I hand the phone back to her and turn around to face the class. They all look a little intimidated, something I haven't seen on a face in this room since Debbie stopped teaching. I'm torn whether I like being looked at like this or not.

"Class is starting," I say. "Let's go."

The dancers find their places on the floor. I tap Spencer's shoulder to let him know that he needs to take over. He claps his hands and heads to the front of the room while I exit. Elise chases me into the hallway. "Hey, Grace. I'm sorry if I upset you. I didn't mean to. I'm so impressed. Jealous like crazy, but so impressed. It's one of the best videos he's got, in my opinion. And it's so sexy. Are you two together now?"

I do my best to smile graciously at her. "Thank you. It was fun. We… we got carried away because the dance was so physical. That's all."

"Is he a good kisser?"

"You're missing class," I tell her.

She shuts her mouth to stifle a giggle, and it makes me want to laugh at this whole thing, too. Maybe I'll come dance after all. In a minute, though. I need a moment to get myself together. Elise dashes off and joins the rest of the class in floor stretches. I make my way into the office with the intention of plopping into my cozy chair. I see the blanket folded innocently over the back and veer toward the rolling desk chair instead. My cell phone is on the desk, and I easily navigate my way to watch the video again. Why this version? Why didn't he post the one with the final pose the way he choreographed it? Why didn't he tell me he was going to do this?

The landline phone for the studio rings. I think about letting the machine get it. There is a dance class going on, and we don't run out to answer phone calls. After three rings, I remind myself that I'm helping run this joint and should probably not ignore customers. I pick up the receiver.

"Grace?"

"Your timing is interesting," I say to Art, recognizing his voice. "I'm watching the video of us right now."

"It came out so good I couldn't bear not to post it. I hope you don't mind."

I'm not exactly sure what to say to this. "I guess not, although my students are looking at me cross-eyed now."

"As well they should," he says. "The whole world should

know you're vibrant and sexy. Not just a quiet ballet teacher, but a woman with a fire burning inside."

"Is that what I am?"

"Yes, and so much more."

He's good. I already feel weak. "It's Wednesday," I remind him.

"I know. I'm sorry for not calling sooner. My meeting was today and only got out a couple hours ago. I was waiting to see if I'd have something interesting to share with you when we got together. Then I realized I didn't have your number because I was so dizzy with you I forgot to ask."

"Dizzy with me, huh?"

"Yes, so much so. I'm surprised I made it back to my hotel in one piece."

I understand exactly what he means. I felt the same.

"I tried calling Debbie, but I couldn't reach her. All of my communication with Spencer was through my assistant. I finally found the number for the studio, so..." He takes a big audible breath for effect. "Here I am at last. Thank you for picking up. Please say you will still see me tonight."

"I thought you were standing me up. I didn't bring a change of clothes."

He has a quick fix. "Go home and change. I'll come pick you up."

I'm not sure I want him at my place. It's too soon since Tyler was there. "How about I meet you?"

"Come here, to my hotel. There's a nice restaurant downstairs."

"When?"

"As soon as you possibly can."

I grab my purse and coat. Stopping briefly at the door to the dance room, I shout to Spencer, "You're on your own tonight."

Spencer throws his arms in the air. "Go get it, baby!"

The class cheers and whistles. I've never seen a ballet class so lively. I wonder if they'll even keep dancing after I've left or if the whole thing will devolve into a big gossip fest about Art and me.

I don't care.

I head home and change my clothes faster than an actress backstage between scenes and touch up my makeup. I'd bought a new dress on Monday for this date, not wanting to wear anything I'd worn around Tyler. It's a pretty cap-sleeved white dress with a print of red poppies. Like most of my dresses, it has a full skirt. I wear a red leather jacket over it and a pair of red pumps. My lipstick is also a bold red. I'm usually more a neutral shade kind of gal, but tonight I feel like doing everything with more flair.

I'm in the Hollywood Roosevelt lobby within an hour of our last conversation. He's impressed.

"I expected to wait much longer," Art says, as he approaches from the elevator and greets me with a warm hug. "You look beautiful."

"Better than when you last saw me?"

He thinks about it. "I have images of you from the other night that will forever haunt me." A sly smirk deepens one of his dimples. "But this is nice, too."

I'm not sure what to say, so I choose a coy topic change. "I've never been here before. I live only a mile or two away, and I've never once stepped inside this building. It's gorgeous."

The lobby is decorated to reflect Historic California/Old Mexico. Its ceiling is two stories high, with balconies looking down and archways leading off to the corridors and ballroom. The floor is a shiny red tile, dark leather sofas and armchairs are tucked along the perimeter, and a beautiful water fountain is the centerpiece. I want to stand there awhile and take in all of the details.

"This building is nearly a century old. If you get quiet enough, you can hear the echoes of Hollywood legends walking about." Art says, taking my hand.

"Do you think it's haunted?"

"I have no doubt of it." He leads me toward one of those lovely arches. "I was wrong. They don't have a true restaurant in the building, but they have a lounge that has some delicious looking appetizers on the menu. That would be fine with me, but if you'd rather have a full meal, we can go somewhere else, or I can order room service and we eat upstairs."

Having not planned on this date becoming reality, I had eaten a salad and a yogurt before going to class. I'm not starving. Also, I'm not sure if I'm ready to go to his room—yet. I do hope we'll wind up there eventually. "Appetizers and drinks sound lovely."

The bar has a different kind of beauty to it. The walnut décor is dark, and the green walls are decorated with a hunting theme, including some mounted animal heads. Looking around, I'm not surprised to find that the only other customers are men in suits.

"Do you want to go somewhere else?" he asks, noting my scrutiny.

"It's fine. I can drink wine with Bambi's dad looking down at us."

We settle in a booth and order drinks, calamari, and some chips with salsa. By the time the food comes, we're on our second glasses and the small talk has gotten easier. It doesn't matter to me much that he's talking about how he dreads going back to the cold November weather after all this sun, because I'm enjoying the hell out of watching him talk. His face is so handsome, and now that I'm able to take time to keep my eyes on him, I see a small scar on his jawbone, a little mole on his forehead, and the hint of gray in his eyebrows. Every imperfection makes his gorgeous brown face more perfect to me. His lower teeth are a bit crooked, and I love that, too. I'm not sure why finding out that the most astonishing looking man I've ever made love to has flaws excites me.

"You were going to tell me about your meeting." I dip a chip into the salsa. "It went well?"

"It went so well," he responds. The fresh thought of it makes him beam. "They're hiring me to choreograph. I can't tell you the name of the project yet. It's still hush hush while they finish working out the details. It was going to be a feature, but now they're fairly set on the concept of a limited series. They're pitching to HBO or maybe Netflix. Maybe FX. A limited series would use more dances than a feature..." He pauses. "I'm sorry. It was like you popped the cork out of the champagne."

"I think we should be having champagne. Congratulations!"

I love that this man who has choreographed for Broadway

and is considered a huge success in his field is as excited as a newbie to get a job.

"I've done some small work for film before, but this will be a huge project. The biggest thing yet. And I owe you so much for helping make it happen."

"Me?"

He looks at me like I'm crazy. "Of course, you. The dance we did. They loved it. Said it was exactly the style they were looking for. They lost their shit about you. No kidding. When I told them a bit about you, one of the producers asked me for your number."

"Alas, you didn't have it to give," I say.

He smacks his head comically. "I know. I'm sorry. I have it now, though."

I debate the question in my mind for a moment, but it finds its way out before I fully decide to allow it. "About the video...?"

Art grimaces. "I guess I should say sorry about that, too, but I'm not."

"You're not?"

He finishes off his Irish Mule and signals for another. "When I was editing the video on Monday, I decided the second ending was better." I start to reply, but he keeps going. "I know. I said that my vision for the piece was that it was about how the passion of love dwindles and in the end a couple stays together but isn't as passionate. That was what I was originally going for with the final pose. It's just that... Well, that kiss was so hot, Grace. It burned up the camera. I had to use it." He gives me a weak smile. "I edited out anything you might consider inappropriate."

"One of my students showed it to me."

"At least your students are grownups. Imagine if you taught little kids. They'd be like, 'ooh, Miss Grace'."

I cover my mouth with my hand to keep from spitting out my drink. I swallow and then say, "It was almost like that, anyway."

"Good. You deserve a little scandal." He pauses and lets the silliness float away. "I am sorry if it embarrassed you. I'll take it down if you want me to, but... it was just a kiss at the end, nothing else. Nothing too racy. The dancing was brilliant, though, and I had to put it on my channel. I'm proud of it. Even more so now that this bit of choreography won me a gig that's going to change everything for me. My subscribers are eating it up. Did you read any of the comments?"

I did read a lot of them, actually. They were full of adulation for him and compliments about me. A lot of people wondered who I was, but he hasn't answered any of their questions. He's keeping me a mystery.

No, I won't make him take it down. I'm proud of it, too.

"Will the project film here? Do you know when it will shoot?"

The light in his eyes diminishes. "They still have contracts to work out. Casting and all kinds of stuff to arrange before I join the team. I think most of it will be in New York. The plot has a lot to do with the history of modern and contemporary dance."

"Makes sense."

I don't know why this upsets me as much as it does. I never expected to have any kind of future with this dynamic man. It's just that for a split second I thought I might get to keep him a minute longer.

Art reaches across the table. I bring up my hand and take his. "They want me to stick around for another day or two to finish up some details, so I have to change my flight back. I was wondering if—"

"I'd like to see you again while you're here. Of course." I squeeze his hand. I'll take as much time with him as I can get.

"Not what I was about to ask, but yes. That would be wonderful." He runs his thumb along the side of my hand. My skin tingles. "I wanted to know if you'd like to come to New York with me. If you have time to get away for a few days. I'd love to show you around. We could see a musical. What do you think? I'm planning on leaving late Friday or Saturday morning."

I've always wanted to see New York. Go to a Broadway show. I remember being so jealous of Tyler when he went back in the day. Somehow, I've never made it happen. I haven't traveled much of anywhere in my life. Extending this fling a few more days wouldn't be terrible.

It isn't smart. I don't want to fall for this guy. I'm still licking my wounds from Tyler. If I take this adventure with Art, it'll hurt when I leave again. Can I handle more pain?

I need to stop thinking about Tyler. That relationship was never meant to be. Sure, I thought him showing up in my life again after all this time was some sign that we were supposed to wind up together. My parents were on board with that theory, but they also had second chance success. Debbie warned me not to make too much of it. She was right. Tyler had always been ambiguous about his feelings for me when we were kids, and he wasn't much better about expressing them as an adult. It was time to stop kidding myself about where that relationship was heading. He and I would never have worked out.

When we were teenagers, he invited me to spend the summer with him in Phoenix. I should have done it. I should have taken that chance. It might not have made a difference in what he ultimately decided to do. But then again, maybe it would have.

I didn't take the chance, and I've always regretted it. I'm done being that cautious girl.

This dynamic man across the table from me has such an earnest longing in his soft brown eyes. He's waiting for me to say something.

"Yes," bursts out of me before I fully commit to it. Then I go with my impulse. "Yes. I would love to go with you. Absolutely."

"Whew," he says. "For a second there you had me worried I'd misread you."

"You did not," I say. I put up a finger to our waiter. "Check please."

Tipsy from the Chablis, I allow Art to lead me up to his elegant room.

*2018*

We were all in the middle of our barre work. Debbie had given us the usual combination of exercises to do and then repeat on the opposite side. She called my name and beckoned for me to come over to the corner where she had sat down on the piano bench. It was rare to see her dance or demonstrate a movement anymore, but I'd never seen her sit during a class. I rushed over as fast as I could without drawing too much attention. The girls stayed focused on their movements.

"What is it?"

"I'm feeling…" Debbie moved her hand as if to erase what she was about to say. "I just remembered that I told Jamie I'd meet him for dinner. I forgot about it when Spencer called to tell me he couldn't teach tonight. He's probably waiting for me and wondering what's happened. Do you mind taking over the class?"

"Teaching it?"

Spencer had taken over nearly all of the teaching these past three years, but Debbie still stepped in from time to time if he was unavailable. Even though I could tell it was hard for her to get through a whole class anymore, she never once talked about hiring another teacher or asking me to do it. I'd been a student there for fifteen years, and I knew everything about how she ran her classes. Many times, I'd thought about asking her if I could try leading a class. I always chickened out at the last minute; afraid she'd say something demeaning. I could always imagine her dismissive tone, "And what makes you think you have any business teaching a class full of professional dancers? They've been dancing since they were children…"

I'd remind myself that most of these dancers were only in their twenties, so in all honesty, I'd been dancing about as long as most of them and more than some. Still, I never could get past my fear of her sneering rejection.

"What did you think I meant? Babysitting?"

I shook my head. "No. I mean, yes. I'd be happy to take over."

"Good. Do the Liszt combination. I don't think any of these girls have done it before. It'll help Helen over there work on her balance. Good Lord, she needs it."

I glanced over at Helen who was struggling a bit to keep her supporting ankle strong.

"Sure. I can do that." I'd have to adapt a step or two. I wasn't sure if I remembered it exactly. It'd been a while since we'd done that one.

Debbie sat still, not getting up and not saying anything further. I couldn't imagine how much pain she was in. It had to be more than anything I could ever tolerate. She was brave, not allowing anyone to see her suffering. Her neck was so tense, and her chin jutted out obstinately. I could tell she was willing herself to overcome whatever was so bad that she had to sit.

I lean closer to her. "Do you need help?"

She didn't nod. She didn't say yes. All Debbie did was make a firm moment of eye contact and then avert her gaze to her lap. She was struggling and too proud to say it. I put out my arm, and she used it to pull herself up. With her leaning against me, I helped her walk as smoothly as possible across the floor to the doorway. The girls turned their heads to gape. Debbie shouted at them all. "Focus!" All their heads snapped back into place. When we got to the door, she said to the class. "Do the whole thing again, *en l'air*. Don't be lazy."

As soon as we crossed the threshold, I closed the door behind me, muting the piano music coming from the speakers. The dancers weren't school kids. I didn't need to watch them to make sure they were still dancing. If they weren't, it was their money wasted.

"Do you need help getting downstairs? Can you drive?"

We headed toward the office. "I'll have Jamie come get me."

It seemed like forever before our tiny steps got her to her desk chair. She collapsed into it and closed her eyes.

"What do you need, Debbie? What can I do?"

As usual, her first instinct was to bark at me, "I need you in the classroom. Obviously. That's what I asked." She put one of her gnarled hands up to her forehead, her eyes still closed.

I stepped back but didn't leave. "Could you, for once, Debbie, not be a complete bitch to me?"

She whimpered and lowered her hand. Tears ran down her cheeks. I knelt by her side.

"You're really hurting, aren't you?"

"Please, Grace. Not now. I can't."

I went to the small fridge in the corner and pulled out an ice pack. "Where do you want this?"

"Give me my phone so I can call Jamie."

Following directions, I put the ice pack away and retrieved her cell phone from her purse. Her hand couldn't hold it tightly, and she struggled to pull up Jamie's number.

"Let me do it," I said, taking the phone from her. I called up her son and asked him to come as soon as he could. When I put the phone back, I said, "He'll be here soon."

She closed her eyes again, and I put a tissue in her hand. A moment before I left the office, I heard Debbie whisper. "Thank you, Grace. I don't know what I'd do without you."

In my life, I'd never heard words that struck me as deeply.

I stepped back into the dance room to a barrage of questions from the worried dancers about Debbie's condition.

"She's fine. Now, back to your positions. I want to see two *grand battements*, *développé*. Four times to the front, side and *derriere*. Let's go." I hit play on the CD player and counted them off.

### Present Day

The ringing of my cell phone wakes me in the middle of the night. It's the default tone, so I know it's not my parents or any of my close friends. I'm about to turn it off when I notice the time is 1:45. I've never gotten a sales call at this time.

"Are you going to get that?" Art murmurs beside me. The ringing has woken him, too. He'd fallen asleep spooning me, with his arm over my waist.

I hit 'accept' and put the phone to my ear. Jamie is shouting on the other end, and I have to pull the phone away.

"Oh, God! Oh, God! Grace, are you there? Oh God!"

"Jamie? Jamie, are you okay? Is your mom okay? Calm down and talk to me."

I'm sitting up, my knees clenched to my chest. Art puts a hand on my shoulder to comfort me.

"Grace! Spencer isn't answering his phone. I need one of you to come here. It's Mom. Mom's in the pool. Please, Grace. I don't know what to do."

"I'm coming," I say without hesitation. I'm already out of bed, picking my clothes up from the floor. I see that Art is propped up on one elbow watching me. His face is full of concern. "What is she doing in the pool? Let me try Spencer again for you."

I'm picturing her having a hard night of sleep and needing her soothing waters. Maybe she's had too many of her pain pills or too much to drink, or both, and is being too stubborn for her son to handle. I'm not sure if I can help.

"She's not moving, Grace. She's not moving. Oh, God, Grace. I think she's... Please come."

My blood turns to ice blades that shred through my veins. I can't move. I can't breathe.

"Grace?" Art jumps out of bed, catching my phone as it topples out of my hand. "Grace, what's the matter?" He puts the phone to his ear. After a moment of listening, Art says, "You need to call 911. Grace is on her way."

He puts the phone down and stands in front of me, taking both my hands. "Breathe, baby. Take a breath."

With his guidance, I take a couple of slow, deep breaths to clear my head. My whole body is trembling. "Art, I have to go."

"I know. Do you want me to come?"

"No," I say quickly. "She'd be embarrassed..." I'm worried about how Debbie will feel. I put a hand to my mouth to keep from screaming. Tears gush from my eyes. Art pulls me into him for a tight hug. I allow it for a second and then push him away. "I don't have time. I'm sorry."

As fast as possible, I put on my clothes and rush out the door, promising to call him as soon as I know something.

When I was drifting off after our lovemaking, I had thought about going home. I live less than a five-minute drive from this hotel. Staying the night had never been my plan. I convinced myself I'd rise early and get home before morning traffic. I wish now I hadn't stayed. I'd be five minutes closer to Debbie's house right now. My car is valet parked, and waiting for it seems like an eternity. I race down Hollywood Boulevard, grateful that the lights are in my favor as I whiz past all the iconic locations of this tourist haven.

The door is unlocked when I get to the house, and I hear sirens coming up the hill behind me. I run straight through the house to the backyard. Light spills out from the living room to the patio. Otherwise, the only illumination out here is the glow from the underwater fixtures in the pool.

Jamie, wearing only a white T-shirt and boxer shorts, rushes toward me. He's soaking wet with pool water and tears. I hold him at the elbows, trying to stay calm in the face of his panic.

"They told me they'd get her out, because I… I couldn't lift her out. My own mother. I can't…" He collapses to the ground, sobbing. I touch his head gently and can't stop myself from looking in the direction of the pool.

I'm expecting to see her floating on the top, like the last time I saw her. She isn't visible to me at first, and I'm confused. Cautiously, I move closer to the pool. I'm a heartbeat from seeing something I know will haunt me forever, when I hear a man say, "Police. Move back, ma'am."

I pivot to see two police officers leading two E.M.T.s with a stretcher across the patio. Jamie stands aside, and I go to be with him. I put an arm around him while the four men stand at the edge of the pool and take in the situation and speak to each other in voices too quiet for us to hear. At a nod, they break apart. One of the E.M.T.s goes into the pool, while the other kneels at the edge. One of the policemen surveys the area around the pool, while his partner comes over to us, notepad in hand.

Jamie answers a bunch of questions basically explaining that he found his mother this way and he did not know how long she'd been out here. He came down to get a snack and saw that the back door was open.

Right about this time, Spencer joins us with a bunch of apologies. We all answer questions while watching the awful scene of our friend's body being retrieved from the bottom of the pool. They don't bother with chest compressions. It's clearly too late.

Debbie is not in a swimsuit. She's in a silky nightgown of her favorite shade of aqua-blue. It's clinging to her form like wrapping on a precious gift. It hits me that Debbie was fully aware of what that gown would look like as she floated in the water, the material delicately drifting around her like a jellyfish. This is a woman who has danced her entire life, and she loves a good costume. She wore this particular gown on purpose, so that she would be beautiful, ethereal even. Perhaps Debbie didn't realize that she would sink.

I shake the thought away. No. She didn't come out here to kill herself. She was hurting, like her son said. She wanted the comfort of the water, and she didn't take the time to put on her bathing suit. It probably hurts to pull on a tight bathing suit when your fingers are aching and swollen. This was easier. Maybe she simply fell asleep while relaxing.

The police officer seems satisfied with Jamie's answers and the level of his grief. There isn't any evidence of foul play. We're permitted to follow the stretcher to the ambulance and watch them put Debbie's body inside. There's no siren as the ambulance disappears down the hill. Before the police leave, Jamie is told that they'll be in touch with the coroner's report and that they are very sorry for his loss.

Lights are on in the bedroom windows of the neighboring homes, but the quiet of these early hours of the morning has slipped back to take hold once more. Spencer takes Jamie upstairs and helps him into fresh, dry clothes. I make some coffee. The three of us sit on Debbie's favorite red velvet sofa in the living room holding each other until the sun comes up, no one speaking, no one allowing the truth to be uttered. Debbie is gone.

# CHAPTER
## Fourteen

I didn't go to New York with Art. After I'd had a chance to get home and clean up, I called and told him what happened. He offered to be there for me if I needed him, but I didn't need comfort from someone temporary. I told him that I had to help Jamie and Spencer and didn't have time to see him. On Friday night, he flew back to New York. We haven't talked since. I do check his YouTube channel from time to time. The likes on our video are at over twelve thousand now. He hasn't posted anything new yet.

The coroner's report came back quickly and revealed that Debbie had a dangerous combination of alcohol and OxyContin in her system. Her death was labeled as accidental drowning as she probably stumbled into the pool unawares. Suicide was ruled out.

I had my suspicions about the truth of that report, but I was grateful for the words on paper. It meant that Jamie would receive the life insurance owed to him. Spencer and I were both convinced that Debbie had it all planned out. For one thing, her lawyer showed up quickly with a will and all of Debbie's prede-termined plans for her funeral and what to do with her remains.

According to her wishes, we arranged a lovely memorial service at that Methodist church where she was apparently a longtime, if lapsed, member. The pews were full of former students that I knew and many more dancing colleagues of hers that I didn't. I saw several famous faces in the crowd from Broadway and film. Jamie pointed out the Hollywood studio executives that had known his father.

Of all people, Sally, my old teacher from Razzle Dazzle turned up. She'd thickened up considerably over the years. We hugged, and I asked if she was still teaching. She sighed and said that she'd quit years ago. Her oldest of three kids was a high school senior now, and she was too busy running all of them around to have a job that kept her busy in the afternoons and evenings. She's an office assistant at a middle school now. I think finding out I was still dancing after all these years made her sadder than the death of our friend. She mumbled her sympathies to me and left quickly to find her seat.

I sat between Spencer and Jamie in the front pew and held their hands through the service. I'd been asked to speak on behalf of the studio, but I begged off and let that job fall to Spencer. He did a touching eulogy about Debbie's contribution to the dance community and what she meant to all of us. It was followed by a video slideshow he and Jamie put together of images from Debbie's career. It was enthralling to see this woman I'd only known as bitter and broken, youthful and glowing with life. I'd rarely ever heard her laugh or seen her smile a genuine smile. Now, I watched pictures flash by of a dazzling, exuberant person in gorgeous pose after pose. Each picture tore at my heart because I'd never seen any of them before that moment. I knew she'd been a professional dancer with many credits. It's one thing to know that and another to see it. How I wished I could've seen her perform like that. Even once. I wondered if Jamie had any videos I could borrow. I also decided right then and there that we would get some of these pictures printed and framed to decorate the studio.

Spencer struggled not to cry as he made his way through his speech and the video. I went through several tissues. When he rejoined me, he buried his face in my shoulder, and I held him tightly while his shoulders bobbed up and down. Jamie's girl-friend, Laurie, sang "Candle in the Wind" because "Tiny Dancer" had been used for the video. Another thing I didn't know—Debbie was an Elton John fan. I thought again of the video and the wonderful best friend in my arms. I'd never seen him dance professionally either. Shame on me. Once we were back on stable ground emotionally, I'd force him to show me any and all videos he had of his work.

To my surprise, my parents came to the memorial service. I'd told them about it but didn't expect them to show up. After the service concluded, they gave me the tightest hugs I've ever received from them.

"I wish I'd met her," Mom said in my ear. "I know she meant a lot to you."

I wish she had, too. Debbie should have been like a sister to me because of our ages, but she always felt more like a mother figure. I looked up to her and learned from her. She had that uncanny way of reprimanding me while simultaneously encouraging me. In her way, she'd shown more support for me than my own parents ever had. They'd never met. There had never been a reason to. Dancer's Room didn't do recitals for my parents to attend. They never expressed any interest in coming to the studio to watch me dance or see where I spent all my time. Even when I moved away from them to purposely live closer to the studio, they didn't ask to see what all the fuss was about. Mom's only response was to worry about my safety, while Dad saw the promising growth for his realty business.

I led them to a bench outside. It was chilly out, a northern breeze blowing brittle leaves off the trees. Mom and I sat while Dad stood with a hand on her shoulder. "We've already read the will," I told them. "Her lawyer met with us right after it happened because she had arranged things ahead of time so Jamie wouldn't have to."

"So young to have lost both parents." Mom patted my knee sympathetically. I fought the urge to push her hand away.

To my father, I said, "I have some matters to discuss with you as soon as things settle."

"Anything you need, sweetheart," he said.

All the money Debbie had inherited from her husband went to Jamie, along with the house and other property. Debbie left the dance studio to Spencer and I. It turned out that she had kept all the earnings from the studio separate from her regular finances. Years ago, her husband had purchased the entire building that housed the dance studio, and all the other businesses within it have been paying rent to her. We'd always wondered how she kept the place afloat with so few students. Now we knew. I was hoping my father could help me learn a bit more about my new status as a landlord and what that entailed. There was a lot of paperwork to sort through still.

Mom was delighted that all my years at the dance studio hadn't been wasted after all. She did a fair job trying to cover up her excitement while I was in the midst of my mourning, but her energy definitely escalated. Dad was less impressed and had a few things to say about how this was going to be a major distraction from my real work. He wasn't wrong. I didn't care about his opinion, though. I needed his help.

Spencer and I took Jamie to release Debbie's ashes at Lechuza Beach, her favorite spot in Malibu. According to the letter she'd left with her lawyer, she always regretted not spending more time at the beach. She moved to California in the early nineties and rarely ever drove to the shore. Once her RA settled in, it was too painful to walk on the sand, and she couldn't bear looking at the ocean if she couldn't put her feet in it.

Jamie never knew this until the will was read. It made him furious. As her ashes dissolved into the Pacific Ocean, he shouted after them. "I could've taken you here! I could have made this happen for you any time you wanted! Why didn't you say something? Why did you always have to suffer?"

Spencer and I stood with him until well after the sun went down that evening. When we arrived at his house to drop him off, he panicked. Hyperventilating and wild-eyed, he told us he couldn't go back in the house. I stayed with him in the car while Spencer gathered some of his things. Jamie stayed with Spencer for two nights and then found a college friend willing to put him up for a while in his apartment.

By the time I met my parents for dinner later in the week, I'd added the agenda of needing to sell Debbie's house for Jamie and finding him another. He refused to live in the house haunted with the ghosts of both of his dead parents. Jamie had plenty of money to purchase a house outright. I showed him my favorite little house in the Valley that no one seemed to want. To my disappointment, he didn't want it either, and we wound up signing a contract on a condominium in Burbank near the film studios. Jamie said he didn't want a yard to deal with, so this was ideal for him. Plus, knowing he could walk past the Warner Brothers lot any time he wanted would give him motivation to finally finish his book.

If the dance studio hadn't been my life before, it was all-consuming now. I neglected the majority of my realtor duties and focused all my time to making improvements to Debbie's Dance Room. We took a couple of months to do major repairs on the structure of the building, including a new roof. We had the building painted eggshell white and got a fresh new awning over the entrance to the studio—aqua-blue. The new matching sign hung proudly above it. We got rid of the nasty vape shop that was behind on their rent and upped the rent on the lawyers. Spencer is still seeing Jeremy, who has been a rock through this whole experience, so we lowered the rent on the hair salon a smidge and told them to keep it under wraps. We've reached out to a chiropractor/massage therapist who works from home on a lot of dancers we know to see if she wants that now vacant retail space. It should be a no-brainer for her, in my opinion.

The biggest thing has been adding another dance space. We broke through the wall at the end of the hallway past our office and cleared out the attic space no one was using. While putting in the floor, we went ahead and upgraded the dance floor in the old studio, hallway, and office. My next job is arranging for a new bathroom upstairs, so we don't have to keep using the tiny one in the foyer.

Right after the new year, Spencer got our website updated and we started our new schedule of classes. The place is hopping from three to nine every night of the week now, plus Saturday mornings. We're scheduling master classes once a month on Sundays and are about to have our second one here at the end of February.

Our most popular class, the one that has boomed to the point of having to turn people away each week, is our contemporary/lyrical on Friday evenings. It's all because of Arthur Montoya's video. Lovely Elise answered a question in the comments wondering who I was with my full name and that I was her ballet teacher at Dancer's Room in Hollywood. Even with us changing the name of the studio, people have found us. Everyone wants a little taste of Art's dance style. Spencer and I do the best we can for them. We most definitely are not Arthur Montoya. No one has complained yet, and we're thinking about adding a second more advanced class and hiring a teacher that specializes in that style. I've thought about contacting Art and seeing if he knows someone to recommend, but I haven't been brave enough, or drunk enough, to do it yet. This might wind up falling on Spencer.

We've been so busy that we sailed through the coldest, bleakest months of the year and didn't even notice. It's almost March now. Sunny spring weather is already making each morning lovelier than the next. Every now and then, I wonder what Tyler would think of all of that has happened. Would he consider what I've helped create here a success? Would he be impressed? Or would he still think I was obsessed with learning a skill I'd never used to perform? Was being paid to perform the only validation of talent?

From time to time, I also wonder if he's seen the video and what he thinks of it. Did it excite him to see me dance like that or to notice the huge number of likes and comments? Did it make him jealous to see me so physical with Art and passionately being kissed by him? Silly me, I occasionally skim the comments to see if he's left one. Dumb, I know.

It takes everything I have to resist the urge to look *him* up, to see if there's anything new going on with *Wildcats* or other exciting projects. I haven't heard from Alan Bergman's office at all about auditions, so that helps prevent me from asking Carla about Tyler.

Sometimes I wonder if he ever bought a house. If he did, he found another realtor to sell it to him.

Tonight is Friday. We're twenty minutes into class. Spencer and I co-teach, going back and forth on who is leading the combination for the night. It's my turn, and I've choreographed to a Billie Eilish song to prove that I can pick music that is not from the 1900s. We're working on some across-the-floor movement when a man and a woman appear in the doorway. He's in slacks, a long-sleeved shirt, and a tie. She's wearing a pencil skirt and blouse with a pair of three-inch stilettos. They are clearly not here to dance. It's also way too late for them to be here about business. Perhaps they're interested in that available space downstairs. I glance at Spencer and he nods for me to take care of it.

I greet the people and lead them into the hallway, shutting the door behind me.

"Can I help you?"

The woman introduces herself as Hannah Evans, and the man with her is Jared Rosby. "You're Grace Fuller," she says. It's not a question, so I don't answer. "We've watched your dance with Arthur Montoya. It's incredible."

This is a first. No one has sought me out that wasn't intending to dance with us before. I'm not quite sure what to say.

"Thank you. That's kind. I'm in the middle of teaching a class right now."

They seemed pleased to know this fact. Hannah says, "Yes, we looked up your schedule online, and we were hoping to watch a little bit. I hope you don't mind the intrusion."

"It's packed in there," I tell them. "You'd have to sit on the floor." I gesture to her outfit. "I'm not sure how comfortable that would be or if you'd be able to see what you're looking for. May I ask what this is about?"

"We should have led with that, my apologies," Jared says. He's a pleasant fellow, balding and a little on the plump side. I'd put him in his forties and her in her late thirties. Neither of them looks like they're interested in enrolling in dance classes. They don't share a last name, so I doubt they're looking into this place for a child. "We work for Angela Semple Casting Agency. She's currently casting a film about the life of Martha Graham, the innovator of—"

"Modern dance," I finish for him. I know who Martha Graham was. "So, you're scouting my class?"

Hannah raises an eyebrow. "We're scouting *you*, Ms. Fuller. Angela has shown interest in having you audition for the role of Martha."

Did I hear that right? "What? Me? I'm not… Really?"

They both nod, enjoying being the bearers of good news.

Jared tells me, "We've seen you dance, obviously, but we wanted to see you in person as well. We were curious what you looked like in person."

"Which is very lovely, by the way," Hannah says. "You're stunning. But would you mind letting us watch your class for a while? It'll give us a sense of how you move and sound. Don't think of it as an audition."

How could I think of it as anything else? All the liquid from my body has evaporated. I remember this feeling from when I was nineteen. It's not something I cared to feel again.

Hannah puts a hand on my arm and squeezes like we're friends. "Don't be nervous." It must show. "You've already passed the first cut. Trust me, we wouldn't be here if Angela didn't think you had something. That dance was glorious. I wish I could move a tenth as well as that. My mom made me quit dance classes when I was eight because I didn't practice."

My mom made me quit dance classes because we were broke after Dad left. I bite back the urge to respond with that fact. "Let me figure out where to put you. Do you mind taking off your shoes? We recently got new floors."

They both comply and hold their shoes on their fingers as I open the door. The dancers are spreading out to their spots.

"Oh good," Spencer says. "We're ready for your routine. You should have seen Gayle's leaps today. Am I right, ladies?"

All the dancers cheer, and Gayle blushes. I'm sad I missed it. They must've been something impressive. She's been struggling for a while to get a good split on her *grand jetés*. Spencer looks over my shoulder at the guests with a questioning expression. I give him my best "I'll tell you later" face. He doubles back with his, "Ooh, a fun secret" face. I don't want to make the girls nervous by explaining who these people are. I'll let them gossip about it later.

I have Hannah sit on the piano bench, and Jared sits with his legs crossed on the floor between her and the mirror. They're blocking our music station, but we can work around it. For a second, I reconsider the piece I'm about to teach. The girls prefer lyrical style to modern dance, and that's what I have for them tonight. If these people are here to see someone who can do Martha Graham's signature brand of dancing, this is the wrong choreography to showcase that for them. For a moment, I consider pulling up a combination I taught last year that is more on point for Hannah and Jared. I haven't practiced it, though, and I'm not sure if I remember all of it. I don't want to mess up either.

The girls stand impatiently, fidgeting with their clothes and rolling their necks and shoulders to stay loose. These kids paid for this class and deserve the dance I created for them.

"Okay, here we go. I want everyone to start facing right. Legs in second. We're going to *plie* and then rise, lifting the right leg…" They follow me flawlessly, as if they are inside my head seeing it as I do. It never stops amazing me to see, within minutes, dancers able to do entire dances that never existed before.

When Spencer hits play for me to try it with the music, several of the dancers holler out their approval of the song choice. I sneak a peek at our visitors. They're enjoying themselves. I don't know if I'm doing what they need, but I'm giving this class my all.

At the end of class, the dancers peel out, some stopping to thank Spencer and I, a couple letting us know they'll be here on Sunday for the master class. I tug on Elise's fingers to keep her from leaving and pull her in for a hug. "Thank you," I say to her.

"For what?"

"I'm not sure yet," I confess. "I know it's all because of you, though."

At last, the room is empty except for Spencer, Hannah, Jared and myself. The casting agent representatives are standing now, still holding their shoes, and talking quietly with my best friend. I approach like I'm checking to see the damage on my car after a rear-ender.

"So…?"

"Wonderful," Hannah says.

"Extremely," Jared agrees. "You're a great teacher. Dynamic energy. Both of you. I wish to hell I could dance."

"Oh, me too," Spencer says, but Jared misses the suggestion. I pinch Spencer in the thigh to let him know this is a time to behave.

Hannah pulls a card out of her purse and hands it to me. "We do apologize for the intrusion and hope we weren't too much of a distraction. We'd like you to do a reading for the movie. It'll be next Wednesday. In New York."

"New York?" I repeat, baffled.

Jared clarifies, "We'll pay for your travel. It's cheaper to bring you there than the whole team here."

"Do you have an agent?" Hannah asks. "I'm not going to lie. This whole thing will be a lot easier if you have representation. This is a huge role, and there will be a lot to negotiate."

"I have an agent," I say slowly, not totally sure if that's true or not. I'm feeling like Alan would be into helping me with this opportunity. Of course, he could also be a dick about it.

"Perfect," she says. "Have them contact Angela and work out the details for next week."

We lead them to the hallway. As he slips his shoes back on, Jared says, "It would be helpful if you familiarize yourself with any videos you can find on Graham. I'm told there's not a lot out there, but anything is better than nothing."

Spencer's gaping mouth through all of this is making it difficult for me not to laugh. He is trying so hard to piece it together. I love how these two are talking to me like this is an ordinary thing to be doing. Just fly off to New York to audition for the lead in a film. Do people really have this life? Has Tyler ever done this? I wish I could ask him.

What would Debbie think of all this?

We all shake hands, and the two of them leave. Spencer looks like he's about to explode, so I fill him in on the details.

"This is amazing!" he screams. "Are you going to do it? Please, God, tell me you're going to do this."

I hold my breath and look into his dark brown eyes, making him wait on purpose before finally saying, "Why the hell not?"

# CHAPTER
## *Fifteen*

In fifty years, I'd only left California once. I'd rarely taken a trip longer than a weekend. Those had all been to hike at Lake Arrowhead or visit the beach in San Clemente. Disneyland. Sea World. Most of these trips had been when I was younger, with either of my parents when they were divorced or both of them when they remarried. The rest had been by myself. Like when I went to Arizona that one time. It was also the only time I'd ever been on a plane.

I wanted Spencer to come with me, but it was too short notice to shut down Debbie's Dance Room for a couple nights. Plus, we were getting in the groove with our new schedule and didn't want to disrupt it. When I told Mom what was happening and forwarded the link to the dance Art and I did, she immediately called me, crying uncontrollably, and offered to tag along. She paid for her plane ticket and an extra night at the hotel, so we didn't have to return so quickly. The rest of the travel details were handled by Alan's office.

Carla responded immediately to the text I sent her on Friday night. She used a lot of exclamation points and heart emojis, which made me laugh. I guess this put me back in her good graces. I met with Alan on Monday morning at his office. He was beyond thrilled at this unexpected change in my status quo, even paying for prints of my headshot to take with me and making sure I had sides from the script emailed to me well ahead of the audition time to read and practice in my hotel room.

Mom wanted to be a tourist as soon as we got to the city. Between being tired from the travel and my nerves, I didn't want to do much. I compromised with one stop—the Empire State Building. We had a nice dinner and spent the rest of the evening hanging out at the hotel. I promised her we'd do something fun after the audition was over because we didn't have to fly back until the following morning. Maybe we could get cheap tickets to a Broadway show.

The support she's shown me during these past couple of days reminds me of the mom who came to every performance of my high school shows. The one that helped with the bake sales and stitched costumes. The lady that didn't discourage me from choosing Theatre for a major in college, even if she didn't think it was a great idea.

I'd forgotten about that woman. For some reason, I got it in my head that my mom didn't approve of anything I did, but I was wrong. My mom always wanted the best for me, and she rolled with the choices I made. She just showed more enthusiasm for the ones that made sense to her. I wish I'd understood this years ago.

The good thing about doing an audition out of town is that it limits my choices of what to wear. I spent a ridiculous amount of time picking my outfit while packing, and now I'm stuck with no recourse. I put on a plain, black, old school, sleeveless leotard and a pair of footless nude tights. Over that, I wear a stretchy cotton olive-colored dress with a full skirt that hangs below my knees. The sleeves are capped, and the rounded neckline is low enough for a bit of my leotard to show. I choose to wear flat slip-on shoes, but I have ballet slippers, toe shoes, jazz shoes, and character heels in my dance bag.

I don't look a thing like Martha Graham. After studying dozens of photos of her from youth to old age, the only thing I can accomplish is affecting her style. She was a big fan of those solid color loose-fitting dresses and bare feet. She had dark hair, not red, and wore it pulled back off her forehead, usually in a large bun. My hair isn't long enough for a bun, on purpose, but I do slick it back, the hair gel making my hair appear more auburn than copper. I darken my eyebrows, thicken my eye shadow, put on some lashes, and use some contour to sharpen my cheekbones. I top the look off with the reddest lipstick I've bought since the eighties. This is the best I can do. I hope they see what they need to.

Mom comes with me to the auditions, holding my hand the whole way and as we enter the building on 43rd and ride up the elevator to the third floor. The entrance to The Angela Semple Casting Agency is glass, as if to say that all of the workings inside are transparent. I love the deception. I give my name to the receptionist, and an intern leads me to a waiting room down the hall. Another intern hands me a printed version of the audition script.

Everything about this so far has a drastically different feel than auditioning for that arthritis medicine commercial. The people who work here are efficient and don't waste time on smiles or pleasantry. My competition is much more clearly defined. Every woman here is within five or so years of my age and all doing their best to affect Martha Graham with their choice of attire and make-up. Two of them have got the look pegged, including the big brown bun. I smooth back my red helmet self-consciously as soon as I sit down. Every actress in the room somehow manages to avoid looking at any other actress. It's quite the dance of eyelids and neck turning.

I can tell my mom is uncomfortable. No one else has a guest. All of these women probably started acting when they learned to talk and had grown out of needing their stage moms years ago. Hell, most of these women were probably now stage mothering their own little actresses.

"I'll be fine if you want to walk around. Times Square isn't far from here."

"Are you sure?"

I nod bravely. "Use the app I put on your phone, so you don't get lost. Okay?"

She stands up and then leans over to give me a quick hug.

"You've got this," she whispers, and then winks at me. Once she's out of sight, the nerves kick in way harder than before. Her holding my hand was more powerful than I thought.

I breathe slowly through my nose and focus on the script in my hands. I've read it so many times over the past twenty-four hours, I have it memorized. I have no intention of putting the script down when I get in there. I'm not that brave.

At ten o'clock, all nine of us are asked to come into the audition room to learn a dance. Half the girls panic slightly. They aren't dressed to dance and either have a change of clothes in a bag or, in two cases, nothing to change into at all. In fairness to them, Carla didn't say outright that we would have to dance at this audition, and I'm assuming their agents didn't clue them in either. I was chosen to come here because they'd already seen me dance. The only reason I wore the dance clothes under my dress was because I thought it was something Martha would do. She struck me as the kind of person who always wore something to accommodate dancing at a moment's notice.

Kind of like how I choose most of my outfits.

I can dance in the dress I'm wearing. It'll allow for full range of movement. Still, I voice the question everyone wants to know, "Do we need to change?"

The young lady leans back into the room, asks, then comes back to us with, "They want you to learn it first, and then people can change if they want to before you do it by yourself." I hear the two women in tight skirts grumbling to each other as they enter the room behind me. A couple of butterflies in my stomach shut their wings and die.

It's not a dance studio, but there are floor-to-ceiling mirrors attached to one wall and the roomy rectangular space is wide open. The floor is cement, which will cause us all to have shin splints if they make us dance for any considerable length of time. Only half of the fluorescent lights in the ceiling are lit, leaving a bright pool of light in the middle of the room but not on the ends.

"Put your things along the wall," a voice says to us from the left as we enter. Along the dimly lit entrance wall is a six-foot conference table covered with headshots and notepads. On the back of each headshot is a resume. I'm sure these women have more credits than can fit on a page. Who in here has been on Broadway or in a national tour? Who has been on TV? Featured in a movie? I don't recognize any of their faces, but that doesn't mean they aren't working all the time. Why else would they be here if they didn't have agents getting them through the door?

Then there's my resume. This guy named Chad at Alan's office helped me type it up. It's got so much white space. He made my high school and middle school musicals sound like they were real regional theater shows by using the names of the streets my schools were on as the names of the theaters instead of the schools themselves. Yep, I had the lead in *Sweet Charity* at McKinney Theater in Los Alamitos. Stretching the truth, much? According to Chad, I was indeed a Theatre major at Long Beach State University, not a dropout. And he played up my whole existence at Debbie's Dance Room to make it look like I was some ballerina superstar who has worked with dozens of successful dancers and choreographers. You bet he wrote down as many as I could name. At the bottom, he said I could do accents well, impersonations, and ride a bike as special talents. I'm not sure if I can do accents because I've never tried, doing impersonations is a stretch for what I'm actually capable of, and I've never owned a bike. I hope directors don't fact-check these things.

A video camera on a tripod is set up at the far end of the table. The four people sitting behind the table introduce themselves as we line up side by side in front of them. The tall woman with impressive blonde locks on the end stands and introduces herself as Angela Semple. Next to her is Claire Bonnett, the writer, who only holds up a hand when she's introduced. Mark Franco, the producer, smiles and crosses his arms. The director, Elias Grant, stands and puts out his hand. We each step forward and shake it in turn.

There is a fifth chair. It's empty.

"Our choreographer is…"

"Right here."

I know that voice. Art enters the room while opening a fresh can of diet soda. He walks in front of the table, and after taking a couple sips, puts his soda down.

Oh, those butterflies hadn't died. They were lying in wait and are now frantically winging about in my belly.

"Sorry," he says to everyone. "I woke up early to add a new move to this choreography and needed a little caffeine to kick into gear. Nice to meet all of you ladies." He does a mini-bow. When he raises his head, he catches for a split second when he sees me. Then he moves right on. "Now, we've seen all of you dance in some form or another, but we want to see you do a little bit in this specific style. If you can make two lines of four and five facing the mirrors, that would be perfect." Art notices the actresses who aren't dressed in loose clothing. "This might be difficult in those outfits."

He spins around and puts his hands on the table. I hear him questioning Angela, but he's keeping his voice low. Her response must satisfy him because he turns back around with a grin on his face and claps. "All right. Those who need to change, there is a ladies' room down the hall. Sheryl will show you where. The rest of you take a moment to stretch. Quick. Quick. Please."

The dancers who need to change dash out of the room, led by Sheryl the assistant. The two girls in their tight skirts shuffle to the back. One of them mutters something about how she "might as well leave". I start to pull my dress off, but Art steps toward me and says, "Leave it on. It's perfect. You look absolutely perfect."

"Is this the project that you used me for?" I hate the way that came out, but it isn't entirely wrong.

He nods and walks past without another word. Either I've insulted him or he's making a point of not showing favoritism. If the other women auditioning recognize me from Art's dance video, they aren't showing it. I look dramatically different than I did that night. The team behind the table all know who I am, and I'm sure they have some suspicions about what happened after that fade to black kiss.

We're a few counts into the choreography when the actresses join us, now in their full dance attire. It only takes them a moment to get caught up. Everyone dances so well, revealing that our class back in L.A. needs to step it up a level. I'm not well trained in modern dance. It doesn't come naturally to me like it does these other women. My ballet skills keep me from looking like a complete shlock, but I'm not keeping up. I'm floundering so badly and can't stand looking at my reflection in the mirror. Honestly, the only thing keeping me from walking out in shame are the two poor ladies in the back row who can't do any of the kicks or wide lunges. I feel kind of bad for them, but a competitive spirit has risen in me and also loves that they've narrowed the odds.

As if the production team hadn't just seen all of us dance, we're all sent back to the waiting room while they call us in one at a time to perform the dance solo. I'm not first, thank goodness. It gives me a moment to gather my wits. Although, waiting might be more excruciating than being first to be judged. I can't tell anything from the faces of the women as they exit the room. Everyone is so good at passive expressions. I want smug or proud or embarrassed or mad. They offer me no clue as to how well they did with their dancing. They're also close-lipped, not offering a tip or piece of advice.

My name is called, and I head back into the room. It feels darker, but I suspect that's my terror playing tricks on me. My heart is racing so fast, I fall off time in the middle of the routine, following my pulse instead of the rhythm of the music. Art claps his hands to pull me back on track. It works, but I'm mortified at the mistake. I try to show off to make up for it, but I don't get the air I want on my barrel turn. I can tell I slouched on my high kick. I never do that. Ugh. Oh, and was I supposed to be doing something with my face? I'm sure it was expressionless. I land in the final pose and manage, at the very least, to hold it until the music stops. I'm feeling confident Art won't be posting this video on his channel.

I stand straight as the production team takes turns saying rote compliments. Art avoids my eyes and says only, "Well done." He's lying his ass off.

I'm offered a bottle of water and told to wait again. I agonize as I sit here, knowing I haven't done my best. Dance is my talent. My only talent. Untried but true. It's what got me this audition in the first place. They aren't going to hire a person to play Martha Graham, the inventor of modern dance, who can't dance. Now everything depends on my acting ability. This is beyond terrifying. I haven't got a prayer.

*Calm down. Calm down. Breathe. I can do this.*

Spencer helped me practice back at home by having me imitate Martha Graham's voice patterns from the few videos we found on the internet. I was always good at imitating actors when I was younger. The skill came back to me naturally when I put some effort into it. I read my script two more times while I wait, Martha's deep voice in my head.

I'm asked back into the room to read. Art is sitting behind the table now. He's not in charge of this part of the audition. I'm told to stand a couple feet back from them to be more in the light. Elias Grant tells me a bit of what is happening in the film right before this scene starts and a gist of what he's looking for from me. He emphasizes authenticity.

"I want real. Not mimicry."

In this scene, Martha has retired from dancing and has been admitted to a hospital for depression and anorexia. A nurse is trying to coax her into eating, but she refuses and instead begins lamenting being too old to do her own dances.

I can't help it. I sneak a glance at Art. He nods almost imperceptibly. *You can do this*, he's silently telling me.

I bolster my confidence. This is it. This is my only chance.

Angela reads the scene from her seat in a fairly monotone style. I stand still and read my lines in response to her. I'm not a trained actress. I've never taken a class on auditioning. All I know is how Martha Graham sounds, and stands, and gestures. And I absolutely know how she's feeling. So, I give it my all and hope it's enough.

Angela reads the cue for my final line. "Perhaps it would help to watch some recordings of your dances. To see what you've created and remember—"

I cut her off. "I believe in *never* looking back. I don't indulge in nostalgia or reminiscing. I don't want to see a dancer made up to look as I did thirty years ago, dancing a ballet I created. I think that's a circle of hell Dante omitted."

I finish, and the team is silent for a moment, absorbing the rage and heartache that Debbie taught me to know so well. Wiping tears off my cheeks with the back of my hand, I wait for directions.

After a long moment, Elias says, "Very nice, Ms. Fuller." The others nod. Art smiles, allowing those dimples to reign over his face.

Angela seems pleased. "We'll be in touch."

I leave the room, and the next woman is called in for her turn. I guess I'm done. The women who read before me left, so I take it I'm supposed to leave now, too. Just like that. The moment is over.

I grab my dance bag and purse from where I left them under my chair in the waiting room and fish out my phone. I'm about to call my mom when I notice there's a text waiting for me. It's from Art. One word. "Incredible."

A swell of emotion chokes me. I definitely don't want to cry in front of these actresses. I bustle out of there and call my mom once I'm out of the casting agency office and down on the ground floor again. A few minutes later, I meet my mom in front of Johns of Times Square, and we gorge on some delicious pizza while I tell her all about it. I'm alternately thinking I blew it and aced it, my brain teeter-tottering so much it hurts.

Mom finally says to me in her reasonable way, "Grace, if you don't get it, then the worst thing that happens is that your life didn't change today. It stays the same. And right now, your life is pretty good."

It is pretty good.

I'm not sure it's end-of-the-movie good anymore. Tyler might have been right about that.

After lunch, we get in line at the TKTS booth and hope we'll luck out and get tickets to something spectacular. Spencer told me to look up some of our dancer friends that live in town and see if any of them could show us around. I had thought about it, but now I don't want to. All I want is to have a great time hanging out with my mom.

# CHAPTER

## Sixteen

It's been three weeks. Carla keeps telling me to stay calm. This is a major project, and sometimes it takes a while. This is the same lady that explained to me last fall that no news means no job. I fully assume at this point I haven't gotten it. I've been tempted to call Art so many times and get his take on everything. To prevent myself from doing something stupid like that, I deleted his number from my phone. I'm sure I could track it down again, but I like believing it's lost forever. Besides, the man should've contacted me by now. His silence is more proof that I've failed.

Alan's office has sent me out on two other auditions. I've been a good girl and gone to them. One of them looks promising. A local commercial for a law firm. I'm up for the part of a woman injured in a car accident. Now that I've got my million-dollar settlement, I can do amazing things like run with my dog at the park. I think I'm getting typecast.

On the same topic of old ladies getting second chances, my mom came up with a brilliant idea while we got late night pie and coffee after the oh-my-gosh amazing show we saw in New York. Why not offer a beginner's ballet class for what she calls "women of a certain age"? She's a true genius.

I started teaching the class on Mondays and Wednesdays at eleven in the morning. I'm calling it Boomer Ballet. It's for people my age and older who are interested in dancing. It's easy and gentle. The women, who are mostly in their sixties and seventies, are loving it. We're only on the second week, and the attendance has grown with each class. A couple of the ladies are long-retired professional dancers. Most of them thought it would be a pretty way to get some exercise. One nice lady told me she used to teach Aerobic Dancing back in the eighties and misses that fluid dancing style of workout. "Everything else is all jumping and so hard on my knees."

I make them take it seriously. They're required to wear solid color leotards with pink or nude tights and ballet slippers. Yes, I make them tuck the ties inside the slippers. However, I also have a box full of tutus and dance skirts that used to be Debbie's, and all the ladies get as excited as little girls to wear them. I'll confess, I wear one, too. I've always wanted to wear a tutu like a real ballerina.

I adore these ladies already and wish I'd thought of doing this sooner. Best of all, Mom drives all the way to Hollywood twice a week and takes the class. She's not bad. Pretty darn graceful. I guess I get it honest.

What hasn't happened is going back to teaching Friday night classes. I haven't been ready to face any of those students yet. They'll have tons of questions about the audition. Spencer assures me that they won't judge. They've all been through auditions themselves and know how it goes. I'll get there, but I need more time to lick my wounds.

Spencer and I are sitting at Stomping Grounds having coffee instead of a proper lunch after my Wednesday morning class. I usually go to lunch with Mom, but I begged off this time because Spencer and I need to have a work meeting about plans for summer and the possibility of doing our first showcase performance. After we get past small talk about Mom and the Boomer Ballet ladies, Spencer falls quiet, his expression dour.

"What's up?" I ask. "Is it Jeremy? Oh no…"

He sighs heavily and pulls the newest edition of *Hollywood Reporter* out of his messenger bag and plops it on my lap. "I thought you might want to know." He points at a headline.

Kate Hudson to Star in Biography Miniseries about Famed Choreographer Martha Graham.

"Kate Hudson? Really?"

"She was good in *Glee*. Remember?"

Spencer and I binge-watched *Glee* together. I remember well how good Kate Hudson was during her brief stint on that show. I remember being surprised to find out she could dance.

I throw up my hands, doing my best brave face. "Well, what did I expect? She's famous. And she's younger than me. By like a decade." I hope he's buying my nonchalance.

Spencer takes the magazine back and folds it in half. "She wasn't the first choice. I read the article, and they originally offered it to Gwyneth Paltrow. Also a *Glee* alumni. She's older than you."

"Not by much. I looked it up once. I'm neck and neck with Amy Adams. Did they offer it to her?"

That makes him laugh. "No, thank goodness. I'd have had to picket the studio."

"Why did Paltrow drop out?"

"You want to read it?"

"No."

Spencer gives me the highlights. I only half listen, not caring about why one movie star did or didn't want to be in a TV series. I'm thinking about the eight other very qualified actresses who were at that audition with me. Did any of us ever have a real chance at this? What was the point of having us audition if they always knew they would use a big name? Was there a quota of non-name people that had to be turned away before the producers green-lighted the salary for a celebrity? Why did the production company spend the money to fly me all the way out there and put me up in a hotel?

I have to wonder if Art had something to do with that as some sort of gift to make up for our bad timing. If so, I'm nothing but grateful.

"Wouldn't it be perfect if they train her for the movie at our studio? I could totally see that happening." When I don't laugh as whole-heartedly as he anticipates, Spencer checks, "Are you okay?"

I sip my coffee and lick the foam off my top lip. "I guess I should be upset, but I'm not. I never expected to get it. Can't get let down when you're not hopeful."

I can tell by Spencer's expression that he's not buying what I'm selling.

Alix brings over a plate of biscotti. "Your favorite," he says. "On me."

"Pity food?" I ask, taking the treat from him.

"I was eavesdropping. Sorry. You guys are the only people here, so…"

I give his arm a squeeze. "Sit with us. Are you on spring break right now?"

Alix starts to sit, but his mom barks at him to get back to cleaning up from the morning rush. He gives us sad puppy eyes and runs off to the kitchen.

"I love that kid," Spencer says.

I agree. I love Alix and Rhonda. I love my old ladies at the dance studio. I love my mom. I love Spencer. "I simply can't feel down right now because I didn't get a part I wasn't good enough to play, anyway." I didn't mean to say that out loud, but it's already escaped.

"You were and are good enough," Spencer says. "Don't ever believe anything else."

He gives me a big hug in those extra-long and muscled arms of his, and I snuggle into his shoulder. "Thank you."

"Always."

We sit like this for a few minutes, not saying anything. It's all I need at the moment. Spencer ruins it when he whispers, "My coffee is getting cold."

I smack him softly and break away. We each drink from our mugs, and while I eat a little more of my delicious biscotti, Spencer gets out his iPad and opens the planning calendar. We get busy discussing when we want to do this showcase and what we want it to look like.

In the middle of a debate about whether or not to include the new Boomer Ballet ladies, my phone plays, "Our house, is a very very very fine house…"

"Saved," I say, taking my phone out of my purse.

"My dad is bigger," Spencer teases in his best tough boy voice. He can't quite pull off school bully.

I stand up as I answer and walk toward the bulletin board. Dad rarely calls, so I'm assuming he needs my full attention. It turns out that I'm right.

"Guess what? That darling house you love so much has finally sold! I need you to meet the buyer to sign the papers."

It's like making a sudden left turn. I've slacked off a lot with my real estate business these past couple weeks, not following leads or answering my emails. I wonder who was so doggedly determined to buy this house from me that they gave up trying to reach me and went straight to the retired owner of the company.

"Wow. That's amazing. You want me to still take the commission? Sounds like someone else did the heavy lifting."

"No. The buyer said you were the contact, but he couldn't get in touch with you."

His voice sounds free of judgement. I'm glad I can't see the judgement on his face.

"What time?"

"Five tonight," Dad says. "At the house. He wants to walk through it one more time to be sure it's what he wants. I got the sense it was a done deal, though."

"O-okay." Doesn't sound done to me. Five o'clock is a terrible time to get to Sherman Oaks. The traffic over the hill is so bad. I hope this isn't a waste of my time. I don't share any of these thoughts with my father. No reason to ruin the rare moment of him being pleased with me.

"Hey, Grace?" Dad pauses for a moment like he's deliberating what he wants to say next. I expect it to be some practical advice that I don't need.

"Dad?"

"I think this one's a good fit. It's going to work out. I know I don't say it enough, but I'm really proud of you."

My "thanks" comes out as almost a question. I hardly

expected my dad's praise at the moment. I'm waiting for the backhand criticism, but it doesn't come. Just a sweet good luck and goodbye.

I hang up and check the time. It's almost three o'clock. It's not like I break a sweat teaching my dear ladies, but I'm hardly looking my best. "Spencer, I've got to run. I've got a client to meet about a house."

I swallow down the last of my coffee, grab the last biscotti, and dash out the door. Spencer calls after me, "This means your opinions on this schedule are forfeit, right?"

Thirty minutes later, I'm standing in my bedroom in my underwear, pulling outfits out of the closet and tossing them on my bed. I don't know what to put on. I forgot to ask Dad who the client was. It would be helpful to know what outfit would go over best.

I only know it's a man. Was it that divorced dad with the teenage son who'd be living with him half the time? Wear something a little more alluring. Was it one of the guys from the newlywed gay couple? Wear something snappy. Was it the man looking for a place for his mom that would be closer to his own house around the corner? Wear something modest. Was it the soon-to-be father? Couldn't be. The pregnant mom was clearly the one making decisions in that family.

I'd shown the house to a few men over the past half year. None of them struck me as particularly interested. The yard was too small. The street too busy. The jacuzzi too much trouble. The open room design was daunting for most of them because they couldn't get their heads wrapped around not having a bunch of walls dividing up the space. None of them saw it the way I do—this amazing space for dancing through life.

I sink to the floor, leaning against my bed and staring at my half-empty closet. I don't know what to wear because I don't want to wear anything. I don't want to sell my house. *That* house. I don't want to be a real estate agent anymore.

What do I want? It's stupid. It's been proven to me time and time again that it's stupid. Why do I keep thinking I could be anything more than a regular person with a regular job?

I didn't get the part in the movie. So what? Stop pining about it. It was never going to happen. It was ridiculous to ever get my hopes up. I'm nobody with no formal acting training. Quitting thirty years ago was the smartest decision I ever made. It saved me decades of heartache from rejection after rejection. Didn't it?

Still, for a moment there. For one moment, I thought something big was happening. It passed by so fast, I barely grasped on long enough to hold it as a real memory instead of a strange, fleeting dream.

All I have left is ballet. Dancing is enough to fulfill me. I don't need anything else. I do what dancers my age do: I teach dance. I'm proud of it. I love it, actually, and I'm trying to figure out how to make it work as my full-time gig and let the house selling go by the wayside. It'll happen. I have plans.

In the meantime, I could use this commission. The house isn't cheap—another reason it hasn't been selling—and my percentage will be substantial. I need to get off the floor and get dressed. Fine. I reach over my head and decide I will wear whatever my hand grabs first. With a tug, I pull a dress, and it tumbles over me to land in my lap. My only gray dress. With an A-line skirt that stops above the knees. I usually pair it with a pink cardigan rather than the suit jacket that came with it. Why not? It couldn't be more perfect for my mood.

With a grunt that betrays the age of my bones, I push myself up. My bed is a mess with clothes. Two of my favorite dresses are right on top. I could put on that yellow one with the full skirt that I love so much. No. Stick with the gray. Dress like a damned professional, not like a little girl who loves dresses she can twirl.

Although a good twirl might pick up my spirits.

I get dressed and fix my makeup and hair. Before I leave, I snap a selfie and send it to my dad. He replies with, "Looks great. So proud of you." I'm sure he is. Right now, anyway.

As expected, the traffic is horrendous. I'm glad I left early. If I get there on time, it will be a miracle. I wish I had the client's phone number to give him a heads-up that I'm on my way. I think about calling Dad and having him do it, but it feels weird to have my father do any more intervening on my behalf. If the client wants the house bad enough, they'll hang for a minute.

It's eight minutes after the hour when I turn onto the street. The sun is low in the sky, behind the house, still an hour or more away from sunset. A car is in the driveway. As I pull closer, I recognize that BMW. I also recognize the man sitting on the steps leading up to the front door. My impulse is to speed away, and, honestly, the only thing that keeps me from pressing down that accelerator are the kids four houses down playing soccer in the street.

I turn off the radio. It sounds like people yelling at me, and it's mixing with the clanging of my brain freaking out. The noise is so distracting, I can barely focus on my driving, and I do the worst street parking job in the history of vehicles. I think I'm a good three feet from the curb. I'd straighten out, but I don't want him to watch me doing it.

Tyler stands as I get out of my car. He looks incredible in a short-sleeved button-down tucked into belted tight jeans. In one hand, he holds a small bouquet of flowers. Pink carnations. In the other hand, he holds a bottle of white wine.

My heel catches on a crack in the driveway. I smooth out the skirt of my dress. Did all my lipstick come off on the can of soda I'd been drinking in the car? Shit, I shouldn't have put the window down for so long. My hair looks like a wildfire, I'm sure.

"I'm sorry I'm late," I say as businesslike as possible. "Traffic coming from Hollywood. So, you've decided on this house?"

"Hello, Grace," he says, making a point of starting our conversation at the correct place.

"Tyler," I respond cordially, doing my best to keep my smile natural. "What made you change your mind? It's been a while since you looked at this one."

"I'm fine. How are you?"

He holds out the flowers for me to take. I don't take them. I cross my arms and stand on one hip. "No. This isn't how it works. You don't get to pretend that we're going to have a normal greeting like nothing has happened. I'm here to meet a client about a house. That's what I was told. Unless you lied to my father, which wouldn't surprise me."

It makes sense now, why the customer went through my dad. There's no way Tyler would call me directly after all this time. He knows I'd hang up on him. My dad fully knows what's happening here and kept it secret. We'll be having some words later.

Tyler puts the flowers and wine on the ground and steps toward me. A soft breeze sends me a whiff of his cologne and a dozen memories fly by with it. "Look, I'm sorry for the go-around. I wanted to see you. And I *do* want the house. That's not a lie. I'm prepared to sign for it and put a down payment."

"You could've used another agent with the company."

"You showed me the house."

"You were the person who walked out on me and never called again."

Tyler runs a hand through that thick hair of his and hangs it on the back of his neck. "You're right. I was mad and frustrated. I was trying to do something for you, and it backfired badly. I figured you didn't want me around, so I gave you your space. It took time to work up the courage to call you again, and by the time I figured out what I wanted to say, I saw that video of you and that choreographer. It was shared in a Facebook group I'm in about New York theatre."

I bite my lip and look at the grass. I'm not sure how to respond.

"Your dancing was extraordinary. I knew you could dance, but I had no idea you were that good. I mean, it blew my mind how good you were." He pauses and then adds, "Then there was that kiss."

I dare a glance at him. His shoulders are tight, and his face scrunched up like a little boy refusing to eat his peas. I can't help the breathy giggle that escapes. "Yeah. That wasn't planned."

He takes a step closer to me. "Did it work out? You and him?"

"Oh no. That was not a… He's in New York." I swallow hard and wonder if that wine on the front porch is cold. I'd really like a glass right about now. Shit, I'll drink straight from the bottle.

"Arthur Montoya is his name, and he's the choreographer of a movie I auditioned for recently. I don't know if Alan or Carla told you about that."

"They did," he says. "It's the other reason I wanted to see you. I have some interesting news for you."

I can't begin to imagine what Tyler is talking about, but I'm not surprised that our agent told him all about my business. "Why don't we go inside?" I suggest. "I've got the house staged with some furniture. It'll be comfortable. And we can open that wine to celebrate your new house. That's why you brought it?" I move past him and open the lock box on the front door.

He follows, picking up the flowers and wine. "I did bring it to celebrate, but not for the house."

We go inside. It's a little dim, but I don't want to put on the glaring overhead lights. There's a simple sofa set with a bland rectangle coffee table in the living room area. I direct him to sit down while I fetch some of the clear plastic cups I always leave in the kitchen. He's opening the bottle with a corkscrew he must've brought with him and pours us both ample servings. We click cups and drink, although I'm still not sure what's the big occasion.

"Sit down, Grace," he says.

I sit in the armchair, letting him have the sofa to himself. "I'm listening."

"Okay, first off, I want you to know that I have nothing to do with this. I found out about it this morning."

"All ears," I say.

He puts his elbows on his knees. "So, Carla calls me this morning with some great news. Apparently, *Wildcats* is getting great ratings, and the fans are loving my character. It's been decided that I'm going to have a bigger storyline in season two."

Why doesn't it surprise me at all that this whole thing is about him? Tyler's success. It's not exactly what I want to be listening to at the moment. It never fails that he's on the fast track while I'm hitting a wall.

"That's nice, Tyler. Congratulations." I raise my glass and take a long swallow of Chardonnay.

"No, no," he says. "That's not what... Listen. What I have to say isn't about me. It's about you."

I don't get where this is going, but I'll be patient. I finish my drink.

"The writers are going to give me a love interest in the show, but they want it to be an enemies-to-lovers thing and evolve slowly. The woman will be a new staff member at the high school who teaches dance and leads the cheer squad. We're always fighting over use of the gym and football field, and our differing opinions of how to treat the students. You know, stuff like that."

"Again," I say, "congrats. Sounds fun." I reach for the bottle to pour more in my cup.

"They want you to play the teacher."

"What?" I almost drop the bottle. I'm positive I haven't heard him right.

"Carla was about to call you, but I begged her to let me be the one to tell you." He takes a big breath to build up the anticipation. "You're going to be a regular on *Wildcats*. I mean, if you want to. I get why you might not want to work with me, but it's such a good part—"

He's rambling, so I cut him off. "I haven't tried out for it. How could I be cast?"

"That's the fun part, the connection to your..." He clears his throat. "To that dancer."

My chest hurts from the pounding of my heart. My adrenaline is so high, I think I could shoot through the roof. What is happening right now?

Tyler puts his cup down and kneels next to my chair, looking up at me. "Carla said you had an audition for that Martha Graham miniseries. Well, it turns out that the casting director for that film is the same as for our show. Angela Semple. She's who cast me when I was still in New York. When she heard about this role, she called Alan's office immediately and said she wanted you."

"This is crazy."

"Call Carla, if you don't believe me."

"It's after five. The office is closed."

Tyler pulls out his phone and punches Carla's personal number. He hands it to me.

Carla answers, "Hey Tyler. How's it going?"

"It's Grace," I tell her.

Carla squeaks. "Did Tyler tell you? It's so amazing. Are you excited?"

"I'm not sure."

"You should be," she assures me. "Angela Semple said your audition in New York was impressive, and she was distraught to not be able to give you anything in that show. This role in *Wildcats* popped up, and she said she couldn't think of anyone else she'd rather have do it."

"Just like that?"

"Just like that." When I don't say anything, Carla goes on. "There are details to be hammered out, and it doesn't start shooting for a couple weeks. We'll have you come in tomorrow or Friday and discuss it. Keedoke?"

I hand the phone back to Tyler in a daze.

As he pockets his phone, he puts up his other hand in a boy scout salute. "I swear on my life I had nothing to do with this. But I couldn't be happier." He takes both of my hands. "I know acting isn't your passion like it is mine, but please, *please*, say you'll do this. Give it a chance. Make this the last house you ever have to sell."

I stick out my jaw. "I was already doing that. I'm planning on working full time at the dance studio." I expect him to spit at that idea. There's so much that's happened since we last saw each other that he doesn't know.

Nothing about his excitement diminishes. In fact, he looks even more jazzed. "That's amazing. There's no reason you can't keep working at the studio and also do this show. We'll figure it out. I'll help, if you want. I'd love to start dancing again."

"I doubt you're at our level," I tease.

"Oh, I guarantee I'm not." He's holding my hands again. He lifts them to his lips for a gentle kiss. "I want us to be together again. Not only so we can work together, but because I love you. God, I love you so much. I knew it when we were kids, but I ran away from it. I thought my plans were more important than love. I don't feel like that anymore. I've had a few months to come to terms with my feelings about you, and I know I don't want to live without you. I don't want to let you go again."

The sun hits the window at that perfect angle that spreads an incredible golden glow across the room. I'd forgotten how much I adored this effect. It's like magic.

"Tyler, I…"

His smile falters, and he doubles his efforts. Those bright blue eyes shine. "I'm going to buy this little house that I know you love, hoping that someday you'll come and live in it with me. We'll finally have that real movie ending. With the house and the kids—"

"Kids? I'm a little past having kids. Sorry."

His hands ceep up to my elbows. "Then we'll adopt. Or foster. Or just get a couple of great dogs."

I'm laughing outright now, and I think I'm crying, too. I lean toward him, and his arms slide up to my shoulders.

"I love you, Graceful."

"I love you, too," I confess. I always have. I'll tell him that later.

He scoops me into his arms and spins me around the open floor plan. I point my toes and throw my head back. This is the best dance ever.

Don't miss out on your next favorite book!

Join the Satin Romance mailing list
www.satinromance.com/mail.html

# Acknowledgments

Thank you for reading my very first full-length women's fiction/romance novel. Up until now, all of my romances have been short stories or novellas. Finishing this novel was a challenge I gave myself in 2020 while in quarantine, and seeing it published is a dream come true. Thank you so much to Nancy Schumacher for encouraging me to write in this genre and accepting this novel to be published by Satin Romance Books. I'm also appreciative of my editor Emma Lockley and for the gorgeous cover designed by Caroline Andrus.

This story was inspired by a conversation I had a few years back with a woman that used to do theatre with me in high school. We were messaging about a Broadway show on tour, and she mentioned that she danced with one of the people in the cast at a studio in Hollywood. Now, this woman was a senior when I was a freshman. Doing the math, this meant that she was 51 years old taking professional level dance classes! I had to know more. She wrote: "It is my love. If you remember, in high school I had completely clutzy and awkward movement..." (No, I don't remember that. She was the star of *Annie*, our spring musical.) "At 24, I started the intro to basics class and slowly worked up, six days a week, for 27 years. This all started because I needed to lose weight."

My mind was blown! Being the collector of stories that I am, I immediately responded with: "Well, someday, if I ever start writing grownup books, I might make a character who learns ballet as an adult. What a great story! Thanks for sharing with me." And here we are, six years later. Lynn Balsamo, I hope I did you proud!

I'm no stranger to dance myself. Like Grace, I took ballet as a child but stopped while still fairly young. I'm not entirely sure why my mom pulled me from Irvine Dance Academy, but I think it might have had something to do with the fact that I didn't practice enough. All I know is that I started taking jazz classes from a high school student who lived down the street—in her garage. After that, my only dance training came from the dance classes my high school offered, the high school show choir, Disneyland Parades, and simply doing musicals. In college, my Theatre Arts degree required us to take ballet and tap. I was actually getting pretty good at ballet, but I never got on pointe because I broke my foot onstage during a production of *Peter Pan* where I was playing Wendy. My dance professor was very upset when I showed up with my crutches. I didn't do ballet again for another twenty years, that was when I got cast as Sheila in a production of *A Chorus Line*. I wasn't great at it, but my friend and the show's choreographer Kate Adams Kramer helped me not embarrass myself. It's been another decade or so since then, and I can only dream about dancing like Grace.

As mentioned, I went to school for Theatre. Unlike Grace, I did, in fact, graduate. I went to Los Angeles and pursued that dream for a while. I even got my SAG card. Then I got into singing with a couple different acts and finally decided writing was my big dream. When I moved to Tennessee in 2003, I auditioned for a local community theatre show and got cast. It rekindled my love of theatre, and I've been addicted to doing shows ever since. *Anything but Graceful* will be published in the month between me performing in one musical and then getting ready to direct another (an original musical written by me called *Songwriter Night*.) It's hard to do both theatre and be an author, but I love both creative outlets too much to quit either of them.

I met my husband doing theatre, and our combined kids (all grownups now) also dance, act, and sing. My daughter just got her own Theatre Arts degree and was going through all of her college frustrations, challenges, heartaches and triumphs while I wrote this novel. It brought back a lot of memories, and it was all very helpful for creating the backstory for Grace and Tyler. I'm so thankful for my family and their support.

I hope you enjoyed this novel. It's my intention to write more in this genre. So, if you'd like to help me out and show that you want more books like this, please leave a review and recommend it to your friends.

## THANK YOU FOR READING

Did you enjoy this book?

We invite you to leave a review at your favorite book site, such as Goodreads, Amazon, Barnes & Noble, etc.

### DID YOU KNOW THAT LEAVING A REVIEW...

- Helps other readers find books they may enjoy.
- Gives you a chance to let your voice be heard.
- Gives authors recognition for their hard work.
- Doesn't have to be long. A sentence or two about why you liked the book will do.

# About the Author

Driver likes to dip her toes into all kinds of writing genres from children's fiction and YA fantasy to adult romance. Her sweet romantic story "The Ticket to Her Heart" is published in the Satin Romance Books anthology *Second Chance for Love*. She's also published six young adult novels with Fire & Ice Young Adult Books, including her paranormal teen romance about the power of love letters, *All the Love You Write*. With a degree in Theatre Arts from U. C. Irvine, it's not surprising that in addition to writing, Driver is also a theatre actress and director. She can often be found singing in a musical theatre production somewhere in the Nashville vicinity or at least belting out showtunes in her car.

Visit her website and sign up for her newsletter: www.dgdriver.com

facebook.com/donnagdriver
twitter.com/DGDriverAuthor
instagram.com/d_g_driver
tiktok.com/@dgdriver
bookbub.com/authors/DGDriver

## Also by D. G. Driver

### Available from Satin Romance

**Novels**

*Anything But Graceful*

**Anthologies**

*The Ticket to her Heart*, featured in Second Chance for Love: A Romance Anthology

### Available from Fire & Ice Young Adult Books

**Novellas**

*Passing Notes*

**Novels**

*Lost on the Water*

*All the Love You Write*

*Dragon Surf* (with Jeni Bautista Richard)

### The Juniper Sawfeather Series

*Cry of the Sea*

*Whisper of the Woods*

*Echo of the Cliffs*

The Juniper Sawfeather Trilogy Boxset

Can't get enough of June?

Read the **FREE** short story prequel

*Beneath the Wildflowers*

in Kick Ass Girls of Fire & Ice YA Books